THE SOUND OF RAIN

OTHER TITLES BY GREGG OLSEN

NOVELS

Just Try to Stop Me

Now That She's Gone

The Girl in the Woods

Run

Shocking True Story

The Fear Collector

Betrayal

The Bone Box

Envy

Closer Than Blood

Victim Six

Heart of Ice

A Wicked Snow

A Cold Dark Place

NONFICTION

A Killing in Amish Country: Sex, Betrayal, and a Cold-Blooded Murder

A Twisted Faith: A Minister's Obsession and the Murder that Destroyed a Church

The Deep Dark: Disaster and Redemption in America's Richest Silver Mine

Starvation Heights: A True Story of Murder and Malice in the Woods of the Pacific Northwest

Cruel Deception: A Mother's Deadly Game, a Prosecutor's Crusade for Justice

If Loving You Is Wrong: The Shocking True Story of Mary Kay Letourneau

Abandoned Prayers: The Incredible True Story of Murder, Obsession, and Amish Secrets

Bitter Almonds: The True Story of Mothers, Daughters, and the Seattle Cyanide Murders

Bitch on Wheels: The True Story of Black Widow Killer Sharon Nelson

If I Can't Have You: Susan Powell, Her Mysterious Disappearance, and the Murder of Her Children

THE SOUND OF RAIN

GREGG OLSEN

THOMAS & MERCER

Text copyright © 2016 Gregg Olsen
All rights reserved.

Published by Thomas & Mercer, Seattle

www.apub.com

Amazon, the Amazon logo, and Thomas & Mercer are trademarks of Amazon.com, Inc., or its affiliates.

ISBN-13: 9781503941960
ISBN-10: 1503941965

Cover design by Jason Blackburn

Printed in the United States of America

For Judy, because she's a fighter

PROLOGUE

I look at my sister and I want to laugh out loud. She stands in her kitchen pouring a really good chardonnay. Her wrists, like her ankles, are perfect. Her fingers slender and adorned with the *Tiff*—the rock on a platinum hoop that Cy "surprised" her with as an engagement ring a few years ago. I could have had a ring too. I could have had a husband. A child. In that order.

Now, I have nothing. Literally. Nothing.

"You can only stay here one night, Nicole," Stacy says, holding the wine to the light and swirling it like she's some fucking sommelier. A beautiful one. She's light, with blond hair and sapphire eyes. I'm darker, with hair that I wish looked like hers in the sunlight. With eyes that are merely brown, not copper.

I'm sitting on a barstool in her kitchen while she hovers over me. "Right," I tell Stacy. "One night. That's all."

"Just *you*. Not your dog. Shelby has to stay in your car."

I hate her.

"That's fine," I say, though it really isn't.

She finally offers me a glass of wine and I take it. I'd like to guzzle the whole bottle, take some pills, and forget that I'm grateful for all that she's done for me. She's like a praying mantis, clutching me in her arms and holding me tight while she eats my head and tells me that she's doing all she can to "lift me up."

"Stacy," I say as we move out of the kitchen to her Room & Board walnut dining table, the light flashing on our glasses as the sun rides low in the sky, "I know I can beat this. I know I can get my shit together."

Stacy lets my words hang in the air while she continues to swirl her wine. It's a trick. She leaves the gap of silence for me to grovel. But I don't fall for it.

Her move.

"I hate to say this," she says, "because I've never been about judging anyone. That's not who I am. You know that, Nic; you above all others know that I've never, ever been one to judge."

Such a liar.

"I know," I say into my suddenly empty glass. "I know."

"I've thought about it." Her blue eyes roll over me before she looks away. "I think that enabling, you know, stalling the inevitable is only going to hurt your recovery. You needed to hit bottom. That's what the books say. That's what your counselor says." She stops, sips.

I stay mute because I know her. She's going to fire a full round at me.

"You're still seeing her, aren't you?"

I nod. Inside I ask God how it is that this woman in front of me, who has been my best friend since the day she was born, can be so fucking condescending.

And yes, I think, I'm still seeing my counselor. Like you really care.

"You have to recover all on your own," she goes on. "I've been reading up while waiting for yoga. Gambling is supposedly a disease. And the choices you've been making up to now are all on you and this disease. You can only recover if you hit bottom and know that the only way to daylight is in acknowledging or whatever."

"Right." What else can I say? She has everything and I've lost everything. Stacy has the upper hand. The tables have turned. She pretends to be sad, but I know she really loves every minute of this personal waterboarding.

The odds of our continuing our relationship once I get well are very, very slim.

"I don't have any money," I blurt out in a Tourette's-like spasm.

She floats her glass in the air and looks for a coaster ("Arts & Crafts tile, 1914, repurposed as a coaster!").

"I couldn't give you another dime," she says. "Cy says the Bank of Sonntag is closed."

"What will I do?" I ask, again Tourette's-like.

"You will find your way back. I have faith in you. To help you any more than I have would only delay your recovery. The things you've done are big. Damaging. Hurtful to all of us. You need to own this. Cy and I agree on this. Besides, we are very busy people and having you here will add a layer of stress to our lives. Stress we don't need at the moment."

I look at the bottle. I feel so diminished just then that I don't even have the confidence to reach over and pour myself another, let alone smack my sister over the head with it.

She picks up the bottle, then her glass, and heads for the kitchen.

I sit still for a second.

"God, Nic, are you coming? You need to get off the pity pot and help me get dinner going."

When she disappears, I get up and drag the jagged edge of the terra-cotta tile coaster over the impeccable matte surface of her dining table. I leave a very good gouge, which I hope she'll discover the day after I'm gone.

That night I find myself in Emma's room. Stacy's husband, Cy, is out of town pushing Microsoft security products at a tech conference in Bologna, and my sister has given in to little Emma's insistence that she sleep with her mom in her parents' bed. The guest room was besieged by painters earlier in the day, so my one bag and I have been banished to the four-year-old's lair. Queen Elsa from *Frozen* stares from every corner. I wish I were frozen. That's it. Frozen like some billionaire with the hope they could bring me back when they'd finally figured out how to stop my compulsive habit.

I've smuggled Shelby into the house, and I know that this is my last night with her. Maybe ever. I don't know if I will take her to the Humane Society or stand in front of the Safeway and beg for someone to take her home. She's warm, like a hot-water bottle. I can barely look into her eyes because at the moment she's the only one truly in my corner. She knows that while the mistakes I've made cannot be undone, they don't define who I am inside. If I look into her soulful brown eyes, I'll start crying again, and I'm no crier.

While Elsa and Shelby watch over me, I go through my wallet. My police ID. My frequent winner's card from the Snoqualmie Casino. My canceled credit cards: Nordstrom, Saks, American Express. I know I should cut them up, but something in the back of my irrational brain tells me that in cutting them up I'd lose even more of who I am.

Who I was.

I read one of Danny's endless stream of letters to me.

Nicole, I'm sorry for what I've done. I'm sorry that I dragged you down with me. I want you to know that. No matter what happens. None of this is your fault. I wish I could hold you again.

I shred it on the spot, wondering if I should toss it in the air like confetti or flush it down the toilet.

I think the toilet.

I hold the Snoqualmie card in my hand and remember the time that all the machines came through when I really needed it. I'd been put on administrative leave at the homicide unit and decided that it was time to remodel the kitchen. Who does that? Someone in deep denial, that's who. Pending the outcome of an investigation that I was sure wasn't going my way, I had faced weeks of having no income. I had fallen from grace. The workers that redid my floors were decent young men. They hadn't deserved the likes of me.

"I'm sorry," I told the foreman. "I have a cash-flow issue at the moment." He was young and I thought I could push him around.

"I need to be paid," he said, his features carved in a block of sandstone.

I can't.

"Right," I said. "Of course. I just don't have the money."

He stepped closer. I couldn't push him around. Pushing around someone as right as he was, when I was as wrong as I was, wasn't a winning proposition.

"You said you did," he said.

I stepped back. "That was then."

"That was two weeks ago. What do you mean 'then'? Fifty percent down, the rest on completion. You owe me six thousand five hundred dollars."

"I understand your terms," I told him, "but as I said, you'll have to wait."

He wasn't going to give me any slack. I could feel it, and I was right.

"I will give you twenty-four hours," he said.

"Then what?" I probed. "Then what will you do?"

Stone-face said, "I will come here and rip out everything we've done."

I stared hard at him. "You wouldn't. You know that I'm a police officer, don't you?"

"I know you *were* a police officer."

He got me.

"Right," I said. "I was."

That night, I had gotten into my car with eighty dollars in my checking account, and I had driven to the casino at Snoqualmie, east of Bellevue. It's a straight shot on I-90. No stoplights. Just a long expanse of pavement toward the foothills of the Cascades. I knew that I could win, because I hadn't won in a very, very long time. My chances were good—if I stayed smart, stayed focused. My favorite machine wouldn't let me down. This was my chance. I could do this. I'd reminded myself over and over that God would take care of me. I was a believer. I prayed. I promised that I would never, ever ask again.

God had heard all of this before.

The casino was perpetual Christmastime: lights blinking, happy faces everywhere. Smoke formed a light haze over a couple of players that I recognized, but had never spoken a word to. They sat at their favorite machines, cigarettes dangling from their lips and eyes laser-focused in front of them. I hoped they would lose. I know that isn't kind, but inside I was sure that there had to be losers in order to be winners. I needed this more than they did.

My card loaded with my last eighty dollars, I made my way across the floor to a *Masterpieces and Double Diamonds* machine. I had always liked this one. Its mix of iconic artwork and gemstones was a step up from the *Dukes of Hazzard* or *Tic Tac Dough* machines that occupied the people across from me. I was better than that. I'd studied art history before going into law enforcement.

When I think back at that musing, I realize how I rationalized every little thing that I did.

I sat there all night. I had to pee. Bad. But I didn't dare leave my machine. I knew that Mona Lisa would smile on me. And if I stepped away for a single second, she'd get mad. I slowed my heart rate. I was calm. The chrome-plated button was like my police-issued Glock, cool to the touch. Power beyond power. As the early evening morphed to late night, I was inside of my own space, pushing the button, rolling the images of diamonds and rubies and old master artwork at my will. I was up. Rembrandt! Picasso! I was down. I told God that this really would be the last time I'd come to the casino—though in my mind I meant, *this* casino.

Not *all* of them.

I only broke my concentration one time, when an annoying young woman squealed at her big win four chairs down. *God,* I wondered, *does that mean this row is dead and there's nothing for me? Don't you do this to me. Don't!*

Four hours later I had $6,700. I was on fire. I was the goddess of my row and people gathered around me to revel in my reflected greatness, my aura. I was a magnet. I had something that night. I had done what I had to do. It was a high greater than any I had known. The kind of feeling that pulses with electricity at every sensitive part of your anatomy. I sat on the casino toilet with my money in one hand, at last relieving myself. I squeezed the wad of cash like a foam stress ball while I emptied my bladder.

I'm a winner. Squeeze. Squeeze. *That's what I am!*

I pulled my car into a spot right next to the door at Walmart in nearby Issaquah. *Lucky spot!* My high waning some, I scurried through the aisles, loading my cart with toilet paper, soap, and dog food for Shelby. Ten minutes later, the rush was all but gone. I knew exactly what I was doing. I glanced in a mirror by the women's underwear. I no longer looked like myself. My clothes were dirty. My hair, limp and unstyled. My late mother's words about my looks came to me then.

"You aren't exactly beautiful, but you are memorable."

Stacy was the pretty one. I was supposed to be the smart one. The memorable one. Now I was pretty sure I was memorable for all the wrong reasons.

I stocked up at Walmart because, while I would pay that foreman the next day, I'd need the supplies to tide me over as I fell under the spell of my own weakness. I'd go to another casino, a place where no one knew my name, but where everyone occupying a seat in front of a machine knew my kind. The men and women who only unlatch themselves from their chairs when midnight strikes so they can line up at the ATM and withdraw more money they can't afford to lose.

A little girl, dark haired and blue eyed, passed by me in that nearly empty Walmart. Her mother, a tweaker with peanut teeth and a rainbow complexion, tugged at the girl to keep her moving.

Then the girl looked right into my eyes.

My knees weakened and I grabbed the handle of my cart to steady myself. She wasn't Kelsey Chase, of course. She could have been her sister. Her twin. I wondered if God had sent that girl and her miserable mother to Walmart to chastise me for lying to him. I wondered if that girl's appearance at Walmart was there to remind me of the biggest failure of my life.

Nothing happens by chance.

As I look up at Elsa in her beautiful, blue-and-silver gown in Emma's perfect bedroom, a tear threatens to roll from eye but I stop it. I know that I will go lower than I have gone until now but not so low that I won't survive this. Shelby nuzzles me. I won't let her sweet nature make me cry. I can't love anyone. Tomorrow, I'll get rid of her because she's a burden. She'd be better off without me.

Whatever.

Dogs aren't allowed in the women's shelter.

That's where I'm going.

As I close my eyes and feel Shelby's hot little body against the small of my back, I think about Kelsey Chase like I almost always do. Like I probably always will. She would be four next week if she were still alive. She would be smarter than Stacy's daughter. She'd never be interested in this *Frozen* crap. I'm as sure of that as I am that I let Kelsey down. I try to think about something else, but she never lets me. A knife inserts itself into pink, unblemished skin. Red blooms over perfect white, Egyptian cotton sheets. A smear of a darker shade mars the floor.

Avenge me.

BOOK ONE

BEFORE MY UNRAVELLING

CHAPTER ONE

"She was only in the car for a little while," Angela Chase says as we stand outside her midnight-blue BMW sedan, cordoned off with the familiar bumblebee-yellow crime scene tape. The color scheme clashes with the holiday decor of the Factoria Target store that looms above the scene.

Christmas is two days away.

A girl is missing.

Everything is wrong with this picture.

A small crowd circles around the BMW and some young blues push them away, but they contract with the wind. Some are angry that their loved ones are on lockdown in the Target.

"I had the seat warmers on," Angela says. "She was by herself for only a minute or two."

"Tell me once more what happened," I say.

The mother of the missing girl looks right at me. Her green eyes flash a kind of anxiousness at me. She's still holding a Target bag. Son Samuel, five, clings tight to her hand. He's carrying a Target bag too and trying hard not to cry while the world shatters all around him.

"I want to go home," Angela says. "Samuel's chilly and my husband will be angry if I don't get home before he does."

"He's on his way here," I tell her.

Angela lets out a sigh. "That's perfect," she says. "Just perfect."

As we stand there in the cold and wet, my eyes land on one of the other officers helping with the search. No words needed. This mother doesn't seem concerned about her missing daughter at all. She's more concerned about what her husband will think if his dinner isn't ready when he arrives home. I wonder about their home life. Expensive—obviously Burberry—coat. Car I could never afford. Hair and makeup just so. I have no idea what her home life is like, but, by the way she's acting, I know for sure that I'd never want to trade places with her. She's evasive at a time when other moms would be clawing at the yellow tape and screaming at us to find her daughter.

"I know we've gone over this," I say, "but let's do it again."

"I can't. I'm too upset. I'm cold. Samuel needs to get home. He has Montessori tomorrow."

"Mrs. Chase, your daughter is missing."

Angela's Target bag slips from her fingertips and smacks the wet pavement. She's beginning to crumble. In a strange way, I'm glad of that. I was beginning to wonder where she was storing her feelings. Or if she had any at all. As if his mother's release of emotions has freed him to do the same, Samuel cries now. The rain starts up, and an officer brings a pair of red Target umbrellas.

"We'll do our best to find her," I say.

As we stand there, the rain rolling off umbrellas, a man pushes through the soggy crowd. He's tall with dark, wavy hair that brushes his ears. He's wearing a long, black overcoat, and his shoes are expensive and likely ruined from the swelling puddle that has suddenly surrounded us like a moat. Samuel runs to him and Angela follows, coils her arm around him.

"She was acting up, Julian," she says, crying without tears. "You know how she can be. We were doing just fine. We were. And then all of a sudden she pitched a fit. I had shopping to do. I had to get some last-minute gifts. I brought her back to the car and told her to sit, and Samuel and I went back inside. I swear to God, only for a minute. Just a little minute."

Julian Chase tells his wife that everything will be all right. He's sure that Kelsey's fine. "She must have gone back inside the store," he says. "Remember the time she hid in the pantry?"

Just as I introduce myself, the shoppers trapped inside Target are released. Some look relieved as they emerge. Others appear angry at the inconvenience. All of them look over at the group of us huddled by Angela Chase's blue BMW.

"I heard they left their kid in the car and now she's gone. Who leaves their kid in the car?" a woman asks, loud enough to ensure that Angela hears.

"Yeah," says her companion, who's older and angrier, "there's even a law against it."

"No sign of her," says Bart Collins, the officer leading the search inside the store, when he joins us. He's in his forties with anvil-heavy eyebrows and sympathetic blue eyes. He's wearing a jacket over his maroon shirt. His khakis are mottled with the spray from a shopper's bright-red cart whizzing past us.

Julian Chase stiffens at the statement. "She's got to be in there," he says, his eyes sweeping over the people pouring out of the store. "I'm going to go get her." He breaks free from Angela and moves toward the doors. An officer, fresh out of the academy and completely earnest, stops him.

"You can't go in there, sir," Bart Collins says.

"You can't stop me," Julian says, trying to get past the officer. "It's my daughter that's missing."

Julian Chase, an executive with an international video streaming company, is one of those take-charge types. I knew it the second he made his way toward Angela, pushing past onlookers and gawkers like they were bowling pins and he was anything but a gutter ball. But the cop stands his ground.

"Sir, you have to let us do our job."

He stops and looks at Officer Collins. He is at once scared and angry. Taking charge was a mask. Taking charge was his attempt to ensure that he wasn't just standing in the rain, waiting for someone to tell him that Kelsey was still gone.

"Then do your fucking job!" he demands. "Find my little girl! You're terrifying her mother and brother." He notices Collins's heavy brows narrow, and he reels in the torrent of emotion. The fear. The confusion. The urgency. "Sorry," he says, his voice dropping. "Just find her."

◆ ◆ ◆

An empty Target store is an eerie place. Wide aisles. Pops of red everywhere highlight the corporation's branding, but with Christmas so near, it's red and green on overload. A disquieting starkness fills the space. Even Mariah Carey's signature Christmas tune can't lift the mood. Not a single person pushing a cart or wandering aimlessly for that last-minute gift that will make their Christmas perfect. A woman with a tag that says "Sherry, team leader" passes the surveillance tapes over a red laminate counter and she doesn't look all that happy about it.

"It's standard procedure," I say, though I know some businesses would balk and wait to be served a warrant.

"Not that," she says. "I get that. Target's corporate policy is to work with the police whenever we can."

I write down her name.

"Just can't believe that someone lost her kid here in the store," she says, picking at a crusty stain on her khakis. "Just makes me sick to think that we've got some pervert shopping here. Right before Christmas too. Makes me sick. Really."

"We don't know what happened," I say. "But I can promise you, we'll do our very best to find her."

Sex offenders. Years ago nobody paid them any attention. They were imagined as wild-eyed weirdoes who lived alone or in their mothers' basements, boogeymen who prowled schoolyards, playgrounds, and carnivals. They were around, but no one ever saw them. All of that changed with the Internet and the registries that share the details of their crimes, their pictures, and their addresses. Sex offenders, it turned out, were the guy—and sometimes the gal—down the street.

"About those tapes," Sherry the Team Leader says, "they aren't the best."

"We're used to lousy black and white," I say.

She gives an uneasy smile. "It's not just that they're crappy. It's that, well, some of the cameras have been on the fritz."

"Some?"

"Most."

"All right," I say, trying to contain my disappointment. "I'm sure we'll find what we need."

"I sure hope so."

The members of the Bellevue Police Department have scrutinized every inch of the store, including the storage trunks that might have held a little body. No sign of Angela and Julian Chase's little girl.

She's simply gone.

An Amber Alert is issued, telling everyone in Washington—everyone who watches TV, owns a phone, or listens to the radio, that is—that Kelsey Chase was last seen in the parking lot of the Target store at the Factoria Mall in Bellevue, a suburb east of Seattle. The three-year-old has dark, curly hair, weighs twenty-nine pounds, and is thirty-four inches tall. When her mother last saw her she was wearing a pink wool coat, a white-and-pink checked sweater, blue jeans, and a pair of Elmo shoes.

◆ ◆ ◆

With Christmas in two days, the investigative unit is short-staffed. Danny Ford, my partner in more ways than one, goes to the Chases' while I stay at Target finishing up with the forensic team as they measure, photograph, and prepare to tow the BMW. The lab will process it for fingerprints, trace evidence, and biologicals. The car, for all we know, is the crime scene. As I stand there, lights flashing blue and red on the shiny asphalt, a few people gather. A couple brings flowers, creating a makeshift memorial faster than a female blowfly laying eggs on a newly dead body.

Which is very, very fast.

A woman with her teenage daughter in tow comes up to me after depositing a bouquet of red carnations with the Safeway sticker still on it.

"I hope you arrest the mother," she says.

She's dressed in all black—a uniform of the elite or someone in perpetual mourning. Always hard to know for sure on the Eastside.

"You are, aren't you?" she asks. Her tone is exceedingly bitter and she seems to be emboldened by her teen, who bobs her head up and down.

I only nod. I'm not sure what to say. Or rather what I *should* say.

"Isn't leaving her kid in the car unattended against the law?" the mother asks.

"It is, Mom," the daughter says before I can respond.

They move on and I stand there as the tow truck pulls away with the BMW.

What kind of mother does leave her child in the car like Angela Chase did?

Danny texts me from the Chases' house only a few miles away.

```
Angela Chase took a sleeping pill and
went to bed and Julian said she'll come
in to talk tomorrow. Looked around the
house. Nothing. See U later.
```

Who takes sleeping pills hours after her child goes missing?

Angela Chase is like no mother I've encountered. *Frantic* is the word that defines most. Unhinged. Desperate. Most guzzle coffee. Have to be forced to eat so they don't pass out. The whole time the investigation goes on, they stay focused on what's happening, make sure that the police are doing everything.

Angela? She isn't like that. Not at all.

Angela took some pills and tucked in for the night.

Chapter Two

Danny and I roll the tape on a monitor in one of the evidence storage rooms back at the Bellevue Police Department. Danny and I have a complicated relationship. Too complicated. He's not my boss, though he acts like it. He's a few years older and has more experience, but part of me thinks there's something inside of him that sees me as a threat.

Sherry, the Target team leader, was right. The tapes *are* lousy. We sit there in the semidarkness poring over the videos, first from camera one, the unit by the front door.

"There she is," I say, recognizing Angela Chase by her expensive designer coat. She came in with a crowd, and it was hard to see if the children were with her. "It looks like she's holding Samuel's hand, but I really can't see him. I don't see Kelsey at all."

"I'll slow it down," Danny says, reaching for the controls.

Even in super slow motion, I can't get a decent read on anyone other than Angela. "Go to the next camera," I say.

"Yes, ma'am," Danny says. "I like it when you're so assertive."

Actually, he doesn't. Not at all. He prefers it when I just follow his lead. He only said that because he wants to remind me that he's always in charge. He's my superior. I'm one level below him at all times. Soon this case, *my* case, will be *his* case. He'll tell me that the news media will be better served by hearing from a more seasoned investigator. That it doesn't mean I'm not leading things, but it's better, he'll say, for the community.

I know he'll do that. I know I'll let him. My relationship with my own father has put me into the category of women who acquiesce to win approval. It's the part of me that I hate the most, the first element I'd change about myself if only I could. My mother left my father, sister, and me when I was seven. Stacy was only four. I was so afraid that we'd be abandoned by our father too that I did whatever I could to hold us together. That meant never pushing back, because I didn't want to make him unhappy in any way. I lost some of what I might have become. Stacy was younger. She missed Mom, but she hadn't felt abandoned. I wouldn't let her. She was my baby. I know I did a good job raising her, because she has everything that I ever wanted. She knew how to grow up and live a life.

That's something I'm still trying to do.

"There's Angela," I say, tapping my finger on the screen. She's standing near a Nate Berkus bathroom accessories display and staring upward at the camera.

"That's kind of weird," Danny says, looking at me.

I agree and then Angela disappears from the frame.

We stare at the images from the next six cameras, three of which approximate a South Dakota blizzard. In the final tape, we catch only one glimpse of Angela and Samuel as they stand in line at the checkout. It is so fleeting that we freeze the image frame by frame, hoping for something more.

I look over at Danny.

"No sign of the kid," he says.

"The manager was right. These tapes are terrible. They aren't going to help us find Kelsey at all. I'm not even sure she was even there. No one saw her."

Danny taps his finger on a reporting officer's stack of statements collected from the people who were stuck inside while the store was on lockdown. "One witness says she saw all three of them. Said that the little girl was being a brat and her mom was threatening to spank her right then and there."

I reach for the statement and read.

"You're right," I say. "She says that she saw the mom take the girl and the boy toward the front door."

"Yeah, right out to the car, where she left the kid."

"I don't know. Maybe this witness got it all wrong. She's the only one out of dozens interviewed."

"Probably," Danny says. "All I know is that if I was a betting man, and you know that I am, I'd put money on some molester freak who was looking to make his Christmas a lot jollier."

"That's gross."

"I'm just saying what I think happened."

I read more of the statement and look up at Danny.

"She says the little girl was wearing a blue coat."

"Mom says the coat was pink," Danny says.

I put down the report. "Says the girl was a blond."

"Witness wannabe," Danny says.

I change the subject to something useful. "We need to interview the parents again."

"No shit," Danny says.

"The mom's stonewalling," I say. "Excuses. Says she's too stressed. Needs to pull herself together."

"She probably does."

"Her little girl is missing. What part of that doesn't light a fire under her?"

"Yeah," Danny says, "that's probably the worst thing that could happen to a parent. She's strange, I'll give you that. But she's not the type to ditch her kid."

I call and get her voice mail again.

"Ms. Chase, this is Nicole Foster of the Bellevue Police Department," I say. "We really need to take an official statement from you. I know this is a really hard time, but we need your help to find Kelsey. Call me back."

CHAPTER THREE

The next morning is Christmas Eve. Still no word from Angela. Or her husband. Their daughter's story is featured on the top of all three of the Seattle TV morning news programs. A missing child during the holidays is tragic.

And ratings catnip.

Danny and I pull up the sexual offenders registry. He hovers over me and picks at a sugar cookie left over from the Records Department's holiday party the day before.

"What?" he asks, thinking that I'm judging him. "I'm hungry."

Which I'm not. At least not now. "You're dropping crumbs into my keyboard," I say. "That's all."

He shrugs. "Sorry."

I know he's not. Danny's never been sorry about anything in his life.

Kelsey's been missing only a few hours, but we all feel it in our bones that this case is the worst kind.

The kind that seldom has a happy ending.

There are more than a dozen hits within a two-mile radius of the Factoria Target store. The number doesn't surprise. The area around the mall is a hodgepodge of apartments, condominiums, single-family homes, and, a rarity on the Eastside, a mobile home park. It's the mobile home park—Lake Washington Mobile Estates—that sucks up most of our attention. It's right next-door to the mall; a trail used by residents connects the neighborhood with the Target parking lot. The map print-out of the registry looks like the page has been splattered with blood. Each red dot indicates where an offender lives.

"Jesus," Danny says, "looks like a fucking molester convention in there."

I'm poring over the report of who lives where, and more importantly, who did what to earn them a spot on the registry.

"We can rule out the man/boy love crowd," I say.

Danny drops more crumbs. "No shit."

"That's this one. The one here. And these here," I say as I take a sharpie and black out the red dots. "That leaves four."

"We can remove her and her," Danny says. "Doubt those sick bitches did anything. They like boys."

I nod. I remember one of the women on the registry. Her name is Sally Ann Meriwether. She's now in her forties and has been living in the trailer park since her release from prison almost five years ago. She'd been a Sunday school teacher at St. Louise, a Catholic church on the eastern side of Bellevue. She'd had sex with two teenage boys.

"She was pretty hot," Danny says.

I give him the look.

"Well," he says, "I understand she was a predator, but if I were those boys, I doubt I'd have complained."

This is a conversation we've had before. "They were victims of a predator," I say.

"I get that," he says, mockingly. "Right. A predator."

That leaves us with three doors to rattle. Three men, aged nineteen to seventy-five, are about to go through the drill, which comes as a price they pay for their crimes. No matter what they did, no matter how they excused it, none can escape what they've done. It follows them like a long shadow wherever they go.

◆ ◆ ◆

The entrance to Lake Washington Mobile Estates is anything but grand. Someone made an attempt to mark the neighborhood with a home-made sign on a sheet of painted plywood—the shape instantly reminds me of its origin, a basketball backboard. The elements and no home-owners' dues have taken their toll. The *W* on *Washington* has faded away. A playground with some swings and a monkey bar is just beyond the sign. Danny makes some crack about the playground being akin to a candy dish for the offenders who call the neighborhood home. I don't answer. I keep thinking about Kelsey and how she's been taken somewhere. How she could be trapped in one of the mobile homes.

"Holy crap," Danny says. "They sure do up Christmas here."

"That they do," I say, acknowledging the abundance of Christmas lights that engulf just about everything. The lights outline decks, spray over bare-limbed trees, and twist up flagpoles like a Christmas light kudzu vine invasion.

"The power bills must be crazy high," Danny says.

"I imagine so."

I don't tell him that I did some of my growing up in a place like this near Hoquiam, a perpetually struggling mill town on the Washington coast, a place where the sky and water are grayer than a gull's wing. All year. Every day. I don't mention that my mother, who had far grander ambitions than Hoquiam could offer, left my father and my sister and me. I hold back that, while we had no money, Dad insisted on putting up the biggest light display in town. It didn't matter that the utility bill might not make it through the holidays. He took the risk. "Be some pretty big-time grinch to cut us off at Christmas," he'd tell Stacy and me.

I don't tell Danny all the things about my past because I promised I'd keep it all inside. Stacy made me. She told me that I would have no family if she had to explain our past to Cy. So I never say a word. I don't talk about the time the lights were turned off and we cooked dinner on a camp stove in the backyard. I never breathe a word to anyone that my father is still alive and suffering from Alzheimer's in a government-paid care facility in Aberdeen. The difference between Stacy and me is that I think all that happened to us has made us better somehow. That there's something good to be found amid the chaos. Something more understanding. Compassionate.

I like to think that's true.

The wipers on Danny's SUV need changing. The lights from the Christmas decorations send streaks of color over the windshield, making it hard to find the right house numbers.

Nothing is sadder than a trailer park on a drizzly December day.

At least that's what I think as we make our way through the narrow streets with questions for people who, by whatever luck or misfortune, have had their stay right where they were while Bellevue grew up around them. Blue tarps keep drips at bay. A child's Big Wheel sits next to a car that I doubt has been driven in years. Its wheels dig into the sodden soil as though the earth is trying to suck it out of view.

"I talk. You pay attention," Danny says.

All right, asshole, I think.

"Got it," is what I say.

Danny is the acting lead of our investigative unit and my lover, both attributes I question on nearly a daily basis. He's handsome in the way that cops sometimes are. His body is his hobby. His phone is full of selfies in front of the mirror of his Bellevue condo. There's nothing pornographic about the images, but he's definitely fixated on his appearance. He's a narcissist, and I wonder what it says about me that I'm willing to sleep with a man whose eyes constantly look past me in search of his own reflection.

We're working in teams under the direction of our lieutenant, Evan Cooper. Other pairs are working the residents of Space 47 and 102. Danny and I are going to Space 23. We're looking for Alan Dawson, but there's no answer when we knock. We ring the bell. Look in the windows. The TV in the front room is dark. The Christmas tree is glowing. We wind our way around a junk pile and some firewood to circle the perimeter of the mobile home, but we find no indication that anyone's home.

"Wonder where the hell Dawson is," Danny says. "I'd like to button this up before the feds get involved. This is my case."

My case, he says. I let it go.

"It's Christmas, Danny," I say, indicating an inflated Santa in the neighbor's yard. "People go places. They spend time with family."

He dismisses my words. "Pervs sit around and watch porn. No matter what the day is."

I think of saying pervs are people too, but I resist. "Maybe so," I say instead. "Let's ask the woman next-door. She's watching from the window."

Her name is Viola Richards. My dad would have said she has a pretty face, so as not to insult her for her size. I imagine she's a hundred pounds overweight. Her hair is a silver bun. She wears two small Christmas bulbs for earrings.

A retired schoolteacher, I think, though I hope not. I hope a teacher's pension would provide for a better retirement home than this mobile home park.

"Dawsons are gone," Viola says from the front door after we show her our ID and tell her we're out on a routine investigation.

"Where to, ma'am?" Danny asks.

"I have no idea. Charlene has a sister in North Bend. Has nothing to do with her folks. Maybe they went up there to the sister's place. Can't be gone long. Left me a note to feed the cat." She looks over at the Dawsons' place, then back at us. "You're here about that girl, aren't you?"

"We're just out on a routine investigation, ma'am," Danny says.

"Routine, my ass." Her tone is brittle. "I know what you're up to. Every time there's a whiff of something that involves a man and a young girl, you make a beeline for the Dawsons'."

"It might seem that way," I say, "but that's not true."

"No need to bullshit a bullshitter," Viola says.

All right, maybe not a retired teacher, I think. I've never heard any teacher talk like that.

"Why don't you people just leave them alone?" she asks. "Alan did his time. And if you ask me, he didn't deserve it. He's a good kid. Charlene stands by him. It's just bullshit that you people have to come over here every few months and shake this place up like the people who live here are trash."

"No one thinks that," I say, wanting to tell her that I used to be one of those people. When we were in a place like Lake Washington Mobile Estates, we didn't think of ourselves as trash, either. Because we weren't.

"I see it every time someone comes in here looking, like you're doing now. You think that someone like Alan is garbage for a mistake that he made. It's not right. He's not the kind of guy that would hurt a fly."

"No one is saying he is," I say.

"You are," she says jabbing her finger at me, then at Danny. "The both of you. You think you're so much better. I taught school at Enatai Elementary for thirty-three years." Well there you go. My instincts were sound after all. "The parents there had boatloads of money. They showered me with gifts. Told me that I was the best thing that ever happened to their family. Some even said I was like a part of their family. But I wasn't. I knew it."

"I'm sorry," I say.

Viola picks up a yellow cat. She says the cat—"Tracks"—belongs to the Dawsons. Tracks purrs and she holds him close to her cheek, taking in the vibrations of a very content animal.

I hand her my card and ask her to call me when the Dawsons return.

"I probably won't," she says. "I'll tell them you came by. That much I'll do."

I thank her, and Danny and I start to leave.

"You know something, detectives, you and I aren't that much different."

I hold my breath a second. I don't know how she could have sensed my past. I haven't said a word of it. I only thought of it.

"How's that, Ms. Richards?" Danny asks. "How are we alike?"

"You don't see it yet," she says, setting down the cat. "There will come a day when you do. The people who are so happy to see you, the ones who treat you like you're one of them, will abandon you. You're called a public servant for a reason. That's how those people that have those fancy cars and water views think of you."

Danny shrugs. "Maybe so."

"It's not a maybe," she says. "It's a fact."

When we get back in the car, Danny turns to me. "What a total bitch," he says. "We come around trying to work a case and she pontificates about our standing in the community. Such bullshit. I bet she was the world's worst teacher. I bet the parents at that school couldn't stand her."

I don't tell Danny what I think. I just don't need to go there right now. But I'm pretty sure that Viola Richards is right. Stacy would agree with her, that's for sure. She'd remind me that as long as we pretend we come from a decent family, people will treat us like we are one of them. God knows Stacy's Cy, for one, is all about appearances. I wonder if Danny would be with me if he knew where I came from.

It's late and we're hungry. Danny suggests dinner. I know where this is going, and while it feels very, very wrong, I acquiesce.

Chapter Four

While we drive east on I-90 to the Snoqualmie Casino, we talk about Julian and Angela Chase. We talk about the things that don't add up. The fact that Angela refuses to talk to us. How she complained about her husband being mad if she didn't get home before him. How the lab tech's report indicated that no other fingerprints than Angela's, the children's, and Julian's were found on the BMW.

"Something so wrong with that family," I say.

Danny keeps his eyes on the road. "Every family is fucked up. You and your sister are deep into a love/hate relationship."

"And I get the distinct impression that you enjoy pointing that out whenever you can. Danny, you don't need to remind me."

"I don't think Angela Chase is the type to off her kid," he says. "My money's on the pervert in the trailer park."

He's talking about Alan Dawson. "He was seventeen when he had sex with the fifteen-year-old," I say.

"He's a pervert."

"Maybe," I say. "But having sex with your underage girlfriend, now his wife, is a far cry from kidnapping a little girl."

"Who says that he hasn't done it before and we just missed it? Slimeballs like that get away with shit all the time."

Lieutenant Cooper texts us that the others in the park have checked out. All had decent alibis. Alan Dawson still hasn't turned up. His sister told police that he and his wife had already left when they did a door knock in North Bend.

◆ ◆ ◆

That night I win a hundred dollars on the slots while Danny loses almost $5,000 at the blackjack table. I know that my victory is a small one, but I know better than to rub it in his face. He doesn't like being one-upped by anyone. He blew a gasket when one of the guys was promoted over him at Bellevue PD. Said it was because the other officer was Asian and there had been pressure to increase the diversity of the department. I'm not so sure. I never said so, but I thought Ken Yamamoto was the far better candidate.

I wander the casino while Danny stews at the bar, commiserating with the other big losers of the night. This place might even be sadder than Alan Dawson's trailer park. Giant, fake evergreens fill the ballroom, and enormous gold-and-red balls hang from streamers that move ever so slowly as people make their way to their favorite chair, favorite barstool, favorite waitress. The casino marketing team is promoting a holiday theme—The Twelve Days of Christmas Rewards. All the hype and sparkle pushes me to think back to the previous Christmas Eve at Stacy and Cy's and how Emma delighted in the old My Pretty Pony set that I had brought her.

"I found it in Dad's stuff," I told my sister.

Stacy looked at it. No smile. Just a look. "We could have bought her a new one, Nic," she said, sipping her chardonnay from a Baccarat crystal goblet. It was, after all, a special occasion. It was one of the days when I, the spinster aunt, was invited to be a part of the family.

Emma latched on to the plastic replica of a little girl's dream of a stable. One with pink horses, purple manes, and jewels that never lose their luster.

"This is the one we played with," I said to Stacy. "Remember?"

She eyed the set. "Did you Lysol it?"

"I dusted it. I didn't think it needed to be disinfected. It was in storage. In a box. No one but us touched it."

Stacy made a dismissive face and guzzled her wine. She'd probably get drunk and go to bed, leaving me talking to Cy about all the things he had to do at Microsoft and how there wasn't enough time in the day or night to be as important as he was. It's the way our gatherings had been going. He talked. I listened.

Sure enough, that's pretty much how it went down. Though that day was a little different, and I was glad about it. He was distracted. He kept looking down at his phone.

"Everything okay?" I asked.

"Yeah. Just another shit storm in China. They want to take over the world, but they can't put together a phone worth a damn. Sometimes I wonder why I even bother."

He tapped out an answer to a text.

I considered telling him I had breast cancer, just to see if he was even paying attention to me, but there was no point in that. I was a piece of furniture that came with his wife. The hope chest with nothing in it. Nothing useful.

"Cy," I said. "I think I'm going to take off."

He looked up. "Huh? It's early."

"I'm working tomorrow," I said, fishing for my coat and purse on the massive entry table by the front door.

"That sucks."

I rolled my shoulders as I pulled on my coat. "Someone has to."

"What's your boyfriend up to? Aren't you going to spend the day with him? It's Christmas, for crying out loud."

"We're working a case."

"Good night, Nicole," he said, looking down at the solitaire game on his phone.

"Tell Stacy and Emma Merry Christmas," I said as I pulled the door shut and headed for my car.

CHAPTER FIVE

Julian Chase sits across from me and Danny in the interview room. We've tried three times to get him and his wife to come in to make a formal statement, but Angela is a roadblock.

"She's too upset," her husband tells us. "She can't even eat or sleep. You're making things very difficult for her. Do your job and find Kelsey. My wife already told you everything she knows."

We push, in a nice way at first. We tell her lawyer that we are sorry. That we understand that nothing could be worse than having a child disappear. That we care about finding Kelsey. She's our number one concern right now. That we need her help to find her. Then we shift tone, telling the lawyer that Angela looks bad. Indifferent. Maybe even guilty.

And yet Angela still balks. She puts up a wall. She tells us to spend our time looking for Kelsey and to leave her alone.

Now, finally, we at least have Julian Chase down here.

Kelsey has been missing for forty-eight hours. It's the day after Christmas and the Bellevue Police Department looks like a silver-and-gold bomb has been detonated, the remnants of wrapping paper from the holiday gift exchange that netted me four gift cards.

Gift cards, I know, are for people that no one really knows. The teacher. The bus driver. The officer two cubes down from mine.

"I'm worried," Julian says, struggling to come up with the words.

"We understand," I say.

"Is the FBI helping?" he asks. "They should be helping to find Kelsey."

"We've reported to the National Center for Missing & Exploited Children," I tell him. "It's not a federal case. No ransom claim has been made."

He looks beat down. Dark circles underscore his eyes. Even the wavy hair that had repelled water so handily when we stood in the parking lot at Target has flattened.

Danny enters the room and takes a seat, and I ask if Julian wants coffee. He says he does. So does Danny. I leave them alone and return with a couple of cups and some creamer and sugar packs. I want some too, but I only have two hands.

"How are you holding up, Mr. Chase?" I ask.

"Julian," he says. "Not good."

I nod and push the packets of creamer and sugar across the table.

"Black's fine."

Danny speaks up. "You said on the phone that you thought your wife wasn't telling you everything."

He sips his coffee. "Yeah. We've gone round and round about it. It's been rough. It's like she doesn't want to even talk about it."

"What has she said?" I ask.

"The same thing she told you at Target. Kelsey acted up. She took her to the car. Left her there and then, well, when she came back she was gone."

"Right," I say. "That's what she told us."

"What are you thinking, Julian?" Danny asks.

Julian addresses me. "You're a woman. You wouldn't do that to your kid, would you?" He looks at me with kind, penetrating eyes.

"I don't have any children, but, if I did, I wouldn't," I tell him. "You're right. I don't imagine many moms would."

Julian looks down at his coffee.

"She never really liked Kelsey, you know."

The words come at me, but they are so very hard to process.

"No," I say. "I don't. What do you mean? Was Kelsey abused? Are you telling us that you think your wife might have done something to your daughter?"

Silence fills the interview room.

"She never really took to Kelsey," he says. "Samuel's everything. He has been from the day he was born. Kelsey, she came into the world with a mother that didn't seem to bond with her."

I think back to my own mother, how she was so willing to just walk away from Stacy and me. We were nothing to her. And yet, every day until we were in our teens, we looked for her wherever we went. The mall. At school events. I even thought I saw her at the DMV the day I got my driver's license.

It wasn't her, of course.

"I don't know what happened," he says. "I can't even sleep, you know. Even saying this to you makes me feel as though I'm going to the worst possible place and, honestly, I don't want to go there."

More silence. Danny and I stay quiet. We want Julian Chase to talk. We want to follow his words.

Julian stands up. "This is a mistake," he says. "I shouldn't have come. God knows that Kelsey is out there somewhere. Someone has her. We have to find her. Bring her home. My wife—"

"Please stay," I tell him. "Please help us find her. That's why you're here, isn't it?"

He sinks back into his chair.

"Yeah. That's why I'm here."

Over the next 45 minutes, Julian fills us in on life with Angela. She was born in France to an American father and French mother and holds dual citizenship. She comes from money. She works at a boutique in downtown Bellevue part-time "because she wants something to do." She speaks five languages. She occasionally blogs about gluten-free baked goods. She placed in the top ten in the Miss Washington Teen USA pageant. They met online.

"She'll consider this a betrayal," he says as he continues dumping her biography in the interview room. But he goes on. "She's obsessive-compulsive about cleaning," he says, holding those words in the air for a moment.

"You're thinking of something," I say.

His eyes latch on to mine. "Yeah," he says. "When we got home from Target that night, the house smelled of bleach."

Danny glances at me, but says nothing.

"Is that unusual?"

Julian looks away. I can see that he's close to breaking. "Yeah. It is. We don't have the housekeeper on Wednesdays."

"Maybe she altered her schedule because of the holidays?" Danny asks.

Julian doesn't think so. "I called Marta," he says. "She told me she wouldn't be coming until after the holidays."

"You've made some pretty big statements about your wife," Danny says. "Something else to back it up, besides a clean house?"

Danny's tone surprises me. It's more than a little confrontational, given the circumstances. I shoot him a quick glare.

He gets the message and I'm all but certain he'll bring it up later.

"The Christmas gifts," Julian says, looking at me. I can tell that he's drawn to me. He knows that I actually care about Kelsey. Danny cares about the case. *His* case.

"What about them?" I ask.

"That night, I couldn't sleep. I just sat there in my chair looking at the Christmas tree and wondering where in the world Kelsey was." He starts to get emotional just then. It's a quiet cry, the kind men do. No real noise, just the tears and the struggle to stop them from pouring from his eyes. "She told me she went shopping for stocking stuffers at Target."

"Yes," I say, urging him to continue in the gentlest way that I can. "She told us that."

I watch him fight those tears again. He sputters. He's doing everything he can to keep going.

"There wasn't anything for Kelsey in those bags."

His wet eyes stay on mine.

"You said that she favored Samuel. Maybe she was doing that again."

He shakes his head slowly. "No. She specifically said that she was shopping for *both* of them. Why would she only get things for Samuel?"

"She was mad at Kelsey," Danny says. "She pitched a fit in the store."

Julian takes a beat to find some composure. He puts his hands on his face and pushes back a little. He locks in his best attempt to keep it together. "Right," he says. "But she told me *both* kids."

"Both," I repeat.

"What are you getting at, Julian?" Danny asks.

Julian ignores Danny. He looks at me. He thinks I somehow understand what he's going through.

"I don't think that Kelsey was ever at Target," he says, his vocal chords tightening and his words coming at us nearly in a whisper. "I think my wife might have done something with her."

CHAPTER SIX

We linger, scanning the space around the double-wide that is our destination once more. A carved sign proclaims who lives there: "The Dawsons." Danny swings open the torn screen door and knocks.

A woman in her twenties answers. She's dressed for work. I recognize the uniform. She works for Panera Bread. She's pretty, with strawberry blond hair, green eyes, and a swath of freckles over the bridge of her nose. Her teeth are crooked but white. If I'd seen her outside of this mobile home park, in something other than her uniform, I would never have guessed that she'd married a sex offender.

"Charlene Dawson?" Danny says.

"I figured you'd be here," she answers. "You people always come around when something like this happens." Her tone is stiff, but more resigned than angry.

"I'm Danny Ford and this is Nicole Foster; we're detectives with the Bellevue Police Department," he says. "We're here to talk with Alan. Is he home?"

"He's at work," Charlene says, inching the door closed.

"No, he's not," I say. "Officers have been to the body shop. He's out."

Something flickers in her eyes. "I can't help you," she says. "I have to go to work. Why don't you just do your job and leave us alone?" Anger has crept into her voice.

Danny sticks his foot onto the doorjamb so she can't close it completely. "Where is he?" he says. "Or do you need to come down to the department and make a statement?"

"I have to work. And I don't know where he is right now. Why can't you people understand that what Danny did ten years ago has nothing to do with the missing girl at Target?"

"He's a sex offender," Danny says. "He's always going to be our first stop. That's the way things work."

Her face is suddenly red. "Leave us the hell alone!"

I pull back slightly, my hand instinctively brushing against my holstered gun as she reaches for her purse behind her, but she just grabs it and pushes out the door.

"I'm going to work," she says, slamming it shut and storming away down the steps. "Alan is a good man," she calls back at us. "You people continue to make the same mistake over and over. He's not a predator. I love him. I always have."

Charlene gets into her car, an old Toyota that struggles to turn over. Through the foggy windows and the smear of water over the driver's-side window, I catch a last glimpse of her. Her face is now red, and I'm all but certain she is going to cry all the way to Panera Bread.

Danny twists the doorknob, but it's locked, and we head back to the office.

◆ ◆ ◆

Alan Dawson was eighteen and attending classes at Bellevue College when he was arrested and convicted for statutory rape. His victim was Charlene Canter, a fifteen-year-old student at Sammamish High School. Her father, a low-level manager at Boeing, was the type of man who had done everything by the book but never seemed to get anywhere. When his wife left him and their children for a man with a higher pay grade, he had appeared to adjust. While no one could see it, though, his anger had become one of those jagged, subterranean fault lines unknown until the earth decides to shift. When he'd discovered that Charlene was having a sexual relationship with Alan, he made a beeline to the police and reported it.

Alan, as the reporting officer told the sergeant on duty, wasn't the "brightest bulb in the chandelier" when questioned. He admitted his involvement with Charlene, though he said he didn't know it was illegal.

"We're both teenagers," he said. "Boyfriend and girlfriend. I really love her."

"That's what all pervs say," the officer who took the statement said.

Eventually, Alan pled guilty and was sentenced to two years in the penitentiary at Monroe, an hour northeast of Seattle. It was one of those stories that went mostly unnoticed and unreported. When he was released, he and Charlene got married and moved into his mother's trailer.

And though they'd made a life for themselves, there was one little thing neither could escape: Alan's crime put him on the sex offender registry.

The list, police like to say, that keeps on giving.

◆ ◆ ◆

When I see her later at the police department, Viola Richards stands stiffly at the front desk with worried eyes and a black plastic bag. Alan Dawson's neighbor and staunch defender is now suddenly transformed into an adversary. She called earlier to say she had found something.

"What?" I had asked her.

Though she'd made the call, silence filled the phone.

"Ms. Richards?"

"I'll bring it to you," she said, her voice clipped and distracted. "It isn't good. It isn't good at all."

I persisted. "What did you find?"

But Viola had hung up. I sat there at my desk for twenty minutes wondering if I should get in my car and drive over to Lake Washington Mobile Estates.

And wondering what she had found.

Viola is wearing a light-pink jogging suit that I suspect owes more to her size than the fact that she's been out jogging. She sees me and turns away, toward the door.

"Ms. Richards," I call to her.

Again, as on the phone, a pause.

"I shouldn't have come," she finally says, slowly turning around to face me. I can't be sure, but I think she's been crying. Her dark-blue eyeliner is smudged.

I keep my eyes on hers and indicate to her to follow me.

"I really shouldn't have come," she repeats. Her hands are jittery and the bag makes the crackling sound of plastic against plastic.

Against whatever was inside.

We go to a small room adjacent to the front desk. It's not an interview room used by the department for interrogations, but one set up to offer clerical and other administrative job applicants a place to fill out paperwork—from the days before everything was done online.

She puts the bag on the table. It's black, with yellow handle-ties that look like a fancy bow.

A present.

Not one Viola had wanted to find, I'm sure. Not one she wanted to bring to me. Yet that's what's happening. I offer coffee or water. She declines. She doesn't want anything. She wants to be anywhere but here.

I keep my eyes on hers as I untie the loops of yellow plastic that keep the contents secure in their black, plastic cocoon.

I peer inside. What I see takes my breath away. I know exactly what it is.

"Where did you find this?" I ask her.

Viola stares at the bag and then clasps her hands to stop from trembling. Her world has been rocked. Everything she'd wanted to believe has been challenged. "Detective," she says, her voice halting, "I'm sick about this."

"Ms. Richards," I say, pushing gently, "where did you get this?"

Viola Richards doesn't break down, but she's on the edge of it. She tells me that she was taking care of the Dawsons' cat, Tracks, while they were away.

"They keep Tracks in the bathroom when they're gone because he's the kind of cat that claws up the furniture when he's angry—which is all the time when Charlene isn't around. I opened the door to feed him, and the little shit got out. He was like a bolt of lightning. Ran right out the front door and under the porch."

She stops to take a breath. She's looking at the bag now. She's remembering how it felt when she made the discovery.

"I feel sick," she says.

"I know," I say. "Did you find it under the porch?"

She nods. "Yeah. That's where I found it."

I think she's going to throw up. She'd loved her neighbors. She had been convinced that Alan was innocent of any wrongdoing. She'd even said so on the local news. I can tell that the part of her that sees good in their love story is now not so sure anymore.

"I remembered what the little girl was wearing from the TV," she says. "My grandson has the same shoes . . ."

She stops talking and presses her shaky hand to her abdomen. Her skin is ashen. By handing me the shoe, she knows that her life has changed forever. Yet I sense that Viola Richards is less concerned with what will happen to her. She was devoted to the Dawsons. She loved them. She was sure that they were underdogs that would prevail in life one day.

Not anymore.

"Do you need to use the bathroom?" I ask.

She lifts herself up from the chair. "Yeah, I think I'm going to throw up."

The evidentiary value of the Elmo shoe Viola recovered while cat sitting is questionable. It wasn't collected properly and a defense attorney would have a field day if the shoe ever found its way into a courtroom. Christine Seiko and her team ran it through the gauntlet of lab tests and were unable to pick up any DNA.

"It's like it was wiped clean," she says. "Some hairs. Not surprisingly, feline."

"Kelsey was wearing shoes like that when she went missing," I say.

"Right," she tells me as we look at the shoe, now tagged and missing a piece of fabric that a forensic lab tech cut out for additional analysis. "There are a lot of shoes like that running around."

She laughs at her line.

I smile, a reflex more than anything.

Danny is practically turning cartwheels in the break room. He'd been working out at the fitness center and the veins in his neck plump like ziti in vodka sauce—his favorite at our Italian place. Danny likes to be pumped up. He likes to be the center of attention. It's who he is. He always wants everyone to see that he's tough, smart. I think there is a gentle side to him, a softer side; I'm just not sure where it is and whether

Gregg Olsen

I should keep looking for it. I don't know if he's my last chance. But he could be.

He's pouring himself a cup of coffee and regaling the officers, including our lieutenant, with the Elmo shoe and what it all means.

He glances at me.

"Look, we don't need to use them in court," he says, as though I'd already voiced my doubts. "We've got leverage now to push that perv to the wall. He killed Kelsey Chase. Dawson's one sick fuck. Can't wait to wipe that smug look off his face. Once a perv always a perv."

I hate to break up his little party, and I know I'll hear about it later, but I have to say it.

"There's no proof the shoe is Kelsey's."

He shrugs and rolls his eyes a little. He's dismissive. "I was doing this when you were still in the academy," he says. "I know what I know."

I want to kick him in the balls and let him know that I'm not going to let him do that anymore. I can imagine the tip of my shoe going right to where it would bring him to his knees.

"There's proof enough," he says. "Enough to rattle his fucking cage and see what falls out."

"There are a million shoes like those," I persist. "It could belong to anyone."

The others feel the unspoken tension and all but our lieutenant file out of the break room.

"Doesn't matter who the shoe belongs to," Danny says. "We have it, and we're going to use it to nail the motherfucker."

"Let's bring him in," Cooper says.

"Let's crush the piece of shit," Danny says.

Chapter Seven

The air in the interview room is stagnant. Quiet. No one is saying anything. Danny and I sit on one side of a long, white Formica-topped table that looks like it belongs in a hospital cafeteria. Alan Dawson, wearing a Metallica T-shirt, black jeans, and boots, stares vacantly into space. I smell the cigarettes and coffee that seep into the air with each nervous breath he takes. He's six feet tall, 175 pounds. His hair is longish, not because he favors the style, I think, but because he doesn't go in for regular cuts. Unlike Danny. I haven't seen Danny's hair grow a quarter inch. It's like he has doll hair. Always the same length. Alan's eyes are dull brown and empty. Only the bead of sweat on his upper lip betrays the nervousness that I'm sure he's experiencing. He's been in a room like this before. Few people are happy repeaters. Those who make return visits seldom do so willingly. Alan sits alone. No lawyer. Charlene is outside in the waiting area. She hugged him before he followed us into the room. I can smell her Jennifer Lopez perfume, clinging on his shirt.

"You know why you're here," Danny says.

"I'm not stupid," he answers.

I hold back. I told Danny before the interview that I'm fine playing good cop, but I will not be mute cop.

"No," Danny says. "No one says you are. You're here because we're on a fact-finding mission. You understand that, right? You're here because you told officers that you want to help."

"Yeah," he says. "I know all about that. But there's one thing you need to know. I don't know nothing about that little girl."

Danny tightens the muscles in his arms as though he's about to slam his fist on the tabletop. But it's an act and I know it. Half of what we do in this room is an act. We lie. We cajole. We promise. We pretend like we care. And indeed we do. We care about making a case and righting a wrong. Danny's more gray area than I am, but when it gets right down to it, I don't ever complain about his sometimes strong-arm tactics.

"That's fine, Alan," I say. "We just need to go over some things. You know how some people are about procedure," I say, glancing over at Danny as though I'm irritated.

Danny puts a photo face down in front of Alan.

I offer Alan coffee or water, but he shakes his head.

Over the next three hours, we talk. We argue. We plead. We worm our way inside of Alan's head, and we try to extract exactly what we're looking for.

Answers.

Truth.

The story.

For his part, Alan teeters between being resolute and being unsure of himself. There are two Alans in that room. We want the weak one to gain ground. We want the Alan who came here of his own accord to push aside the Alan who wants to save himself from another stretch in the penitentiary.

"You have a thing for young girls," Danny says, pretty much out of nowhere. "Some guys do. Maybe it's something that's suppressed deep in our DNA. In some guys, it bubbles up."

"What?" Alan says, suddenly alert. "You're sick. The girl you're talking about was a kid."

"Look," Danny says, "I know that you didn't mean for things to get out of hand. You seem like a nice guy. Yeah, you've had your problems, but hell, we've all been a little fucked up now and then."

Alan doesn't respond for a beat. He looks down at the surface of the table and then over to meet my eyes.

"Talk to us," I say. "We're here to help you. There's a way out of this, and by doing the right thing, no matter how hard it is, you'll feel better."

"Help me? Neither of you gives a crap about me. You don't give a crap about the truth, either. If you did, you'd get out there and look for the killer."

"Who said she's dead?" I ask.

Alan blinks. "No one. Just thinking that probably happened to her."

"Why would you think that?" Danny asks. "Unless you know something about it."

Alan runs his fingers along his neck, loosening his shirt collar. "Everyone thinks she's dead. That some pervert took her and killed her."

"I know who that pervert is," Danny says. "I'm looking right at him."

"You have nothing on me," Alan says. "Because I didn't do it. I didn't do nothing to that little girl."

"We have the little girl's shoe. Came from your place."

He looks puzzled. Not fake, but real. Or maybe he's just looking confused or ambushed.

"I don't know what you are talking about," he says.

Danny gets right up in Alan's face. "The fucking shoe you tried to hide. The shoe you took off the girl, along with her other clothes, when you molested her."

Alan looks at me for support, I think. But I don't give any. I'm not the red-faced aggressive cop that Danny revels in being. I know that his working out at the gym is not to impress me. Not to get looks from other women. It is for moments like this. The muscles in his neck are a fire hose.

"Why are you doing this to me?" Alan asks.

49

Danny's on fire. "Why did you fuck and kill a little girl?"

Like he's been hit, Alan just sits there before speaking. "I didn't. I didn't do nothing like that."

"You make me want to puke," Danny says.

Alan seems to be about to crumble. I'm expecting him to ask for a lawyer, but he doesn't.

"You have me all wrong," he says. "You have it in for me."

"The world picks on you, Alan. Is that it?" Danny makes no effort to hide his contempt. I've seen it when he doesn't get his way in the office or when he loses at the casino. Here it is again.

Alan Dawson is floating on a raging sea. He's trying to stay afloat. But he's going down.

"Cops pick on me," he says. "Charlene and I were in love. We're married. We're going to start a family. But you just won't stop, will you?"

"We'll stop when you tell the truth," Danny says, leaning closer. His breath is hot against Alan's face. He takes that moment to overturn the photograph. It's instantly recognizable as Kelsey Chase. That same photo has been shown on all the local news outlets—TV, radio, print, and especially the Internet, where crime blogger Lane Perry has used it to grow the audience of Eastside Crime Watch.

Alan pushes back his chair. It's as if the sight of the little girl repels him.

"Where is she?" Danny pushes.

"I don't know," Alan says. "I've told you. I don't know nothing about the girl or her shoe. I swear it. You can ask Charlene. She'll tell you."

"She told us she didn't know where you were the day Kelsey went missing," Danny says.

"I stayed home sick. I had the stomach flu."

Danny pushes his chair back. "Really?" he asks. "You can do better than that, Alan. You can think up some other excuse."

"It's the truth."

"You didn't see a doctor, did you?" I ask.

Alan shakes his head. "I don't have insurance. I stayed in bed."

"I bet you did," Danny says, now in disgust mode. "You make me want to puke."

"I didn't do nothing to her. I swear it." He looks over at me, and I pretend to be sympathetic by nodding slightly.

My phone vibrates and I look down at the text. I show it to Danny.

"Just a second," he says. He gets up and goes outside. "Stinks in here." I'm alone with Alan.

"Sure you don't need something?" I ask.

"I need to go. I don't want to keep Charlene waiting."

I don't tell him that he can leave at any time. He hasn't been arrested. He came in voluntarily. I'm not convinced of his guilt the way Danny seems to be. I also don't tell him what the text just relayed to me, that another pair of investigators grilled Charlene and she's left in tears.

"Just tell us what happened?" I say, lifting my eyes to look at the two-way mirror.

"Nothing," he repeats. "Nothing happened."

"Was it an accident? Is that what happened? Did you only mean to talk to her and she got scared? Did you try to quiet her? I bet that's what happened."

Tears roll down Alan's face, but he doesn't make a crying sound.

"You people will never let me be free," he says. "You people think that one mistake—which wasn't a mistake—means that a person is trash. You think that I'm nothing. That I'm a freak. I had sex with my girlfriend when she was a week shy of her sixteenth birthday. I was seventeen and a half. *You.* The press. You all report that she was a fifteen-year-old girl and I was an eighteen-year-old man. We were only a little over two years apart in age. Two fucking years."

I know that if her father hadn't pressed charges with such vehemence, things might have gone another way. But I don't say that. I say, simply, "It was against the law."

Alan wipes his eyes on his Metallica T-shirt. "I didn't know. I really didn't."

"You know that's no excuse. Not knowing something isn't legal is not a defense."

He doesn't say another word to me. I know that, until that point, he thought I was an ally of sorts, or at the very least, someone who would actually listen to his point of view. Someone with an open mind. But, like Danny, I'm here to find out what happened to Kelsey Chase.

Nothing else matters.

After a few minutes of silence, Danny returns and takes a seat. His expression is grim. He has a folder in his hand, and he lets out a sigh. It's as if he's brought with him the key to the mystery of what happened to Kelsey.

And it isn't going to make Alan Dawson the least bit happy.

"You need to be straight with us," he says. "The parents of a little girl need to know what happened to her."

"It was an accident," I say, looking at Danny.

Alan, his forehead now wet with perspiration, doesn't say anything.

"An accident?" Danny repeats.

"I don't know," Alan says, teetering on losing it. "I don't know about that at all."

"Do you really want the death penalty, Alan?" Danny asks. "You know you get your choice. Noose or a needle."

Somehow the mechanic with the sex-offender status finds his resolve. "I didn't do nothing," he says. "I've told you over and over. I never *saw* her."

Danny shoves his body back from the table, in so doing sliding the table into Alan, nudging him, rattling him even more. "You diddled her, and you killed her," Danny says, his words so icy they'd splinter in a good breeze.

Alan wraps his arms around his chest. The sleeve of his T-shirt rides up just enough to expose a tattoo for the first time. It's Charlene's name over a red rose.

"I didn't," he says. "I didn't."

Danny puts his hand on the file folder. I've seen this move before, though I have never used it in an interrogation. To me, it always seemed just a little over the line. Legal, but not right.

"We have proof, Alan," Danny continues. "I thought you'd want to do the right thing without having to be pushed into a fucking wall. For once in your fucked-up life, can you do the right thing?"

"I never saw her. I swear it!"

"Goddammit, Alan! Let's get real," Danny says, now on full-court press. "You have the power to fix things and make them right. We just got the DNA results on the sheets from your bed, and we know that Kelsey was there."

His face tightens. "That's a damn lie!"

"You are the liar. DNA doesn't lie!"

Alan blinks. He's crumbling. "Maybe I blacked out? Maybe I don't remember anything?"

"That's it," Danny says, shifting his tone to something approaching civility. "You don't remember," he says. "But you know she was there, wasn't she?"

Alan looks lost and utterly confused. Tears stream down his cheeks. "Yeah, I guess maybe she was," he says. "I guess she had to be. I don't know how. Honest. I don't. I never saw her. I never did. I want to go home."

"You're free to leave, Alan," I say, still surprised that he hasn't asked for a lawyer.

Danny gets in a last shot. "Free for now."

We watch as Alan collects himself and makes his way down the hall and out the door.

"What was in the file folder?" I ask.

Danny opens the folder and pulls out a single sheet of paper.

"Jimmy John's," he says. "Cal's calling in an order. Turkey Tom, right?"

My smile is an uneasy one.

"Yeah, that's my go-to."

♦ ♦ ♦

The next morning, when I come back from a run to the bank to move some money from one dwindling account to another, it's all backslapping in the office. Danny is in the center of the rest of the team. He is holding a signed confession. It is typed rather than handwritten.

"What's this?"

"Alan Dawson. Admitted most everything."

This is the first I've heard of it. "We pressed him pretty hard yesterday," I say.

"Yeah. We did."

"But he didn't admit to it, Danny."

"To me. He admitted it to me."

Just then Evan Cooper strides over. Lieutenant Cooper is forty-nine. He and his wife Deanna have four girls—going into his office is like going into a girl power kiosk at Bellevue Square. A dozen pictures of the twins and their little sisters adorn the surface of the credenza behind Lieutenant Cooper's desk. He's balding, has a sandbag over his belt, but he beams like a searchlight whenever he talks about his girls. He's the reason I'm a detective.

"We need more like you," he told me one day.

"You mean under thirty?" I asked.

"More diversity," he said. "One day someone like you will be running the place. That's as it should be."

I knew he meant that a woman could be in charge. Or maybe even should be.

"Good work, Foster," he says to me now, seeing me for the first time in the circle of admiration orbiting Danny.

"Thanks," I say, though I'm not sure why.

After everyone leaves and Danny and I are standing in his cubicle alone, I reach out, take the paper, and look at the statement.

On December 23, 2014, I was home alone. I went over to the Target to kill some time. I had been feeling sick and stayed home from work. I did not have it in my mind to do anything other than look around. Maybe get some popcorn or something. I had done all my shopping for Christmas already. When I started back home I saw a little girl crying in the window of a BMW. She was alone. I asked her where her parents were. She said she didn't know. I asked her if she wanted some help in finding them. She said OK. I did not plan to do anything to her. I don't know why I did, but I got her out of the car. I told her that her parents might be nearby and we'd have to look. It was raining, so I picked her up so she wouldn't be cold. We couldn't find her family anywhere in the parking lot, so I took her to my house through the trail in the woods. I fell asleep and blacked out. When I got up I found her in my bed. I don't know what happened. I got so scared. I didn't want to go back to prison. I didn't know what to do. I didn't want my wife to see the girl at our house, so I wrapped her in a sheet and took her to the parking lot south of the East Channel Bridge. It was getting dark, and no one saw me. I put her body in the water, and I went home. I am sorry for what I did. I am sorry that I have disappointed my wife and the people who believe in me.

 Signed,
 Alan Dawson

"When did he say all of *this*?" I ask.

 Giving me an exasperated, dismissive look—*God, he can be such a jerk*—he takes the paper from my hand. "Just now. I took another run at him."

I realize there must be something wrong with me to put up with Danny Ford. He is no good for me. Not in my life. Not at my work. But like limpet on a beach rock, I'm seemingly stuck.

"I didn't know he was coming in, Danny. Why didn't you wait for me?" I ask. "We're a team. At least I thought we were."

"You know how things are," he says. "You have to seize the moment. Strike when the iron's hot. He wanted to talk. I did the interview."

"That was some good, quick work," I say. "Must have been some interview."

"I'd like to say that I was in rare form—in fact, I did say that to Cooper—but really, just right time, right place. He was ready to spill. You'd have had the same outcome if you were here."

"But I wasn't."

He nods. "Right. But so what? What matters is that that fucking piece of shit is going to pay for what he did."

I state the obvious. "Right, except there's nothing to back up his words."

"We don't need Kelsey's body to prosecute."

"We need something."

"We have the shoe."

"We don't know that's her shoe."

"Lab says DNA—his and hers—says it is."

"I didn't know."

"See what happens when you run an errand?"

"Let's go look for Kelsey," I say.

CHAPTER EIGHT

The East Channel Bridge connects Bellevue to Mercer Island, a real estate agent's dream, with homes along its Lake Washington shoreline worth upward of tens of millions. *Each.* The wind is wicked, but at least the freezing rain that the weatherman with the baritone warned of this morning is merely a sputtering of regular rain. I tug at my coat as Danny and I emerge from his vehicle next to the crime techs, who had arrived before we pulled into the parking lot littered with beer cans and cigarette butts. The hum and thump of commuters as they cross the bridge to the island, then on to Seattle across another bridge on the other side, plays over the scene like a teen's amplified bass. The lake is more than 200 feet deep in places. The water, inky black. The muck at the bottom hides countless sunken boats, seven airplanes, a few coal cars and ferries, and undoubtedly numerous bodies weighted down and consigned to the depths.

"Hey Nicole," Christine Seiko calls over.

Christine and I started at Bellevue PD at the same time. She's two years younger and twice as ambitious. She's been promoted to supervisor of the crime lab, married, and become the mother of a darling little boy in only a few years. I can find myself deep in a pool of jealousy some days, upset that none of that has yet happened for me. Clawing for a life ring. But not today.

"Hey," I say. "Anything catch your eye?"

Christine shakes her head and at the same time acknowledges Danny. I get the feeling that she's not all that fond of him. I make a mental note to ask her about it later. But I know I won't. I already know he's bad for me, the same way I know that the idea that chocolate is good for you is just that, an idea.

"I doubt we'll find anything," Danny says. "The weather's been a bitch and this place has seen more action than a frat house." He points the toe of his shoe to indicate a purple condom.

Christine nods then gets back to work. She and her team have mapped out a grid and are doing all they can to scour every inch of the area around the boat launch to see if Alan left anything, anything at all, behind.

Danny and I talk about the case, we make dinner plans, and he promises never to cut me out of the investigation again.

"I'm sorry, Nic," he says. "I just got lucky and went with it."

"It isn't that I don't think you did a great job," I say, "but, you know, it just makes me think that you didn't think enough about me and how I could help with the investigation."

I know if Christine and her team weren't there, he'd wrap his arms around me, flexing those muscles as though the action is to transmit his love to me. "I'm sorry, Babe," he says. "Lesson learned."

I give him a quick smile, despite the fact that I loathe it when he calls me that at work.

Ninety minutes after we arrive, Christine pronounces the scene clear.

"Nothing," she says. "I didn't think we'd find anything. Our guys are going to drag the area around the boat launch in case he weighted her down with something. Wouldn't take much. She's pretty small. A couple of fist-sized rocks could send her into the mud."

I look at Danny. "Did Dawson say anything about that?"

"No. He didn't get into what he did after he brought her here."

It occurs to me that Danny didn't ask.

I'm pretty positive that I would have.

"Lake doesn't give up much," Danny says. "There's more crap down there than a junkyard. Make that a couple of big junkyards."

Christine turns and starts for her black SUV. "Yeah," she says, "if he didn't weight her body with something, then it's probably floated off somewhere. And if that's the case, we'll have to wait until someone calls it in."

I scan the shoreline, the magazine-worthy houses on Mercer Island on the other side, the remnants of the cattails that poke through the shallow edges of the lake like the broken bristles of an old scrub brush just north under the gloom of the stretch of Interstate 90 that feeds traffic from Seattle to Boston. I want more than anything in the world to find Kelsey just then. It's an ache inside. It's a ticking of a clock that reminds me every second that she's out there. She's gone. I know that. But it's more than that. She's lost. She needs me to find her.

We get in the car and Danny looks over to make sure no one is looking, then puts his hand on my shoulder as though he needs to steady himself as he backs up. Our affair has been like that. A game in a way. We pretend that no one knows about us, but I doubt it's that big of a secret. Danny's a talker. I know that.

That night we drive east to the casino along that same stretch of the interstate that passes the spot were Kelsey was dumped. I'm thinking about her all the time we're there and wanting more than anything to talk about it, but Danny's in too good of a mood to share my angst. He wins a thousand dollars at the blackjack table. I pull the handle of a slot that I knew was a mistake the second I inserted my game card.

Whospunit is the name of the machine, a kind of murder mystery game that just keeps my mind on what happened to the little girl who occupies my thoughts. I drink a gin and tonic and watch my balance go to zero after an all too brief flurry of winning.

We have dinner and then we go to my place. I like it when Danny spends the night, though I'm pretty sure I want something more than he can offer. We kiss and fall onto the bed. It's the kind of winner-take-all sex that is his specialty. At times I wonder if this is something we're doing together or something he's doing to me. When I finally climb on top of him, I feel it's less me taking control and going for what will please me than about him actually being willing to give me something.

We kiss and he rolls over. The relationship is a complete and utter loser and I know it.

CHAPTER NINE

Lieutenant Cooper appears at my desk. He's holding his phone like it's sharp and hurts. His face is grim. So grim, I wonder if something has happened to one of his girls.

"I think we might have found her," he says.

He doesn't need to tell me who.

"Call came into the King County call center an hour ago." He lowers his phone and presses the play button of a recording.

"Hey, I found something up here just off the trail near Rattlesnake Ridge," a man's voice says. His tone is urgent. Upset.

"Is it an emergency?" asks the dispatcher.

"Could be. Hell, I don't know."

The dispatcher prompts the caller for more information. She takes down the man's name, his address, and confirms his cellular number. She does it all in a monotone that suggests a script is taped on her computer screen and she's taking care not to miss anything.

There's no "What the fuck do you mean it *could* be an emergency? Why you calling me with this bullshit?" Just a dull-voiced, "What did you find, sir?"

"A body," Darrell Hamilton, thirty-three, says, swallowing some air. "I think I found a body. Looks like a little kid. Hard to say, might be some rotten garbage some shithead campers left here."

"Can you get a better look?" the dispatcher asks. "Can't send law enforcement out for a sack of garbage."

"Hell, do I have to?" the man says, a twinge of fear in his voice.

"Come on. Help me out, okay?"

"Fine. Just a second, it's hard to get to."

He huffs a little, the sound of his feet crunching the crusty edges of a snowbank are picked up by the receiver. Next, the sound of his body weight shifting the refrozen and thawing snow finds its way into the mouthpiece of his phone.

"Oh God," he says, his voice rising. "Oh God!"

"Darrell, calm down." He has her full attention now. "What is it? What do you see?"

"It is a body," he says. "It's a body. A little girl, I think. Want me to unwrap it? It's wrapped in a sheet."

"No. No," the dispatcher says. "Do not touch anything. Stay right where you are. I'm sending someone right now. Do not, I repeat, do not touch anything. Please back away from the body."

"Yeah," he says, "I did. I'm back on the trail now. Who the hell would do something like this? Who in their right mind would do this?"

"All kinds," she says. "There are all kinds of people in this world. I'm going to put you on hold for a minute and let my supervisor know what's happening. I want you to stay on the line until I come back."

Her tone has completed the shift from rote indifference to unmistakable concern.

"All right," he says. "All right."

◆ ◆ ◆

I don't choke up at the news. I don't know why. I wonder if it's because I've already mourned Kelsey Chase's death. I steady myself and get in my leased car to make the notification. Danny is taking some training at the academy in Burien and I know he'll be disappointed that he's missed out, but the discovery of a body has already made the news. Google alerts ping my phone like popping corn.

Julian and Angela Chase live near the top of Somerset, a hilltop development that affords residents gorgeous views of the Olympic Mountains, Seattle, and Lake Washington. The Chases live in a 1960s house that has been completely restored into what it once had been. But better. The word *swanky* comes to mind and swanky is a word that I don't think I've ever said to anyone. Samuel, the five-year-old who was with his mother shopping at Target the day his sister disappeared, answers the door. Immediately a hand comes from around him and latches on.

"Samuel, you must never answer the door! I've told you that a thousand times."

It is Angela. She looks at me and without a word waves me inside. She's changed her look. Her dark hair has been cropped short since the last time I saw her. She's wearing dark slacks and a white cashmere sweater. Her earrings are definitely statement pieces—the statement being that she has money. A lot of it. She reminds me of my sister just now. Not in her coloring, of course. But in that she's perfect in every way. But now, with the news that I've come to bring her, far less so. I want to put my arms around her and hug her like a friend. I want to tell her that I'm so very sorry for her loss.

"Is Julian home?" I ask, though I don't think so. He works downtown and keeps long hours. It's the middle of the day.

"No," she says. "He's never home."

Words stick in my throat a little. I need to tell her something so very terrible, but I somehow think there's a way to soften the blow. It is such a stupid thought. I look over at Samuel, who is playing with an empty AmazonFresh box.

"We need to talk," I tell her. "This is very bad news, I'm afraid. We need to talk alone."

She leads me into the kitchen, where a young woman I take to be Angela's assistant is busying herself with paperwork I assume to be associated with Angela's gluten-free baked goods blog or the boutique she's opened in Bellevue. The girl looks to be about nineteen. Her hair is blond, long, and fashioned in a fisherman's braid.

"Mariel," Angela says, "could you take Samuel to his room?"

When Mariel has disappeared from view, I ask if she might be expecting Julian sometime soon. They both need to hear what I have to say.

"We're not saying anything publicly," Angela says after Mariel disappears from view, "but Julian and I are separated."

"I'm sorry to hear that," I say as I follow her to the kitchen table and sit. She offers me coffee, tea, water, whatever I want. I decline. "You'll be hearing some news today about a discovery made near North Bend."

Her green eyes fix on mine. "Did you find Kelsey?"

I shake my head a little. "We don't know. But the body is a child's. A girl. About the same age and size as your daughter. We can't be sure until it's been examined. I'm really sorry to bring you this news."

The green eyes don't blink. They don't well up with tears. Her mouth tightens a little. "How did she die?"

"We don't know that, either."

"Did he molest her?"

"Sorry," I say, firmly. "We don't know."

Angela's mouth tightens more and she turns away toward her magnificent view. It's a steel-gray afternoon. The clouds over the Olympic Mountains push down hard on its jagged ridgeline.

"You don't seem to know much, Detective Foster, do you?" she asks, still facing away. "I know you think that you do. Wandering in and out of other people's lives with a badge that gives you all-access anytime you desire to poke your nose into something."

I didn't see that coming. I know grief and shock mix sometimes into a kind of toxic brew that can lead to unpredictable results, but still. "I'm just doing my job," I say, though the words feel hollow. Even to me.

"I don't want to see her," she says. "I just want to forget this all happened. I want you to leave. I need you to leave. You have no idea how it feels to have your name all over the news, smeared by innuendo, your marriage torn apart by lies. I had to cut my hair and change Starbucks because of the mess you and your people put me through."

"We were just trying to find out what happened to your daughter," I say, getting up from my chair.

"You know the way out."

"Are you going to tell your husband?"

She stays fixated on the view. "*You* tell him. I know you like him. You have his cell. Call him."

Her words come at me like the round from an AK-47. I do like Julian Chase. I feel sorry for the man. His wife has not made the best witness to their daughter's disappearance. She's been all over the map with her story. At one point while we stood outside the Target, I'd asked her if she was on any medication.

She was holding a coffee that the victim's advocate had given her. She sipped and sneered at me as we stood by the car. I'd offended her.

"Medication is for the weak," she said. "I wonder what *you're* on." She took another hit of her apparent drug of choice, never taking her eyes off me. "And if you're not on anything, you should be," she went on. "Women like you—running around and acting as though you care about everything and everyone—you waste oxygen meant for those who matter."

I'd hit a nerve, which surprised me. I didn't think she had any.

CHAPTER TEN

The day after Kelsey's body is recovered from Rattlesnake Ridge, Danny and I receive electronic copies of the autopsy report from the King County Medical Examiner's office in Seattle. We read at the same time from our respective cubicles. I can hear Danny murmuring about how twisted the killer is and how he's going to nail him, but I tune him out and focus on the report. The cause of death is asphyxiation. Petechial hemorrhaging, the rupturing of the tiny blood vessels in Kelsey's eyes, indicates that her air supply had been forcibly cut off. There was another injury—a cut in her abdomen—but it was small and not the cause of death. However, accompanying pictures showed a small red bloom of blood on the white sheet in which she was found.

Surprisingly, while the three-year-old's anus had been dilated, it was as a result of the freezing conditions. There was no sign of sexual abuse—the basis we assumed for the abduction. Her internal organs contained ice crystals, indicating that she'd been frozen solid while on the ridge. While she weighed a little less than when she was first reported missing, her stomach contents indicated that she'd had a meal of tater tots and a hamburger before she died, which differed from what Julian said his wife told him their daughter had last eaten.

"Pizza," he'd said. "She took the kids out for pizza before going to Target."

A tox screen indicates she'd been given a fairly large dose of dextromethorphan and an antihistamine—both drugs found in Dimetapp, a children's cold medicine. Yet, according to the examiner's report: "The victim did not show any indications of respiratory inflammation."

Danny appears in my cube. "Must've drugged the kid," he says. "Dawson was home sick, remember? Gave her a big old shot of Dimetapp, knock her out before he molested her."

I look up. "I doubt that," I say. "The M.E. says no signs of molestation."

"Who knows what he did to her? Lots of stuff freaks can do to someone and can hide it when they've been doing it as long as Dawson has."

I don't want to have that conversation again. *Why* does he have such a hard-on for the guy?

"Dimetapp is for kids," I say. "Charlene and Alan don't have any."

"Kids only?"

"Right," I tell Danny. "Parents use it to zonk out their kids all the time."

He folds his arms and pulses his biceps. He does that a lot. Nervous tick? Aggressive move? I've never been sure.

"Didn't know you were such an expert on kids," he says.

I'm not, of course, but I have a niece and was a kid myself once. I don't answer him.

I read on while he hovers and flexes.

The final item on the report indicates that the sheet that had been used to hide and transport Kelsey had been turned over to Christine Seiko for examination.

I hunt her down in the hall. No smile on Christine's face, no hello. She looks at me with apologetic eyes.

"What is it?" I ask.

"There's nothing on the sheet except a spot of Kelsey's blood. No fluid. No trace—except some fibers that match the fleece worn by the hiker who found her."

"I don't get it," I say. "Whoever killed Kelsey is the luckiest perp alive."

Christine nods. "I guess, but honestly, I'm baffled. The sheet and body were clean-room quality. Whoever did this to Kelsey really knew what they were doing."

I think it before saying it aloud. "Like he's done it before."

"Right," she says with a sigh. "Someone who has had some practice."

Chapter Eleven

A week later, Christine Seiko and I meet for coffee at the Denny's closest to the office. It's an old-school cop hangout, a place where we don't need to worry about someone freaking out if they catch a glimpse of our guns. She messaged me that she's been troubled by something and wanted to talk.

We settle into a booth along the front windows. The restaurant has seen better days. The booth's cracked vinyl has been repaired with duct tape. The faux-oak grain of the table has been rubbed off by countless elbows and sliding plates.

"I hear they'll be closing soon," Christine says.

"Too bad. Lots of memories here," I say. "Not all good. But a lot of them."

We motion to the waitress.

"Just coffee," Christine says.

"Me too."

"Something's bothering me about the Dawson case," she finally says as the waitress leaves. "The evidence doesn't point to him."

I nod. "It isn't any single bit of evidence that we're looking at," I say, "it's the sum of every piece that puts Alan Dawson right where he belongs."

Christine sips. Her glasses are new and I want to say that I like them. But I don't. She's undeniably uneasy. "I understand, Nicole. But there is zero physical evidence on Kelsey's body. Not a hair. Not a skin cell. No fluids."

"He was careful," I say. "He'd been in prison. He watches *CSI*. I don't know how, but he knew how to sanitize her body so that he didn't leave a trace of his DNA."

Christine holds my gaze. "That's what I'm getting at, Nicole. It wasn't just that there was none of his DNA on her body, her clothes, or the sheet she'd been swaddled in. There was *no one's* DNA. Do you understand how remarkable that is?"

I know she didn't mean to be condescending just then. It isn't her way.

"Not impossible," I say.

Her phone rings, but she ignores it. "Wouldn't you expect to find her mother's DNA on her?" she asks. "Her brother's? Maybe even an unknown sample from someone who brushed up against her in the Target?"

"I don't know," I say. "I guess so."

I ask for more coffee. I've gulped down my cup. Christine has barely had any at all. I feel nervous, but I don't know why.

"He confessed, Christine. He admitted that he took her. That he killed her."

"I looked at the confession," she says, challenging me a little. "He never said he killed her. He never used her name. He never once said any of that. I went back to reread the confession," she says. "I thought that maybe Danny or you missed something. Maybe he'd indicated how he'd managed to hide her body and dispose of it without anyone seeing. In North Bend, of all places too. Seems like a long way to go. He told us over by the East Channel Bridge, remember?"

Of course I remembered.

"He had family in North Bend," I say. "He was there the night she went missing."

Christine shakes her head.

"I don't think he dumped her on Rattlesnake Ridge that night. I looked at the weather report for the two weeks after Christmas. It was raining in the mountains, Nicole. There's no way that body stayed frozen until it was discovered."

"Are you working for Alan Dawson's court-appointed lawyer?" I ask, my tone more defensive than I mean it to be.

"Thanks," she says. "I thought we were friends."

"We are. It's just that—I don't know. I'm not sure what you are getting at."

"I'm warning you that something isn't right. Dawson may have done the crime, but if you ask me, he wouldn't even know what eight-hundred-thread-count Egyptian cotton was, much less have any of it on hand."

I look blankly at her.

"The sheet that Kelsey was wrapped up in was Boll and Branch and, as sure as I'm sitting here, didn't come out of someone's bedroom at the trailer park."

"That sounds suspiciously elitist," I say.

"Not meant that way. Just a fact."

I set down my cup. "They all have iPhones and flat-screens. You'd be surprised about the priorities of people who don't have much money."

I watch as Christine sinks into the ratty booth. She knows me well, and I can see she's assessing. Analyzing.

"I could be wrong," she says, looking away. "There's a first time for everything." She looks up just then and forces a smile that has more to do with keeping the peace in our friendship than being self-deprecating.

I pay the bill and we walk out to our cars. I end by telling her that I like her new glasses. She says something about the earrings I'm wearing. I'm not exactly sure what happened there, but I know that something is wrong.

Danny never told me about the sheet. Before I ask him about it, I think that I should review the tapes of Alan Dawson's confession.

The Records department at the Bellevue Police Department is enormous, new, and very, very well organized. Everything has a place and everything is in its place. Before joining the department, I worked for a city east of the mountains. Its records and exhibits were kept in plastic storage containers, old U-Haul boxes, and for some reason—proximity to a defunct orchard I imagine—vintage apple crates.

Don Cudahy runs the Bellevue PD records department. He's been there forever, seeing it through something that might have been like the apple crates of my last job to the state-of-the-art facility it has become. He buzzes me in. He's in his late sixties, with snowy-white hair and cheeks so pink that they suggest a permanent state of blush. He is trim, quick, and helpful. All the things more than thirty years in a government job should abate.

"What can I do you for?" he asks.

"Hi Don, I'm following up on the Dawson case."

"Congratulations on that one. Confession. Saves the taxpayers' money and keeps our pension safe. Case closed."

"I'm not so sure."

He clicks a few times and stares at his computer screen.

"Hmmm," he says.

I lean in. "What is it?"

He looks at me over the round rims of his glasses. "Must be a mistake."

"What?"

"The tape was checked out but not returned."

"Who has it?"

"*You* do."

On March 1, against my better judgment, which I realize is not so great these days, I decide to make a call to blogger Lane Perry. He baited a hook and I'm biting. While the office staff, cops, clerks, and the powers that be move past my cubicle, I listen to his latest voice mail before I dial.

"Detective Foster, Lane Perry here. I have big news I'm about to break, and I need your comment."

He's been a festering wound in my side for weeks, never letting up, always pushing for an interview that I'll never give. I've provided all the right reasons. Ongoing investigation. Not what the family wants. Too soon. Department policy. None seem to sway him from trying to call me. His approach has always been the same. He doesn't think that Alan Dawson was the killer, and he wants me to comment on that.

As if I ever would.

I dial his number.

"This is Detective Foster. Returning your call. What's up?"

His voice is an excited one, but then, it always is that way in his voice mails. As though he only knows a single mode. His words rush at me. "My source tells me that Alan Dawson committed suicide this morning."

"No comment," I say.

"Detective, I'm about to push the button to make my post live. I really need a comment from you. He said he was coerced and framed. He planned on suing the police department."

"No comment," I repeat, hanging up. I look for Danny, but he's still not in. I try him on his phone. No answer. I dial the jail and the superintendent confirms the suicide.

"Wasn't he on suicide watch?" I ask.

"Yeah, but around here all that means is that we take away sharp objects and look in every fifteen minutes. You can do a lot in fifteen minutes if you put your mind to it."

Chapter Twelve

I think about Kelsey before I go to the door. She's always there, inside of me somehow. I think about her final minutes on earth. I know she was scared, because she had to be. She'd been snatched away from her life, taken in the dark, and then discarded by some kind of evil she never could have imagined. I wonder if she called out for her mother. For her father. For Samuel. I wonder if she knew what was happening to her the minute she was abducted from that Target.

If that's what really occurred.

I stand there in front of that gorgeous quartersawn fir door and steady myself. I knock.

Julian answers. He's dressed in faded gray jeans and a black T-shirt. He looks casual in a way that I haven't seen him. He looks calm at first, until he realizes it's me disturbing his morning.

"I expected Angela," I say, looking at my wrist, though I don't wear a watch. "I thought you'd be at work."

He shrugs a little. He hasn't shaved today. I notice how tired his eyes look. What happened to his family continues to take a toll. He's already lost some weight. "Taking some time off," he says.

I'm here to drop some more bad news on a family who has endured the worst kind of loss. I was there at the funeral at Sunset Hills Memorial Park. Some park. It was raining and the crowd was packed in around the tiny gravesite, a sea of black-coated mourners. It was hard to tell where the tears ended and the rain began. If anyone had asked, I'd have told them that I was there as a department representative. As though we provide that kind of public service. I was there because I knew that what was happening to the Chases was far from over. Burying the remains of their beautiful little girl wasn't the end of anything. Not really. While there would be no trial, there would still be media intrusions. People like Lane Perry would trade innuendo for clicks.

I follow Julian inside and he shuts the door. In the foyer are several boxes. Some empty. Some brimming with toys and clothes. I don't say anything about what I'm seeing. I can't imagine what it would be like to pack up your daughter's bedroom. How it would feel to sort through the tiny reminders. I don't even want to know. As my eyes scrape over the boxes, I notice that the contents so carefully packed away closest to where Julian stands are women's shoes.

"She's moving out," he says, acknowledging my unasked question.

"Sorry," I say, not telling him that she'd already told me of her plans.

He crosses his arms over his chest. "Yeah," he says. "Her choice, in case you are wondering."

"It's none of my business."

He motions me to the kitchen where he pours me coffee. I notice a shot of whiskey goes into his cup.

"Are you all right, Mr. Chase?"

"No," he says, drinking. "And I won't be if you keep calling me that. Julian. Please."

He slides into a chair and I do the same. I face him and give a quick nod. "Right."

"Things haven't been right between us," he says. "Not for a long time."

I think about cutting him off and stopping the conversation, but I don't. I think about the reason I came there, but I hold it inside for now and listen. Julian tells me that no matter what the evidence showed he hadn't been convinced that Angela was telling the truth.

"She didn't seem despondent on Christmas. She told me that she was putting up a front for Samuel. That she didn't want to ruin his special day. That we didn't know what happened to Kelsey and she was sure she'd turn up."

I let his words soak in. The pause allows him to say more, but he doesn't.

"She was in shock," I say, though I don't mean it. I go back to how she acted in the parking lot on December 23. I would have put money on her being the best suspect. She was too, too . . . too controlled, and too concerned about things that didn't matter. She'd completely dissociated herself from her missing daughter. I wished that I'd asked to see the contents of her shopping bags back then. I wished that I'd have thought to ask her how a mother in her right mind leaves her three-year-old girl in a car unattended.

But I didn't.

"She moved to a condo in Kirkland. Took Samuel. Says that she's not ever coming back. She was a bitch before I married her. My mother told me women like her don't get nicer as time goes on. Guess Mom was right."

"I'm sorry."

"Not your fault," he says, drinking that whiskey-infused coffee.

People self-medicate all the time. My dad did. I know that when I sit at the slot machines and wait for Danny to win big at the tables, I'm doing the same thing. I'm trying to find some solace, some comfort, something. I press the button and the lights flash, the colors drill into my retinas and I feel a rush. I feel better.

"I came here to tell you something," I say.

He studies my face. "This can't be good."

"I don't know how to frame it for you," I say, before I blurt it out. "Alan Dawson committed suicide early this morning."

Julian doesn't say anything for the longest time.

"Suicide," he finally repeats. "Why would he do that? He said he was innocent, that he was going to prove it in court. He seemed like such a convincing liar. Wasn't he supposed to be on suicide watch?"

I nod before echoing the words of the superintendent at the jail. "They can only do so much. They looked in on him every fifteen minutes."

"How?"

"Hung himself with his bedsheets."

The words *bed* and *sheets* stay with me.

"Why would he kill himself, Detective? He gave that interview to Eastside Crime Watch just last week. He said that he was innocent and that he hadn't confessed to anything. That the confession was one big lie. He threw some shade on you and the police department. You saw that, right?"

Of course I did. *Everyone* did. The department's PR flack told us to ignore Lane Perry's blog and focus on ensuring justice for Kelsey.

"No one knows what someone else is thinking," I tell him. "You know that, don't you?"

I'm referring to Angela, not Alan, but leave it unsaid. Julian knows that I don't like or trust her, and I'm all but certain that's our common ground. Now, and back when Kelsey first went missing.

"Do you think Dawson could have been innocent?" he asks.

I don't want to answer that. I think of Christine and the evidence. The bedsheet that she was sure would never have come from a part-time mechanic's home.

They might come from a home like *this*.

"One thing that's bothered me," I say, "was the bedding that the killer used to transport Kelsey."

He gulps more of what I suspect is more whiskey than coffee.

"What about it?"

"Nothing," I say, not sure why I don't want to go all the way with it right then. Danny would consider me disloyal. My lieutenant would say that I shouldn't discuss the specifics of a case with a grieving family member. "Generalities," he'd say. "Be vague. The less they really know the better they are for it. No matter how much they beg. Telling them any details whatsoever could compromise the case."

I don't care about any of that right now. I tell him.

"They were Egyptian cotton. The best money can buy. Eight hundred thread count."

He sets down his boozy coffee. "Angela has a thing for sheets," he says. "What color?"

"White."

He leads me to what appears to be Angela's office. It's a bedroom painted in pale pink with a closet that holds perfectly folded stacks of towels, tablecloths, and sheet sets.

The sheet found wrapped around Kelsey's body had a satin piping. I scan the closet for the shimmer of fabric. Nothing. I run my fingers down the stacks, searching. Nothing. I turn around and notice for the first time that the wall by the door we entered through is covered with photographs of Samuel. He's standing next to the windmill at Marymoor Park in Redmond. He's pulling a wagon. He's holding a blue Seahawks football. Close-ups. Group shots in which he is the undisputed focal point for the photographer, presumably Angela. I feel sick, breathless. I look over at Julian.

He knows what I'm thinking.

"There's one photo of Kelsey," he says, indicating a wallet-sized photo of brother and sister. "I think she put that one up only because she loved Samuel's smile in it."

Kelsey is holding her brother's hand and looking up toward the lens. She is smiling in that way little children do, exaggerated, on cue. Someone said "macaroni and cheese" or something and she smiled so big. Samuel is looking at his sister with a smile too. The photo appears to be recent. Kelsey is wearing the same pink coat Angela described to investigators when she went missing from Target.

I step closer to the photographs, take down the image with Kelsey and her brother and study it. I ask Julian if I can have it, and he nods. My eyes well up with tears. I cannot believe that a mother could love one child over another to this extreme.

I understand favoritism. How one child can be the apple of a mother's eye.

Like Stacy had been.

But this. I hold my words for a beat, thinking how Kelsey must have felt every time she wandered into her mother's office. Was she scanning the wall to find a picture of herself? Did she delight when her eyes landed on this one? Did she understand that her mother didn't love her the way she loved Samuel?

Or did she wonder if her mother loved her at all?

"This is more than not *taking to* Kelsey," I finally say. "Those are the words you kept using, weren't they?"

Julian slides into Angela's office chair, one of those white and chrome Italian chairs on casters. It rolls a little and he steadies himself. I'm unsure if he's had too much to drink or if he's overcome with emotion.

Bringing me to this room had not been an accident. It hadn't been about looking for sheets that might have been there.

"Yes," he says, "that's the way I tried to explain it."

I push. "She hated your daughter, didn't she?"

He notices my tears but doesn't offer me a tissue. I'm glad for that.

"As I told you, Angela didn't take to her. I think she wanted nothing more than to be rid of Kelsey, literally, from the day she was born.

When we were in the hospital and the nurses brought her to us, she whispered to me that she'd never forgive me for not letting her get an abortion. She turned to the nurses with a big smile and said, 'Daddy, here's your little girl.' They all beamed. They had no idea that she was literally handing Kelsey over to me."

"I'm sorry," I say. What else could I possibly say?

He takes the photograph from my hand and places it on the OCD-organized desk.

"I think she did something to Kelsey," he says. "I really do. I think she either sold her or gave her away. I don't think she would actually kill her. Angela wouldn't want to mess up her hair. She wouldn't want to deal with a bloodstain."

A million things cross my mind. None pleasant. I allow myself to wonder about the odds of a man like Alan Dawson coming to Angela's rescue. How she might have wanted to get rid of the inconvenience of a daughter she'd never wanted. How she might have arranged all of it. *Sociopath. Bad mother.* I have experience with both of those labels.

"Are those sheets?" I ask, looking at a carton in front of the desk. Julian leans forward awkwardly and nods.

I find myself kneeling on the floor. I start digging through the folded fabric. I am careful to keep things neat. I always have been. He gets up from the chair and joins me, dropping to his knees too. We start digging for those satin-edged sheets. Our hands touch. I look into his eyes and then, embarrassed for some weird reason, I pull away.

"They're not here," I say, pulling myself up. "I need to leave. I need to tell Angela about Dawson's suicide."

Chapter Thirteen

Angela Chase doesn't answer her phone. I leave a message. I call again. I drive to her boutique. It's one of those clothing stores in which everything is cream, white, or black. Its interior is a gleaming starkness that suits what I think of Angela Chase at the moment. She's gorgeous, but cold. She could be stone. And if she were, she'd be alabaster. Smooth. Flawless. She sees me from the raised office area and immediately descends. *She's like a winged predator,* I think.

"Angela," I say, examining her demeanor, wondering if my own mother was like her in some way.

"Detective," she says. "What are you doing here? We don't carry your size."

Her tone is so friendly that anyone overhearing would have thought her words were given in kindness. In any case, I'm a six. Unless bulimics are her only clientele, I am fairly certain that she stocks my size.

"I'm not here to shop," I say.

"Then why?"

I just come out with it. There's no room for asking how she's doing. How Samuel is. If she misses her daughter even just a little, tiny bit. If her life is perfect now that Kelsey is gone. I tell her about Alan Dawson's suicide and I wait for her reaction.

"You could have called me with that," she says.

"I tried."

"Is there anything else then?"

She's such a bitch. So I decide to be one too.

"I saw Julian," I say. "I'm sorry that you two have separated."

She knows what I'm doing, so she deflects it. She treats Julian like he was a Persian cat hair on a black velvet pillow. She picks and flicks. "It's fine," she says. "The situation with Kelsey only magnified our problems. And you thought we were the perfect couple."

Situation with Kelsey? How about Kelsey's abduction and murder? That's not a situation but a nuclear bomb detonated with the Chases all wrapped around it, I thought.

"I just thought you would want to know before it finds its way into the news."

A shopper listening to us, a size two with plenty to choose from, stalls to take it all in.

"Then the case is closed. No trial. Just over."

"Right," I say. "Just over."

She turns and leaves me standing there. I don't get that woman at all. I head out the door, and a beat later the size two with the big ears stops me in the courtyard.

"I couldn't help but overhear," she says. She's in her forties. She seems nervous and I give her a moment.

"I've been following the story about Kelsey Chase," she says.

"It has been pretty big news," I say, acknowledging the obvious and giving her the opportunity to say whatever it is she has to say.

"You're the detective on the case, right?"

"That's right."

"I meant to call you. I thought of it a hundred times, but my husband said to stay out of it. He told me to mind my own business and that I watch too much TV and spend too much time on the Internet. I admit that I'm fascinated by crime."

"A lot of people are," I say. "What was it that you wanted me to know?"

"It might be nothing."

"That's all right. Just tell me."

"I work at Carson Luggage. Like I said, it might be nothing, but I was working on the morning of December 23 and Angela Chase came in. She seemed frazzled. I mean, I know how these women are. I'm not one of them; I actually *have* to work. They come in the store bragging about the trips they're going to take. A cruise. A private island. Whatever they can say to make the help feel like, well, the help."

"She was frazzled. How do you mean?"

The woman thinks. I can tell she's nervous. What she's holding inside has troubled her.

"She said she was going on a trip and needed a large suitcase. I pulled out several to show her but she said none were right. It needed to have wheels because it was going to be very heavy. She said she wanted soft-sided luggage because she had to put something bulky inside."

She looks around.

"Go on."

A couple walking and talking on their cell phones stops to see where they are.

"Well, I made a joke," she says. "I said what are you going to put in it, a body? She got so mad at me. She stomped out of there. I didn't mean to offend her. It really was a joke. And then I saw what happened on the news."

That night Danny and I have drinks at Duke's. He's on edge about something, and I don't know what it is. I tell him about the woman from the luggage store, and he cuts me off.

"Look," he says, setting down his empty scotch. He motions to the waiter to bring another and looks at me. I shake my head. One is enough. "You need to leave this alone. It's over."

"Something isn't right," I say. "I can feel it."

"There you go *feeling* something."

The go-to dig he uses to shut me down. He builds me up, then tells me that I'm wrong, that I've misconstrued something. That I've let my intuition get in the way of authentic police work. This is one of those times when I wonder how in the world I ended up with someone like Danny Ford.

"Dawson is dead," he says. "It's over. He couldn't stand the guilt of killing that kid. You know we had him dead to rights. You saw the confession."

Confession. Oh that. I read it. I wasn't there when it was made. You did that all on your own.

"About that," I say, a little unsure where I'm going, but deep down knowing that it's a place fraught with consequences. "I went to look at the tape, and it was missing."

He reaches for his third scotch and drinks. There is no eye contact, just a glance that barely washes over me. He swallows some more.

"Checking up on me, were you?" he asks.

I was. Now I know it.

"No," I lie. "Not that. I just thought maybe we'd missed something. He had an alibi. Charlene was adamant that she called him from work and that he was at home the whole time."

Danny stares straight ahead. "Cell phones can ring anywhere there's a tower," he says. "Wherever he took her."

A beat of silence, then a girl laughs at something her date said. An exaggerated and desperate sound. I look in her direction, glad for the slight break it gives me. It buys me time. I think very hard about what I'm going to say next. Danny is a marginal boyfriend, a so-so lover, and, most importantly, a formidable opponent.

As I sit there, Laughing Girl pelts the bar with another laugh. Her date must be very, very funny.

Or she is very, very desperate.

Swipe left.

As for Danny, I wonder if I care about him just enough to let this slide.

"Landline," I finally say. "The calls that Charlene made were to the landline at their trailer. Alan doesn't have a cell phone. They couldn't afford one."

Danny rolls the shrinking, rounded ice cubes around the bottom of his empty glass and stares at me. "Doesn't matter," he says. "Dawson's guilty. He's got a record of molesting girls."

"Charlene Dawson was fifteen, almost sixteen," I say. "She wasn't a three-year-old, Danny."

He doesn't say anything for what seems like the longest time. The waiter looks at us, and I nod. There's tension here. I need a second gin and tonic after all.

"The confession wasn't real," I say.

Danny stays silent.

"And now he's dead."

"Guilt will do that to you," Danny finally answers.

I gulp my drink the instant it's set in front of me, maybe to keep from throwing it into Danny's face. I want to get up and walk out of there right now. I have made a mess of my life up to this point. This was another misstep. I never choose the right guy. It's like I'm on some kind of never-ending hunt to find the worst man in the room. The one I'll go home with. The one I'll lie to myself is different from the others. Danny Ford is another in the long list of the bad choices I've made. I'm about to enter my midthirties, and it occurs to me just now that I'll need to have my eggs frozen.

"I can't keep this to myself," I tell him, my heart rate escalating. "You know that."

He turns away and refuses to look at me.

"I'll tell them that you were part of it," he says.

And there he is. The real Danny Ford has emerged. The man sitting across from me is no different from the creeps that we collar every day. Before Dad lost his mind to the haze of Alzheimer's, he told me that cops and criminals shared the same DNA. He's right about that. I see that now. I will take Danny down if it's the last thing I do.

"Why did you do it?" I ask.

"Because I knew he was guilty. You know it."

"I don't."

"You did. You allowed this to happen. Now you're pretending that you're something special, something high and mighty, when you and me—we're the same. We didn't go into this job to let the scum of the earth overtake the world like some goddamn plague."

"Alan Dawson didn't do it."

"So what if he didn't? He's still scum."

"How can you sleep at night?" I ask as I get up to leave.

"Fucking you puts me to sleep just fine."

I get up to leave. I'll let those be the last words he says to me.

◆ ◆ ◆

I turn the ignition and wait for my car to warm up. My hands are cold and my heart is racing, but I'm not falling apart. In some ways, I feel free. Our relationship was going nowhere. I knew that when he didn't balk about my spending Christmas with Stacy and Cy. We'd been lovers for a year and a half. *Lovers.* Wrong word. He fucked me. He gave me just enough to make me think that we were going somewhere. That he was almost to the point of having me move in. He took me to the casino because it looked better for him—like he didn't have a gambling problem when he had a girl on his arm. At work he used me too. Whenever I uncovered a promising lead, he was there to take credit for it.

I put the car in gear and pull into traffic. I'm alone, but somehow it feels crowded in the space of my car. I can feel the presence of others. I look in the rearview mirror. The backseat is empty, of course. It's a trick that my heart is playing on me, and I know it. As I drive I feel like Alan Dawson and Kelsey Chase are with me. I know that I have let them both down.

Something is happening to me. I lay in my bed late that night, feeling the vibration of my phone like rolling thunder as Danny texts me. I turn on the white noise machine on the nightstand. I pull Shelby close but, hot water bottle that she is, she doesn't comfort me at all. Danny's texts have unnerved me. They are like that hard, needlelike rain that hits your face as you scurry from your car to the doorway of the Starbucks to buy a drink that's overpriced, not very good, and served by someone who robotically reads your misspelled name from the cup and tells you to have a super day. I get up and drink some Nyquil even though I don't have a cold. I need something to help me sleep. I try to avoid my reflection in the mirror. Eyes are shot. Skin's breaking out. Seeing the consequences of a conscience only makes it worse. Back in bed, I pick up my phone and scroll though Danny's predictable tirade. They are a dartboard of emotions. He cajoles. He threatens. I imagine how he feels, like building a house of cards in a tornado corridor.

```
You are not perfect.

You'd be nothing without me. You know
that, don't you?

Answer me, Nic.
```

I'm coming over.

I'm not letting you walk away from us.

You don't know what you're getting yourself into.

You can't be such a goody goody.

Bitch.

I love you.

Keep your mouth shut.

No one wants to hear what you think.

I can't see. The screen on my phone is blurry. I pull Shelby closer. This is all I have. And I'm about to risk it all. As I bury my face in my pillow, I think about what I have to do.

Chapter Fourteen

It has been months since Kelsey's disappearance. I'm looking at my lieutenant and the faces of the men from Internal Affairs just now, and even though I've invited this scrutiny, I feel like I'm starting to drown. I want nothing more than to get the hell out of the little conference room and back to the slots that relieve my stress the way a heroin addict surely must feel when the needle slips under their skin. The sudden rush is indescribable. It's the kind of relief that only someone in absolute pain can even comprehend.

And even then they'd come up short.

It's a hot potato game that leaves my fingers burned. I reiterate that Danny falsified Alan Dawson's confession. That Danny discarded the videotape of it. They push back, noting that as Danny's jilted lover, I can hardly be unprejudiced against him. That he dumped me because of my gambling problem. That my behavior has been erratic. It's like an out-of-body experience and I'm hovering over my interrogators. None of this should be happening.

"Your accusations are serious, Detective," the thin one finally says.

"Why should we believe you?" says the fat one.

I look for help from Evan Cooper, but he just sits there. I want him to say something about how he knows me, how he trusts me, but he's mute.

"Why would I lie?" I finally ask.

"Sometimes a lie is the easy way out," says the fat one.

The room constricts, and I think I hear the sound that the slots make when I win, but I'm not winning now. I'm losing.

"I didn't take the tape from evidence."

"Detective Ford says you did," thin one says.

"What reason?" I ask. "Why would I ever do that?"

The fat one folds his arms and his shirt buttons strain over his stomach. I hope they pop. I hope the button hurls into my eye and permanently blinds me. Then I could sue. Then I could get away from this humiliation.

"We can't divulge everything right now," he says.

◆　◆　◆

I feel sick, and I look for a friend. Someone who will tell me it will be all right. In the lab I find Christine. She looks up from her computer. She's startled; I hadn't meant to sneak up on her.

"You practically jumped out of your skin," I say, apologetically.

The crime lab supervisor touches her mouse, and the screen goes to the screensaver of her son with a soccer ball and the biggest grin in Bellevue. "Just doing some online shopping while we wait for the autopsy," she says, barely looking at me.

I saw what was on the screen.

The Eastside Crime Watch, the guilty pleasure that our lieutenant has asked us to refrain from viewing at work.

"That leech Lane what's-his-name logs our IP address," he's said at least twice, referring to the blogger Lane Perry. "I don't like it when he reports us among his readership, especially when he has a hard-on for whatever it is we've supposedly done."

I could call Christine on it right now. In a joking way, of course. But before she closed it, I saw that she was making a comment. I wonder what she was saying. I know that I've had a thing or two that I've wanted to say to Perry—none of which I'd want tracked back to the Bellevue Police Department's IP, that's for sure.

"Trying to find a decent car on Craigslist," she says, doubling down on the online shopping lie.

I stand there looking at her, wondering about the reason for the lie. I don't challenge her. I'm already in trouble here. I don't need any problems with the last true friend I have in the department.

"Just wanted to see if you wanted to go to lunch," I say.

She looks at me with her gorgeous almond eyes, then over to the overflowing in-basket that commands the space next to her desk phone. "Rain check, Nicole. I'm in the middle of something. Tomorrow or Friday?"

She's brushing me off, and it stings me.

"Sounds good," I say.

I know that as time goes on, as Danny sinks himself deeper into the hole he's digging by throwing me under the bus and denying what he did, others will treat me the same way. Doing something wrong and lying about it is about as low as one can go. Not being aware of what's happening right in front of your eyes, though—that's unforgivable.

That afternoon I scan Lane Perry's blog. There's a post about Kelsey's case, but it doesn't offer anything. Not really. Lane's over-the-top prose trashes Angela Chase's failed food blog. She's written a story about a low-calorie eggplant pizza that she said was "guilt-free." Lane copied the post and added his own rejoinder: "The only thing guilt free is the pizza, not Target Mom!"

I read the comments to see what, if anything, Christine wrote. But there's nothing there.

CHAPTER FIFTEEN

Evan Cooper reminds me of my father. Never more so than at this moment, as my lieutenant watches me pack my things in the humiliating ritual prescribed by Human Resources and the powers that be. It isn't his formidable physical presence that takes me back to my childhood. Cooper is barrel-chested, thick-necked, and has eyebrows that need a lawnmower. His forearms are firewood thick. My father was slighter in build and had sandy, curly hair. As awe-inspiring as Evan Cooper is, it is softened with a sweet and slight lisp that I know he's fought with speech therapy since he was a child. It's that vulnerability that reminds me of Dad. Dad was tough, but when he looked at you, really looked at you, you could see that under the veneer of father, provider, and husband beat a tender heart.

He stands in front of me blocking my view of those in the Bellevue Police Department who suddenly loathe me. The switch was sudden. The instant that word got out that I suspected Danny Ford had messed with the evidence and lied to everyone about it, I'd gone from colleague to pariah. In a matter of a single day, I went from being part of the police department to part of a problem. Sympathetic nods turned into blatant avoidance. Even Shelley in Records—whom I'd helped get a promotion—pretended she didn't see me when we were the only two people in the break room. I did the right thing. I know it. Yet in the Circle of Blue, I've betrayed them all.

"Only personal items, Nicole," he says as I put my desk calendar into the evidence box the department has provided.

"It's mine."

He shakes his head. "No. Department issue."

I keep my eyes on the calendar. "I have some notations, phone numbers I need to keep."

"Sorry. You'll need to leave it."

"Until I come back," I say, glancing at him and hoping for some affirmation.

He nods.

The moment feels very false just then. I don't know if I will be back. Danny and I have been put on administrative leave. He made good on his unspoken promise to screw me one last time. Figuratively, of course. Though nothing indicates that I had any knowledge that he'd tampered with evidence at the time, I'm guilty of not reporting my suspicions sooner. I own that. It is what I did.

"Got everything?" the lieutenant says.

I'm not crying, but my vocal chords feel stuck in a low gear, and I can't quite speak.

"Okay then," he says, "I'll walk you out."

My cubicle had a window. I fought for that space that overlooked a row of old Douglas firs, planted by some homeowner before the city bought the property and tore down the old house that had sat in decay for decades. The old lady who had lived there was a classic cat lady. She had dozens of them. Every now and then someone would complain to the city that she was a nuisance. That the place was an eyesore. That she stood in the way of progress. Before Hoquiam, when we lived on the Eastside, my sister and I used to ride our bikes over to the old lady's place, leave them by the firs—though they were much smaller then.

Gregg Olsen

Her name was Mary. She didn't care what anyone thought of her. In a way I admired her for that.

When I come back to work at the police department, I tell myself, I'll push out whoever takes my place by the window. The view won't matter to them. Not like it does to me.

"I'm going to try to sort this out," Evan Cooper says.

We stand next to my car.

I choke out a single word. "Thanks."

"I know you were only doing the right thing."

I balance my sad carton of personal items, which amounts to nothing more than a few desk photos, a coffee mug, a hot pot, and a box of Earl Grey tea. He takes the box while I open the car door.

"I was trying."

The lieutenant, my mentor, hands me the carton and turns away. He doesn't say anything more. I allow myself to think that he's fighting the urge to tell me everything he's thinking. I've been to Cooper's for dinner. When his youngest daughter was born, I went to the hospital to see Deanna and their new baby, Carly. This is not just an employee getting the boot for something she shouldn't have done. It's deeper. Evan Cooper knows me. He knows Danny. I would never put ambition before the truth. His frame disappears from view as I slide behind the wheel and turn the ignition. The wipers send a pair of gray arches over the windshield. I sit there for a second before I put the car into gear and drive out of the parking lot—past those fir trees.

Doing the right thing feels like shit.

CHAPTER SIXTEEN

We sit there looking at the big plasma screen. It's so large that I wonder how in the world they got it into the house. Tear out a window, maybe? Cy tells me its dimensions and how he's the first person in the United States to have one—a Microsoft supplier in China gave it to him.

My brother-in-law holds a drink in one hand and a remote in the other.

"I've synched it up with my phone," he says.

My sister sits next to her husband on their robin's-egg-blue sofa while he cues up his photos from his recent trip to Thailand. Emma is on my lap on the sofa. She's freshly bathed and smells better than anything I've ever smelled before. Her strawberry blond hair is fragrant, with the lightest touch of jasmine. I know that the shampoo is not all that makes this girl sweet. She is completely innocent. She isn't tortured by parents who are at odds with one another. She sees beauty in the ugly. When her father fills the immense screen with the tight-focus image of an insect, its eyes a kaleidoscope of greens and purples, she says, "Pretty!"

"I took mostly people shots on my downtime," Cy says.

Emma beams at her father. "I like the bug, Daddy."

"Bugs are yucky, Emma," Stacy says from her perch next to Cy.

I give Emma a soft little hug. "I think they are pretty too."

"You would," Stacy says, in a tone that reminds me that she's my younger sister. No matter that she's further along in life—a husband, daughter, beautiful home.

We sit rapt as Cy flips through images of children playing in a broken fountain, running across a green landscape. They're clearly crushingly poor, but the images are lovely, intimate. Cy is great at whatever he does—the man's an achiever, as neither he nor Stacy will hesitate to tell you—but he's truly a fantastic photographer. Graduated with honors as a computer science/business double major at Washington State, but still found time for a minor in photography and a shelf full of awards for his work. I'm sure he earned every one. The kids on the mammoth screen in front of us have been brought back whole. As Emma and I watch the slide show, I can't help but think of all of the children who had gone missing or were being abused in our own country while far away—a world away, really—these little ones were laughing and taking in all the goodness they could find. Even without a beautiful house or the world's largest TV, they found something wonderful to be happy about. A boy with a monkey. Children everywhere. A little girl, a year or so younger than Emma, is shown getting out of an outdoor tub.

"Naked girl!" Emma says. "Just like me!"

We all laugh.

Stacy reaches for Emma, stealing her warm little body from my arms. "Daddy's show is over," she says. "Time for bed."

Emma makes a face and wriggles from my lap.

I die a little inside. My sister has a way of snatching the best moment from me when I least expect it. Always with a smile on her face too.

CHAPTER SEVENTEEN

I am lost. Alone. And there is only one place that calls to me. This is how it starts. The Snoqualmie Casino is only a short drive away. I've seen others find comfort, solace, even a smidgen of meaning in the chair in front of the glory of a slot machine. God knows I could use some comfort.

I keep the letter that came from the police department in my purse. It's a kiss-off. A Dear Jane. A Thanks for Nothing. An end to everything I wanted to be. I'm so deep inside my head that I'm at the freeway exit before I know it.

I see the back of the same heads as I make my way to a row of machines that call to me with a magnetic pull that is fierce and undeniable. In two seconds my card is inside the machine, and I'm on the ride that I love more than anything.

A young guy enveloped by a cloud of Axe sits next to me. He smiles. Even though I am dead inside, I smile back. The Bellevue Police Department has terminated my employment. There will be no getting around it. No appeal. No arbitration. I am no longer a detective. I am no longer anything at all. All of this is my doing and I know it. My union rep said we could fight it. And yet, I just couldn't. To fight it would be to lay naked all that I'd done. Everyone would know that I'd bounced checks, borrowed money, and lost it. Friends like Christine would have to testify against me. Say that they'd seen me, far more than once, come to work in the same outfit as the previous day, looking beat and wired at the same time after a night at the casino. There's no arguing that my judgment wasn't impaired. And Danny. He'd scapegoated me to try to save himself. A coward. An ass. For all the good it did him. He ended up pleading guilty to giving false statements and to perjury before a grand jury panel convened to review the Alan Dawson case.

"I'm Steve," the young guy says.

"Nicole."

"Come here often?"

"Once or twice when I feel like winning," I say, wondering if my lie indicates there's more wrong with me than merely trying to keep myself from crying or killing myself. I've thought of that too.

A waitress comes over.

"I'll have what she's having," he says. "Another for her too."

I nod. God, he's young. I press the button on the *Masterpieces and Double Diamonds* slot and it whirls to its predictable conclusion. Nothing. I press again.

"I'm in from Boise," he says.

"Idaho," I say.

He smiles. "Yeah. That's the one."

I feel stupid. "Sorry. My mind's somewhere else."

The drinks come. Gin and tonics with brown-edged slices of lime.

I keep playing. The lights start flashing and the fake sound of rain that comes with a win plays through the speakers. Steve continues to play his game but doesn't appear to be winning. I bask in the throb of lights, the sounds. The world constricts a little and I don't think of Danny Ford or Evan Cooper or Alan Dawson. Poof. Smoke. All gone. I feel giddy. This is what it feels like to start over. This is how I'll get through the humiliation of the mistakes I've made. I'll keep winning.

"I'll buy the next round," I say.

"This is my lucky night," he says.

I laugh and continue to press the big red button that seems a part of my fingertip.

I'm on a carousel, and it's spinning faster and faster. I see the brass ring, and I barely try to reach for it and it's mine. I put ring after ring on my wrist. Bangles. I close my eyes and I can still grab a ring. I'm fucking invincible. That's me. "Boogie Wonderland" plays in the disco and the rush of the beat makes me spin faster. More bangles. I'm winning. I'm something.

"You're on a hot streak," he says.

"I'm smokin'," I say, smiling at him, fully aware of my meaning.

"Yeah, you are," he says.

The wheels spin faster. The double diamonds line up like rows of Beyoncé backup dancers. Eight hundred dollars. I don't even need a job. *I can do this,* I think, *for the rest of my life. I'm unstoppable. I'm a Sia song.*

More drinks come. I keep playing. Steve's doing the same, but not with the kind of system or intensity that propels someone from loser to winner. I'm in it. To win it. I'm an advertisement for what gambling can do for someone. It's lifting me out of my funk. It's taking me far away faster than one of those Blue Angels that streak through the sky at Seafair. I know the letter is in my purse, but with all the plates that I'm spinning, I don't care. When Steve puts his hand on my leg, I don't even bother to flick it off. It's possible that he's the reason I'm winning. It might not be the shoes I'm wearing or my mother's ring. When I'm winning I don't want to mess with whatever it is that brought me to that place. I'm at $1,225 now.

"You *are* smokin'," he says.

"You're not so bad yourself," I say, though I don't know why. I feel a little drunk. Maybe that's it. I feel a little high from the game. Maybe that could be the reason? Whatever it is, when he asks me to go to his room, I agree. I tell myself I'm smart to cash out, to listen to the part of my brain that is smarter and more powerful than the thrill of winning. I'm not so stupid as to think that the streak won't cool. The trick is finding that spot when you start to slide, but before you talk yourself into believing you can beat the slump with just one more spin. I've found that spot, and I'm walking away.

When we get up to his room, I use the bathroom. I sit there, thinking about that letter in my purse.

Shit. I knew it would come back to me.

I need to get back to the machine.

When I come out, Steve has put on some hipster music and has opened the wine from his minibar.

I watch as he pours. Chardonnay. Stacy's favorite too. The instant a thought of her comes into that casino hotel room, I see what I'm doing. I'm twisting together all the threads that make up the noose that is my life. Stacy telling me that I'm a bad judge of men. Evan Cooper saying that it was a shame that I messed up a promising career as a detective. I'm flogging myself because I absolutely deserve it. Alan Dawson is dead. Kelsey Chase's killer is out there. I can never get away from Alan and Kelsey, and I know it.

I want to get back to *Masterpieces and Double Diamonds.*

Steve's shedding his clothes. Then he's naked on the bed, and I start dropping my clothes as I move closer to him. The sooner we finish, the sooner I'll get back to winning.

"God, you're hot," he says, watching me undress.

I unhook my bra and the room's AC rushes at me, hardening my nipples and sending me toward the stranger on the bed.

Double diamonds. Boogie Wonderland. Over and over.

While Steve prepares to fuck me, I play the slots in my head. He's young, and I'm grateful that it likely won't take long. He works out, and his body feels like a surfboard: rigid, unyielding. His torso is smooth, save for the wispy treasure trail. His manscaping is precise, like bonsai. *He's pleasantly handsome,* I think, really looking at his face for the first time as he climbs on top of me, condom ready. The cloying scent of his Axe body spray seeps into my skin. I don't care. I just need to get back to the game. I need to get on the merry-go-round and forget every mistake that I've made. Every person I've asked for money. Every dollar I've lost.

His warm breath comes at me.

"You're hot, Nicole," he says. He's tapped out on what's clearly a very limited vocabulary.

"Thanks, Steve," I say, realizing I don't know his last name. I probably should. He comes, and I feign my own ecstasy. I like sex. I really do. But right now it feels different. It feels like I'm just doing it to pass the time. Steve is eager and nice. But I feel nothing for him. He's a diversion.

He wants to talk, but I just want to get back to the floor.

"I have an early call this morning," I say, getting up to retrieve the bread crumbs of my clothing, which lead to the bathroom. It's after 1:00 a.m.

He shifts his lean body on the bed. "Okay. Me too."

I'm thankful that he didn't ask me about my early call. I wouldn't have known what to say.

I should never have fucked Steve. Back down on the casino floor, I lose everything. I withdraw $400 from the two bank accounts that I've created so that I can keep things going in times like these. I ride the downward spiral like a water park slide. It is after 3:00 a.m. before I look around, exhausted and ashamed. Some of the players I know by sight are feeling the same way. A pretty Filipina—who wears nurse's shoes and carries her lunch in a Walmart bag—arrives, plants herself in front of a machine, and inserts her frequent player's card. A pit stop on her way to work. Win or lose, she always smiles. We talked one time about her kids. She is sweet. No one at the hospital where she works has a clue that the casino is her stop on the way in every day. She would never seem to be the one with a problem.

"Not so great this morning," she says after a while, looking over at me.

"Me neither."

"See you later," she says as she finishes her quick, nonproductive game.

I nod, knowing that we will.

"Tomorrow we will be lucky."

Somehow I doubt that very much.

It's already tomorrow.

Chapter Eighteen

My addiction counselor, Melissa Tovar, dresses in that trippy space between bohemian and New Age. I've never seen my counselor without a gauzy tunic and a statement piece of jewelry that didn't say "I Believe" in some way. Doves. Dream catchers. Rainbows. Unicorns. One time when I planted myself on the couch in her office off Bel-Red Road, I swear on my father's life that she wore a pendant that looked like a unicorn ensnared in a dream catcher. No shit. *Really.*

A few days after I screwed a stranger and lost all the money I had, I find myself in front of this kind, patient woman, and I'm so angry that I'd like to pull that unicorn from her neck and stab myself with it.

But of course I don't. Until Danny, Kelsey, and the gambling, I was always in control. I'm going to get back to that place where crumble is a topping and not a way of life.

"You've been making great progress, Nicole," Melissa says as she cocoons herself in a pale-purple afghan and tucks her legs underneath her.

"Not really," I say, holding back. Finding my steady place once more.

"Talk to me, Nicole."

"I can't," I say. "It's all so stupid."

Melissa watches me. I know exactly what she's doing. I don't mind that she's trying to find a way inside.

"When was the last time you gambled?" she asks, her tone not the least bit accusatory.

Even so, I lurch back like I'd been struck by a hot iron. I immediately lie because the truth is so damned embarrassing.

"I'm doing better," I tell her. "Though of course I've been tempted. The other day I was at the Safeway and I passed by a claw machine. It took everything I had to keep going past it."

She knits her brow. "Claw machine?"

"A kid's game," I tell her. "You feed the machine fifty cents and a claw drops down and you try to grab ahold of something stupid like a toy dog with one eye and pull it out."

Melissa doesn't have any children. Almost certainly shops at Whole Foods. She clearly doesn't have the faintest idea what I'm talking about. About the claw. About the things that have led me to her. Especially about Danny.

I fidget a little. I've told her only about our personal relationship. How we made each other feel. He was wrong for me even before the gambling spun out of control. I never told her what a snake he was. The planting of evidence. The confession. All of that. I didn't tell Melissa because the rest of it was bad enough.

"Nicole," she says in that soothing voice of hers. "You need to accelerate your recovery. You need to attend Gamblers Anonymous. Trust me. It will help."

I want to tell her that I can't trust anyone. Not anymore. That I don't want to go sit around with others—the losers of the losers' table.

"All right," I say. "I'll go."

◆ ◆ ◆

Like all first-timers I waited too long, and I know it. I'm making my way into a church basement to do what Melissa says. That my only hope for recovery is from the understanding that I'll gain through my sessions with her and the support of a group of strangers at Gamblers Anonymous.

I count fourteen people sitting on folding metal chairs stenciled with the name of "Aldersgate Methodist" on the back, as though anyone would want to steal them. For a fleeting instant I think about turning around. *Run. Get out. You are not one of them.* Then, in the midst of someone's sob story, they all turn and study me. I'm a mouse on a glue trap. I can't go now.

Without much scrutiny it is easy to see that I've failed in life much sooner than any of them. Which in a way makes me a winner, right? They are all in their fifties and sixties. One man with the whitest bald head I've ever seen has to be much older. His features are driftwood. I'd say late seventies. He points to a seat next to him, and I take it.

I clear my throat. "I'm Nicole."

"Pete," he says. "Welcome."

I nod, and a woman named Darla hands me a cup of black coffee. I thank her and bite into the Styrofoam rim. She's Korean. Hard to say how old. Somewhere in the middle, between Pete and me.

For the next hour, people talk about their lives in the casinos.

One lady wishes that she'd never gone with her ex-husband. "It wasn't a problem for him," she says in a lilting voice. "But, for me, another story. I found myself thinking of nothing else, watching the clock and hoping the hands would move faster so I could leave sooner."

Her name is Peg. She was a schoolteacher. Like most of the people in the room, what she was before she gambled her life away is gone.

"My husband left me when he found out that I'd cashed in our kids' college fund. I'm working things out with my boys. Like everything, it's one day at a time."

Sal was a banker.

Marcia was a radiologist.

Kim, a blond with big green eyes and a nose that suggests a heavy hand by a plastic surgeon, was a real estate agent before she lost her home. "That's ironic, don't you think?" she says.

Everyone nods.

Sandy talks next. She's a midlevel manager at a software firm, leading an engineering group. She's attractive and she occupies that ambiguous gender space that suits her name so well. Her hair is cropped silver. Her jacket is denim. Thankfully, she wears it completely unembellished.

"I was a VP at a big aerospace supplier in LA," she says. "I started with scratch tickets. Then I went online. I've never even been to a casino. I didn't have to. I screwed up my life with my smartphone."

When it comes to my turn, I can barely speak. I'm not sure that I can tell a room full of strangers that I'm going to lose my house. That I still catch myself allowing my brain to add the word *probably* to that sentence. There is no way I can save it.

"I started on nickel slots and graduated to dollar slots," I say. "Every time I pressed the button on my machine, things got worse. I knew it then, and I know it now. But the truth is that just when I think I can stop, I go back."

Pat nods. "We all do that, Nicole."

"Yeah," says silver-haired Sandy. "I quit gambling fifteen times before it took, and the truth is I'm not sure it really has taken. I think about it every moment of the day."

"Me too," says a woman whose name eludes me, even though she just said it. I'm too caught up in my own miserable thoughts to retain anything like that. I don't want to accept that this is a lifelong battle. I shouldn't have gone to the casino with Danny. Danny. Danny fucked my life over in every way possible. I know Melissa would tell me to stop blaming Danny for my choices, but God, I'm not a perfect person. I'm not someone who can say that I fully accept that the blame for the ruin of my life is at my feet alone. Sue me. Tell me that I'm weak. Tell me that I'm nothing and I won't argue. I won't stand up in front of everyone saying that I own everything that ever happened to me. I know that Dr. Phil, Oprah, and any one of those TV judges would tell me that I need to grow up and own it. But Danny is to blame for Alan's incarceration, his death, and the fact that Kelsey's killer is still out there. No one here—teacher, doctor, bus driver—had that kind of push from anyone into the disaster that's become all of our lives.

I look down at my cup. A crescent of Styrofoam is missing. I wonder if I've swallowed it. I probably have. I feel sick as the voices of those in the room ebb toward me like a malevolent tide. It's my turn again.

My mouth moves. I don't even know what I'm saying, but Pete looks at me approvingly. Sandy's eyes are suddenly sympathetic. I feel something in my throat. The rim of the cup? I'm done.

"Thank you for sharing, Nicole," Pete says.

Everyone claps.

I have no idea why.

After the meeting I make a beeline for the door. Silver Sandy stops me. She's wearing Chanel. I expect it was a bottle that she had before she lost everything. I doubt anyone at her miserable software company job can afford the perfume.

"I wanted to catch you before you leave," she says. "I'm not supposed to say anything personal here—you know, nothing about our lives outside this room."

"Right. The rules."

She studies me.

"I read that Eastside Crime blog."

Oh shit.

"I just wanted to say that I don't blame you for what happened with that little girl's case, and the man that was falsely accused. I'm really sorry about it, though. Heartbreaking. Stay strong, Nicole. I hope to see you here again. I'll be here tomorrow night."

I won't be.

107

"Thank you, Sandy," I say. "I appreciate it."

My car takes me to the I-90 on-ramp. In twenty minutes I'm pulling in front of the Snoqualmie Casino. The valet waves over at me like we're old friends. I smile back. I am going down, and I can't pull myself up. I'm in a pool. No, a lake. I'm drowning. No doubt about it. No one will throw me a lifeline. My counselor says that only I can save myself. That presumes there is a reason to save me at all. I load up my ticket with my last hundred dollars. The house is in foreclosure. I'd have to win really big tonight.

Or tomorrow morning.

CHAPTER NINETEEN

Stacy attacks me with that look she really ought to patent. It's a combination of pity and disdain, with just a dash of anger. The anger is only a dash, because Stacy likes to hurt me in small doses. Ridicule by a thousand paper cuts. The waiter brings us bread and water, and I want to laugh at the irony of that. I want to laugh at anything, because the tension is like a steel plate between us.

"You're going to need to repeat that," she says.

Stacy's hearing is just fine. She merely wants me to say it again. So I do.

"The house is about to go into foreclosure."

There. I. Did. It.

"Oh God, Nic, what's the matter with you? You aren't still gambling, are you?"

She knows the answer to that too. I'm a voodoo doll just then and she's sticking pins in me. To her, the pins she inserts into my flesh are like acupuncture. Each one makes her feel better.

"I haven't since Sunday."

"Sunday? Good God, you're such a fuckup. I'm glad Mom is dead, and Dad doesn't know who the hell we are anymore. You'd have broken his heart with this latest fiasco."

I sit there. There really isn't any more to say. I thought I could ask her for help, but Stacy isn't about helping me. She's about proving that she's superior. She's Miss Perfection. I'm Miss Failure. She has a beautiful little girl and a rich husband. I lost my job. Lost my career. Am losing my house. My bank accounts are overdrawn. I've shamed myself with everyone I know, and there are the strangers too. They look at me with some of the same suspicion as my sister. The woman at Moneytree in Crossroads told me not to come in anymore. Moneytree is a last stop for the desperate and the deadbeat. That's who I've become.

The waiter brings her chardonnay and my hot tea with lemon. I add sugar while Stacy sips and sticks in another pin.

"You've made such a mess of things. First Danny. Then your job. And now the house. What the hell is wrong with you, Nic?"

"It's an addiction. I'm getting treatment," I say, though I'd rather hurl my teacup in her face.

"Whatever," she says. "It's like you're self-destructing before my eyes. I don't want to hurt you even more, but you look like crap too. Those roots need a touch-up."

She indicates the part of my hair.

"Thanks," I say, though I want to kill her. "I obviously don't have the money to do a lot of things, Stacy."

Like keep my house, you spoiled bitch.

"Sorry," she says.

She isn't, though.

"What are you going to do, Nicole?"

She wants me to beg. I just sit there and sip my tea. After the waiter takes her order, he turns to me.

"A small Caesar salad."

"Get anything you want," Stacy says. "I'm buying."

She was buying anyway. But she's saying that to make me sink a little lower. I don't take the bait.

"Add grilled prawns," I say.

When we're alone again, she gives her head a shake and pretends to look sad. I've seen that before. She perfected it on our father whenever she wasn't getting her way. This isn't that, of course. Same look. Different meaning.

"I can give you a little money," she says, "but not enough to save the house."

"I don't want your money."

"You don't have much of a choice, do you? I mean, what's going to happen to you, Nicole? Where are you going to stay? You've made such a mess of things. That Eastside Crime blog is something else. It's kind of embarrassing for all of us to have all of your troubles flapping in the wind. So public, you know. Cy says you can't stay with us. He just doesn't think it's a good idea. You know, considering."

I don't even know how to begin with that one. *Considering?* Considering what? I have a problem. It's not contagious. I'm not going to steal from Cy. I love my sister, kind of. I love my niece, Emma, with all my heart.

"Please."

No word has been harder for me to utter.

"No. He's firm on it."

I think she's lying. I think she's the one who wants to see me twist in the wind off the end of a thick rope.

"Just for a little while?"

"Sorry, Nic. I just can't."

"I have some of Mom and Dad's stuff," I say as my salad is placed in front of me. Stacy has Dungeness crab cakes—the most expensive thing on the lunch menu. Naturally. Even as a child, she always took the best—the piece of my birthday cake with the pink frosting roses, the thickest part of the salmon from the barbecue, the top of the popcorn bowl where all the butter resided, the front seat whenever either Mom or Dad drove us somewhere. She was my little sister, and I let her. I loved her. I didn't know that all those years while I was giving in to her every whim she was keeping score and looking for ways to undermine me in our parents' eyes. In the eyes of the boys we fought over.

She made out with my college boyfriend and made *him* tell me about it. Later she told me that he didn't mean anything to her and that by having sex with him she proved to me that he was a total douche.

Kyle Crowley *was* a total tool. But he was *my* tool.

"I don't know where I'll go," I say finally.

"Don't you have any friends that'll put you up?"

I shake my head. The truth is that any friends I had were probably sick of me. I'd borrowed money from them. Or tried to.

"Not really."

"Are you on something?" she asks, spooning some chutney onto her overpriced crab cakes.

The fork I'm using to spear the prawns on my salad would look great dug into her Botoxed forehead.

"Drugs are not my problem, Stacy. Gambling is."

"Gambling is an activity. Not a problem."

"It's hard to understand, I know. But trust me, I have a problem, and I'm working toward recovery."

"If you went to the casino on Sunday then you haven't been trying very hard."

I hold the fork tight in my grip. I wonder if I'll bend it.

"It's one day at a time, Stacy."

She eats. She drinks. She trashes me.

"Mom and Dad's stuff, you say. You have some family things?"

"Nothing of value," I say. "Sentimental."

She's not sentimental at all, but she'll pretend to be. Stacy has always pretended to care about the things that matter to others. For a while I thought she might be a sociopath, but with Emma's birth I could see that there was at least one person on the planet that truly mattered to her.

She gets another glass of wine.

Someday she'll get a DUI and I'll be so happy.

"Do you have any room to store things at your house?" I ask.

She sips and shakes her head. "No can do, Nicole. Cy is a bit of a minimalist these days. He wants me to curtail my shopping because he doesn't think we have room."

I want to say, it's because he doesn't want you to spend all his money on crap you find online.

But I don't.

"Mom's china, Grandpa's chair. A few things, that's all."

The wheels are turning. She's calculating the value of the china. It's Theodore Haviland marked Limoges, France. It's old. A complete set. I know she'll want it because it was the one thing we fought over that I actually got.

"I'll rent you a storage facility for six months," she says. "If you can't make the payment at that time, I'll keep the china and sell the rest."

She's hoping I won't be on my feet. I can't say for sure if I will be.

"Agreed."

I tell her to rent the unit tomorrow. The house goes back to the bank in three days. In three days Shelby and I will be homeless.

"What are you going to do about that dog?" she says, as if reading my mind.

The *dog* has a name. "I don't know," I say. "Will you please take her?"

The check comes, and she flirts with the waiter. He's at least five years younger than she is. She's one-upping me again. Or trying to. I want to tell her I fucked a young guy named Steve at the casino. That even though my roots were showing, I was still attractive.

"Oh no," she says. "Cy hates dogs."

That night I hold Shelby for the last time while Elsa of *Frozen* watches over me.

CHAPTER TWENTY

My eyes are flooded, and I really can't see, but I pass Shelby from my arms to a middle-aged woman at the Humane Society not far from the Target where Kelsey Chase went missing. Shelby looks at me with those brown eyes, and I think she knows what's happening. I let myself think that this woman with her kind eyes understands that my life has unraveled, and my Shelby is better off, that even though I love her, I'm letting go.

I think of the poster that hung in my room when I was a teenager. *If you love someone, let him go* . . . I know that Shelby won't be coming back to me. In a way that's not deep or hidden, I know that I'm giving her away to punish myself for all that I've done.

The house is empty. Foreclosed. *I'm* empty. The things that I once obsessed over have evaporated along with all that I have been. I feel myself falling closer to the bottom of wherever I'm going. The bottom will hurt. But it will be final, and I will find a way to pull myself back into the world.

I park my car at the dealership on Bellevue Way. Blue-and-white balloons bob on a line stretching from one end of the lot to another. A few, beaten down by the rain, sag on the line. The November air cuts through my coat like a razor blade. Holding Shelby right now would sustain me with the warmth that I crave. Yet, she's gone. All that I need or all that I think I deserve is in my rolling carry-on. I wheel it into the lobby, where a young guy in an embroidered dealership polo looks up at me from his blue laminate cubicle. He doesn't pounce. I wonder if he knows why I'm here, that I'm not a buyer but something else.

Something that won't make him a dime.

"I'm turning in my vehicle," I say, thinking that his job is a lot like gambling. He plays the odds, sizes up the prospects, and engages when he thinks he has a live one.

I'm so not a live one.

He knows it.

"Something wrong with it?" he says, opening the silver pouch of a Pop-Tart and adjusting some dealership paperwork that he's fanned out on his desk to review.

"Nope," I say. "Can't make the payments. I called. Said to come in. Here are the keys." I pass the key fob across his desk. I pull the leasing papers from my purse and hand them to him. He eats his Pop-Tart. The scent of strawberries, fake as it might be, takes me away for a second. I think of the summer Stacy and I picked berries at a farm in Fall City. She complained about the heat and said that her back hurt, but she pushed through it. I was proud of her. We ate more berries than we picked and conspired against the row boss that treated the group of mostly teens as though we were prisoners. It was awful and fun at the same time. We were close. Fleetingly so, as it turned out.

"Lease payments too high?" he says, crumbs falling from his lips.

I give a quick nod. "Right, a great car. Just too expensive."

He brightens. He sees a way in. "Can I get you into something else?" he says, thinking for a second that there is opportunity in my downfall.

"I can't afford a car right now," I say, wanting to add, "fuck face" to let him know how I really feel.

"All right then," he says.

I fill a paper cup with coffee from the carafe adjacent to where he sits. There are donuts there too. But I don't feel like eating. My stomach is knotted like an old mop.

I roll my bag to the curb in front of the dealership. I have no one to call. I just sit there. An hour passes. I look at my phone as if someone will call me. *I'm killing myself,* I think, *without even trying.* I'm on the edge of a cliff, and I'm just jumping off. I'm not even trying to grab a lifeline.

And then one comes. Sort of.

"You need a ride somewhere?"

I look up. It's Strawberry Pop-Tart.

"I guess," I say.

"Come on," he says. "I'll take you where you need to go. Got permission from the boss."

I wonder if it's because the dealership manager wants to show kindness or if my sitting there is bad for business. I decide that I don't care. I'm ashamed. It's like I'm watching a movie, and I'm in it. I know that I can change the script. I know that I can fight my way out of this, but not now.

"Angeline's," I say.

"Is that a church?"

Be honest. Be direct. You are down. But you are going to get better.

"No, a women's shelter," I say. "Belltown."

He glances at me, surprised, and then with the same look as the woman at the Humane Society. Pity.

Nothing makes a person feel worse than knowing you've inspired pity. It's a knife in the chest. A scalpel across the neck.

"Okay, then. You have the address?"

"Third and Lenora."

Book Two
Nearly a Year After Kelsey Went Missing

CHAPTER TWENTY-ONE

When I was a girl, the Belltown section of Seattle was a dump. It was the home of what my father called "bums" and "druggies." When my sister and I took the bus from Hoquiam to go shopping in the big city at Christmastime, he told us to stay on Fifth and Fourth, where the major retailers kept things clean, safe, and free of those people he insisted would do us harm. Times have changed. Seriously so. As I wheel my luggage toward Angeline's, I pass condos that top a million dollars with views of the snowcapped Olympics across the Puget Sound, with its ferries skittering like water bugs across a blue tableau that is at once placid and ever-changing.

I give a woman my age at the entrance of the shelter all of my information. Her eyes sweep over me. I'm not better than anyone here, I know that, but the way she studies me indicates that she knows I'm new to this. The women in the line behind me have been at it awhile. The air around them shows it. It's thick with body odor and Suave hair care products. I'm not an elitist. I'm just someone who knows the difference, because until last May, I was someone who would donate to a place like this.

I'd never in a million years think that I'd ever be here.

"You can come back for lunch at eleven thirty," she says.

"Can I just stay here?"

She taps on a keyboard. "No," she says. "We won't be able to place you anywhere until tonight. This is transitional. Day shelter."

"You don't have any place to stay here?"

"A few spots. But don't worry. We'll find you a place. Counseling services are by appointment. Next-door is a copy, computer, and fax center. You need help in finding a job?"

I need help all right.

"Thank you," I say.

I wheel my luggage around Seattle. It's cold. Faces pass me like a slide show. No sound. No hello. I see my reflection in the window at Nordstrom. I used to shop there. The coat I'm wearing is a North Face that I bought at the Bellevue Square location. My reflected face lines up with the mannequin wearing a navy-blue dress with long sleeves and accented by a trio of gold-tone buttons. I know her, I think. She's who I was.

I return to the shelter at eleven thirty and line up. I say nothing to anyone. I just take my sandwich and banana and sit at a table, at first alone. Then two women, one black, the other white, sit and talk. Neither looks at me. They are friends. One was beat up by her boyfriend. The other says something about missing meetings. She's likely got a problem similar to mine. Drugs? Booze? Narcotics? The possibilities spin in my mind like the machine at the casino. I listen and eat, hoping for the spinning to stop. To win at the game I'm playing in my head.

"Who are you? I'm Linda," the white one says.

"Nicole."

"Michelle," the black woman says. "Haven't seen you."

"New to this," I say. My sandwich is tuna. I hate tuna. I eat it anyway and look around the room. Women of all shapes, sizes, ages eat—mostly in silence.

Linda and Michelle assure me every one of them has a story. Some are victims of men. Some are victims of themselves. Some have been in and out of the shelter more times than they want to admit. They seem to be stuck in the transition that Angeline's provides. Gerbils on a wheel. Unable to get off. Starting over is never easy, both my tablemates agree with weary shakes of their heads.

"Don't let them put you at St. Marks," Linda says, looking at her friend. "They kick you out at 5:00 a.m."

"God, and those pews," Michelle says. "Rock-hard."

"Yeah," Linda goes on. "I thought of suing the Catholic church for that, but they have enough problems."

The women laugh a little. I do too. Though I'm only mimicking their laughter. Nothing is funny to me. I thank them for their information and look at the big clock in the dining room. I run through the time line of my demise—Kelsey's disappearance, Alan's confession, his suicide, the internal investigation, my forced leave of absence, and then, finally, the gambling away of every cent I'd borrowed from those who were kind—and stupid enough—to help me. Lunch takes less than twenty minutes. I have to leave the shelter until five thirty.

What am I going to do for five hours?

The answer: The same thing I did this morning. I'll walk the streets, pretending that I'm between flights and will soon be on my way to the airport. I'm going to leave rainy Seattle and go to Hawaii. Cabo. Better yet, Fiji. I'm going to meet my boyfriend and stay in one of those palm-thatched huts that hover over the turquoise South Pacific. We'll have shrimp grilled over an open flame. I'll get drunk. We'll make love. He'll ask me to marry him. I'll say yes. We'll move to Sedona where it almost never rains and the air smells like clean earth. I'll have a baby. I'll make things right with my sister. I'll never go near a machine again.

And I won't even miss it.

That night I sleep on one of those pews at St. Mark's I was warned about. I try to, anyway. The woman next to me snores like a chain saw in need of a good oiling. I shift my body on the pew, but I can't find a position that facilitates comfort. My shoulders ache. I use a Bible and hymnal for a pillow. The blanket the nun gave me smells like someone tried to Febreze it into submission.

I think of the last time I saw Danny. It was a beautiful afternoon in March. I had spent the morning planted in a room with an investigator for Internal Affairs. I'd spilled my guts, but I didn't lie. I didn't exaggerate. I didn't put the blame on Danny for Alan Dawson's suicide, though I agonized about what drove an innocent man to kill himself. I simply told the investigating officer the truth—that I didn't believe the confession was genuine. That Danny had destroyed the videotape because he'd been caught up in a rush to judgment that he'd needed to protect. I saw the truth as my only way to salvage my career.

How stupid I was.

"Now, Detective," the investigator said, "We're aware that you have a problem that you're dealing with right now."

I knew what he meant, though I pretended not to.

"Yes, this investigation is taking its toll," I said.

"Not this investigation," he said. "Your other problem."

"I'm behind on some bills, yes."

"Detective, that's not your problem, is it? It's a consequence of your problems."

Danny had told them about the gambling. He'd told them that my addiction called into question my integrity.

"I have a gambling problem," I said. "But I'm getting help. I'm doing my best to try to pull myself together. I'm not under any pressure to lie for any reason. Why would I?"

The investigator, a self-righteous asshole if ever I sat across from one, didn't even blink.

"Revenge?" he asked.

I got up. "We're done here," I said. "What Danny Ford did to Dawson made my problem worse. It was there before. And God knows, it's here now."

When I left that airless little room, Danny was on his way to Booking. He seemed small, like a teenager. He'd somehow shrunk. He wore a hoodie and jeans and everything about him was diminished, average, and unremarkable. What I'd seen when I looked in his eyes was completely gone. He was nothing but trouble. He looked over at me with a "fuck you" expression that indicated he wasn't done with trying to bring me down for something that *he* did. I stared hard. I wasn't going to back down. He finally broke his gaze, turned away. My heart pounded. I could barely breathe. To be free of him meant that I was truly alone. And to be alone meant that there was no one in my corner. I left the office feeling sick. But free. I was free.

Free also means nothing.

The lobby of the Seattle Westin is on trend, with midcentury modern furniture and a carpet that resembles quartz striations on an endless slab of gray basalt. A cylinder of orchids occupies the low, glass-topped table in front of me. I stow my bag in the space next the table, hoping that it's out of view. While I know that people in hotels are traveling, I feel that everything about me telegraphs that I'm one of those homeless women rolling a suitcase along the streets of Seattle while waiting for a shelter to open a space. I find myself, quite ironically, praying to God that I don't end up at St. Marks again. The pews are hard. The echoing of snoring in the space is nearly deafening. Sleepless nights there blur from one to the next.

I know that my makeup is bad. My hair is dirty. I've clipped it back, but it doesn't hide that I haven't showered in a couple of days. I look like the other women who have no choices, and I also know that all that has happened to me has been my own doing.

On the other side of the lobby, I see a table set up with two enormous vessels of water, one flavored with cucumber slices and the other with slices of lime and lemon. I make my way over, past travelers waiting for their Uber car. They are young. Rich. Attractive. I nod at them, but they don't see me. No one sees me. It's like there is a sonic warning alerting them that I'm a loser, and they shouldn't look at me.

As I fill a glass with citrus water, I notice a couple of hotel employees as they wheel a cart of breakfast menu items. Coffee. Pastries. Linen napkins. I move closer. A sign welcomes a group from Whole Foods. I used to shop there. When the workers disappear down the hallway, I pounce. I'm so weary of oatmeal. So tired of the bitter taste of my failures.

"Hey!"

I spin around. It's a young African American hotel employee. He glares at me and stabs a finger in my direction. I drop my croissant.

"You can't eat here," he says, lowering his voice so that the Uber couple doesn't hear. "You have to leave. Take your things. Get."

Mom used to rattle the window and yell "Get!" to any dog in our yard. "Get!"

"Sorry," I say, keeping my eye fixed on the croissant on the edge of the table. "I'm going."

He points again. This time at the object of my embarrassed stare. "Take that with you," he says. "Can't put it out now."

I think I see kindness in his eyes. I'm not sure. I can't read anyone anymore. I take the pastry and fetch my luggage and slink out of the Westin. Back to the shelter. As I roll my suitcase over the cracks and seams in the sidewalk, past the young guy with a golden retriever and a sign asking for help, I count each bump. I turn each bump into the push of the play button on my favorite machine. The images of the Old Masters spin before me. The spinning stops and in my mind's eye I catch a glimpse of Edvard Munch's *The Scream*.

That pretty much sums up how I feel.

CHAPTER TWENTY-TWO

Everything around me reminds me of my problem.

The hat inverted next to the young man with a guitar, a dog, and a sign that says "Anything Welcome." The dollar bills float on top of a random splatter of change. I think back to the time when I was out of money and so desperate to feed the machine that I returned to my car in the parking lot and nearly tore apart the seat because I'd dropped some coins there coming through the drive-through one time. I was absolutely crazed. I had to find those quarters. I cut the back of my hand on the undercarriage of the seat. A big slice. But when I found the money I was so happy that I didn't even care that my hand was bleeding like the top of a Maker's Mark bottle. I just hurried back inside and bought a dollar ticket. I pressed "Play" and all of the anxiety that enveloped me just drifted away. Somehow I managed to win and keep going. *God really did want to help me,* I thought. He was looking out for me.

Going to make everything all right.

When I see a letter carrier, I go back to how desperate I was in the fall. How as the creditors lined up, the résumés stopped pulling in responses, and the foreclosure that I thought I could stay was all but an inevitability, I was desperate to get my unemployment check. The casino was waiting for me. It was going to be my day.

It was going to be *my* day. Every day.

The mailman always delivered around 10:00 a.m. That time was no good. I was missing the morning. Someone else on my machine might use the good spins. I got in my car and circled the neighborhood, looking for the red, white, and blue Jeep and the slowpoke behind the wheel. I pulled up behind him and got out.

He recognized me. I'd waited by my box every Monday that the last of my admin leave checks arrived. My online banking account had been suspended—for misuse, the lady on the phone had said. The look on the postman's face was neither incredulous nor pissed off when he saw me. Just the flat countenance of a government employee who'd seen my type before. The check crasher. The person who needed money that very second. He probably thought I was on drugs. I know that I would have.

"Got my check?" I asked. "I'm heading out of town and wanted to run some errands."

My excuse didn't fool him. At least I didn't think so. I'd lied to strangers more often than I told the truth. Embarrassed, I guess. Ashamed that I'd fallen so hard. So low.

"I'm not supposed to give it to you. It's supposed to go in the box."

"I know. Just this once. I'm in a real hurry."

"Okay, Ms. Foster," he said. "This one time." He fished for my check in a plastic tub in the back of the Jeep. "You want these too?"

It was a bunch of bills. One was stamped "Final Notice."

I shook my head. Bad news like that would weigh me down. I was going to win, and I didn't want any reminders in the backseat of my car telling me that I was a loser.

Once I learned his route, I got the check earlier and earlier. I didn't tell him that I was going out of town or had a sick aunt or any of the bullshit that I'd used on others to cover where it was that I was going. It was none of his fucking business.

The memory plays in my head as I move the Bible under my neck on the tortuous pew and try to turn down the noise in my mind. Shut off the slide show. Get some sleep. Stop thinking about him.

Stop thinking about her.

The next day at the shelter is more of the same. Dragging my luggage like it's Shelby on her leash, I wander around Seattle. I miss her so much. I consider calling the Humane Society to see if she's all right, but my phone is dead.

I still have no real plan to get my life in order. I want to get on a bus and head to a casino, but I have no money. And I know that the casino is black quicksand just waiting for me like the most beautiful beach in the world. Beckoning. I smell the scent of plumeria and coconut oil. The beach wants me. It's begging me to step onto its hot sandy surface so that it can swallow me in one big gulp.

And drag me to hell.

As I walk through the cold rainy morning between holiday shoppers, I see more women like me. All pull luggage; all walk among the office workers and tourists as though they have some place to go. I never noticed them before. I wonder if anyone notices me. I hope no one does. My hair is wet and stuck to my head. My clothes damp. It's like the worst of camping.

That night I sleep in a bed at a shelter down an alley near Second and Stewart. It's a communal space, like the sleeping porch at my sister's sorority. Or maybe an army barracks. They have a TV with rabbit ears in the main sitting room. Forty women command that space. Some stare blankly at the screen as old Tom Cruise and Julia Roberts movies play. We sit and stare because we have to use up our time. We eat at five thirty. We go to sleep at nine. The staff turns off the lights, and we lay on our beds. The girl next to me starts to cry.

"You okay?" I ask.

Silence.

"Are you okay?" I repeat.

The blanket holding her stirs some. "I want to go home," she finally says.

I shift my weight on the metal-framed bed and lean closer. "What's your name?"

"Stella," she says. "My mom and dad threw me out. Said I was no good. Trash. Said that if I didn't get my shit together, I'd never amount to anything. Like dropping me off here is going to teach me some big lesson."

"Maybe it will."

"Yeah," she says, "like how much I really do hate them."

I don't ask for details. No one here likes to give any. They hold their secrets like a winning hand.

"I haven't got any money," Stella says. "Do you have some?"

Would I be here if I did?

She is about twenty with curly black hair. Her skin is a golden tan, like an almond shell, I think. She whimpers into her scratchy pillow and I reach over to touch her shoulder.

"I don't have any money," I say. "I'm sorry. Did you talk to the counselor?"

She shrugs a little. Even in the dim light of the cell phone she clutches I can see she's a beautiful girl. Her eyes are pretty and resonate with a kind of sharp alertness. Her ears are pierced, and she wears over-size hoops that move like wind chimes when she speaks.

"Yeah," she says. "I did. I already have my GED. I just need money. I'd do anything for money," she says, now looking into my eyes.

I pull away.

"I'm sorry, Stella. I wish I could help you. The truth is you have to help yourself."

"You should be one of them," she says, indicating the counselor that wanders the rows as we settle down in our miserable existence and swim toward the black of sleep. She turns away.

I hate how I'm so free with advice. With everyone. Except myself.

I stand outside a Starbucks in downtown Seattle in my damp North Face coat. The guy who works at Sleep Country knows I'm one of those homeless women with carry-on luggage going around and around the block, and he saw something in me to hand me a five-dollar bill for a latte. I have no shame. I stand there drinking the macchiato like it's a liquid Thanksgiving dinner, and I have some reason to be thankful. The pavement glistens after a cold rain, and I hover next to the window, watching throngs of shoppers pass by.

"Detective?" a man's voice calls to me.

My heart sinks. I haven't been called that by anyone in a long time. I don't want anyone to know that's what I was. Some of my girlfriends from the shelter might overhear.

My face is stone. I pretend not to hear.

"Detective Foster?"

It's one of the two men I never wanted to face again.

I turn around. "I'm not a detective anymore, Julian."

Julian Chase is wearing a black raincoat over a suit that looks so soft I want to reach out and touch it. His necktie is royal blue. He's lost weight since we last saw each other. It looks good on him, heightening the handsome angular features that make his face. His eyes take me in questioningly.

"I read about that," he says. "I'm sorry. How are you?"

"Not great," I say.

He looks down at my luggage. "Going somewhere?"

"No. Not anywhere."

He looks me over. His eyes are like some kind of optic scanner and he's pulling in the bits of information that will tell him that I'm a wreck. That I'm not going anywhere, because I have nowhere to go. My clothes are not fresh. My hair hasn't been styled in weeks. Maybe more. Once you start giving up a regimen you no longer can mark the time between when you last had something done. Every six weeks is an easy reminder. Every now and then soon turns in to not doing it anymore. Whatever it is.

"We should talk," he says. "A lot has happened."

"I can't talk about it," I say, stepping away and pretending to search out someone in the mass of people ping-ponging from one retailer or coffee shop to the next. There is no lifeline for me to grab at.

"Seriously," he says. "We need to."

I stand there unable to say anything.

He touches my shoulder. "Are you okay, Detective?"

I am not okay. I am standing in front of a Starbucks with a charity macchiato with the father of the little girl none of us could save, whose death none of us could avenge.

"I will never be okay," I say, looking him in the eyes for the first time. I want him to know that I mean it. "I think about Kelsey every day. I'm so sorry about her." My hand is trembling, and the cup falls to the pavement. A spray of frothy, white milk splatters on his impeccable shoes and his not-so-black-now raincoat.

"Crap," he says.

"God, I'm sorry." I bend down and start dabbing at his feet with the crumpled napkin I've been clutching since I heard his voice.

"Stop it," he says. "No worries, Detective."

I look up. My eyes have puddled. "Please," I say, my voice a soft croak, "don't call me that. Don't ever call me that. Call me Nicole."

He reaches down and helps me up. I pull myself together. Or at least I try to. "We need to talk," he says. "Come with me."

It's like I'm sleepwalking. I don't really want to follow him. But I can't stop. I owe him something. Something more than I can ever give him. He takes me to his car, a new Range Rover. I get inside. My feet are frozen. Damp. My hair is wet. I imagine that I don't smell very good. At once, my mind races back to Kelsey's case. The car. The makeshift memorial and the woman and her daughter and their sad bouquet of supermarket flowers. Almost a year.

Julian turns on the ignition and mankind's greatest invention, heated seats, work their magic.

"What happened to you?" he asks again. "After the Dawson thing."

He's being kind by not being specific.

"I had a problem, and it got worse. It's an addiction problem."

"Is it drugs? I know a good therapist."

"No. Not drugs." I look at him. He's not judging me. "Not sex. Obviously not overeating. Gambling. I'm a gambling addict."

It feels good in a way to tell that to someone who sort of knows me. Strangers don't care. Loved ones judge you. Someone like Julian Chase can take me or leave me. I was important to him for something that I didn't do right. He could actually hate me, and I wouldn't blame him one bit.

I tell him my story. I talk about Danny and how we went to the casino. How it was an outlet to relieve the stress of a long day. Unwind. How over time it became something greater than that.

"It was my safe haven," I say, though the words sound ludicrous, even to me. "My way to forget the mess I'd left behind."

I don't say Kelsey's name. I know that he understands.

"Alan Dawson didn't have anything to with Kelsey's death, did he?" Julian asks.

I watch a young woman push her stroller past our car.

"Let's go for a drive," I say.

"Where do you want to go?"

"Away."

As we pull into traffic the heat pours over me. I look over at him. There's an uncertainty to his gaze, but I continue to sense that this man is decent and understanding.

"I don't think he did," I say.

"I've wondered," Julian says. "I admit I've considered that. If he was framed by your partner, that meant he was innocent."

"Yeah," I answer. "I think he was."

"Nicole, help me," he says, looking into the rearview mirror as we merge onto I-90.

"Help you?" I ask. "I can't even help myself."

"We need to find out who killed Kelsey. The police won't help. They tell me that Detective Ford fucked things up, but that doesn't mean Dawson wasn't guilty. It was just an example of an overzealous cop giving the evidence a nudge."

"Some nudge," I say.

"I've made a nuisance of myself down there. Nuisance, by the way, is the word your boss, Evan Cooper, used. Said that if I continue to be a nuisance by checking up every week, they'll have me arrested."

"Cooper hates all the negative attention Danny—and I—have brought to the department. He was blowing smoke."

"Right. I guess," he says, as we pass over Mercer Island and onto the East Channel Bridge. I look over at the landing on the shoreline where Alan Dawson's trumped up confession led us on a fruitless search for Kelsey's body. I doubted the confession at that point. But Danny was someone I loved and looked up to. Stupid is how I feel just now.

"Where are we going?" I finally ask.

"You're going to stay with me, Nicole." He looks over to assess my reaction.

I just sit there and stare out the window.

"Nothing weird," he says. "Don't worry. I think we can help each other. Clearly the two of us are alone in this."

"Right," I say. "How did you find me?"

"Confession," he says. "Your sister. Your sister saw me outside my office and recognized me from the media. She told me what happened to you and where you were."

It's hard to know if Stacy was gossiping or being nice.

"That was nice of her," I say, though I wonder about my sister's motives. She's an expert at slipping needles and pins into Twinkies and feeding them to the unsuspecting. At finding a way to plead ignorance by putting the listener on the defensive:

> *There's something genuinely wrong with you if you think that's what I meant. Seriously messed up. You might need to see someone. I'm saying that as someone who cares about you and is very, very worried.*

"I can't stay here," I say as the garage door rises and the Range Rover pulls beneath a small, plastic ball hanging from the ceiling. When the ball rests on the hood, Julian turns off the engine, unhooks his seat belt, and faces me.

"The way I look at it," he says, "you don't have that many options. And that's fine. I don't, either. I want to find out who killed my daughter. I'm drafting you."

I get out and see the midnight-blue BMW that Angela had driven to Target the night Kelsey disappeared. It takes me right back to that sodden December the year before. So much of my life had been defined by that case.

"You can drive it while you're here," Julian says. "For some reason, Angela didn't want it any more. Too many bad memories, maybe."

That night I find myself sleeping in another child's bedroom. This time, it's Samuel Chase's, a space decked out with a *Cars* theme. The bedspread is Lightning McQueen, and the lamp next to the bed has a Mater shade. My hair is wet from a shower, and I'm wearing one of Angela's left-behind nightgowns. If that didn't amp up the sickness that I feel in my stomach, I don't know what would. Julian and I talked for only a short time after we arrived and ate some pizza. Then I told him I had to lie down. I want to see this strange arrangement as an opportunity to fix all of the things wrong with my life. I want to undo all the things that left Kelsey's killer free. I'll take that first step tomorrow.

I'll go see Alan Dawson's widow, Charlene.

Chapter Twenty-Three

I turn into Lake Washington Mobile Estates in the midnight-blue BMW that used to be Angela's. It would be more appropriate for me to crawl on my hands and knees for the part I unwittingly played in the events that led to Charlene Dawson's husband's arrest.

And death.

I've drawn my gun before, and I did so with steely resolve. I've faced down a pack of rabid, knife-wielding teenagers. One time I shut down a gas station robbery while on my way back for coffee and wrapped it up while the cup was still hot. Nothing intimidated me. I was fearless once. Now I'm a second-guesser. A person who can't move from Point A to Point B because she's too stuck on the reasons she landed at A in the first place. I'm going to shake that now. Or try to.

Charlene opens the door, wide and without any fear of who might be standing under the aluminum overhang to challenge her—to negate the love she had for Alan, to say that she was an enabler, the wife of a pervert, the lover of a child killer. She's cut her hair short, but her eyes are the same. They look right through me with the force of a broken and bitter heart. She holds a towel in her hand. I imagine that she'd like to wrap it around my neck. I'd probably let her.

"You have a lot of nerve to show up here," she says.

I don't really have any nerve. I stand there silently.

"Speak," she says.

I open my mouth and move my lips. The words that tumble out are pathetic, weak. "I need to talk to you."

Charlene's fingers tighten on the dish towel.

Good, she really is going to strangle me, I think.

"You *need* to talk to me? You *need.* I'd laugh in your face if I knew how to laugh anymore. You have no idea what you've done. You and that prick Danny Ford."

I stand there as she pummels me with words meant to hurt. And they do. In another life, I'd have flung them right back at her. I'd have defended myself. I'd have told her that she was a self-centered bitch. I'd have made some comment about how her holier-than-thou attitude was her way of covering up her own insecurities.

"I'm very sorry about Alan," is what I finally say.

She holds the towel in both hands now, clutching it. I see that she's doing that to steady herself. I know I'm not welcome here. I know that I am a reminder of the worst thing that ever happened to her. And to be fair, I know that she has not had it easy for a very long time. The worst things in her life were handed to her in endless doses. Ending up in this trailer park with a man who'd done time for loving her was only the middle of a burning fuse ignited a long time ago.

"You broke him," she says, tears now falling.

"I'm sorry," I say once more because it's the only word that seems to fit. It's a weak and useless word, I know. But it's all I have right now. I want to tell her that I don't think it was a suicide, but I can only fix one disaster at a time. I can try to make amends and hope for justice for Kelsey.

"You and Detective Ford pushed him to do it. I know it. I know that he was innocent. He never would have done anything to that little girl. He wasn't like that at all, but you made it seem that he was."

"Charlene," I say, "I'm here to help. Really. You can be angry, and I deserve that. You can blame me, and I'll take that too. I understand it. I accept it. Please, let me come in and talk with you."

She looks younger than her years as she stands there in the doorway of her double-wide. I wonder how much her appearance had played into the media's obsession with her case as a teenager. She barely looks twenty now. At almost sixteen, I imagine she looked closer to twelve. Her eyes are green and the wispy blond hair she wore clipped back when I saw her heading to work at Panera the morning I ruined her duct-taped-together life is now cut short and asymmetrical, with bangs that swoop to the right. I wore my hair like that before I went with the Bellevue Bob—the style that half the women I know have adopted. Functional. Banally pretty.

She leads me across floorboards that give slightly under our weight to the kitchen. It's spotless. The whole house is. She retrieves a pair of mugs from a shelf above the sink. I see one that drives an ice pick into my heart.

It says: "World's Best Husband."

Charlene sees me reading it. Her eyes fasten onto mine. "I got it for Alan at the mall when we first got married. He drank his coffee out of it every morning. He broke it one time. Somehow. Anyway, Alan replaced it with another one just like it. I noticed the price sticker on the bottom. $7.99. I would never have paid that much for it."

I don't say anything, because there's nothing to say.

"Cream?"

"Black is fine."

"Why are you here?" she asks as she pours coffee and sits across from me.

"I told you."

She slides the World's Best Husband mug to me. I know she's doing that to make sure that I don't forget what happened.

I never will.

"I don't buy it," she says. "You're here because you want something, right? I don't know what it is. Forgiveness?" she asks, measuring the expression on my face. "If that's what you're selling, I'm not buying."

"I don't think your husband had anything to do with Kelsey's murder."

My words hang in the air.

"You came here to tell me that? I already know that. I knew the second that goddam confession came out that he was pushed into making it."

"I wasn't there when he made his confession," I say, as though my absence would absolve me from everything that happened.

"You were a part of it," she says. "You. Detective Ford. Most of the news people. All of you were trying so hard to get what you were after that you didn't care about the truth."

"I care about the truth," I say.

She waves the back of her hand at me, flicking my words to the floor. "You do *now*. I read about what happened to you. How you weren't officially blamed for what happened, but you were fired anyway. Seems like a cover-up to me."

"No cover-up," I tell her. "Just a fuckup. On my part."

Charlene Dawson pushes some newspaper clippings toward me. They skitter across the table top. Headlines play out my worst moments. Public moments, anyway.

Dawson's widow says 'no' to suicide claims

Detective on leave from Bellevue Police Department

Ford pleads no contest on obstruction charge

Ford sentenced to prison for falsifying records, confession

Detective resigns, seeks treatment for gambling addiction

I've memorized the articles, but I keep my eyes on the papers. Charlene's studying me. She's looking to see if there is any part of me that she can trust. Her eyes say that she hates me, but I feel that despite her words to the contrary, she does want whatever I'm selling. After all, she's alone.

"I'm moving from here," she says. "Down to Eugene. We have a new store opening, and I'm going to be assistant manager. Should be manager, for all that I do for the store I'm at now. But whatever."

The shift in tone feels better. "That'll be great, Charlene," I say. "A fresh start."

She looks to the window then back at me. Her eyes are wet. Shiny. "That's what my mother says. All of a sudden she and Dad are acting like Alan never happened. I'm their little girl again. Makes me sick." She pauses to drink. "Can't wait to get out of here."

"You saw Alan," I say, bringing her back to the reason I'm there, "after he was transferred to King County."

Her eyes stay fastened to mine. "Yes, I did."

"How did he seem?"

She looks at me like I'm from another planet. That whatever he was feeling should be obvious to me. "Upset," she answers. "He was hurt. He wanted to make sure that I didn't believe anything that you people said he'd said. I told him that I would never. He didn't even have to say a word to me. I would never believe it. I still don't."

"He was upset."

Her eyes are no longer wet. They send a glare in my direction. "Not suicidal, if that's what you're getting at, Detective."

She's hurling something at me. I deserve it.

"Charlene. I'm not a detective."

"Right. You're not. You've lost everything too. Are you here for some kind of therapy?"

I am, in a way. She's a keen observer.

"I don't think your husband had anything to do with Kelsey's murder."

"You said that already."

My cup is empty, and she pours me more coffee.

"Are you sure Alan wasn't suicidal?" I finally ask.

She stirs powdered cream into her coffee. The air fills with the scent of French vanilla. It makes me think of my dad. He loves that flavor.

"No. Never. In fact . . ." She keeps stirring that creamer. It's a big, pale-brown whirlpool in the center of her cup. She is looking down at it. She doesn't want me to see all of the hurt she's holding inside. People like her live with a shell. I know that because I'm one of them too.

"He told me not to worry," she says, her voice catching in her throat. "He told me that everything was going to be all right. He said that the cops had made up everything, and he had proof. There was a camera recording the entire interrogation. He never said anything about dropping off that little girl's body."

The tape. Alan Dawson knew about it. I wondered if he knew the recording had vanished.

"You know something else?" she says. "I called the Bellevue Police Department and told the officer that we'd be millionaires, and someone there would go to jail. I told them that whatever they thought they knew, they were fucking wrong."

"Do you remember who you talked to?" I ask.

She stops stirring her coffee. "I wrote down the name. I tossed it, though. Just burned a whole bunch of stuff. My parents made me.

Told me that I needed to move on. Move on? To where? Alan was my whole life."

I have no words to console her. *Sorry* seems so lame. Yet it is all I have. I get up to leave, and as I open the door, she calls out to me.

"Cooper. It was Evan Cooper that I talked to."

◆ ◆ ◆

As I drive up the hill to Julian's house, I pause by the water feature that marks Somerset's grand entrance. Some kids have poured dishwashing detergent into the agitating waters resulting in a billowing mass of bubbles. An empty Costco-sized bottle of Dawn is flattened by a Mercedes that passes me. Bubbles spill over the perfect, brick water receptacle onto the landscaping, meticulous even in winter, and finally onto the pavement. It's like a white, undulating blob that is swallowing everything in its reach. I need this moment. Breathe and think. I think about Charlene Dawson and the mess I helped make of her life. I wonder if she'll ever recover after losing Alan. A palpable ache is the undercurrent to every word that she says. I have no idea what that kind of devotion and love feels like. I've had times in which I felt a twinge of something more than comfort, something deeper than lust. My counselor, Melissa, told me that the slot machines were a replacement for genuine attachment to another human being. She said that something inside of me was broken and that fixing it wouldn't be easy, but it could be done.

"Just like the GA program," she said while we sat in the overstuffed leather chairs in her tasteful but comfortable office on Bel-Red Road in Overlake, "your recovery is one day at a time. You can get better. You can learn to accept yourself and others. You can find a way back to loving someone."

While I know she's a counselor, a cheerleader to help me find my way to a real life, I always feel empty whenever our sessions are over.

I think about Evan Cooper. How he mentored me but admired Danny. How hard it must have been for him to know that Danny was going down on that confession. How sick he must have felt when he found out for the first time that the tape was missing. I can remember how his facade cracked when the Internal Affairs detectives swooped in and did what they were supposed to do. Danny was out. I was trashed. Cooper was humiliated. None of us would ever be the same.

I ascend the hill and turn into Julian's driveway. The garage door is open, and as I pull in I notice the row of boxes marked with Angela's name sitting along the perimeter. I stop with the nose of the hood under the hanging ball. I find it hard to get out of the car. I sit for a second.

Just then Julian emerges from the door to the house. He's wearing jeans and a tan V-neck sweater. His eyes are kind, concerned. He doesn't look at me in any weird way at all, but I feel weird. I'm wearing his wife's cast-offs, clothing that she deemed "last season" and left behind. I'm sleeping in his son's bedroom. I'm trying to pull myself together, patch up my life. The only way to get there is to find out what really happened to Kelsey Chase.

"I have something to show you," he says.

CHAPTER TWENTY-FOUR

Julian leads me to the kitchen and offers me something to eat. I'm not hungry. How could I be? He pushes a sheet of paper across the glass-topped table. Just then I notice that the underside of the glass is marked with the small fingerprints of the children who no longer live in this blandly classy house on the hill. The surface is pristine—not a mark on it. I imagine that Julian has left those sad little reminders in place intentionally.

Underneath the table is a Windex-Free Zone.

"Samuel made it," he says of the child's drawing that he's placed under my gaze. "Angela didn't want me to have it."

I study the drawing. In blue crayon it shows a car with three people inside. The car, I think, resembles Lightning McQueen. It has a face. A sad one. Tears ooze out of its oversized headlight eyes. The figure in the front seat is a woman with large, green eyes and curled lashes. Angela. In the window of the passenger seat behind the driver are two faces peering outward. One is larger than the other. One has longer hair. Samuel and Kelsey. The boy's mouth is a straight line, like the mother's. The girl's mouth is another matter. It's an open circle. She appears to be calling out to someone or something.

Screaming?

Outside of the car, an animal with large teeth and a tail somewhere between a rat's and a raccoon's hovers over the scene. It's a monster animal, a Sendak with true menace. The figure's chest is colored red by a series of hurried strokes.

"What's that?" I ask, tapping my finger on the creature.

"A mutant cat," Julian says. "That's what he told me."

"Mutant cat," I repeat. "When did he draw this?"

Julian leans in closer and looks at the drawing, something that he's probably done a thousand times. "A few days after Christmas, I think. I found it under the tree when we were taking it down."

Samuel had said little to anyone about what he'd seen that night in the parking lot. At first, I'd wondered if he was somewhere on the spectrum—autism, Asperger's, something like that. But a child psychologist who had interviewed him said he was neither. He was traumatized by the events that ultimately made him an only child.

That's not to say he saw anything, the police department's go-to psychologist wrote in a report that ended up buried in the file after Alan Dawson's case abruptly ended with his suicide. *He may merely be traumatized by the actions of those around him, postabduction.*

The finger pointing at his parents was fair and in its own way unremarkable. His mother and father were at war, albeit a kind of secret, guerilla-type battle that was mostly unknown to anyone but them. They lived in a beautiful home with a dazzling view. They drove nice cars. The veneer of their life together was the essence of who they were as a couple. And what they were as a family. Somerset was no different than many of the fashionable neighborhoods east of Seattle. Keeping up appearances was the true cost of living there.

"I showed it to Angela," Julian says of the drawing. "She grabbed it from me and threw it in the trash, saying that she just wanted Samuel to forget what happened. That he'd need to move on from this or be scared for the rest of his life."

Julian's words stun me.

"Move on? Kelsey had barely been gone for a week. Everyone was traumatized."

He tightens his lips. I can see that he's thinking carefully about what he's going to say. "Right," he says, in a tone that feels confessional. "I knew it. Deep down, I knew it."

I don't blame him. I trust him. He was handed something very ugly, and he didn't want to believe it. But I push a little anyway, to make sure of what I'm hearing. "Knew that she was part of it," I say.

He slowly nods. "Yeah. I don't think the killing part. I can't think that."

"You say she didn't want you to have the drawing?"

"Right. She put it in the pile of wrapping paper we were about to burn, and I pretended to put it in the fireplace. Instead, I hid it from her."

He didn't trust her. Even then.

"Did you ask Samuel about the drawing? What he might have meant by what he made?"

The two of us sit there in silence. He indicates coffee, but I decline. The schoolhouse clock, an antique down in the alcove off the kitchen, ticks like a machine gun.

"Did you?" I say, nudging but wondering if I was being too insistent.

Julian finally exhales. "That's just it. I *did*. He told me the mutant cat took his sister."

We both know that didn't happen. Somewhere in Samuel's brain he'd contorted the images that he'd collected by observing something that frightened him beyond his ability to cope.

Maybe to even recall what it was he saw.

"A child's brain draws connections between fantasy and reality in ways that we can't always understand," I say. "Sometimes details are more clear as time passes. Sometimes memories fade. What does he say now about that night? Anything?"

145

"I wouldn't know, Nicole."

"You haven't asked?"

He fidgets in his chair, but keeps his eyes locked on mine. "I haven't seen my son in months. Angela won't let me. She's shut me out of his life."

Months. He hadn't mentioned that.

"Haven't you agreed to a parenting plan?"

"That's a laugh. She defiant. She's said every nasty thing that she can to the court, and I've been scrutinized like a bug under a microscope. Whenever I win a point, she has her lawyer trump up another complaint. Do you know what it's like to be betrayed by someone you thought you knew?"

He sees the look in my eyes.

"Sorry," he says. "Of course you do."

"Not the same, but enough to get where you've been."

I ask him the question that I've held inside since he showed me the drawing.

"Julian, why didn't you tell us in the beginning? Why hold that back?"

He looks away.

"You don't have kids, do you?" he asks.

I shake my head.

"If you did you'd probably understand. I just didn't want to believe it. That she was involved. Really. Now I'd kill her if I could get away with it. Like she's gotten away with what she did to Kelsey."

"We don't know what she did or didn't do," I say, though I find myself thinking about the Target video, the luggage she supposedly bought, the lies she told the people at the scene, and how no one really saw Kelsey in that parking lot.

It's a dark place, so I change the subject. "How is your son? Do you know?"

Julian shakes his head. His emotions are on a steady simmer. I tapped a button that was stupid to push.

"I have no goddamn idea how he's doing," he finally says, his words now coated in anger, "except for what I read on the Internet."

◆ ◆ ◆

That night Julian leaves for a business trip, and I find myself alone, unsure if I'm a guest, a house sitter, or a problem that will only add to the collection he's already been handed by his wife. He's loaned me his iPad, and it takes only a swipe of my fingertip to the favorites folder to find a link to Eastside Crime Watch. I scroll down and find a post about Kelsey's case. It's an update without any real update. Lane Perry is a master at making nothing into something. This rehash says that though the case is closed, "sources" indicated that Kelsey's abduction and murder have some lingering questions.

One year later: Why doesn't Target Mom talk?

The story, if one could call it that, covers the bizarre behavior of the victim's mother after the crime. In over-the-top, histrionic prose Lane Perry doesn't outright say that Angela Chase had been involved in the crime, just that she was a supremely bad mother.

Lane apparently thinks his readers are sharks, and it's his job to dump a bloody, stinking bucket of chum for them as often as he can.

What kind of a mother leaves her three-year-old child alone in a car?

The blogger notes the custody battle between Julian and Angela and this time he tosses a grenade in Julian's direction.

My mother always said where there's smoke there's fire. Just what is it about Mr. Perfect that his wife knows and we don't? She's repeatedly told the court that he's harboring some dark proclivity. Abuser, maybe?

I scroll down and thank God that Lane has let my thread of the story die a withering death. Danny's conviction and my public shaming had been good for a month of stories. The worst of it came when

Lane published a photo of me coming out of the casino at four thirty in the morning.

Disgraced cop continues losing streak

In what I knew was an indication of my own poor character—and proof that Lane was probably correct about me—I was glad that my dad had Alzheimer's. At least he didn't know any of this happened. Not like Stacy.

I click on the comments section of the Bad Mother post. Angela Chase has no shortage of haters. The first is a posting by someone with the handle Uptown Girl:

> *She's a total bitch and everyone here in the complex hates her. Her baby is dead, and what does she do? She shacks up with a fitness trainer. I don't even go to the pool anymore, because whenever I'm there she and the trainer are practically screwing in the hot tub. Not cool.*

I'd like to talk to Uptown Girl to see what else she could tell me. I'm tempted to post a comment underneath hers, but I resist.

Next up is a comment by QTpie:

> *I used to work with her. There was something really weird about the way she just kind of hung in the background of every office conversation, not saying anything, but just kind of stalking us. Seemed like she didn't know how to be a real person but was trying to take lessons. We had a party the day she quit to become a food blogger. Everyone in the office came. Even Angela. She didn't know why we were celebrating. She thought it was to wish her well. Wish her well? We wished her gone.*

Tammy O posts one of the more fascinating comments, a glimpse in time that I'd never heard about.

> *I went to the memorial someone started in the parking lot at Target, and I swear to God Angela Chase was there just watching. It was about a week after Christmas when everything was blowing up on the news. She stood like a statue a couple of cars away. At first I thought she was there to thank everyone for caring, but she wasn't there for that at all. She was there to shop at Target. Who does that? Who goes shopping at the place their kid was taken?*

Sea Star chimes in:

> *I told that cop that lost her job about the luggage Angela wanted to buy at my shop before her daughter went missing. I swear on a stack of bibles that there was something really off about Angela. I'm not saying she was going to put that kid in a suitcase, but really, that's what I felt at the time.*

I shared the substance of the conversation with the luggage store worker with Danny, but it didn't fit the case and was discarded along with a thousand other leads that didn't align with the Dawson narrative he was busy promoting.

Bellevue Bob, a regular on the site with more than two hundred postings, added:

> *That husband of Angela's is no prize either. I know him from college. He was a skeeze back then. Whenever I see him on TV looking all sad about his daughter or the fact that his wife won't allow him custody, I think there's something really off*

*about him. Look at me. I'm a victim. Blah blah blah. Grow
a pair, buddy. I live in the same neighborhood as the prick.*

The next comment breaks my heart. It was posted by Charlene
Dawson. She didn't change her name.

*Alan Dawson is not a pedophile. Someday the cops will wake
up and admit what they did was wrong. That they accused
an innocent man of a terrible crime. All of you should leave
Angela Chase out of this and let her grieve. Don't be such a
self-righteous judge of things that you know nothing about.*

Crime Fan 666 posted:

*That father just likes the limelight. Reminds me of those people
who go on TV and cry about how they've lost something so
precious but really inside they are happy for the attention.
Remember the old Ramsey case? The parents boohooed for
years.*

To which AnnieT responded:

The Ramseys were not boohooing. They were innocent.

Crime Fan 666:

Innocent my ass.

I read on, scrolling through the smears that come so freely from
those hiding behind their computer screens. So easy to be snarky and
cruel when you're anonymous. I wonder if the neighbor would say any

of what he'd written to Julian's face. Or if the condo neighbor would tell off Angela while she and her lover simmered in the hot tub.

Of course they wouldn't. No one speaks the truth to anyone anymore. Lies either by omission or purposefully have become our national pastime. Backstabbing is an Olympic sport. Or at least it should be.

I hear a tone from the iPad that I set next to Lightning McQueen to charge overnight, but I ignore it. It's 9:00 a.m., and I need to pull myself together. I've been using the shower between the kids' bedrooms. This morning I decide to wake up in the shower of the master bath.

Julian's bedroom is magazine-spread neat. His bed is perfectly made. It's a snowy field of white that makes me think of the postcard our mother sent me and Stacy from a film festival in Telluride. She'd written on the back that she'd met a very important producer that she thought would help her with her big break. Closing the card, she'd written that she missed us.

I knew she didn't. Dad knew it too. He let us put the card on the refrigerator. I realize now how much seeing it must have hurt him. How whenever Stacy bragged to someone in front of our father that Mom was a big movie star had to have been another dagger in his shattered heart. There was only one gift that came with Alzheimer's: Dad's memory stopped before Mom left us. When he could still speak, he talked about her like she was in the next room making her world-famous green-chili enchiladas. I played along. How could I not?

I stand in the shower looking at myself in Julian's shaving mirror. I know that I look a little like my mother—in the eyes. Not as large and pretty as hers, but the same shape. My lips are thin like my father's. Genetically, I'm a kind of mix of the least remarkable things about their faces. My dad's wrists. My mother's small, pre-implant breasts. When the DNA Vitamix was on full when we were conceived, it was Stacy who'd lucked out. The steam fogs the mirror, softening my look. I am not my mother. I'm not my sister. But I am beautiful too. I'm not a loser. I'm a winner. I'm never going to gamble again. *Never.* I'm never going to look for a man to solve my problems.

To make me complete.

I will fall in love one day. Or maybe I won't. And if I don't it won't define the rest of my life.

The water is hot and it feels so good. At once it soothes and refreshes me.

I know what will define me.

Kelsey. Finding out who killed her. It's the reason I wake up in the morning. It's the reason I'm here.

Chapter Twenty-Five

If there was any kind of truce with my mother, it came in the days before her death. I'd graduated from the police academy and Stacy was setting her hook for Cy. We were not close then, but we were closer than we'd be later in life. Our mother had ovarian cancer, and I'd talked to her a few times on the phone from her place in California, but the conversations were stiff and stilted. She had no interest in what I was doing.

"Oh Nicole, this police thing is such nonsense," she said during our last call. "How in the world do you expect to raise a family? Or meet someone? Petty thieves, traffic-law violators all day long. Honestly, what are you thinking?"

I just let her go on pelting me with more of her motherly-soaked-in-cyanide advice. Her words were that pretty, deep-blue box of Morton sprinkled into a gash that didn't heal. My mother was the girl in the yellow slicker, leaving the sparkle of salt all over me. Deep down, I wanted the same things she wanted for me. To be complete. I wanted to have a family, and wanted to believe that I would, someday. That somewhere in the wreckage of my own childhood there was something good. There had to be.

Finally, though, on this day, instead of just taking her mean remarks like I always did, I put my lips up to the blowgun that was my phone.

"Why did you leave us, Mom?" I asked, for what I knew was the umpteenth time. It was my go-to to hurt her back for whatever she said, whatever she did. This time I was the Morton girl.

"Water under the bridge," she said without so much as skipping a beat. "Nicole, I can't be everything to everyone. I need to be true to myself."

"We were little kids," I said.

"And now you're not."

I held my breath. *Was this the best she could do?* "So, you're basically saying just get over it," I said. "That's your final word on it?"

"I'm dying," she said, trumping me as always. "You can think whatever you want when I'm gone. You can twist your story into a wringed up, tear-and-snot-soaked Kleenex. Or you can just let it go."

A week later, Stacy and I flew down to Calabasas where our mother had lived in a small bungalow at the end of a long, dusty road. Stacy cried the whole way on the flight from Seattle. I didn't shed a single tear. Stacy said she couldn't imagine a life without our mother.

I had tried to forget her from the day she left us.

Our mother's home was a shrine to herself. Above the fireplace in the inglenook was a large, framed image that showed her standing in a field, wind stirring her hair. Her blouse unbuttoned as though she'd hastily walked into the frame from some tryst. She was undeniably stunning.

"She was so beautiful, Nic," my little sister said, looking at the black-and-white photograph that Mom had commissioned when she'd fled Washington to start a modeling and acting career in Los Angeles.

"She was," I said, though when I looked at the photo I could see no life in her eyes. She was pretty, but cold. Like a kitchen appliance never used.

"Mom really loved us, you know," Stacy said, slipping a silver-framed photograph of herself taken by her latest boyfriend into the open jaws of her purse. It was the only photograph among more than two dozen that excluded Mom in the frame.

Loved us? I didn't argue with Stacy. To challenge her on this was a losing proposition, I knew, besides just being unkind to my younger sister. She'd always been the favored one. She'd been the one that ran to the phone whenever Mom phoned, and I was the one who got on the call for a few awkward exchanges before Stacy would pop back on and chatter, laugh, and drown herself in the bitter, always conditional love of the woman who left us to appear in films and TV. Her IMDb listing was full of roles in which her character's name appeared to be "uncredited."

"I'm going to make a scrapbook," Stacy said, leafing through more glossy headshots in a box on the glass-and-chrome art deco desk by a window. "Mom was so busy." She held up some old issues of *TV Guide* in which our mother had folded back pages and circled listings in which she appeared.

"Great idea," I said, though inside I wondered if Stacy had any clue that her completely misplaced adulation for our mother only served to drive us further apart.

The excavation of her things in her bungalow in Calabasas proved that.

Among the photographs our mother had collected in a hatbox from a haberdashery on Rodeo Drive were scenes from our life before she vanished one afternoon, and our father told us that she wasn't coming back. She played favorites with her photographs, like she did in everything. Stacy—who our mother always called by her full name, Anastasia—was represented in the rubber band-webbed packets by a margin of three to one. In most homes, the firstborn is over-represented in the family album. Not in our mother's. Maybe I was Kelsey to Mom's Angela?

"Look, Nicole," Stacy had said, her eyes brimming with tears, "remember when Mom and Dad had that pony at my second birthday? It's one of my happiest early memories."

Yes, I remember that, Stacy. And the time Mom forgot my birthday because she needed to try out for a dog food commercial, I think.

"That was such fun," I said.

I love my sister. That had never been in doubt. And yet there were times when she'd say something—on purpose or otherwise—that left me wondering if she cared about my feelings at all. She, like our mother, was the center of her own universe. I merely drifted somewhere else on my own.

It was easy to join the legion of Angela Chase haters as I read more online about her, as I absorbed more of who and what she was by listening to her husband, wearing her clothes, sleeping in her son's bedroom. My mother was an Angela Chase kind of figure. She had been beautiful, conniving, sexy, beguiling, and devoid of any real ability to love.

They would have been best friends. Before one killed the other, of course. In the worlds of women like my mother and Kelsey's, there can only be a single dominant bitch.

On the Alaska Airlines flight home from LAX to Sea-Tac, Stacy managed to get drunk on the free chardonnay a sullen flight attendant poured into clear plastic cups as though she was doing us both a favor. *Maybe she was.* Stacy told me that she was almost certain that Cy Sonntag would ask to marry her. He was handsome and successful, a local Seattle boy with an MBA from Stanford. She was sure that our mother would have adored him.

"He's everything I've ever wanted," she said. "He says I could be a model."

"I'm happy for you," I said. And I was.

"I know it's hard for you," she countered. She reached for the call button and pressed it. The doorbell ding-dong alerted the flight attendant with the wine bottle from some no-name vintner. Stacy held up her empty cup for a refill.

"I said I was happy," I repeated.

"You're so brave, Nicole. You really are."

She was taunting. Like our mother. She was reminding me that I was older, had no prospects, rich or otherwise. I didn't take the bait. Instead, I pretended to be enthralled by the view outside my window. The golden light from the setting sun ran up a river like a rising ther-mometer. I told myself to stay calm. The temperature would drop. I could be cool. I could make it through this flight without telling my sister that her support for me was the thing that I dreaded the most. She was Hitler encouraging Jews to take a hot shower ("You've had such a long journey."). She was Jim Jones telling his followers to slake their thirst with FlavorAid ("It's so hot here in the jungle."). She was the hunter who killed Bambi's mother to thin the herd ("Mother Nature needs a hand now and then.").

And yet with our mother dead, our father inside the rapidly dim-ming tunnel of Alzheimer's, Stacy was all I had.

Lucky, lucky me.

Chapter Twenty-Six

Outside Samuel's window is a rain chain fashioned of tiny, copper buckets. As the rain rolls off the roof, it collects in the first bucket, rolling it over into the next, and so on. The sound of the rushing water and striking of the continual sequence of the little copper is pleasing in its constant rhythm. The vibration calms me. Distracts me a little. I keep my head on the pillow and stare out at the blackness of the night as the rain flows down the chain. I think of the people in my life since I was sucked deep down into the maelstrom of my own disaster. The smug kid with the world's faintest goatee at the Moneytree who made me feel like a drug addict for getting a cash advance on my unemployment. The middle-aged woman ensconced in the casino's cage, supremely aware that most who appeared before her were regulars. The Asian man with the flat affect that told me I had four days to vacate my home—unless I wanted the police to be there to lend a hand. The Bellevue Police, of course. And finally, the young women at Angeline's who lay stiffly in their beds at night, wheels turning, thinking of an escape from the lives that hold them captive. I think of Shelby too. I wonder if she's a hot water bottle for someone else. I hope so. I miss her so much. I miss her more than I miss the flickering of the lights and the sound of a winning push on my favorite slot.

Tomorrow I'll do two things. I'll take the money that Julian left for me in an envelope by the stove, and I'll buy some new clothes at Macy's. Maybe even Target. I'll need to do that because tomorrow I'm going to talk to Angela Chase. I don't want her to look at me in her old clothes and assess which one of us wore it better. That's not a battle I can win, and I know it.

As I drift off listening to the rain flow down those copper buckets, I think of Kelsey. I feel her moving in her brother's room. I hear her small voice, her laugh. I've never seen her in life, of course. Yet from the photos and the videos Julian has shown me on his phone, she's come to life in my thoughts. I purposefully try to think about something else, as though I can control where my dreams will take me. And yet, I find no other subject to take my mind off of Kelsey Chase. I know that when sleep comes I will hurl through that tunnel, a pinprick of light leading me to her. I will see her little face, bruised and inert. I will see the red on the white cotton sheet that shrouded her wilted frame when the hunter stumbled across her on Rattlesnake Ridge. All of that will visit me, I know. The price I'll pay for something like sleep.

I linger in the parking lot of Acadia, the condominium complex in Kirkland that Angela and Samuel Chase now call home. It's four stories. New. Expensive. The top two floors, I think, have expansive views of Lake Washington. As shoppers and employees headed to work brush past me, they completely ignore my presence. I'm glass. Not in the same way that people pretended not to see me as I pulled my carry-on luggage around the streets of Seattle waiting for a shelter to open. This is a different kind of avoidance. At Acadia, it's exhibited by young ear-budded phone-swipers, all fixated on wherever they are going. They emerge from the building alone too. No couples. Just one solo person after another.

Through the annoyingly small cutout on the lid of my cup, I suck in hot coffee from the shop across the street. And I wait.

It's Angela's day off from the boutique. I know she has to come out sooner or later. I have plenty of later.

My Macy's attire—jeans, a sweater, a coat—has boosted my spirits a little. It's embarrassing to admit that something as small as a new sweater could feel life changing. One of the women at the shelter was ecstatic that a new pair of socks she'd been given still had that plastic wire that holds the pair together. Those socks were a big deal. When I think of things like that it makes me feel even more foolish about the demise of my old life. *It was my doing.* When some of the girls at the shelter were talking about boyfriends or husbands that had beat the shit out of them, I just nodded knowingly. I let them believe that my pitiful circumstances were aligned with theirs. In a roomful of other gamblers, I have the courage to admit the reason I'm there. But to lose everything to a machine is indefensible when among those who'd been victimized by another.

I have no visible scars to share, and I know it.

Then, finally, as my coffee passes to that lukewarm temperature that invites a toss into a trash can, I see Angela emerge from the gleam of Acadia's front door. She's not alone. Samuel's with her. And so is a man.

The fitness trainer with whom she'd outraged her condo neighbor in the hot tub, no doubt.

Angela's head is down in that way celebrities pose when they pretend to avoid the stare of a TMZ freelancer's lens. She's a woman who lives to be noticed. Like my mother. Angela wears all black under a cherry "look at me" coat. She swings what I'm all but certain is a Prada bag like it's ballast to steady each step made by her nail-spike heels. Samuel is in jeans, a dark-blue hoodie. The fitness trainer appears to be in his late thirties, is dark-complexioned with a light stubble on his chin. He's handsome. An accessory, like that Prada bag. His head is shaved and I see the dimples in earlobes that indicate he ditched earrings a while ago. His arm is a python around Angela's impossibly tiny waist. His white teeth float in the air like Alice's Cheshire cat.

"Angela," I say as I move in her direction.

Immediately, the man pushes Angela and Samuel behind him. "No media!" he says. His tone is sharp and aggressive.

"I'm not media," I say. "She knows me. I need to talk to you, Angela. It's about Kelsey."

Angela barely looks at me with those big, green eyes of hers. She turns to the man. "She's that cop that got fired."

His eyes brush over me. "Leave us alone," he says.

Cheshire cat is now full-on fangs.

I ignore him. "Angela, we need to talk about the drawing."

She looks at me blankly.

"The one Samuel made."

As if she'd been jolted, she suddenly waves her arms and swings that status purse of hers. She's agitated. This is more life than I saw in her the day Kelsey went missing.

"I don't know what you're talking about. You are scaring my little boy!"

I drop to my knees so that I'm eye-level with the little boy. "I'm here to help," I say, but the man she's with puts his palm toward me. His hand is large. A baseball mitt.

"Don't touch me," I say.

I realize I have no standing here. And yet I almost want him to shove me. I want something to happen. If he assaults me, maybe the police would haul him in and start working the case. Wishful thinking, I know. Never got me anywhere except on the losing side of the casino slots.

Samuel looks hunted. Scared. I don't want to frighten him. He draws inward.

I turn to his mother. "Angela, you've got to help me." I'm pleading now. "We have to find out what happened. Samuel has a right to know what happened to his sister."

"The case is closed."

"It shouldn't be," I say.

She doesn't respond. Instead, she looks at the man. "Let's get out of here."

Samuel's gaze is now fixed on me—not at his mother or the man that's inserted himself between all of us. I notice for the first time how much he favors his mother. There's maybe a little of Julian in the wave of his hair, but, really, he looks like Angela. It makes me think of Stacy, how she appropriated our mother's beauty while I inherited our father's features.

"A monster took my sister," Samuel says to me, dead serious.

Angela grabs the boy's hand, jerks him close. "Shut up," she says. "We don't talk to strangers."

I stand. My heart is pounding now. I pull the drawing from my purse and hold it out to the boy.

"Do you know who the monster is?" I ask as the trio hastens toward a white Lexus. Its headlights flash once, and I hear the sound of the locks rise.

"Your daddy misses you," I call out as they vanish behind the tinted windows of the car.

"Piece of work, those two," a voice behind me calls out from the entrance to Acadia. It's a young man.

"Yeah," I say. "You know them?"

He nods. "Can't stand them. None of the tenants can."

"The hot tub thing," I say.

"You don't know the half of it," he says.

"Tell me," I say.

He considers me, then indicates to follow him into the lobby. It's a dimly lit space of white Barcelona chairs and glass tables and crystal pendant lights that hang from the ceiling like a thousand icicles.

"You're police, right?" he asks.

"I was," I answer. "Not anymore."

His name is Marco Denton. He's the assistant manager. He's young, but he reads the news sites. I know the look of recognition when I see it, but he's kind enough to avoid throwing it in my face. I like this guy. For whatever reason, he's aching to dish the dirt on Angela Chase.

I want Marco Denton to dump it all over me. Bury me. Pile it on. Every speck of Angela dirt is what I want. I'm an open grave. Fill me up.

He's a gift, lit up for me like a pulsing row of double diamonds.

We sit across from each other on the Barcelonas. It's a conversation area I can't imagine ever hosting a conversation. Acadia's people scurry out. Nod only if they have to. The elevator pings incessantly as they're delivered down. It's only a four-floor building. Yet no one takes the stairs.

"She's a total bitch," Marco says, looking around to make sure we're alone. He's going to tell me something, but he's going to be careful. "I mean, that chick thinks she's all that and everyone else is someone to serve her. And if you're not serving her, she looks at you with a kind of glare that asks you not to breathe too much air. Like you're nothing."

Pretty much the best analysis of Angela Chase that I've ever heard.

"I'd say you're a psych major," I say.

He grins. "No. Computer science. But thanks. I can read people pretty well. But seriously, Angela Chase is a walking billboard for a screaming bitch. No real reading needed on that one. One look at her, and you'll figure out that the best way to deal is to get away as fast as you can."

He likes her about as much as I do. I like this kid.

"What else can you tell me about her? I'm trying to help her husband. He's been cut off from seeing their son—despite a court order."

His head bobs. "That sounds like her. She's been the renter from hell. My boss, Tracy, won't tell you anything. She's totally by the book. So tight her eyes squeak when she reads a leasing contract."

I'd probably like Tracy. Ethics are good. Not so much, however, when you need to get something out of someone. I have Marco for that. I press him for some details. "So Angela's been a problem tenant?"

"The worst was when she left the water running one time," he says. "Flooded the unit below her. She said that it was a faulty pipe, but when the maintenance guys checked it out they said she'd left the bathwater going. No other possibility. But she flat-out lied about it."

"She does that a lot," I say.

"No kidding," he says, leaning toward me as though he doesn't want anyone else to hear. Maybe by-the-book Tracy. "She's always complaining about someone. Says people are harassing her here. We don't rent to harassers. Except for her and her boyfriend. She told Tracy that she's going to sue if Tracy can't keep a lid on the things."

"Who's the guy?" I ask. "Seemed like a real charmer."

Marco picks some pet hair off his thigh. It makes me think of Shelby, but I can't go there. "Michael Bennett. He's a complete asshole," he says. "Maybe worse than Angela. Something's always someone else's fault. Pitched a fit when someone keyed his car. I mean a major, 'I'm going to have the security staff fired, and you'll have to give me free rent for a year' kind of tirade in front of a bunch of residents at the Friday-night wine tasting. It was fun to pop his bubble on that one."

"How'd you do that?"

Marco leans in some more and breaks into a wide smile. This is a very happy memory. "We have cameras all over this place. Guess who did it?"

I hoped it wasn't Julian, though I wouldn't have blamed him. I'm not even sure if he knows about Michael Bennett.

Marco pauses for dramatic effect. "Angela," he says.

I repeat her name.

"Yeah," Marco says, now excited. "Isn't that awesome? That whack job did it. We told him about it, but he said we were liars and that we'd faked the tape. Let me repeat. *Faked the tape.* Who does he think we are? The CIA? God, what a jerk."

"Awesome that you caught her." I loathe the word *awesome* as much as I hate the phrase *at the end of the day,* but I'm speaking Marco's language. *When in Acadia.* "How'd she react?"

"Angela and that poor kid of hers just stood there while Bennett just unloaded on us."

"Did she deny it was her?"

He leans back in the Barcelona. "Of course she did," he says. "Her excuse was that she doesn't own a coat like the one the chick had on the tape."

I can tell that Marco loves every beat of our conversation. A little spittle has collected at the corners of his mouth. It's more endearing than gross.

"You caught her in a lie, didn't you?"

He head-bobs excitedly. This is Marco Denton's finest hour, and he wants me to know it. "Not only that. I found the coat in the Dumpster the next day. Still have it. You want it? I kept it for the police in case Bennett got them involved. We let it slide because it looks bad to have any kind of crime or vandalism at exclusive Acadia."

His voice drips with sarcasm. I really like this kid.

"Yes," I tell him, "I'll take the coat."

"Sure. I was going to donate it, but I don't know. Just kind of held on to it. Seemed too nice to throw away."

Marco vanishes into the office. While I wait, I listen to some kind of electric violin music as it flows through the sound system and think about what little Samuel said. What he might have said if his mother hadn't muzzled him. He knows something about who-ever took his sister. The monster with the big, scary teeth wasn't an apparition.

It was a person. I'm sure of it.

A beat later, Marco emerges from the office with the coat draped over his arm and some paperwork in his hands.

"Something always kind of bugged me," he says, handing me the coat that I immediately recognize from the rainy day at the Target store where Kelsey vanished. It's the Burberry.

No one throws away a coat like that.

"What's that?" I ask, looking down at the papers.

"It could be important. I don't know. It just seems weird. Working here, you see a lot of weird shit, but this . . ."

His words trail off. He's no longer reveling in telling me what a bitch Angela is and what an ass Michael Bennett can be. His eyes stay on the papers. My eyes stay on his.

"But this what?" I ask. "Marco?"

"It gave me a sick feeling," he finally says. "Michael Bennett rented his unit three months before the maniac and her little boy moved in."

"Why does that bother you?" I ask, folding the coat and tucking it under my arm.

"She came in with him the day he previewed the space. I recognized her from TV."

"She's pretty memorable," I say.

"Yeah. Those kinds of women are. Pretty on the outside, no doubt, but kind of like a poison apple."

I nod. Another apt description of Angela Chase.

"But that wasn't the weird part."

"What was?"

"I'm pretty sure that they came in before that little girl went missing."

My adrenaline surges just then.

"Are you sure, Marco?"

For the first time he looks a little uncomfortable. "I know it was Christmastime," he finally says. "She remarked on our tree. She said that she was surprised our decorations were 'so off trend.'"

"Really?"

He laughs. "Yeah, she said that copper was what all the high-end designers were using and that silver was 'last year's metal.' Like there's three choices for metal-toned ornaments and Tracy made some huge mistake. We laughed about her being such a bitch at the time."

"Are you completely certain, Marco?"

A tone beeps on his smartwatch. "Yep. Shift over. Gotta get out of here. My last day is tomorrow."

Ah ha. A short-timer. That explains my luck in tapping this fount of aggrieved information. "Where you headed from here?"

"Google." The young man beams. "I was an intern, and I actually got hired on. Feels good to be out of the business of smiling all day no matter what shit someone throws at you. I worked in retail before this gig. Hated that too."

We walk out together and I wish him well, but before he heads to his car I ask the question that I know Julian would want answered above all others. "How's the little boy doing?"

"Sam?"

I nod. "His father hasn't been able to see him."

"Yeah, Angela told us to keep an eye out for him. Said she got beat up pretty bad by him, but none of us believed her. I'm sure that's not PC, to not believe someone, but I'd have a hard time believing today was Tuesday if she told me."

"How is he?"

"Okay, I guess," Marco says. "His mother never lets him out of her sight. He's never even been to the park, as far as I know. Feel sorry for him. It's like he's the third wheel in Angela and Dickwad's relationship. Dragged here and there. Never talks. Just complies. I feel sad for that kid."

"Me too."

"You might want this too," Marco says. "It's the lease agreement. It has Bennett's Social, past address, and other stuff if you need it. I don't care if they fire me for giving it to you."

"Because you've already quit."

He smiles.

Looking down at the description of the unit is like a shot through the heart.

Two bedroom. Three residents maximum.

CHAPTER TWENTY-SEVEN

I try Stacy, but she doesn't answer. She's avoiding me. Hurting me that way is one of her favorite things to do. Certainly, she'd never admit to that. She's a classic passive-aggressive. She always finds a way to make me feel as though I'm intruding and so very wanted at the same time. I tell myself that when I pull up in front of her house in Julian's car. Of course she's home. She's always home.

I don't have to take a personality test to know that I'm not a good person. Not all the time. I was a good detective. I was motivated to help others. Getting out of bed in the morning after a long night working a case was never a chore. I honestly couldn't wait to get back to what I was doing because I always focused on how others who needed help—families of the missing or abused—benefited from what I could do for them. How I could right a wrong. How I could fix my own life by doing something for someone who was worse off than I was.

That's what's driving me now, as I sit in front of Stacy's perfect home. I know that as much as she pushes me away, she needs me. I've seen the fissures in the facade of her marriage. I've deciphered the coded language she uses to talk about her marriage to Cy.

"Why didn't you tell me you were coming over?" Stacy says as she opens the front door.

"I tried calling," I say. I don't add "six times," because I don't want to be that sister.

"Oh," she says, "that's weird. I didn't get any messages."

"I didn't leave any."

Emma runs to me, and I scoop her up as my younger sister leads me into the kitchen. She has her laptop open to a video on wontons. On the big block of a cutting board she's laid out some of the most pitifully folded wontons I've ever seen.

"You want some help?" I ask, setting Emma on the counter.

"Would you? I just can't get the hang of it."

"I took a dim sum cooking class in college," I say. "I'll bet it's a bit like riding a bike."

She drinks her wine and I fill the thin pastry squares with dollops of the pork mixture she's made fragrant with ginger. She remarks that I look better. It's only half a compliment. She leaves the room and comes back with a gift card to Gene Juarez. Of course, she still thinks my hair is in need of a styling.

"Someone gave it to me," she says. "I don't like any of their stylists there. The last good one I had, Tatum, left for another salon."

I know she's lying. She's bought that card for me. Stacy's like that. She can't ever be really nice in a direct way. Even so, I'm touched.

"Where are you staying?" she finally asks.

"A friend's place."

She looks at me over her wine glass. "What friend?"

"You don't know him."

"A him?" she asks. "Interesting. I hope you're not jumping back into a relationship."

"Staying with someone when you're homeless and broke isn't about a relationship, Stacy. It's about survival."

"Don't be so touchy. I was just saying."

I finish folding and sealing the little squares, and she invites me to stay for dinner. "Cy will be home around seven. Don't tell him that you helped, okay?"

"I wouldn't dream of it."

"Who is this guy?" she asks.

"The one I'm staying with?"

"Uh-huh. That one."

"Julian Chase. I'm staying at Julian's."

Slowed by the "crisp, not too oaky" chardonnay she's been drinking, Stacy's brain whirls. Her eyes widen. "Kelsey's dad?"

I shrug. "Yeah. I'm trying to help him find out who killed his daughter."

"I don't know about that, Nic," she says. "That seems a little weird to me."

It is weird. I know that. Yet I defend it.

"He needs help. I want to help."

"The case is closed," she says, refilling her glass. "That trailer-park freak killed her."

When I hear my sister say "trailer-park freak," I want to scream. She's like everyone else. They still think Alan Dawson is the killer. The Bellevue Police admitted to Danny's deletion of the records, the fact that the confession was coerced. They sent him to prison. They fired me. After all of that, Alan Dawson is still demeaned and disparaged.

"He didn't kill Kelsey," I say.

"Innocent people don't kill themselves, Nic. They just don't." She pours me a glass, and I take it. "You aren't screwing Julian Chase, are you?"

Of course I knew the question would come, but I still sip the wine to buy some time. Julian is handsome. He is kind. If I could have picked a decent man like him, I'm all but certain my life would have been different. I don't blame Danny Ford for my gambling addiction. I know I can't blame anyone for that. But I can blame myself for loving someone who didn't love me back. I was in a sinking lifeboat, and Danny let it go down. Hell, he punched a hole in the bottom.

"No," I say. "I've done messy and complicated. I'm not about to go there again."

An hour later, Cy breezes in. He's the local boy who's made good. An all-American swimmer at Washington State. An MBA from Stanford. His body is better than most twenty-year-olds, though he's in his early forties. He jogs five miles a day and works out at a CrossFit twice a week. His hair is dark and thick, and his eyes are a very light shade of blue, the color of the kitchen wallpaper in the house in Hoquiam where Stacy and I grew up. I can smell the cigarette smoke on his clothes when I give him a quick hug. I whisper in his ear.

"She still thinks you've quit."

He gives me a sly wink. "She thinks a lot of things," he says. We laugh a little.

Despite his annoying self-absorption and vanity, now and then I've found some ways to like Cyrus Sonntag. Sometimes better than my own sister. Where Stacy never cared one whit about police work, Cy was actually interested in how I worked a case or what I thought about the criminal justice system. Though he'd been promoted up at Microsoft, he'd started in the cybercrime division working with the federal government and state agencies to put a stop to hackers, cybercriminals, and the ever-changing world of information security. On occasions when Danny and I were over and the conversation veered toward shoptalk, Stacy would grow impatient and switch the subject to Pilates or pool tile from Italy. When Cy talked about what he was doing, I didn't need to feign polite interest. I was interested. I knew that whenever Stacy suggested that Cy wanted alone time with her, it was really that she wanted me gone.

I let her take credit for the wontons, though Emma, who happily eats a microwaved White Castle burger and some tater tots, almost blows my attempt at a sisterly subterfuge.

"Auntie made them," she chirps as we sit at the table that I'd clawed the night before I gave up my beloved dog and said good-bye to my house once and for all. I was at rock bottom then. I was glad Cy was away then. I look for the gouge in the wood, but it's gone. My fingers feel for it, but it has vanished. Stacy never lets an imperfection fester.

"I only found the website," I say. "Your mommy did the hard part."

My four-year-old niece looks confused, but doesn't say anything more. My sister gives me a look, indicating appreciation. At least that's what I think it is. I always hope for the best.

The wontons have been prepared two ways, steamed in a bamboo steamer and fried in a deep-fat fryer that I'd get rid of after that night. Nothing is messier. Or worse for you.

Or tastes better.

Stacy's opened a bag of salad and steamed a pouch of jasmine rice in the microwave. She takes a lot of shortcuts for someone without a job.

That's the bitch in me. Sorry, Sister.

"Everything is so good," I say.

Cy smiles approvingly. "Reminds me of a little hole-in-the-wall I ate at in Hong Kong last year. Except the fish bladder part. Thank God, you didn't serve that tonight. Not a fan."

Stacy laughs and pours us more wine. I notice that when she leaves for the kitchen there is a slight pause before the wine bottle hits the granite countertop. I'm pretty sure that she's guzzled some and refilled her glass.

"Did Nicole tell you about her new living arrangement?" she calls in.

Cy dips a wonton in French's yellow mustard and sesame seeds. I seriously doubt that's how they served the dish at the hole-in-the-wall in Hong Kong. "No," he says, looking at me and arching a brow. "I almost hate to ask. But where?"

I don't answer. My mouth is purposefully full of that terrible micro-wave rice.

"She's living with the dad of that dead girl, Kelsey Chase. Isn't that weird, Cy?"

Cy sits up and cocks his head. "Seriously? What's that all about, Nicole? Is that really a good idea?"

The two of them talk like I'm Helen Keller, and I let them.

"That's what I said," Stacy says, making her return from the kitchen.

"That can't be healthy for your recovery," Cy says.

"Yes," Stacy says. "That's what I was thinking too."

Finally I stop chewing; I know it would be rude to shovel another forkful of rice into my mouth as an excuse to avoid jumping into the conversation that is all about me.

"Cy," I say, "it is unusual, I guess. But he offered. I had no place to go."

"You could have stayed here with us," he says, his eyes snagging Stacy's and then looking back at me. "Isn't that right, Stacy?"

"That's what I told her," my sister says. "I *begged* her."

I feel my face grow hot. I remember the scenario quite differently. I recall that my sister very pointedly said to me that I had to leave before Cy returned from Italy. That my being there would only cause them problems. I know a sinking ship when I see one. Their marriage is the *Lusitania* or the *Andrea Doria*. It's certainly not been a Carnival cruise, like the one advertised on the brochure fanned out on the table.

"She did," I say, lying for my sister. I realize then that Cy doesn't know a thing about my staying at the homeless shelter. In a way, that eases how hopeless I've felt. He'd likely not have let me endure all of that if he'd known. "I need to work out my own problems. You know, Cy, part of my recovery."

"That makes sense, I guess," he says.

"Perfect sense," Stacy says.

"Guess you won't be waiting for Danny," Cy says.

"No, I guess I won't."

Cy motions for a drink, and Stacy obediently gets him one. "So what's this guy like?" he asks. "You're not involved with him, are you?"

He thinks I'm a slut. My sister is absolutely the worst person to confide in. She's the first person to betray someone under the guise of someone "having a right to know" about something about which they had no right.

"No. Nothing like that. Just trying to help."

"That case is closed, right?"

"Officially, yes."

"Why do you say 'officially'?"

"Bellevue Police have closed the case. Despite everything that happened during the investigation, they stand firm that Alan Dawson killed Kelsey Chase."

"Sick SOB," Cy says.

"I'm not so sure," I say. "Some things just don't add up."

"Like what, Nicole?" Stacy asks, though I know she doesn't care. She just wants a way back into the conversation. She did that when we were growing up too. My dad and I loved to fish. Stacy hated it. But whenever we were talking about our next trip, she'd find a way to insert herself with some conversation-stopping non sequitur.

"I don't believe Alan Dawson kidnapped and murdered her."

"Who do you think did?" Cy asks.

The truth is I don't know. "I just don't think we have all the facts," I say.

"But there was a major investigation, Nicole," he says. "Everything pointed to Dawson."

I don't want to have this conversation. Not with these two people. And yet I can't bite my tongue. "Danny really fucked things up," I say, immediately regretting my word choice. Emma looks at me, her eyes big, her nose wrinkled. I've been caught, and she doesn't need to wag her little finger at me.

Stacy will do that for her.

"Please, watch your mouth, Nicole. Little elephants have big ears, and I don't want her repeating that word at a playdate."

"You're right about Danny," Cy says, dipping another wonton into a bath of far too-bright yellow mustard. He points to his now-empty small dish of sesame seeds, and Stacy jack-in-the-boxes into the kitchen to retrieve more. And to guzzle, I'm pretty sure. "He's really messed things up. But he's a good guy."

"I thought so at one time too," I say.

Nicole comes in. She seems a little wobbly. I'm a betting woman. So I'd say even money that she was drunk. She sets down the dish of seeds, spilling some on the table. Emma looks at her mother and heads off to watch a Disney princess DVD.

"Cy's right," Stacy said. "Danny has his good points."

I really don't want to go there right now. But I do. "He messed with evidence. He sent a man to jail who was probably innocent."

"Probably?" Cy says. "He was a pervert, wasn't he? He had a record. Come on, Nic, cut Danny a little slack. His life is—" he stops, making sure that Emma can't hear, "—is totally fucked up."

This is a repeat of a conversation we had not long after Danny's arrest. Danny and Cy were in the same frat in college. They'd vacationed together before Cy married my sister. We'd double-dated a couple of times, but we weren't a steady foursome by any stretch. Danny thought Cy was a sanctimonious prick. And while I liked my brother-in-law, I could see Danny's point. Cy could be a total prick. Not to me so much, but to others. The way he talked about his employees at Microsoft made me pretty sure that they couldn't stand him.

And judging by the way my sister acted around him, being married to Cy was no great shakes either.

Cy slides his chair back and stretches his legs. "You know," he says, "you really should go and see him."

"I doubt that would be a good idea."

"Damn it, Nicole, he misses you. The guy messed up. Can't you forgive him?"

I wonder if either Cy or Stacy has pondered where my life has gone since I got involved with Danny Ford. Not that he's to blame for everything, but surely, couldn't the two of them see that Danny and I were toxic for each other?

"Are you in touch with Danny?" I ask.

"Not really. He's called a few times. Collect. I take the calls, of course, but then I have to go through some asinine business-expense reporting at work that's a complete nightmare."

I didn't know they talked. Stacy didn't mention it. I look at her, and she ignores my gaze.

"The guy still loves you," Cy says.

Danny doesn't know what love is. It might be that I don't either. But I'm certain that his idea of love ruined my life.

"You were such a great-looking couple," Stacy adds.

My face is hot again, and this time I cannot stop the explosion. "He royally screwed me over," I say, getting up, composing myself just enough to say good-bye to Emma.

"You know," I say to Stacy as I close their glitzy door ("I went to five door and cabinet stores to find what I thought would give the right first impression"), "you could have kept Shelby. You didn't have to make me give up my dog too."

As I sit in Julian's BMW, air-conditioning on to cool my face despite the chilly evening, I wish that I hadn't stormed out of my sister's house in the way that I just had. Not without telling Cy that I folded all of those fucking wontons.

Chapter Twenty-Eight

The drive to the prison outside of Shelton runs from the Seattle-to-Bremerton ferry through Belfair along Hood Canal. Portions of the roadway seem to be a mere scratch in the evergreens that had been the reason for most of the towns along the way. But as I drive Angela's cast-off car along these stretches, I see gaps in the green. It's almost as though the trees are a false front. A Hollywood set. A dark screen to hide the fact that beyond the wall of green is a denuded, logged-off landscape.

I've been to the prison once before. The police academy in Burien included site visits to all of the correctional facilities in Washington as part of the curriculum. I never thought I'd need to go back. My job was to put people there. Not for social calls.

I wonder how Danny felt when he first arrived.

Lousy as hell, I hope.

On the outskirts of Shelton, I pass by an enormous cross section of a Douglas fir tree that ticks off the history of the world since it germinated nearly seven hundred years ago. A sapling when the plague decimated Europe stands on the edge of an overlook that takes in the Shelton lumber mill below.

Danny Ford is my personal plague.

I pull off Highway 101 and onto the road that runs past a small airport, Sanderson Field. A sign points to the Olympic Grand Prix racetrack. I wonder how many inmates have fantasized about escape plans that involved either of those venues.

It's 4:00 p.m. Visitation starts at 4:15 and lasts until 7:15. I wonder how long I'll be able to sit there with him. He's in an isolation unit, and our visit will be through a glass partition. None of the precautions are designed to protect me or any other visitor. Cops in prison are extremely vulnerable. They eat alone. Peruse the library without the distraction of another human being. They exercise alone. Racquetball, I'm told, is a favorite sport for those incarcerated solo. Danny wrote me a few times after he was locked up, but I didn't answer. The letters were pleading, full of regret and promises that he'd make things right. I threw them away.

One line, however, stayed with me.

I did what I did because I love you, Nicole.

Ruining someone's life. Such an act of love.

I queue up in a line of cars coming into the correctional institution. The minivan behind me is full of kids coming to spend time with their father, I guess. The voice on a speaker by the parking lot directs me where to park and what door to enter. I'm the only car that peels off to the left. Where I'm going, there are no tables to play cards or snacks to share from a vending machine.

The Alder isolation unit is an iceberg floating in the middle of the sea. It is for the most violent offenders. And, that rarity among all those incarcerated, the police officer. Danny Ford is like the last passenger pigeon at the Cincinnati Zoo that I wrote about in a high school paper. Utterly alone.

I show the guard my ID and he hands me a key to a locker.

"Nothing goes inside," he says.

He's about twenty-two. His hair is buzzed. His teeth are Gary Busey large. I wonder if he can even cover them with his lips.

He pats me down, and I pass through a metal detector.

"Visitor for Ford processed," he says into a shoulder microphone. He leads me to a booth with a phone.

I look through what I presume to be bulletproof glass. I catch my own reflection and wish I'd have applied more lip color. I look pale. I adjust my hair a little and sit there. I'm dressed in my other Macy's outfit—black slacks, white blouse, and a jacket that I suddenly fear makes me look like a flight attendant for some regional airline. I find myself wishing that I'd purchased something sexier, then immediately wonder why in hell I would even care. To show him what he's missing? Make him jealous? Why would that matter?

Waiting.

My heart rate picks up. When Danny appears through the glass, my breath stops.

He's aged. Like the president does after a few years in office. But Danny has aged in less than a year. His hair is long now—not perfectly cut. It tucks behind his collar, and I want to think that he's not wearing it in a ponytail. But I think he is. His skin is pallid, and I wonder if he ever goes outside in the yard.

I pick up the phone.

"You look good, Danny," I say.

Inside, I'm very happy that he looks like shit.

"You're as hot as ever," he says, lowering his eyes to check me out.

Good. He can't have me. Ever.

I can see that while he looks beat down, he's been working out. His chest pushes against the T-shirt he's wearing.

Now I'm checking him out.

"I'm not sure why I'm here, Danny," I say.

"Because you miss me too."

"Like I'd miss cancer if I'd beat it," I say.

"Tough-Tough Nicole," he says. "I see right through you."

There was a time when I thought he did. Before everything happened I would have told anyone who asked that I thought that Danny Ford really got me. That it was the concept that he understood me that had made him all the more attractive. I was able to overlook the narcissism and the constant chest thumping about how good he was on the job or in the bedroom. Only a fool would overlook the things I did because I thought that being with someone who seemed to love me was better than being alone.

"It took me a long time, Danny, but I see who you are too."

He lowers the receiver to think. This isn't going the way he wants it to. I know he'll think of some way back to me. Or he'll try.

"Look," he finally says, "you didn't come out here to tell me that I'm a piece of shit, Nicole."

My eyes don't blink. "I didn't?"

He shakes his head and in doing so I see that he does have a stubby ponytail.

"You came to see if I'll take you back," he says.

Even though the statement is the funniest thing I've heard in months, I don't laugh.

"I came to see why you framed Alan Dawson. That's the only reason I'm here, Danny. I couldn't fucking care less about you."

His facade cracks a little. "You don't mean that, Nic."

He's ignored my question. I ignore his attempt to distract me.

"We'd barely started the case, Danny. You wanted Dawson to be the perpetrator. What was that about? Was someone in your family molested? Were *you*? Did you commit statutory rape too?"

"None of the above, Nicole. I liked Dawson because he fit the profile, and he lived practically next-door to where the kid was last seen. That's why."

I keep my eyes on his. "You *made* him fit the profile. You planted the shoe that Viola found. You forced Alan into signing that confession. You goddamn know you did all of that."

Danny barely blinks. Stalemate. I'd forgotten how cold his eyes could be.

"I admitted that I pushed him," he says, trying to switch his tone. "But I didn't make it up, Nicole. He did what he did. I don't know anything about the shoe."

Liar.

"He didn't dump the body on Rattlesnake Ridge, and you know it," I say.

His eyes flicker, but he steadies his gaze at mine though the glass. I notice a smudge on the glass. A handprint. Some couple played the movie cliché. That's not going to happen here. I don't have a gun, of course. And the glass is bulletproof. Even so, I think of smashing it and lunging at that SOB that let a little girl's killer get away.

"People like Dawson never change," he says. "They can't."

"Are you speaking from experience?"

"I'm talking about broken people, Nicole," he says. "People like you."

I want to tell him to fuck off and die, but that's only going to make him happy. He always loved to assess my personality, dig into the roots of my depression, pick apart my relationship with my mother, my sister, and my father. I'd told him too much. I'd given him a portal into every character flaw I possessed. He'd held me and comforted me. I looked up to him. I thought that he was so much smarter than he really was.

All the while he was just a schemer. A user.

"I hate you," I say.

"How's that new boyfriend working out? Jesus, Nicole, even you have to admit that's pretty fucked up."

I wonder if I'm having a heart attack right now. My heart's no longer beating.

"What are you talking about? I don't have a boyfriend."

"Fucking the dead kid's father, that's really something. Off the charts."

"I don't know what you're talking about. I'm not fucking anyone."

"Really?"

His eyes probe mine. I feel right then that I'm the passenger pigeon. I'm the one alone. I'm on the wrong side of the glass.

I pull inside myself. I'm going to take this conversation back to something useful. If I can.

"Did you have something to do with Alan Dawson's death?"

Danny gives me a cold stare. No affect. Just ice. "He killed himself."

He's behind glass, so I push more than I would if he had been standing next to me. I trust him so very little. "You visited him at the jail, Danny, just before the purported suicide."

More ice.

"It wasn't *purported*, you bitch. The pervert couldn't live with himself. I might have rattled him a little, but that's all. I didn't have a goddamn thing to do with what he did after I left."

"Like everything you say," I tell him, "I have a hard time drawing the connection between your words and any of the events you describe. Do you even know the truth anymore?"

"I know you were a lousy fuck," he says.

It's back to that. Danny thinks that nothing hurts like a sexual insult. He's stuck at seventh grade. I've taken the bait before, but not now.

"You know that I'm going to find out what really happened, don't you?"

He glares through the sheen of the wall between us. "You're not that good of a cop."

I suppress a bitter smile. Another of his favorite digs. ("Watch the master and learn, Babe. Only time will tell if you've got it in you to be a real detective.")

"Maybe not," I say. "But I'm pissed off, and anger has always been my best motivator, Danny."

He's still talking, but I'm not listening anymore. He's trying to convince me that he's misunderstood. That I'm stupid. That I'm nothing without him. That everyone knows that I've gambled away my house, my reputation. That I'm not really hot. His tirade almost makes me laugh; instead I just give him one concluding parting shot.

"And honestly, what grown man still calls himself Danny? Please. You're in your forties. Get off the Little League mound and grow up, you arrogant son of a bitch."

That felt so good.

◆ ◆ ◆

My car remains the lone visitor's vehicle in my special parking lot. I look over at the other side of the complex, dimmed by the first blush of dusk. More than three dozen cars fill the lot. I wonder if my visit was the worst of the day. Or if any visit with someone you actually care about is worse because the visit is a weekly, monthly, maybe even a yearly obligation. I'm never coming back.

I reach for my phone and press the icon of a kitten that Emma chose to represent her mother when I got the phone. It rings as I pull out of the lot, passing the guard as he waves me through.

"I just saw Danny," I say before she can even speak.

There's a slight pause, and I wonder what Stacy is doing just then.

"You did?" she finally asks.

"Do we have a bad connection here?" I ask her. "I just said that I talked to Danny."

"I got that," Stacy says. "How'd it go?"

My sister is a piece of work. She proves that little fact to me just about every time we speak. "Why don't you tell me?" I ask her.

Again a pause.

"Stacy?" I ask.

"Are you still there, Nicole? I can't hear you."

Liar.

"Don't pull that crap on me. You can hear me." I look at the front of my phone. Four bars.

"Nic, I think I've lost you."

Then she hangs up.

I immediately call her back, but the call instantly goes to voice messaging.

"Stacy, one of you—*you or Cy*—talked to Danny. How could you tell him that I was sleeping with Kelsey's dad? Why would you even say something like that? It's not even true. I told you that. Honestly, Stacy, you keep giving me reasons to never trust you again. Is our relationship really nothing to you? Nothing at all? Do you give a flying fuck about me at all? I have done nothing but try to be a big sister to you. When Mom left. When Dad got sick. When Mom died. I was there for you. You continually stab me in the back. Really. If it weren't for Emma, I'd be done with you for good."

The last words tumble out with ragged edges, and I know that if I keep talking I'll start to cry. I'm glad for the safety net of leaving a recorded message. She'd have interrupted me with faux outrage that I'd even suggest any kind of betrayal on her part. Or she'd have whined about how hard it was for her to support me when I'd maxed out my cards, lost the house, and ended up in the shelter. Like she'd thrown me some major lifeline. Or my absolute favorite: that I'd never know how difficult it was to be married to a professional like Cy.

I have never used the C-word to disparage another woman in my life, but right now, I know that when that epithet was first used by some hateful jerk, it was tailor-made for Stacy Foster Sonntag.

CHAPTER TWENTY-NINE

The lights are on. Julian is home. I open the garage door and pull inside, again finding that perfect position that aligns the center of the hood with the dangling ball.

The smell of something delicious hits me as I go into the house.

He's in the kitchen.

"I didn't know you cooked," I say.

"Surprisingly, I'm a pretty good chef. Before she had Samuel, Angela cooked something new every other day. This was before she went gluten free. I guess a lot of what she did rubbed off on me."

"She has some good points, then," I say.

"*Had*," he says, pulling a wine glass from the cupboard and setting it next to his already-filled glass. "Second-shelf Cabernet okay? Or are you a white wine drinker?"

I think of Stacy and her ever-flowing chardonnay.

"Hate white wine," I answer. "No health benefits."

I expect a smile back, but instead he looks concerned. "Speaking of health, Nicole, you look like you've been through the ringer."

Danny could utter the same words and they would feel hurtful. When Julian says them, they're compassionate.

"What are we having?" I ask as I prop an elbow on the island that separates the two of us.

"Lamb shanks," he says, opening the oven door and releasing even more of the wonderful aroma of a well-seasoned, slow-braised meal. The air is resplendent with garlic, onions, and thyme. "I got home early," he says, dropping some white button mushrooms in with the shanks. "You were gone so I figured why not make something that takes some time? Cooking gives me a chance to think."

"I saw Angela," I say.

He stops what he's doing and spins around. Mushrooms fall to the floor. "Did you see Samuel?"

"Yes," I answer and add before he asks, "and he looks great."

He picks up the mushrooms, sets them on the counter and takes a drink of wine. I do the same. I'm no connoisseur, but it tastes like a very expensive bottle.

"She's everything the blogs say she is," I say, knowing that he's bookmarked the Eastside Crime Watch blog on the iPad he loaned me.

"Yeah," he says. "You're sure Samuel is all right?"

I wonder how to tell him what I learned or whether I should tell him at all. I've been a bad judge of men. Serious understatement. I know that I wouldn't even consider telling him if I were working the case for the department. But I'm not. I'm working it for Kelsey. Julian deserves to know what happened to her.

"Yes, he's fine for now," I say. "But there are some things you need to know."

We stand there. I talk. He listens. It's nearly like a late-night TV monologue. Without any laughs, of course. I tell him about the scared look on Samuel's face as his mother yanked him away from me. How he'd said that a monster had taken his sister.

"He's still saying that?"

"A monster can be anything to a child. A large, aggressive man. A stranger. Anything."

"Right," he says, as we sit to eat. The food is delicious, but I don't say anything about that. Seems frivolous. "He knows what happened to his sister, don't you think?"

I'm not sure and I say so. "It could be that his memory has been supplanted by things said to him by his mother. She's in total control of your son. I don't think she lets him out of her sight. He even goes to work with her."

We talk about the custody case a little, and he knows that I'm holding back.

"What is it, Nicole?" he asks.

"Julian," I say, "you are a very good cook."

He smiles. "Nice try. What is it?"

"Have you ever heard of a man named Michael Bennett?"

He doesn't need to answer. I see the sick look of recognition wash over his face. He sets down his fork. Hard.

"What about him?"

"How do you know him?"

"He's a sales rep for one of the lines Angela sells at the boutique. I met him one time at her office. A tool. Acted like he was the king of retail and that Angela was going to dominate the market in whatever it was that he was repping at the time. She used to talk about him all the time. Michael this. Michael that."

I drop a little bomb. "I saw him at Acadia today."

"The prick lives there?"

I'm pretty sure he doesn't know. So I tell him.

"He and Angela are living there together."

"Holy fuck!" he says, rising in his chair a little. "With my son there? She's screwing some guy while my son's in the next room over. Her lawyer told my lawyer she was living alone! God, that bitch. She can't do this."

He gets up. His face is now the color of the Cabernet we're drinking. He pours more and faces out at the view of the Seattle skyline,

188

glittery in the cold night air. I step over behind him and put my hand on his shoulder.

"There's no way Michael Bennett is a replacement for you, not so far as Samuel is concerned. You know that, right?"

"Yeah," he says, "I know that. But Jesus, Nicole, how could she do this to us? We lose our daughter and she runs off to the first guy, a sales rep that wants to fuck her. And this is what we have now. A worse mess than we had before."

I lead him back to the table, and we sit. Neither of us is hungry anymore. Our plates peer up at us, but we're done eating.

"I care about you, Julian."

"I know," he says.

"I don't want to hurt you," I say. "But there is something else. Something that I think you need to know."

I can't quite tell, but his eyes look wet. I'm unsure if it is anger or an overwhelming feeling of defeat that has seeped beyond his ability to completely hide his pain.

"What?"

"Michael Bennett signed the lease at Acadia before last Christmas. The week before Kelsey disappeared."

"Okay," he says. "He rented a place there, and Angela moved in with him in the spring."

"That's not the time line, Julian. She was with him when he signed the lease. She came to look over the space. To approve it."

Julian buries his face in his hands, then looks up after a long moment. "So she was planning on leaving me before any of this happened," he says. "Are you sure?"

"The assistant manager remembers very clearly that she was there. She complained about the decorations. They weren't up to her standards."

Julian sits there and stews. "I feel like such an idiot," he finally says. "I never thought she'd cheat on me. Especially with that douche."

"Sometimes people are good at keeping secrets."

He exhales. "Right. That's Angela, for sure."

We sit in silence. I weigh what I'm about to say. I don't know if the man across from me can bear any more of his estranged wife's machinations. I don't know if I want to be the one to poke him with a stick. Another jab in the gut. He didn't deserve any of this.

"I think so, but there's more, Julian," I say slowly, finding the best way to tell him something so dark that I know will crush him even more than anything he's learned up to that point. I let my words hang in the air.

"What, Nicole?"

"This is something the police need to know."

"Please," he says.

"It's a two-bedroom unit, Julian. They leased a two-bedroom unit."

He looks at me, unsure. My eyes stay fastened to his. I know what I'm about to tell him will change everything. It will challenge him in every way imaginable. He'll know for sure that his wife was more than an adulterer, more than a liar.

"Kelsey was never going to live there," I say.

"I don't see how that follows," he says. "They could've been planning on having the kids share the second bedroom."

I shake my head. "I have the rental agreement, Julian. When Bennett rented the unit, he agreed to the terms that two adults and one child would be staying there."

A wounded look comes over his handsome face.

"She's part of this," he says.

CHAPTER THIRTY

It's late. Almost seven. But I know Christine Seiko's penchant for being the first to arrive and the last to leave. I park by the Dumpster where Danny used to sneak a smoke.

I've known Christine for years. We were more than work friends. I went to her wedding to Rick Seiko, the principal at Sammamish High School. I attended the gender reveal of their son, Jared. In a nod to Rick's Asian heritage they had fortune cookies made, inside were slips of paper printed with "It's a Boy!" I haven't reached out to her since my unceremonious dismissal from the department. I don't know where I stand with anyone anymore.

The back door to the lab swings open and she sees me right away. I can't tell if she's happy or annoyed. Christine has the kind of face that goes with her brilliant, analytical mind. She never betrays any emotion until she's one hundred percent certain of whatever it is that she is doing.

I get out of the car and walk to her carrying the Macy's bag.

"I meant to call you," she says.

I want to believe that she means it. I really do. Christine's not a liar. Yet, she hasn't called me.

"Me too," I say, though the truth is that I haven't considered calling her. Shame has a way of cutting one off from everyone one knows. Especially those who might forgive.

"You look good," she says. I see the kindness in her eyes.

I touch my hair. "No, I don't."

"No, really. How are you, Nicole?"

"One day a time," I say. "Today is a good day. And so was yesterday. As far as my problems go."

"Where are you living?" she asks.

"Staying with a friend. Up the hill from Factoria." I don't think I could explain why it is that I am staying with Julian Chase. And really, I don't want to try. "How's Rick? How's Jared?"

She smiles. "Both good. Jared's growing like a weed. Cliché I know, but true."

"I came to ask a favor."

She tugs at her purse.

"No," I say, "not that, Christine. I'm fine. I need help with this." I hold up the Macy's bag with the Burberry coat inside. "This is the coat Angela Chase was wearing the night her daughter disappeared."

She pushes the bag away. "I can't do anything with that, Nicole. You know that. Chain of custody. Contaminated by who knows what. There's no way this could make it into evidence anywhere. Especially—" She stops herself.

"Especially since I've brought it to you," I say.

Christine shakes her head. "I'm sorry, Nicole. I really am. I can't help you."

"Please, Christine," I say. "I don't want to beg, but I have no resources. You know that Kelsey's killer is out there. You know people who kill little girls can't stop at just one." Christine is my only chance. She's the only one who can analyze the coat. "I know you can't do anything officially. And I don't know if there's anything on this coat that would tell us one thing we don't already know about what happened to Kelsey. But it could. It could provide something that could point us to where we need to go." I realize I'm using the words *we* and *us, which* implies that I'm still part of the department that had been my life. It feels like a lie when really it is a hope.

"I don't know," she says. "I really don't want to get involved."

"You know that Alan Dawson didn't kill that girl. I know that you know that as much as I do. I know that you have that same sick feeling that Angela is covering up something. She's refused to even make a statement. What does that tell you, Christine?"

Christine reluctantly reaches for the Macy's bag. "It tells me exactly what you think it does."

I measure every nuance of my friend's expression.

"She's part of this, isn't she?" I ask, hoping for confirmation.

I'm not disappointed by Christine Seiko. A mother herself, she has to place child killers at the very bottom of the pile of human refuse that deserves to rot in prison.

"Yeah," she says. "I'm pretty sure she is. Even Cooper says so, though he won't get off his ass to do anything about it. It's as if everyone here wants all this to just go away. Like nothing ever happened. That's more on Danny than on you."

Her words pour over me. I am so grateful.

"Thanks, Christine," I say.

She sees the emotion in my eyes. But she doesn't linger. Christine was always about getting the job done.

"You were a good investigator," she says as she makes her way to her car. "Collateral damage. Danny damage. That's what happened to you."

"I know you can't promise anything," I say as I follow her.

Christine waves at me without turning around. Her trunk pops open and she deposits the bag on top of her son's soccer gear.

"I can't promise. And I won't," she says. "Call my office line in a few days."

The trunk shuts with a soft thud. I stand there in the parking lot and watch my favorite lab supervisor get behind the wheel and drive away.

My eyes trace the outline of the office before I look up at the window that had been my place. The floor is mostly dark. A man stands in front of one of the windows. I strain to see his face, but I can't make out who it is. The figure is large and blocky. I hope to God it isn't Evan Cooper.

The last thing I need is the lieutenant who kicked me to the curb questioning Christine. I need a break. I need to find out what really happened to Kelsey. I'm not alone. I know that Julian wants to know, as does Charlene Dawson, and now, I think, Christine Seiko.

My group of supporters is small, but growing.

CHAPTER THIRTY-ONE

The web is that dark space that allows people to hate whenever they desire. It allows a woman to trash her neighbors because she hates the color of their house. A discarded lover, the opportunity to post revenge porn. A pedophile to search for victims in chat rooms. These people pass by us every day as we move from home to work or travel somewhere on vacation. They smile at us, when if they could—if they had any little reason at all—they would tear us down. Humiliate. Ruin.

Lane Perry is a ringmaster; a conduit. And while he posts hate for clicks, he really wants nothing more than for his readers to do the dirtiest of the work he needs done.

And they do.

Julian did Lane's bidding, though he had a good reason for it. His wife had stolen his son and, Julian was sure, had been the reason his daughter had gone missing.

"I post under a bunch of names," he tells me as we sit in the living room looking at his laptop.

This disclosure surprises me. "Seriously?"

His eyes meet mine for a split second, then dart back to his computer screen. "He doesn't have as big of a readership as you probably think," he says. "Sure, there are lots of lurkers, but mostly the same people post comments."

"What name—or rather, names—do you use?"

He grins at me. "You'll have to figure it out."

"A guessing game?" I ask. "I don't like games. Not much, anyway."

Julian shrugs and stretches out on the sofa next to me. "I don't either. Let's just close our eyes. Let's forget about everything. Just for now."

Neither of us ever could do that, but we both pretend. Julian and I are good at that. Pretending that everything will be okay has gotten us to where we are. In this instance, I can accept that. Tomorrow, I know, I will start over. My Groundhog Day starts with a missing girl at a Target store and a boyfriend who fabricated a criminal case against an innocent man. I'll look for the missing piece—the one that would have told me the truth before I lost everything.

CHAPTER THIRTY-TWO

Sleep eludes me. I fight for the cool underside of the pillow as though something so simple could take me away from the thoughts that keep me from the rest that I need. So tired. I slide to the edge of Samuel's bed and let my arm dangle and the backs of my fingers graze the tips of the shag carpet. I swing my fingertips over the carpet, feeling the nappy fibers of the lime-green shag. I'm seeking distraction in a house that is a quiet stranger.

I'm a stranger wherever I go now.

I miss the lights of the casino, the blank stares of anticipation on the faces of the players lined up in front of the machines that offer the potential to change their lives. We were all escapees. Whatever had brought us to our favorite chair, our favorite game, at 2:00 a.m. had never been about winning. It was always about getting away from the lives we were living before we were swept inside the open doors of the casino. Right now it is taking every fiber of my being to stop myself from getting behind the wheel and driving to the casino.

I didn't know it at the time, but while I sat there with Danny, I'd wanted nothing more than to be a million miles away from him. He hadn't been the answer. He'd been a part of the problem. I'd settled because I was too afraid to end up alone. I thought that he was better than nothing. Yet I knew. *I knew.* Whenever we made love, I was somewhere else. Sex with him was like the machines that beckoned me with the twinkle of holiday lights. The sound of rain had been an escape. Our compatibility was based on two things—my angst over a younger sister who managed to possess all that had eluded me and our shared interest in law enforcement.

I was a moron then. And I am now. Probably more than ever.

Even though I'm dead tired, I see things clearly. Julian's grief for his dead daughter had brought me close to him. I had a need deep inside to fix everything that Danny and I had done to stall an investigation and let a killer go free. I wouldn't need my counselor, Melissa, to tell me that my attraction to Julian had more to do with my deep desire to repair the problems in my life than to be close with him. And yet, I couldn't deny the attraction.

I carry the loaner iPad to the kitchen where I make some Sleepytime tea, which I greatly doubt will help get me the rest I need. I'm sure that it's an Angela purchase, another example of her trying to show that she's the better person. Natural this. Sustainable that. I'd prefer to take a couple of Xanax and call it good.

I rub my eyes and scroll through Lane Perry's crime blog. His latest post is about the increase in burglaries in the Crossroads neighborhood of Bellevue. Another nonstory. There have always been burglaries and robberies in that part of town, an eclectic mix of newcomers from nearly every point on the globe clashing with the old guard. Lane's playing it as something new, the dark result of an ever-intensifying invasion of outsiders. I know that whenever Lane can post something that even hints at racism, he's got an excellent shot at some decent click-throughs. And for Lane, that's all that really matters.

The tea is terrible. So is the blog. I sip and scroll because that's all I can do right now. A year before, I'd have gotten into my car and driven to the casino. I'd go from tired and weary to indomitable and invincible in the instant the ball of my foot warmed the accelerator. Once inside, the vitality of the casino would be sucked into my body.

I notice Truthsayer has posted a new comment on the last Target Mom story.

Yes, Kelsey's mother is a pile of garbage. Everyone knows that. Target Mom is hiding something. No argument there. But that doesn't make her a killer. What mother would kill her own baby?

Seattle Bob added his two cents.

Ever heard of Susan Smith? Andrea Yates? Moms kill their kids all the time, you idiot.

I love the level of discourse on the Internet. Seattle Bob is wrong. Killing one's own child is exceedingly rare. In cases in which a parent is the actual perpetrator, it's far more likely that the killer would be a father, not a mother.

And in the case that I've inserted myself back into, that would be Julian.

Yet, I know it couldn't be him. Julian doesn't have the temperament. He doesn't hide behind a mask. He'd been an active participant in the investigation. He'd never wavered in his hopes—first that Kelsey would be found alive, and second that her murderer would be brought to justice. He'd defended his wife in the very beginning. Only as he uncovered her lies—one at a time—he'd pushed the investigation in her direction. He'd been hesitant. When I look in his eyes, I can see the struggle. I can see very clearly that Julian just hadn't wanted to believe that Angela had been capable of murder.

Truthsayer answered Seattle Bob's latest jab.

Angela sold that baby. I know it. Someone else killed her.

And in real time, before my eyes, he answers back.

If you know something so important as that why don't you do the right thing and report it to the police?

I sip the tea. It's not so bad, after all. It's not making me sleepy, though. Even the Xanax would have little impact right now with the adrenaline pulsing through my veins as these two strangers face off in a game of dueling comments. While I'm not even allowed to think about gambling, my money's on Seattle Bob. I imagine he's some nerd taking a break from his Xbox console because his mother says he spends too much time on it and that he needs to live in the "real world." Lane Perry's blog, for some, *is* the real world.

Truthsayer posts:

The police are corrupt. Don't you read the real papers? They've botched this case from day one. One cop's in prison, and the other's been kicked off the police force. Trust me, Angela Chase isn't a killer.

Seattle Bob immediately writes:

Go away, troll. Move along. Sick of people like you posting here like you know everything. Our police force isn't perfect, but the men and women in blue do the best they can.

Suddenly I *like* Seattle Bob. It's easy to dump on the police. Much harder, even in the safe space of your own home, in front of our own computer screen, to defend the blue.

Truthsayer takes the last word.

You can say whatever you want, but I know what I know. I know for an absolute fact that Angela didn't kill anyone.

For an absolute fact, huh? I decide to play along. I think a moment, but given the hour, I'm completely out of ideas. I start to create an account with the handle Sleepy Time. Damn! The form requires an email address. I almost stop. I know I can't use my email address. This is such a hassle. I hate the Internet. Finally, I soldier on and create a new Gmail account. Once I've done all of that, I start typing in the tiny box used for posting blog comments.

If you know who did it, why don't you just say so?

Then I sip my cold tea, and I wait. Not a long time. A minute at most.

Because I want to live. If I tell who did it, I'll die.

In my heart I know this is another game player, and I am a complete idiot for posting. It's 3:00 a.m., and since I'm only drinking tea and not a tumbler of Maker's, I have no real excuse for what I've done. There is nothing all right with playing "catch a killer" on the Internet. I linger over the iPad until it fades to sleep mode. Good idea, I think. I'll try that too.

I lay there thinking that night. Unable to turn off the noise in my brain. I give Lightning McQueen a sideways glance. I think about the little boy. His sister. Danny. My father. Mother. My sister. It's like one of the hideous PowerPoint presentations given by the police department's school safety team. They keep showing the faces of those who'd driven drunk. Texted when they shouldn't have. Darted out in front of traffic. Each image flashes first with a smiling face, unaware. Then the next shot, the mangled remains in living, bloody color. My mind does that to me. I see all of the people that way too. I hear Julian get up and walk past my bedroom. He can't sleep, either.

I drop my legs to the floor and grab one of the dress shirts Julian had boxed up to give to the Goodwill. When I snatched it, I told him that I'd be wearing it as a nightgown. He'd arched his brow a little, but just shook his head and shrugged a little.

"Looks better on you than it ever did on me," he says when I join him in the kitchen.

"I don't know. It's a pretty nice shirt."

He's wearing sweatpants and a black V-neck T-shirt.

"Can't sleep," I say.

"Me too. I was going to pour myself a whiskey. I'm going to knock myself out if it's the last thing I do."

He pours some Maker's, and we sit at the kitchen counter. Mostly silently. As I look at him, I know where this is going. I know that I should get up and go to my room, that what I'm feeling right then might go away with some needed sleep. But I don't. I sit there, looking at him and feeling every ache of the pain that he feels.

"I'm glad you're here, Nicole," he says, touching my hand.

I pull back a little. I feel the current going from his body to mine.

"I won't give up," I tell him.

"I know," he says. "I knew from the minute you came here that you were a fighter."

"That's what my father called me."

"That's why you became a cop. You wanted to fight for others. Somehow you lost something, though."

I don't say anything.

"You've found yourself now, haven't you?"

I nod and look past him. I don't want to look into his eyes right then. It has been a very long time since anyone really knew me. This man who's lost just about everything he held dear is more complete than anyone I've dated in my adult life. He should be broken. Instead, he's full of resolve.

I get up and go look at the view. My eyes are damp. The skyline looks like a blurry kaleidoscope. I don't look at Julian when he comes over to me and sets his glass on the table next to mine. His breath is on my neck. I'm finding it hard to breathe. Difficult not to dissolve into tears.

"You all right, Nicole?"

I nod, but don't speak. I suck in some air and stand there waiting for him to touch me.

His hands are on my shoulders. I slip back toward him, feeling his body against mine. He brushes his hands over my breasts and leans in to whisper in my ear.

"If you think this is weird, say so. I want you, but I don't want to hurt you."

I turn around and we kiss. It's a tender kiss. He tastes like Maker's. Danny always tasted like a pack of smokes. Julian's lips are so soft, but I feel the burn of his stubble against my face. Sandpaper. But I don't care if I look like one of those Bellevue women who have had a chemical peel in the morning. He pulls me gently from the window.

In a second, I'm standing there naked while he pulls off his shirt and steps out of his sweatpants. His body is defined, but not like Danny's. Danny's body was built for admiration and attention. The man holding me in his arms is not a poser or pretender.

"You're really beautiful," he says.

"No, I'm not," I say, thinking of my mother and her insistence that Stacy had won the genetic lottery in our family and that I was something less than her. The two of them were two peas in a pod. I was the outsider. The "pretty enough" one.

203

"Hey," he says, in a sweet, low whisper. "You don't get to say that. There are a million things that make you beautiful."

"This is where you tell me I have a great personality," I say, breathing harder and guiding him to where I want to be touched. He goes there. He traces his fingers along the points of my body in the way Danny never did.

"I'm not going to make love to your personality," he says.

We both laugh. It's not nervous laughter, but a kind of relief. He leads me into his bedroom, and I fall onto the white cloud of the eiderdown. He rolls on a condom. I wonder if he's been thinking of this for a while. So prepared. I'm so ready. A second later, he's on top and inside me. His body tightens and mine responds in that kind of chaotic rhythm that I've missed. And while we make love I keep my eyes on his. Just taking in what it feels like to be with someone who wants me for me.

I wake up and find Julian Chase next to me. He's snoring but it doesn't bother me. He sounds like a distant engine; the stopping and starting of generators in a subdivision after a power outage. Comforting. I breathe in the smell of the two of us together and part of me hopes that this is only a dream. My cheeks are still warm from the brush of his beard. I untangle myself from the sheets and sit up. In the dim light from his old-school alarm clock, I see Julian's face. I've never seen him sleep before, and just now I'm sure that our night together has been a good thing. Julian is smiling.

CHAPTER THIRTY-THREE

When I wake up, the shower is running, and I am grateful for the cover it provides as I find my way back to my room, throw on some clothes, and slip into the kitchen. The coffee's already made. Julian set a cup out for me, and I pour the thick, dark Sumatra that I know he purchased because I'd mentioned it was my favorite coffee. He *did* ask.

Last night was wonderful, but what seemed so right in the haze of the Maker's we'd consumed now seems wrought with problems. It isn't that I've fallen in love with Julian. I'm not that kind of moron. Despite some missteps during my casino days, I've never slept around. Sex for me is intimacy, not just an activity. I'm not sure how I really feel about Julian. He isn't Danny Ford. That is clear. He isn't some kind of casual mistake.

At least I don't think so.

I'm unsure if I should make breakfast or if that would make it seem that I'd moved myself from former-homeless-detective-roommate to live-in lover. I don't want Julian to feel strange about what happened. I just want to find out the truth about his daughter. That is everything to me. The question is decided for me as I survey the pitiful contents of his Sub-Zero and see there's nothing I could make him anyway.

Julian appears in the kitchen, dressed for work. His tie is a little crooked, but I resist the instinct to reach over and straighten it.

"For such a huge refrigerator," I tell him, "you've got a whole lot of nothing in there, Julian."

His smile halts the uneasiness that I'm feeling inside. "Guess I'll need to stop at the store. Or you can." He reaches for his wallet and hands me a pair of hundred-dollar bills. "I'd let you use my Visa card, but I'm afraid you might get questioned for fraud, and that would pretty much ruin your day."

"I guess so," I say with a smile back. I don't ask him what he wants for dinner. I don't want to presume that we'll even eat together. It's like the crooked tie. I'm uncertain of the boundaries between us. I don't want to mess up. I've messed up enough.

"What's on your plate today?" he asks, drinking a last gulp of coffee before gathering his things to head out.

"Session with my counselor," I answer. "A group meeting. Pretty much my new normal."

He leans over and kisses me on the forehead. It's a nice kiss. But it isn't the kind that holds any meaning other than maybe he knows I haven't brushed my teeth yet this morning. Or maybe he thinks of me as a good friend. As he disappears, I hope it was the teeth part.

The house near the top of Somerset is empty. I've showered and dressed in the last of my new clothes. Carrying a fresh cup of coffee, I find myself wandering around the place, looking at each room. I haven't been in Angela's office since the day I arrived. I've passed by the closed door a hundred times. It's seemed like a Pandora's box, beckoning me to twist the knob and go inside. This morning, while the clock ticks loudly and reverberates from the alcove down the hall, I go in.

For a second time, I take in the wall of photographs of Samuel enjoying the attention of the camera—an eye that is always trained on him. Now that I've seen Angela Chase in her new life, I know beyond all doubt that she didn't have room for a little girl. She's a lot like my mother in that regard. She couldn't stand the competition. Underneath the perfection of her packaging, Angela Chase is revolting. Twisted. She stomps around in a pricey wardrobe that barely cloaks her hot body. Her hair. Her makeup. She walks into a room and is the mirror that every man looks into and loses himself in arousal. They want her because she wills them to do so. I saw the way Michael Bennett pressed his hand on the small of her back to scoot her away from me in front of the doors of Acadia. It wasn't just to spare her from my questions, but a leering kind of touch too. Despite his harsh words for her, I caught a kind of hunger in Acadia short-timer Marco Denton's eyes too. Angela Chase is repulsive and attractive at the same time. She's the kind of woman who fucks for sport and makes sure she's declared victor when it's over.

I sit at Angela's desk among things she left behind when she told Julian that she needed space, needed time to think about their fractured marriage—a marriage that was dissolving precipitously over the loss of their little girl. Kelsey's sad eyes look at me from her lone photograph until I twist the chair away from her.

The chair is chrome and white leather. It probably cost two weeks' of my salary.

Back when I had one.

I lean back and fall into thoughts of this woman whose clothes I've worn, whose estranged husband I've slept with. Angela Chase has become a part of me. I wonder if the night with Julian was a kind of subconscious battle to win something over her. He's still her husband. She's screwing another man. I don't want it to have been just some pissing match victory.

"You don't deserve him, you bitch."

I sit up straight and pick through some papers from the top of the credenza. Purchase orders and letters, but mostly copies of complaints she's lodged against businesses. Apparently—and not surprisingly—she has some compulsion to keep paper copies of the hate mail she dispatches to suppliers, restaurants, and a beach house she'd rented in Cannon Beach, Oregon.

That last one invites an eye roll. It's that good.

> *If you do not refund me in full I will Yelp you into goddamn oblivion. The hot tub was not sanitized and the complimentary mineral water was not Sanpellegrino as pictured on VRBO. I don't know a single person who drinks Perrier from a plastic bottle. Not only is it false advertising, but you're contributing to the decline of the environment.*

I had no clue Yelp was a verb, let alone a menacing one. Angela could probably make any word an epithet. *I'll kitten you. Don't mess with me.*

A handwritten message on a canary-yellow Post-it catches my eye in the way that crows are attracted to shiny objects. It isn't the color that draws me in, but what's written in Angela's architect-ready script. *Kirk Whitmore—American Life Ins.*

Underneath the man's name is a 425 area code telephone number. Local.

Below the number is Kelsey's name.

The room constricts just then, fun-house style, but without the fun. I wrap my arms around myself to hold my emotions inside.

Money. This was about *money*?

My hand shakes a little as I pick up the landline from the desk and dial the number. A man answers on the first ring.

An exasperated breath fills my ear. "Angela," he says, "I told you that you and your husband should stay off the radar for a while, but I didn't mean to disappear from the face of the earth forever. Jesus, I thought I'd have to send smoke signals or something. I sure as hell couldn't call or email."

The words *your husband* ring in my ears. *Jesus, not Julian too.*

"You there?" he asks.

My voice stays inside of me for a beat, while the room spins. My heart drops like a lead sinker, and I stiffen in the overpriced chair; in doing so I roll backward, nearly falling off the seat. My muscles are so tight, I feel that if I fall I'd shatter into a million pieces. Vacuum-ready dust. Shattered. That's what I am.

Kirk Whitmore of American Life thinks I'm Angela Chase. He's obviously holding a policy for which the Chases are the beneficiaries. It has to be on Kelsey's life. I press my hand against my stomach. I feel vomit rising, but I will it to stay put. I will not throw up right now. Instead, I try to get Whitmore to talk some more.

"We needed to be very careful," I say, testing him a little as I steady myself. "There's a lot of money at stake here."

"No shit," Whitmore says with a laugh.

Who laughs when a little girl is dead? Who are these people?

"Five million dollars is a lot of cash," Whitmore goes on. "And I'd like to get moving on it. My wife and I want to move to Cabo. Found a sweet little villa right on the water. It's perfection. You two will need to come down sometime."

I choke on what I'm hearing. "We'd love to."

I'd love to drown you in the water off your villa.

"I see you're back in the Somerset house," Whitmore says.

He has caller ID on his phone, of course.

"Not staying here," I say. "God no. Just to get some things." I hold my breath a little. Angela would probably prattle on about something she was pissed off about, but I can't. I'm having a hard time talking, a hard time thinking.

Kelsey was killed for money.

And Julian had a part in it.

I wonder if he's the monster his son saw the night his sister vanished. If I've made love with a monster.

I leave the empty house and drive into downtown Bellevue and park in the garage of one of those monolithic office towers made of mirrored finished glass that remind me of the disco ball above the dance floor at the casino. I find Kirk Whitmore's insurance office on the sixth floor. His assistant is a young woman with impossibly long lacquered nails, yet she manages to text.

"Have an appointment?" she asks, barely looking up at me.

"I'm his sister," I say. "Is he with someone?"

She shakes her head. "Go in."

And so I do.

Kirk Whitmore sits behind a large black desk. Behind him, a view to the east catches the snowy tops of the Cascade Range. He is in his late fifties or early sixties. His hair is dyed black and his eyeglass frames and lenses are so thick they swallow his small nose. He reminds me of an owl or something.

Yet he's not an owl. Owls are smart. He's more of a snake.

I don't beat around the bush. There's no need to with this guy.

"I'm here to talk about Kelsey Chase," I say.

He looks at me like I've said something in Farsi. He pushes his glasses up. "Who are you?"

"I'm someone who's about to upend your life," I say. "You sold Angela Chase a five-million-dollar life insurance policy. You sick fuck. Who the hell does that?"

He gets to his feet. "I'm going to call security," he says. "Get out of my office. Now."

I slide into the chair across from him. "Fine. I'll tell them about our conversation. You know, the one we had about your place in Mexico."

His face goes blank, then pink, and I can almost feel the sweat collecting on his brow.

"Don't threaten me," he says.

"I don't threaten."

"What do you want?"

"I want to know why and when you sold the Chases the policy."

His hands are trembling now. His knees might be too because he takes his seat again. His little snake brain works in silence for a while, and then he says, "I knew this was a bad idea." I can barely hear him. "From the minute those two came in. Said they wanted to protect and provide for their kids."

"They were both here?"

He nods. "Yeah. They sat right where you are. Told me that the girl was precious, that they'd never get over losing her, but that if they did lose her . . ."

"They'd have the money."

"I said no. I really did. Told them I couldn't get it through, anyway—though they knew I could. They'd done their homework. Then I told them I just wouldn't be a part of it. But Angela . . . that one can be very persuasive. She promised me . . ."

"A share," I say, the words almost sticking in my throat.

A bead of sweat rolls off his forehead and splats on this desk. I watch as he wipes it away. Biding his time, thinking. Trying to come up with something that didn't make him look as hideous as buying a condo in Mexico from the proceeds of a little girl's murder.

"Are you going to arrest me for something?" he asks. "I'm going to need a lawyer."

He thinks I'm a cop. That boosts me a little.

"It's possible we can work something out," I say. "Tell me everything about the policy and who purchased them."

Whitmore runs through the policy. The face was 2.5 million, but it contained a double indemnity clause in case of accidental death. Most people think of something like a car crash as an accidental death. I know there's another cause that fits into the scenario. I'd worked a case in which a woman killed her husband with rat poison. Her children collected on their mother's million-dollar policy after the trial.

"Murder is considered accidental."

"Yeah. Yeah it is. Honestly, I didn't want to write it up. The Chases were so insistent. Told me not to worry. Told me that they'd give me a hundred-thousand-dollar bonus if the unthinkable happened."

"When did you sell it to them?"

"The week before Kelsey went missing. I told Angela not to make the claim. Not for a long time. It just looked so bad. Then I saw on the news how she was kind of a suspect. Holy shit. I just wanted to curl up and die right then.

"But damn," he said. "She has those pretty green eyes. She works them. Made me think there'd be a share of her too, maybe, though then she'd leave, and I'd wonder where in hell I got that impression." He shakes his head. "Beautiful blond hair. Men and blonds, I guess. I'm getting up there, but I'm not dead yet."

"Angela's hair isn't blond," I say.

He thinks for a minute. "Yeah, I know. She changed it after everything happened."

It was dark at the Target.

I pull up a picture of Angela and Julian on my phone. It's from Eastside Crime. They are dressed casually, beachwear. I'm thinking it's a vacation photo that someone must have leaked to the site. In any case, they are a gorgeous couple.

The kind no one would ever suspect.

"Is this who you sold the insurance to?"

Whitmore leans close to my phone. His thick lenses magnify his owl eyes. "Right. Yes. That's her for sure."

"Him?"

He takes the phone from my fingertips and pulls it closer. "That's Julian Chase?"

I nod.

Whitmore grimaces a little as he studies it. "Then, yeah. I guess. That's who I sold the policy to."

"You seem hesitant," I say, almost hopefully.

"To be honest, what can I say, I paid most of my attention to her. She's the one that was really pushing for it. He just kind of sat there."

"But he signed it?"

Whitmore nods and I stand up to leave.

"You going to arrest me?"

"Not now," I tell him in the coldest tone I can manage. I even jab a finger at him. "Don't leave the country. Forget Mexico. That's not happening. Not ever."

That night Julian leads me to his bed and we make love again. It's all kinds of wrong, but I can't stop myself. I feel as though he can read me. And I don't want him to, so I find myself in his arms with his gentle hands touching me the way Danny never did. I want to believe that he couldn't have had anything to do with the insurance, that Whitmore's poor vision has tripped him up and that it was Michael Bennett who had been there. It has to be Michael.

There were a dozen times that night that I could have confronted Julian, but I let each slip away. First a drink. Then a look. Then a kiss. Then I was gone.

We talk a little after—the kind of small talk that makes me forget for a moment or two that I'm here because I was party to the disaster that was his daughter's murder case; now there is something else that binds us together. Something that I could tell someone about that didn't make them cringe.

Julian drifts off, and I watch him sleep. I feel his breath on my face. His muscular arm drapes over me, but I wriggle out from under it without waking him. I dress. I pace. I do everything to keep my mind off of the one thing that's going to get my mind away from what I'm thinking about him. I'm playing a game with myself and I know it.

I open the garage door manually. I don't want the noisy chain of the automatic opener to reverberate into the bedroom. I can't stop myself. I couldn't even if I tried. The engine turns over and the lights stay off as I back out.

In twenty minutes I pull into the bright lights of my salvation. It's my Cheers. It's the place where even though they don't know my name, they all seem happy to see me. I put some money on my all-but-tapped-out frequent player's card at the cage. The girl wishes me luck. I know I'm going to lose. But right now losing feels better than not being sure about Julian.

CHAPTER THIRTY-FOUR

I am rattled. It can't be about money. It can't be Julian. It has to be Angela. Her and her alone. I just won't let it be.

It has been a couple of days since I turned over Angela's Burberry coat to Christine. Finally, I call her office landline. When she hears my voice, I get the sensation that she's annoyed. As though I'm the last person on earth she wants to talk to. Her tone stings. I know at once she's irritated with me for pressuring her. I've used our friendship to advance an agenda for which I have no official role.

"Look," she says, keeping her voice low, "I can't help you with this. Cooper caught wind of what I was doing and blew a gasket. Threatened to write me up for abuse of resources."

"Holy crap, Christine," I say, "I'm sorry. I never meant for you to get in trouble."

"I know that."

I hate to ask, because I've already caused trouble, but I can't help myself. "Did you find anything on the coat?"

Short pause. "No," she says. "Not that I really expected to find anything. I just wanted help find out who killed Kelsey. Maybe more importantly, I really did want to help you. Against my better judgment, that's for sure."

Again, saying I'm sorry is all that I have to offer.

"I know you were given a raw deal. I've always thought Danny was a complete ass, but I never thought he'd drag you down and get you booted out of here."

"Thanks, Christine."

"I mean it. I knew you had problems, Nicole. I could see you spiraling out of control with the money and the gambling and everything. I never thought any of that was who you were. It was the combination of Danny and you."

Tears well in my eyes and I'm grateful that this conversation is over the phone. "Thanks, Christine," I repeat. I have to ask about the stupid coat again. "Why would she get rid of the coat?"

"Maybe she just got tired of it, Nicole."

"Tired of a coat that cost nearly a thousand dollars."

"She got rid of her little girl, Nicole. She was tired of her too."

The lone email in my Gmail inbox is from Truthsayer123456789a. Apparently many others wanted the same name. I touch the screen and the email opens.

The email contains only three words and a year: *Silver Falls, Washington 1998.*

I write back right away. *What about it?*

I type the information into the search bar and run through the list that comes back. Silver Falls, Washington, is on the Snake River in Whitman County, not far from Colfax. I click on some images showing the rugged beauty of the falls that tumble forty feet into a pleasant swimming hole and rushes away down the river. A few people posted about how they enjoyed camping or day-tripping there. One woman says she and her sister used to hike there and swim when they were children and had recently brought back their own kids.

I keep scrolling.

Finally, on the third page, my eyes catch what Truthsayer wanted me to see. An oblique reference to a dead girl found there in 1998. No name.

I type in "homicide 1998 Whitman County."

The results help me put the pieces together.

On Sunday, April 9, 1998, a couple of local kids found the body of a little girl at the base of the falls. Eventually, the authorities put a name and a story to how the victim got there. She was Lisa Roberts. Her mother, Meg, had brought the four-year-old to Mom's Weekend at WSU and left her with Meg's stepson, Tommy, at his fraternity that Friday night.

I click on a picture of Tommy. A mug shot, so I know where this is going. I read on, taking in the narrative from newspaper accounts and other documents someone thought should be shared.

That night the mother partied the night away with a bunch of frat boys and the next morning when she went to collect her daughter, Lisa was nowhere to be found. Campus police were called first, then the police from Pullman, and finally the sheriff's office for Whitman County was brought in. Lisa had only been missing a few hours when her body was discovered at Silver Falls.

Truthsayer wants me to dig into this case? The age of the victim is close to Kelsey's. So what? It would take me seconds to find the names of dozens of girls and boys killed at age three or four in the state of Washington alone.

Little Lisa Roberts was found in a remote rural setting, not much different from Rattlesnake Ridge. That's two things.

Still, next to nothing tying the cases together.

I read about the trial of Tommy Roberts, the victim's stepbrother. The state put up a case that he'd gotten drunk and messed around with his sister while everyone else was away at a party in another chapter house on campus. The prosecutor painted Tommy as a loser, a young man who couldn't get a date, had very few close friends, was enraged by his outsider status, and took it out on his sister.

The defense had planned to argue that Tommy would never have hurt his sister. There was no physical evidence to tie him to the murder. No DNA—hair, blood, saliva, or semen—was found on the victim. Tommy's lawyer insisted that he'd blacked out from drinking too much, and when he woke up she was gone. He thought that his stepmother had come for her.

Tommy didn't testify at trial. In fact, the trial was halted before the case went to the jury. Tommy pled guilty rather than risk the death penalty.

I click on a photograph of Meg Roberts. She's shown standing outside of the courtroom. She wears a simple skirt and jacket, not a suit, but something very dignified. Her hairstyle is instantly recognizable as the Rachel, the cut made popular by actress Jennifer Aniston. She's very pretty and very, very sad. It's as though the life has been sucked out of her. She's a Madame Tussauds figure. Next to her is either a lawyer or her husband. He's in his midforties, dressed in business attire, and has his hand on her back.

I read on. Lisa had been smothered. The prosecution put up a theory that the little girl had cried out, and Tommy had sought to shut her up. While there was no evidence of abuse, the prosecution floated a theory that a drunken Tommy had engaged in some kind of inappropriate sexual behavior—something that Tommy denied.

After a five-day trial in which the prosecution built a rock-solid circumstantial case, Thomas Roberts, now 20, has been convicted of second-degree murder and sentenced to 20 years in prison.

I search in the inmate database and I stare at what I find.

Roberts, Tommy, paroled December 1, 2014.

Now I know why Truthsayer wanted me to see this.

Tommy Roberts was released three weeks before Kelsey's abduction.

My hands shake as I try to find out more. *Where is he? Was he registered as a sex offender? Nothing. No.* I collect myself for a beat and try another approach. It takes only two clicks and I find out that his stepmother, Meg Roberts, lives in Renton. I copy her address. It's a start. I get dressed as fast as I can and I hope that Ms. Roberts is home. I need to find out everything I can about her stepson.

I need, more than anything, to *find* him. It has to be him. It's the only thing that makes sense. And it makes a *lot* of sense. Or will, when I confront him. Get Tommy Roberts to tell me why he'd killed again. How it was that he took Kelsey. Why he chose her or how it was that Angela found him. She had a new man. She didn't want to be bothered with Kelsey. Had they met in a chat room? Had he gone hunting online for a victim and found Angela on the other side of his computer screen?

Ready.

Willing.

Able.

The scenarios of what might have transpired come at me. I'm sick to my stomach—a queasy mixture of adrenaline and hope—and I decide to try to steady myself by going through the Starbucks drive-through in Factoria and getting a latte and a breakfast sandwich.

I'm staring at the plasma display when the barista says, "Like, whenever you're ready."

It's clearly not the first time she's asked for my order. Still, I can't immediately wedge myself out of my thoughts.

I'm thinking of Kelsey.

I am ready. I can do this.

I snap out of my fugue and give my order. A few stoplights later I'm on 405 heading toward the Renton Highlands.

Chapter Thirty-Five

The wipers on my borrowed BMW slough off the rain as I pull up to the address where the Internet said Meg and Chuck Roberts live. The house is an A-frame, one of those lodge-like homes that suggest the heart and soul of what people outside of the region believe Washington to be. Woodsy. Outdoorsy. Mossy. This house is all of those things, I think as I dodge droplets from an old cedar that envelops most of the property with its drippy, feathered green cover. The door, however, is a bubblegum shade of pink, which amuses and surprises me. Maybe this kind of house had been Meg's husband's dream and the woman standing in the courthouse with her nice clothes and pretty hair was not the woodsy type after all. The paint had been her way of telling everyone that a woman lived there—and a woman with a sense of humor at that.

She answers on my first knock.

"Ms. Roberts?" I ask.

She looks me over. I watch her eyes land on my cheap, but practical, Macy's shoes. She no longer wears the Rachel. Her hair is a stunning shade of silver, and it's pulled back away from her face. Her eyes are emerald and for a second I wonder if she's wearing contacts. So very,

very green. But she isn't. She holds a pair of glasses in her slender fingers. Her manicure is French.

"Do I know you?" she asks.

"No," I say, wishing for my badge just then. A badge opens doors like nothing else and catches people off guard. They have to wonder if they've done something wrong, if something has finally caught up with them. That isn't the case with Ms. Roberts, of course. She hasn't done anything wrong. Yet, even so, I know that the past is about to catch up with her and that what I have to say will be unwelcome.

Twenty years have come and gone. Maybe she's put everything out of her mind. Maybe my being here will spark a painful memory and produce untold consequences.

"I'm here about Lisa," I say.

Her green eyes penetrate mine. She doesn't play a game. She doesn't tell me to get the hell out or that I've got no right to utter her dead daughter's name. Instead, she assesses me and answers with a matter-of-factness that surprises me.

"That was a long time ago. Who are you? Have we met?"

I shake my head. "No. We haven't." I don't mention Tommy's name. It's the natural thing do to, but something tells me that the way in is through her dead daughter. Not her murderous stepson.

"I want to find out what happened to Lisa."

"Go online," she says, switching the weight on her feet and beginning to edge the door closed.

"I did."

Probably against her better judgment, she stops the door's progress. "What's your interest in this? They say my stepson killed my little girl. He ruined my life. I don't know any more about what happened than you do if you read the papers."

"I'm with the police," I finally lie, knowing that if she calls me on it, I'll probably get arrested for impersonating an officer.

But she doesn't.

Her glasses fall from her hand to the floor, and I hurry to retrieve them, press them into her outstretched palm. I feel a slight tremble. Meg Roberts is the picture of perfection, but underneath it all she's shattered.

"Why are you here?" she says, stepping aside so I can enter. "Why now?"

"I'm working a case," I say. "I can't give you any details."

She offers me something to drink, but I decline. I sit in a big cobalt-blue chair in a living room that doesn't look anything like I thought it would. Not a rack of antlers anywhere. Instead, the furnishings are contemporary—modern, without being cold.

For the next hour she talks about the murder, the disintegration of her marriage to a big-box store retail executive, how once Lisa was gone, her life felt empty.

"I just lost the ability to do anything. I couldn't get up in the morning. I popped some pills to get me awake for work, and then some more at night so I could sleep. Chuck said it was Lisa's death that caused him to leave, but I know it was the way I handled it that forced him out."

"The death of a child is impossible to get over," I say.

"How would you know?" she asks from her perch on the edge of a sofa across from me.

"I don't know from personal experience, but I've been around many people who have been left with the kind of hurt that won't ever heal. Not completely. I know that's true."

She watches me. She's deciding. I hope she doesn't push me for more of why I'm there. I'm looking for a way into talking about Tommy.

"Lisa was the sweetest little thing ever," she says.

"She was beautiful," I say. "She looked a lot like you."

Meg smiles a thin, sad smile. Shrugs, crosses her legs, and smooths out a wrinkle in her sweater. "Photos of me at her age," she says. "We could've been twins."

I sit there. I feel for her. Yet I need to know about Tommy. He's why I'm there.

"I saw a picture of you at the trial," I say. "I could see the pain you were enduring in your body language. You were the image of anguish."

She nods. "Of course, I blame myself. I should never have left Lisa alone. I don't know what I was thinking," she says, keeping her eyes on me. She's ashamed, but not so much that she can't own up to what she did. I think about how I averted my eyes at Gamblers Anonymous when telling my story for the first time. She's had twenty years to own her behavior that night, I know, but even so, I give this still-devastated woman all the respect in the world.

"I don't have any great excuse," she says. "I'm sure you know what I did that night. The boy was twenty-one. I behaved like a slut on spring break."

Her hand clenches. She's fighting the tremor.

"You were not the cause of your daughter's death. Tommy was."

She waits a long time before speaking.

"Really? You really think so?"

"He was convicted, wasn't he?"

She shrugs. "Innocent people are every day."

Her unflinching demeanor stuns me. "You think he was innocent?"

She purses her lips. "I don't know."

"The evidence pointed to Tommy."

She stares at me, a flicker of something behind her eyes. I can't make it out. "There really was only the smallest amount of direct evidence," she says.

"So you think he didn't do it?"

She waits a long time before answering. "He might have. It's easier for me to think that he did—at least, that's what I thought at the time. Now, I really don't know. You see the thing about Tommy was that he was always such a sweet boy. When I married his father, Tommy was six. His mother had died, and he really needed me. At the trial they made it sound as though he was some messed up little prick. You know, from a broken home. Jealous of his little sister. He wasn't any of that. If he killed Lisa—and that's an enormous *if*, by the way—it was an accident. If you're here to try to pin some other crime on Tommy, you've come to the wrong place."

"I'm here for the truth," I say.

"The truth," she says. "The truth is what happened to Lisa. It isn't necessarily what the prosecutors and police—no offense meant—promote as the story of what happened the night she went missing."

She's right, of course.

A criminal case is an assemblage of facts and details in an order that presents a story to a jury. Some pieces of the puzzle are magnified and others are diminished. In some cases, pieces are hidden. Or, as in the case of Alan Dawson, tampered with.

Meg gets up and stands next to a table by the window. She looks out at the cedar tree that shuts out so much light that a table lamp is required even during the brightest part of the day. She stoops slightly. She's breaking down a little.

"I knew that boy since he was a first grader," she says. "They made me believe that he'd hurt Lisa, but I know that he loved her. My husband, Chuck; the police; the prosecutor; all of them—they tried to tell me that he was a killer. I went along with them. It just seemed better than admitting to myself that what I'd done had allowed everything to happen."

"Did you tell Tommy how you felt?"

She picks up a framed photograph from the table. It's a boy and a little girl.

"Tommy and Lisa," she says, handing it to me.

Meg's eyes are Christmas now. At once green and red. She's still very beautiful, but in that way that a tortured piece of driftwood can be. There are tiny cracks in her controlled demeanor. She's hurting, and she's letting me see it for the first time.

"They look very happy together," I say.

"They adored each other," she tells me. "That's why all of this has been so painful. Tommy was a sweet kid. He was never a problem. Shy. Kind. Chuck wanted him to do 4-H, but when Tommy found out that raising a pig meant killing one, he quit. Not only that, he didn't eat bacon for a year. Maybe two."

I let her talk it out a bit longer. Meg Roberts is working through it all over again, like I'm sure she's done a thousand and one times over the years. She tells me about how she visited Tommy in prison a few times, but stopped going because she couldn't face him anymore.

"He said he didn't think he could have done it, but he wasn't sure. He just couldn't remember."

"That must have been very hard," I say.

She nods. "Every time I went, I came back here to get an earful about how stupid I was to fall for Tommy's act. Chuck didn't ever go. Chuck didn't love his boy. The pig thing was only one part of their discordant relationship."

There was a war in this A-frame. I can see that now.

"Did you correspond with him?"

"Not really," she says, hesitating. "I know I should have. I heard from him around last Christmas."

"You did?"

"Yes, but I didn't talk to him. I got a letter. He said he'd been released from prison and wanted me to know he didn't blame me. Chuck saw the letter and pitched a fit. I kicked him out on New Year's Day."

"You're separated?"

"The divorce will be final in another couple of months."

I shake my head. There doesn't seem to be anything to say. And the fact is, my mind is elsewhere. I need to find Tommy.

"Where is the letter? Do you still have it?"

"No. Chuck ripped it up and threw it in the fire," she says, looking across the room at the river rock fireplace.

"Did you see the return address?"

She shakes her head. "I did, but I really didn't pay attention to it."

"I need to talk to Tommy."

She looks at me. "Why? What do you need to talk to him about?"

I don't want to answer, so I start for the door. "I need to go," I say.

"Fine," she says. "Police business, right?"

"Right." I turn back at the door. "Did he say anything in the letter about what he was doing, where he was living? Anything at all?"

"He said he earned a veterinary assistant certificate from WSU and was working for a clinic. Tommy always liked animals. He'd never hurt a fly. That's why I've always had a hard time believing what they were telling me. Just didn't seem like Tommy at all. But what do I know? I'm far from perfect too."

CHAPTER THIRTY-SIX

I'd recognize that face anywhere. Lane Perry sits in the booth at the Italian place in downtown Bellevue that Danny and I used to frequent. Perry has picked that location for us to meet because he knows more about me than my closest friends. If I had any left, after what I've done. He's wearing a white cashmere sweater over a checked shirt. His hair is blond and when he calls over to me, I see why none of the photographs on his site ever show him with an open smile. Lane has the tiniest teeth I've ever seen on an adult. Baby teeth. His blue-gray eyes catch my unfortunate stare.

But he ignores it.

"Glass of wine?" he asks.

"No," I say. "I won't be staying long."

His stubby fingers grasp his own glass of merlot and I think how those teeth will turn the color of his gums and disappear. He's twitchy. He's nervous. For someone who plays master of ceremonies for crime news junkies and holier-than-thou haters, he's uncomfortable. Very. That's the only thing I like about Lane Perry.

"This isn't an interview," I say right away, looking down at his phone and his forefinger, ready to press "Record."

"Everything's an interview," he says.

"Put that away, or I'm leaving."

"Party pooper," he says.

Parasite, I think.

Perry sets aside his phone. I'm not stupid enough to think that he doesn't have another recording device at the ready. But I need to talk to him. I need to know who is posting on his site as Truthsayer.

"Sorry about losing your house and everything," he says, his tiny teeth forming a sympathetic smile.

"Yeah. Thanks for posting that."

He arches a brow. "People have a right to know."

I didn't come here to talk to him about that. My blood boils, but I do everything I can to keep a lid on the simmer. "Well, Lane, the truth is that they don't. They don't need to know about everything."

He purses his lips. "I'm doing a public service. I put more information out there than the *Seattle Times.* My readers have an absolute right to know everything that I publish, because—well, they are the people. You work for them."

"Worked for them."

"Sorry about that too. I hear you went and saw Danny Ford."

I don't even want to know how he knows that.

I don't answer.

"How's he doing?" Perry asks.

"Lane," I say, "I'm not here about that. I'm here about Truthsayer."

He grins his tiny-teeth grin. Her lips are the color of the zinnias Mom planted the summer before she left us for Hollywood. I loathe that shade of pinkish red. Perry's skin is clear except for his forehead. He has a touch of cover-up there, soaking up the oil. Trying to make himself look as good as he can. Seeing him in person instead of the Photoshopped visages on his site tells me so much more about him. Lane Perry has always been the outsider. He was the kid with bad skin. Crappy teeth. Though I can't see his belly behind the booth, I suspect he has a middle as soft as the center of a buttermilk biscuit. It's hard to tell if his site is making him any real money, but there is no doubt that it has made him a name.

"Truthsayer is good," he says, sipping his wine and looking supremely satisfied. "Every now and then a commenter comes along and pokes the hornet's nest in all the right ways."

I lean in. "Who is it? Do you know?"

He shakes his head. "I have scruples," he says. "I don't infringe on the rights of my readers to post anonymously. Some are pretty stupid about leaving obvious bread crumbs, but others—like Truthsayer—are good at staying hidden."

"So you've tried to track him?"

"If it is a him, yes. If it is a her, yes. I don't know who the fuck it is, but I do know that whoever is posting under that name knows their way around computers."

"I need to talk to him," I say.

"Good luck," he answers. "I've tried to figure out who it is. If I can't—no offense, I doubt you could."

"What about the IP address?" I ask.

He smiles. It's a patronizing smile. "Honey, that IP is routed through Singapore. Maybe it's someone in law enforcement," he says. "I have a lot of fans at Bellevue PD. Lots of clicks coming through on any story about you, Danny, and the whole Alan Dawson debacle."

He's baiting a hook. I don't bite.

This has been pointless.

"I really need to leave now," I say, putting my palms on the table to lift myself to my feet.

"I have a photo of you at the Angel of the Winds," he says, pressing his hand on mine.

"I'm leaving," I say, yanking my hand from his and rising.

His face turns red. I've embarrassed him. Good.

"I was thinking of doing a post about your problem," he says. "Sort of a look back at the rise and fall of a young—" bitch that he is, he amends it "—*youngish* detective. A dealer I know at the casino told me a thing or two about you that, well, I'm sure would make interesting reading. Lots of clicks, you know."

The doughy little shit thinks he can blackmail me. As though I could be brought any lower. If I'd taken that glass of wine, his white cashmere would be red. Like his little teeth.

"Look, Detective Foster," he says, "I won't publish anything. I promise. I need you to give me an exclusive when and if you figure out this case. I know you're working it. I want that bitch Angela Chase behind bars."

I start away, then turn back. I'm no longer on simmer. My pressure cooker has blown its lid. "Look here, you little prick," I say loud enough for everyone to hear. "Give me the IP address and any information you can on Truthsayer, and I'll spare you the favor of dentures."

He cowers back in the booth.

"You don't have to yell at me," he says. "You aren't very nice."

CHAPTER THIRTY-SEVEN

It feels very strange standing in the lobby of the Bellevue Police Department. The last time that I waited here in this public space was when I first came here for my interview with Evan Cooper. I was nervous and excited. I knew it was the beginning of everything that I thought I'd ever wanted. And now I'm waiting for Evan again. This time I'm no longer looking for a way in, but for a way out of what I've done with my life. I need his help, and I'm not sure he'll give it to me. The receptionist is new, but she knows who I am. At least I think she does. When I presented myself to her, she called upstairs and nodded, then told me to sit.

"I'll stand, thank you," I said, then walked from her station to the window.

Outside, cars go by and it dawns on me that everyone behind the wheel knows exactly where they are going. And then there's me.

I see my former lieutenant's reflection coming toward me, and I turn around slowly and put a warm smile on my face.

"What are you doing here?" he says.

His tone and demeanor make my smile fall like a soufflé.

"Hi yourself," I say.

He's wearing a suit that suggests something important is going on. He's lost a few pounds, and ordinarily, I would have said something to encourage him. He's always dieting. The original yo-yo. Each time is the time that will work. The truth is, the weight never looked bad on him. It made him all the more formidable.

"I told you that I'd call you when things settled," he says. I'm pretty sure that he's scolding me, but I don't push back. "I'm pulling for you to get reinstated," he says, probably seeing the hurt in my yes, "but showing up here and calling attention to yourself isn't going to do you any favors, Nicole."

I exhale before speaking. I'm not here about my job. *My job?* Really? That's what he thinks? At the moment, my job seems lost forever no matter how much Evan Cooper says otherwise.

"I need your help," I say.

His eyes wash over me, then land at my feet. "I can't give you any more," he says.

A knife slices my aorta. If I'm not here to beg for my job back, it has to be to beg for money. My face burns. I only borrowed money from Evan one time, and I paid him back. Granted, I paid him with the loan I got from Stacy, but still. I paid him. It wasn't that he was pressuring me for his money. It was that I saw him every single day, and the knowledge that I was in trouble was always there in his eyes. I played a game with myself that Stacy didn't need the money and that she was family. That was a good one. The truth was I paid the lieutenant back over my sister because even if I did pay her back, Stacy would still remind me about it for the rest of my life.

"I don't want any money," I tell him, doing my best to mask the sting of his words. "And thanks for that."

He looks a little wounded, and that makes me feel better.

"But I do need your help," I say, then hurry on without allowing him to respond. "I don't want you to ask *why*. I just need you to do something for me. Just this once. Never again. I'll never bother you again, but I really need this one thing."

He changes the subject.

"You really shacked up with Julian Chase?" he asks. "That's what I heard."

Word travels fast. I hold my surprise, though I do wonder who told him and if he's bringing it up to derail me.

"I am staying with him temporarily, yes. In case you haven't noticed, the list of people that have offered to help me is pretty short. Julian's a good person. I'm trying to help him through this, and at the same time, it's helping me. I wouldn't expect anyone to understand."

"Well, I don't," he says. "Seriously messed up, if you ask me."

"Good thing that I didn't," I say. "Now, since we've established that I'm fucked up, and that I don't want any money, are you going to help me or not?"

His eyes sweep over me. I think I see a little pity there. It doesn't offend me. It only tells me that I have a shot here.

"I don't know," he says.

It's a stare down. I blink first.

"You didn't listen to me before you let Internal Affairs run me out of here," I finally say. "You owe me one favor."

He stays riveted to me. He's reading me while I read him at the same time. The lieutenant knows I'm right. He has to know it. A little more backbone on his part, and I might have made it through the internal investigation and into counseling before I'd lost everything.

"All right then," he says. "What is it?"

I feel the tension that's making my body brittle dissolve as I hand him a slip of paper with Tommy's name.

His eyes stay on mine. "What's this?"

"I need to find him."

He glances down at the paper, then shakes his head. "Google him like everyone else."

"You said you'd help."

Evan Cooper thinks a moment. I know that at one time he really liked me. I know that standing there in front of that nosy receptionist he's finding his way back to the time when he was my mentor. He knows that I wouldn't ask for something if I didn't need it. For a second, I feel as though he wants me to succeed.

"Fine," he says. "How?"

"Roberts is in the system. He was paroled last year. I need to know where he's staying while he's on parole. That's it. Just his address."

He shakes his head but leaves with the paper. I look over at the receptionist, who's watching me like I might steal something from the lobby. Five minutes later, the lieutenant emerges from the offices where I'd once worked. He's expressionless.

"Here, Nicole," he says, pressing the paper into my palm.

"Thanks."

We stand face-to-face. I expect a word of encouragement from him. I think of telling him that he looks good, and I wonder what he's doing. Diet? Exercise? Or both?

But he doesn't. And I don't.

Instead he makes one thing very clear.

"Don't ask me or anyone in the department for help again."

His tone is sharp. Cold. He's done with me. I see it now. The receptionist probably sees it too. She watches from her desk by the door.

"I looked up that guy's jacket," he says. "You're barking up the wrong tree if you think he's involved in Kelsey's disappearance."

"You don't know that."

"I do," he tells me. "He was pulled over for speeding and given a warning on December 23. In Pullman. He was five hours from here when Kelsey was snatched from Target. I imagine you're chasing down every kid killer from the last twenty years. We did that, Nicole. After you and Danny botched the case, we went back. We still like Dawson."

The tension is back. "He didn't do it," I say.

234

He doesn't budge. "The evidence says he did."

"You mean the shoe?" I ask. "The girl's shoe, Evan? That's all you have, and you know it. You also have to know that the shoe was planted. You have to know that."

He starts to turn away. He doesn't want to revisit that conversation. I don't want to either. We've been over it before. It doesn't matter what he says, anyway. I know in my heart that Alan Dawson didn't do a thing to Kelsey Chase.

Evan Cooper's eyes no longer hold the warmth of recognition.

"You better go now, Nicole," he says.

This feels very final. Different from the day I walked out with my personal belongings in an evidence box.

"Fine," I say. "I will."

I turn and start walking for the doors. I don't look back. Instead I glance at the slip of paper that the lieutenant passed into my palm, and I'm gripping like it's the winning numbers to the lotto.

Below Tommy's name in Evan's familiar scrawl is an address.

145 Wheatland Drive, No. 2, Colfax, Washington.

When I get to the car I'm going to be like one of those drivers I watched from the window. They know where they are going. Finally, I do too. I'm going to head up to Somerset, pack a few things in my homeless shelter special luggage, leave a note for Julian that I'll be gone overnight, take the iPad, and start the drive to the other side of the Cascade Mountains. I'm going to find out what it is that Truthsayer thinks I ought to know about Tommy Roberts and the murder of a girl that I'm all but certain he'd never known. I fish Kelsey's photo from my purse and put it on the dash. I've got this. I can do this. This is not a mistake.

Chapter Thirty-Eight

The snow along the mountain pass is no longer Christmas-card pretty. It's an aggregate of sand, gravel, and ice. It rises from the roadside like a wall, punctured every mile or so by a logging road, a way into someone's winter hideaway or, at the summit, the ski runs that draw thousands from the Seattle area. Once my mother had attended the film festival in Telluride, she'd frequently made the point that Washington had more beauty than any other state, but the people had no vision. Her complaint was that there was no Benetton at the top of our mountain. The thought of my mother's ridiculousness makes me smile.

Once over the Snoqualmie Pass, I plot out the rest of my day as I drive. The late afternoon light illuminates new grass poking up here and there along I-90. The season of renewal. I'm feeling it too. I eat one of Angela's health food bars and drink coffee from a drive-through in North Bend. It's tepid, but I don't mind. I need a lot of coffee. I know it will be dark when I get to Colfax.

The drive is long and monotonous—especially the long stretch on the highway after passing over the Columbia River at Vantage. It's been years since I've been on that highway. One of my closest friends from high school went to WSU, and I went over a few times to see her. Well, to drink and hang out with boys, mostly. I have no idea what happened to Monica. Our friendship faded over the years, like many in my life. I Facebook-stalked her when my world was imploding, but her account was set up so that very little of her life was revealed. I didn't send her a friend request.

I stop only once to get gas and use the restroom. I'm on a mission to find Tommy.

The Palouse Motor Inn is tucked off Main Street in downtown Colfax near an old department store that's been converted into offices and an antique mall. My room is clean and efficient. It's the kind of setup—a kitchenette with a minifridge and a microwave—that suits the traveler on a budget or those who would rather eat in than sit alone in a restaurant or bar. It's too late to knock on Tommy's door. I'm not police. I'm here for help. While there is some urgency to find out what he might know—if anything—there's no call to be rude.

I turn on the heat and log on to the complimentary Wi-Fi. The signal strength is weak, but it is *complimentary* and I sit patiently while Eastside Crime loads. I scroll down, but there's nothing new posted in the comments section by Truthsayer or anyone else for that matter. I look in my Gmail account. Nothing there, either.

I call Julian, and it goes to voice mail after a few rings.

"It's me," I say. "I'm guessing you're still in transit. Hope you had a good, productive trip. I'll be back in Bellevue late tomorrow. Bye now."

That night I dream of Kelsey again. The little girl who haunts me is alive this time. She's playing in the park with her brother. My mind is taking me to the photo of the brother and sister—the one Angela left in the house—and it's playing like a helicopter parent's video. The kids are laughing. Kelsey is in a swing and Samuel is pushing her. It's gentle and sweet. She begs to go higher and he obliges, but only a little. She's a pendulum in my mind, swinging back and forth, laughing and smiling. She's here. She's gone. Here. Gone.

Really. Gone.

The apartment complex on Wheatland Drive is tidy, but older. Whoever manages the place is doing a very good job at maintaining it. I imagine that many of the people who live here are doing the very same thing. Maintaining it. I have a feeling that Tommy Roberts is.

It's early. Before six. I sit in my car by the steps to his upper floor unit in a space stenciled with "Welcome Guests." I'm neither. I watch as his door swings open. It's Tommy, all right. Although he's spent nearly half his life in prison, he looks very much as he did when the newspaper photographer from the *Statesman Examiner* captured him in court. He's slender, about five foot eight, I think. His hair is still thick and blondish. He wears a neatly trimmed beard that is more hipster than lumberjack. He's wearing jeans and a hoody and carrying a Tupperware lunch box and a thermos of what I expect is coffee.

I get out of my car as he makes his way down the steps.

"Tommy?"

He scans me like a bar code. "Do I know you?"

"No. No, you don't. Tommy, I need to talk to you."

"What about?"

"About you," I say.

He sweeps past me to his car. It's a ten-year-old, dark-green Subaru Forester. In the back is a dog crate.

"Are you from the paper?" he asks, opening the car door and placing his lunch box and thermos on the passenger seat. He's no longer looking at me. "I told your editors that I just want to be left alone. I don't want to be an example of the system doing something right, because, well, it hasn't done anything right."

"No," I say, moving closer. "I'm not from the paper."

I stand motionless, thinking. I know he wants more of an explanation. I don't have a good one, so I throw out a little truth and little lie.

"I'm a police officer," I say. "I'm working another case."

Tommy twists his body toward me, and shoots me a hard glare. "Why don't you people just leave me alone?" he says. "What happened to Lisa was a long, long time ago. Leave her be. Leave *me* be. I've served my time."

"I need your help."

"That's really funny," he says. "You people tortured me for twenty years. You fucked with my brain and twisted my memories until I wasn't sure what I did or what I didn't do. I have news for you: I didn't kill my sister. I know it."

He slides behind the wheel, and I grab the door before he can shut it. My fingers nearly get caught, but he stops closing it just in time.

Tommy couldn't hurt a fly.

"I know," I say. "I know you didn't kill her. Someone else did. And, Tommy, whoever it was may have done it again."

His eyes flash. "I can't help you," he says.

"You can. You need to help me. Tommy, I saw your mother. She believes in you."

"You saw Meg? She's my stepmother. Or was."

"Yes, I saw her. She never once referred to you as a stepson. She still thinks of you as her son. She knows you could not have hurt Lisa. Someone else did."

"I've got to get to work."

"I need to talk to you."

"I'm busy."

I refuse to budge. "You're not that busy, Tommy. You're not too busy to make this right, and you know it."

"I don't know."

"You do. What time to do you get off work?"

"Four thirty today."

"I'll meet you here then."

He turns the key, and the engine ignites. "All right. I guess so. I'm telling you, I don't remember much, if anything, from that night."

"Understood. See you tonight."

239

◆ ◆ ◆

While I wait for the time to pass, I drive to the key locations of the Lisa Roberts murder case. First to the university campus and the chapter house for Sigma Chi. It was the last place Lisa was seen alive. The night she went missing, Tommy was purportedly watching her inside the fraternity house that uses the Norman Shield as its symbol. Online the chapter boasts Brad Pitt, Luke Bryan, and David Letterman as famous alums. Brothers forever. I find it odd that none of the so-called brothers came to Tommy's defense at the trial.

Not a single one.

The house is nothing special as far as Greek Row goes. No faux Tudor or Monticello-like architecture here. Instead, the last place Lisa was seen is a white, craftsman bungalow with a metal roof. There's no point in going inside or even getting out of my car. It has been twenty years since everything happened. The house has been abused by hundreds of young men since then. It has probably been remodeled a time or two. It is no longer a crime scene, just another place where something terrible once occurred.

I drive around campus and am struck by how young the students are. Without children of my own, I've found the time difficult to mark. It just was. One year would bleed into the next. When Emma was born, I could see my sister Stacy maturing because she had to do so. She had a little person to take care of, and that seemed to make her life more significant than mine. It seemed to reverse the roles we'd always played. Though of course in her eyes, she was always more important than I was. I always rolled my eyes at the way she saw herself. So like our mother in that way. Yet in a very real way, though I never said so, I know she has passed me. I have more in common with the young people milling around the campus than I have with Stacy. While I'm no longer young, I have nothing but the future ahead of me. Nothing that I feel I can hold onto.

The sun feels good on my face. The air is warm. I close my eyes and hear the voices of the students all around me. They are songbirds. They chirp away at the serious and banal. There is no off/on switch. I wish I could trade places with them right now. I wish I could start over and select a path that will lead me to wherever I was meant to go.

I slept well last night, but I drift off.

My phone buzzes me awake, and I know it's either Julian or Stacy— the only people who have this number.

It's Julian.

"Hey Nicole," he says. "You okay? Where are you?"

Julian's not a phony. I know when someone is asking me how I'm doing only as a precursor to getting whatever it was that they want from me.

"I'm fine," I tell him, fully alert. "I'm over in Pullman."

"What's going on there?"

"Probably nothing. But like I told you, I have to go where the evidence leads me."

"What's the evidence?"

"An old case. Just has some similarities to Kelsey's."

"Really?"

His voice is full of interest, but I can't tell him much. "Total long shot, but sometimes long shots pay off big-time."

"What's the case?"

"A girl. Murdered in 1998."

"That's a long time ago."

"Right," I say. "It is."

I don't tell him how it was that I found the case. It would sound so foolish. *I got a tip from a mysterious commenter on the Eastside Crime Watch.* No. I also don't tell him that part of my going away is to get away from him. Not because I don't have some feelings for him . . . not that. It's just that we crossed a line and I don't know how to get back to where we were.

"Do you want me to come to Pullman?" he asks.

"No," I say. "No. I'll be back tomorrow."

I edit myself from saying what first came to mind: "I'll be back *home* tomorrow." The use of the word *home* would only serve to underscore the weird feelings I have about Julian and me. Evan Cooper's question—*You really shacked up with Julian Chase?*—has played on my brain like the bass drum I hear some college kid banging from the open window of a music room.

"Are you sure?"

"Yes."

"Are you safe, Nicole?"

It feels as though he truly cares about me. But I've never been a good judge of that. Danny will always be Exhibit A proving that.

"I'm fine," I say. "Will call you if I find out anything."

I hang up, and while a couple of sorority girls roll up their pant legs and the bottoms of their tank tops to expose their flat stomachs to the sun for the first time of the year, I dial Stacy. I'm a big believer in keeping my enemies close. Even—and maybe especially—those who supposedly love me.

"I thought I'd check in," I say when she answers.

"Where the hell are you? I thought you were coming over to help me with those stupid Swedish meatballs that Cy likes so much."

"I'm out of town until tomorrow."

"Where?" she asks, prying in that snide way she's always been so expert at. "You and Mr. Chase in Cabo or something?"

"No," I say stiffly. "I'm just working the case."

My sister always puts me on the defensive. And I let her. Someday I will stop that record on repeat. Not today.

"Okay," she says. "Fine. You do that. I guess I'll have to make these fucking meatballs without you. If Cy doesn't like them then this whole thing is on you." She's in Drama Queen mode.

"I'll take full responsibility," I tell her.

But honestly, who can't make a simple meatball?

We hang up, and I return to my car and calculate whether I have time to get to Silver Falls and back before four thirty. I drive pretty fast. I can do it.

Though not yet full-on spring, it feels like it. Skunk cabbage erupts from a ditch that runs the length of the turnoff from the highway. Ferns unfurl their spiral fronds. Trilliums flop toward the sunlight. It is quiet at Silver Falls. No one is in the parking lot. I walk over to the rocky edge where someone dumped Lisa's body. I haven't seen any crime-scene photographs, so I'm not sure exactly where she was found. The paper said she was near a swimming hole at the base of the falls. There is only one, some forty feet below me.

It had to be right *there*.

I don't have enough detail to try to imagine what played out the night Lisa was dumped here. I can't go to the police to see the case file. I can't ask the prosecutor's office. I can only ask the one person who was convicted what he thinks occurred. There's a big problem with that, of course.

He doesn't remember anything.

Chapter Thirty-Nine

It's the smallest one-bedroom apartment I've ever seen. I've been in studios that were more expansive. And yet, as I sit there nearly knee-to-knee with Tommy Roberts, I see that it's all the space he needs. A small couch, a single chair, a barstool. Through the slit of the open bedroom door I see a mattress on the floor, made up with an extra blanket folded neatly at the foot. I wonder if the small space gives him comfort; if his years in prison made him used to a tight fit. A swaddled baby sleeps through the night. A man who's spent almost all of his adult life in a nine-by-twelve-foot cell might feel lost if given too much room.

Or it could be that he continues to punish himself for whatever it was he did or didn't do.

He offers me a diet cola, and I accept. He drinks one too.

"I know you're here about Kelsey Chase," he says.

My adrenaline pumps. I haven't mentioned her name to him. "How do you know that?"

"Google, Detective. I mean, former detective."

I nod. I'm glad he knows who I really am. I've never been a facile liar. "Right," I say. "Google."

As he sips his cola, I notice a jagged scar along his forearm. Self-inflicted, or an injury? He sees where I'm looking.

"I got cut up pretty bad," he says. "That's pretty much what happens when you're branded a baby killer."

His eyes are unflinching. He is measuring my reaction. He wants to know if this uninvited stranger in his room is here to hurt him or help him.

"I'm sorry," I say.

"There's nothing for you to be sorry for," he says. "Sorry is for losers, anyway. At least that's what I need to believe. I've spent my entire life being sorry for something I didn't do—at least I don't think that I could have. Or would have. I've seen guys on the inside who could, who've done that and worse. They percolate hate from every pore in their bodies. It's like the air they exhale is thick and dark. They're bad to the marrow. I've never been like that. It's not in me."

I wait to see if he'll say more. I don't want to push too hard because I can tell that despite his insistence that he has started over and is trying to put the past behind him, he hasn't managed it yet.

The past is who he is.

"Look," he tells me, "I don't really know why you're here. I said I'd talk to you only because you mentioned my mom's name. You caught me off guard, Detective."

"Call me Nicole," I say. He knows I'm no longer with Bellevue Police. "I wouldn't be here if I thought that I could get the answers I'm looking for anywhere else."

"Right," he says. "Though I know you can't. No one in law enforcement around here would help you. Not just because you've been kicked off the force in Bellevue. Because no one wants to revisit my case. One of those network news magazines tried to get something going on my story, but they were completely stonewalled."

This interests me. "What was their angle?"

"That I might have been wrongfully convicted. That's what the producer told me. I had some hope on that, you know. But I've learned in the past twenty years that hope doesn't get you very far."

Over the next two hours, we talk about his family. About his father, his stepmother. He opens a bag of tortilla chips and a jar of salsa. I offer to take him to dinner, but I'm glad that he says he's not very hungry. I just want to talk. I don't want any distractions. His story fascinates me. Finally, he tells me about the night that his mom left Lisa with him at the Sigma Chi chapter house. They watched TV and she played with her stuffed cat. One of the fraternity brothers from the house next-door offered him a beer, and he drank it. He might have had another, but he wasn't sure about that.

"I hadn't eaten all day," he tells me. "I just let the day get away from me. The party scene wasn't my thing. I only joined Sigma Chi because my dad had been a member, and he insisted. So when everyone was going out, I didn't mind staying with Lisa. I missed her."

Tommy stops, and I can see that his eyes have puddled. He turns away and wipes them, so swiftly he probably thinks I didn't notice. He *hopes* I didn't. As an inmate he'd had every bit of dignity stripped away from him, piece by piece, until there had been nothing left but the shell of what he'd been. His tears tell me that he's fighting his way back to being who he was before Lisa vanished and was found at Silver Falls.

"Your mom says the same thing," I say, giving him a chance to breathe. "She says that you and Lisa were very close."

He takes a chip from the bowl, doing what smokers do: using that chip instead of a cigarette to buy some time to think. "Yeah," he says, taking a bite, "we were."

I push gently. "What happened, Tommy? What do you remember?"

He stays silent for what seems like a very long time.

CHAPTER FORTY

His story comes at me in a kind of stream—no, a river—of consciousness that I suspect flows directly from the night Lisa went missing. His words are heart-wrenching. Tommy consumes the rest of the chips and another diet cola as he touches on one thing after another.

"Mom showed up. She had to shake me. It was morning. I could barely open my eyes. I felt so sick. The front of my shirt was wet. I'd puked on myself. I was disoriented. She had her hands on my shoulders and she was screaming at me. Over and over. She was yelling, 'Where's Lisa? I can't find Lisa!'"

Tommy says he could barely remember the night before. They'd played some games. He had a beer or two. And then they went to sleep.

"I really do remember that," he says, looking to see if I'm with him or not.

I am.

"It isn't something that I made up later to make myself feel better. Lisa was sleeping on the sofa that folds out into a bed. She was safe when I passed out. I know that for sure because I saw her sleeping. *I saw her.* She didn't wander off. She was taken."

I ask Tommy about the time line. "Your mom testified in court that she didn't come for Lisa until eight the next morning. That she'd spent the night at the sorority three doors down."

He nods.

"I know that. I know she said that."

"But it wasn't the truth."

"Look," he says, "I don't blame her. I don't think she would have said that if my dad hadn't used her for a punching bag. She'd have admitted where she'd really been, but she was more afraid of him than she wanted to help me. Didn't she tell you about my dad?"

I shake my head. "No, she didn't."

"Figures," he says. "That's what we talked about after I went to prison. Whenever she came to visit, she told me how sorry she was and how she was going to make things right for me. I always told her that I was glad she was alive and that it didn't matter anyway. They found my vomit on Lisa's body. They had me with that. I pled guilty because it was the easy way . . . the way to spare Mom and me."

He excuses himself and slips into the bathroom, just a few steps away. He shuts the bathroom door, but I can hear the stream of his urine as it meets the water in the toilet bowl. I hear him flush and wash his hands. When he opens the door, I see what I'd expect to see—a perfectly folded hand towel next to the sink. Everything in his life is in order. Everything but what happened to him and his sister nearly two decades ago.

"I want you to know that I still love my mom, and I forgive her," he says. "She did something with some guy that made her feel young again or something. Maybe to feel loved or just wanted. I don't know. She did something that night with a boy she'd never see again, and it cost her everything that mattered to her. She lost a whole lot more than I ever did. I lost my freedom. And while that seems huge—"

"It is," I say.

"Maybe so. But I have that back now. My mom doesn't have Lisa, and she never will."

There's nothing I can say to that. He's right, of course.

"Do you have any idea what really happened to her?"

"They said she was abducted and murdered. No rape. That's all I know. That was the only saving grace in the whole nightmare. I was never labeled a child molester."

"Do you have any theories?" I ask, before stating the obvious. "You've had almost twenty years to ponder it."

He doesn't bristle. Tommy just shrugs a little. "Ponder is hardly the word," he says. "For the first ten years, it was all that I could think about. Day and night. Alone or with the other inmates. I expect that some of the other guys thought I was slow because sometimes they'd talk to me and have to repeat themselves to snap me out of my stupor."

"And what did you come up with?" I ask.

He closes his eyes a beat. *Remembering*, I think.

"Mom's Weekend was crawling with people," he says. "I have no idea who would have done such a thing. The police didn't look for anyone once they matched my vomit to her body."

"Right," I say. "That was a key piece of evidence tying you to your sister. It was on her body, right?"

He shakes his head.

"No. Not on her body. It was on the sheet that the killer wrapped her in before he dumped her into the water below the falls."

The tiny apartment shrinks to matchbox proportions. I now know why Truthsayer has sent me here.

"Wrapped in a sheet?"

"Yeah," he says, catching the shock on my face. "Like that little girl in Bellevue. I thought that's why you're here. That you think there's a copycat or something."

I stand up, bumping my knee against the little table that holds the bowls of chips and salsa. They fall to the floor. I frantically—too frantically, I imagine—start to help clean up. Tommy touches my hand.

"I got this," he says, trying to calm me. "It's okay."

I want to speak, but I can't. I can't say anything. The bedsheet didn't mean copycat. It meant signature. Whoever killed Kelsey might have done it nearly two decades before. The victims' ages were close. The mothers were distracted. Angela was caught up in a relationship with Michael Bennett, and Meg was in the throes of a one-night stand with a college frat boy. While it was clear that both mothers differed in their devotion to their children, both were preoccupied enough to let something terrible happen. Neither child had been sexually assaulted. Both had been dumped in an area that was remote, but easy to get to. Out in nature.

"If the same person killed both girls," I finally say out loud, "why wait all these years to attack a second time?"

"Maybe he was in prison and got out," he says.

He's testing me.

"I know you didn't do this, Tommy."

Tommy makes a face and rolls his shoulder a little. Says, very quietly, "Thanks."

"Why did you plead guilty?" I finally ask. "It was the middle of the trial and you just stopped it all. You pled guilty when you knew you didn't do it."

He leans back and closes his eyes as if he's exhausted. I know he's not tired, but is just going back to that time.

"There was a part of me that thought that I might have done something, even though I knew that I never could. They told me over and over that if I pled guilty I'd be free one day. The reason was my mom. I didn't want her to have to say what she'd been doing that night in open court. That was part of it. But not all. They told me that if I didn't, I'd never see the light of day again. I'd probably get shanked and murdered in prison. Baby killer. I wanted to be free. I wanted a chance to live. Just like Lisa, I'm sure. Whoever killed her, ignored her cries. They just did what they wanted to do."

"You saw no other way out?"

"They told me I'd serve eight to twenty years. I believed them." He shakes his head darkly. "I'll tell you one thing, that's the last time I ever did that. I don't believe anyone. My mom. My dad. No one."

"I want to make things right," I say.

He smiles. It's a faint one, but I think it's genuine. "I know."

Before I leave, Tommy tells me the one thing he says he's never told anyone. His reason for holding it back is clear.

"I don't think it means anything," he says. "And after what happened to me, I don't ever want to turn someone's life upside down by accusing them of anything."

My spine stiffens and I lean forward to the edge of the chair. "What is it, Tommy?"

"It's probably nothing," he says again. "But I heard from a girl soon after I went to prison. She'd been at WSU when I was there. She sent a letter and said that she'd come to visit, but never did. I was excited at the time, but later, after I learned that being in the papers draws weirdos like flies to ripe banana, I discounted it."

I know he's right about that. Whenever we started any case that grabbed some media coverage, we'd get deluged by crazies absolutely sure they knew who the perpetrator was. We were obligated to chase down every lead, of course, but honestly, using the police to gain attention or settle a score is a low blow.

"What did she tell you?"

"She said that she was a TA in the Fine Arts department and one of her duties was to empty out the trash from the darkrooms."

"Sounds like a custodial job."

Tommy nods. "Pretty much. She said she found something in the trash, and she needed to talk to me about it."

"What did she find?"

"She didn't say. Like I said, she told me that she was going to see me in person, but she never showed."

"Do you remember her name?"

"Yeah. I had to put her on my visit list. It was Lauren Bradshaw. She's still in town. Works at the university in the same department. I thought of paying her a visit, but I don't know . . . I got this great job at the animal hospital here, and . . . well, I just thought it was water under the bridge."

More like a deluge, I think.

"I'll find her. I'll let you know what she has to say."

Tommy shrugs again. "It's all right. I stopped hoping a long time ago. I just want to live, remember?"

◆ ◆ ◆

That night the ice maker outside my motel room hums all night long. I listen as the ice drops into the chute, then into the receptacle. It's going nonstop because I'm surrounded by a group of hunters who I'm absolutely sure are going to be unable to do much hunting the next day. It's after 2:00 a.m., and they are still at it. I pound on the wall, but it only gets them going. If I still had my badge, I'd go over and knock on the door, flash it around, and I'm fairly certain they'd calm down for the night. Instead, I lay here looking at the ceiling.

I scroll through text messages sent by Stacy and Julian while I was with Tommy. Neither had much to say other than they hoped I was okay. I *am* okay. I'm feeling better than I have in a long time. I feel like I'm getting somewhere.

I just don't know where that *where* is.

And finally, when I can no longer bear another minute of the noise next-door, the raucous hunters settle down. It's an opening of silence. I take it. I drift off to sleep. No dreams. Just slumber.

CHAPTER FORTY-ONE

Lauren Bradshaw is in her early forties. She's dyed her short hair coal-black and her neck is encircled with a dozen silver chains, some with small charms dangling from them. Stars and moons, I think, from where I watch her through the glass of her office door in the Fine Arts Building, off Stadium Way on the WSU campus. She motions to me, like she's expecting me. I wait until she finishes talking with a young man with equally black hair and a Cry Freedom tattoo just below his clavicle.

She can't possibly think I'm a student, though when I think about it, I might resemble one. I barely slept last night. My hair is in one of its uncooperative moods. No matter how much cajoling and product I used, it's left me with the bedhead look that is only sexy when you're twenty. And there's the sweatshirt that I purchased at the Bookie to stretch my meager wardrobe. It was half off.

Go Cougs!

"Sorry about that," she says, as Cry Freedom brushes past me. "Jeremy was having a bit of a meltdown over his collage project."

"Lauren Bradshaw?" I ask.

She lets out a sigh. "You're not from the *Daily Evergreen*, are you?"

I shake my head no. "Sorry. I'm here to help out a friend of mine. I think you can help me."

She suddenly seems wary. I watch her step back from the doorway and I follow her into her office. The space is overstuffed but organized. I have never seen so many art books in my life. It's as though every corner of the world, every era, is represented on the shelves that run the length of two walls. I could get lost in her collection. On another day. But not right now.

She doesn't offer me the chair across from her desk, but I plant myself in it anyway. I'm here. I'm going to get what I need. This is my Nagasaki moment.

"I need to talk to you about Tommy Roberts."

Her dark, flinty eyes spark and she looks at the door, still open. "I don't know who that is."

She's lying.

"Yes, Lauren, you do."

She sits there mute. I only had to mention his name, and he was right on the top of her mind. She didn't need to sit and think about this name, this blast from the past. He was right there. I suspect that she's never been able to suppress whatever it was she'd wanted to tell him, but couldn't.

"I can't get involved," she says. "I'm not tenured."

"What does tenure have to do with it?"

"You obviously are not in academia. Just who are you?"

I tell her my name and I say that I'm an investigator working on Tommy's case. It's true. I am.

"Tommy's served his time," she says.

"You're right," I say, "he has. You know all about him, don't you?"

"I've never even met him."

"But you wrote him in prison, didn't you, Lauren?"

Her eyes stay on mine as she gets up to shut her office door. She touches one of the lowest-hanging chains that hang from her neck with her fingertips. Her fingers are lightly stained with nicotine. Her nails are short, gnawed on. She's a nail-biter. She fidgets the slender, silver rope chain. She's literally grasping at whatever it is that I know she will tell me.

"Yes, I did. I wrote him one time."

"Why did you do that, Lauren?"

"I wanted to help him. And I did."

"How did you help him?"

"I saw an article in the paper about prisoners working with guide dogs, and I knew that he loved animals. I had the dean of the Veterinary Medicine program send him information on the correspondence course that we offer to young people who can't afford or are unable to attend the university for whatever reason."

"He was convicted of the murder of a little girl," I say. "Why in the world would you want to reach out and help a man like that?"

She wants to smoke and pulls a lighter from her desk drawer. I watch as she fiddles with its uncooperative flint.

"I knew he didn't kill that girl," she says.

"Tell me what you know."

I don't beg. I don't have to. I can tell that this woman is tired of carrying the burden of what she knows. Two decades is a long, long time to face yourself in the mirror when you know you've made a terrible mistake.

She starts talking. Her words are staccato at first, but they become more fluid. Tears come. She shuts the blinds and finally lights a cigarette. An air purifier whirrs, sucking in the smoke.

It was early in the fall after the Lisa Roberts murder and the trial that sent Lisa's brother, Tommy, to prison. The temperatures were in the high 90s, nearly triple-digit. The sororities and fraternities had already rushed new members and the drip, drip, drip of new freshmen on campus had begun. The deluge was to come the following week. Lauren was a TA for the Photography chair at the time with the unenviable task of cleaning out the wet darkrooms.

"You'd think it would be cool in a dark place, but the AC wasn't working, and I practically passed out it was so stifling," she says. "But you have to do what you have to do. There aren't many jobs in the fine arts—as my mother and father rightly pointed out—and my only hope was to teach."

It seems that she got to where she wanted to go.

I prod her, and she goes on.

Her job was to go through all the cabinetry, rinse out the trays, wipe down the counters, and make sure that all the chemicals were fresh. There were a number of wet darkrooms, and this took a little time. Just prior to the start of school, the department had held a workshop for some high school students in Spokane.

"Those were the worst," she says, lighting another cigarette. "Seriously. I must have hauled out a hundred Bud Light cans from one of those rooms. I can't imagine that they did any actual photography because they had to be three sheets to the wind. Maybe four or five sheets, if that's even a thing."

"You found something, didn't you?"

She blows smoke into the air-purifying machine that I seriously doubt has fooled anyone.

"Yeah, I did."

◆ ◆ ◆

It was getting late and Lauren was in the midst of a cyclone of debris and seriously re-thinking her life as she scrubbed, organized, and emptied the trash from one room to the next. Until that moment, she'd loved the smell of the developer and other chemicals. They'd always smelled like an integral part of the creative process. By 10:00 p.m., she'd had too much of a good thing, and she considered getting some Vicks for her nose, autopsy-style. She'd stopped glancing at the contact sheets and left-behind film, because from what she'd seen they were left behind for good reason. There wasn't a single new Diane Arbus or David LaChapelle among them. Not even a Leibovitz.

It was hot and she was hungry. Lauren was about to call it a night when she slumped to a seat on the just-swept, gray-speckled linoleum. She was like a lizard, taking in the cool of the floor. She rested her eyes and tried to remember what it was about the arts that had attracted her so much. Her parents were engineers. Both of them. In their own way, they were very creative people—but creative within the confines of the needs of an industry. Her father was in computer science. Her mother in aerospace. Lauren wanted a life that colored outside of the lines, but still drew people in. Sitting there, resting, all angst and self-absorbed contemplation, Lauren saw the negatives.

It was a strip of seven images, stuck to the bottom of one of two darkroom trash cans that had been stacked together. If she hadn't been sitting on the floor, she wouldn't have seen it. Neither would she have taken the time to hold it up to the light.

I have no idea where this is going. The office is a haze of smoke now. The little portable air purifier is unable to keep up with Lauren Bradshaw and one of the habits she uses to soothe herself. Another is on display too. Between puffs she chews a fingernail—and she doesn't do so surreptitiously. She's beyond that now. She just wants to get this over with and get me out of her office.

Before the smoke alarm sounds.

"I wish I'd just thrown it away without looking at it," she says. "Looking at it ruined my life. Have you ever seen something that you just knew you shouldn't have?"

I nod. I don't tell her, but I once walked in on my mother and a man that she'd hired to fix, ironically so, our plumbing.

"What was on the negatives?"

Though the blinds are drawn, she looks toward the window. "I wasn't sure at first."

"But later," I say, "you became sure?"

"Yes. I made a print."

Lauren Bradshaw starts to unravel now. She's taking herself back to the darkroom. No amount of nicotine, no nails to be chewed can placate her now. She stubs out her cigarette and waves the last curl of smoke in the direction of the air purifier.

I give her a moment.

"There were some pictures. Black and white. One showed a boy passed out. The others showed a little girl. She was posed. Naked. She looked so scared. I could just feel the fear coming from her."

My heart beats so hard in my chest that I wonder if Lauren can feel it. *Hear* it. She's looking at me, measuring my response. I cannot hide what I'm feeling.

"Did you know who the boy and the little girl were?"

She plays with her chains. She's still back in the darkroom.

"Not at first," she says, sucking in more smoke. "At first I thought it was just some school assignment from the workshop that summer. I was pretty sure that it couldn't be real, because if it was, well, I knew that it was child pornography. Can you imagine? I knew that even looking at something like that was against the law."

Lauren says that she went to the department chair with the negatives.

"I showed him, and at first he looked at me the way he always did, like I was bothering him or something. He suggested that they were probably part of a conceptual project and that I needed to be more open-minded."

Open-minded? I don't even say the words. She knows that's what I'm latching on to.

"Right," she says after a pause. "Like I was some bumpkin from Tacoma who didn't know true art. I felt like I was about two feet tall."

"Humiliated."

She puffs. "I pushed back a little, and his tone shifted. He told me that small-minded people like me might not belong in an art program."

"But you knew what you had, Lauren. Didn't you?"

She nods. "Yeah. I was pretty sure, but my mom and dad were engineers. No nonsense. Everything can be proved. I risked a lot in the eyes of my family when I told them I wanted to be a photographer." Her phone rings, but she ignores it.

I remember how Stacy rolled her eyes when I told her I wanted to be a cop. She'd acted as though serving the legal system put me in a kind of limbo, as far as social standing was concerned. She begged me to be a lawyer, because, as she put it, "at least you'll be rich and useful."

"At some point you determined that the images on the film were of Tommy and Lisa Roberts, didn't you?" I ask Lauren.

"Right," she says. "Of course, I followed the story through the trial. It was big news here. I didn't think in terms of the photographs being Tommy and Lisa until I made the print. I made the one of Tommy sleeping or passed out. Whatever he was. I never made a print of any with Lisa in them, because, well I wasn't going to do that. I knew that if I did, I'd be guilty of a crime. Believe me, I was sick to my stomach at the thought of being so close to something so evil."

"How do you mean?"

"I knew that whoever had taken those pictures had probably killed the little girl. From the sequence of the images, I had some serious doubts that Tommy was involved in the crime at all. He was in the photographs."

"Passed out."

She nods. "Right. And since he was in the photograph—"

"You knew someone else had to be there to take the picture."

Lauren looks right at me. Maybe for the very first time. Direct. Fully aware.

"Not just someone," she says. "I saw a reflection on the TV screen just beyond where Tommy was laying. I'm pretty sure there were two others there. I tried burning in the image, but I never got enough detail to see who it was."

"There were two of them?"

"I'm not completely sure, and I wouldn't swear to it, but yes, two."

It's too much to hope for, but I ask her if she still has the print she made.

"I shredded everything," she said. "I kept it a long time. I don't know why. Probably to torture myself. I knew that it could help Tommy, but I also knew that it could ruin my career. You have to believe me. I wanted to do the right thing. I just couldn't."

It always comes down to that. A career.

There's no point in beating her up, but I find myself unable to hold back.

"Two things, Lauren," I say, keeping my tone as professional as possible. "One, Tommy wasn't Lisa's killer, and you probably could have proven it."

"He was already in prison," she says. "I couldn't have gotten him out. Not on the photo."

"You don't know that, not really."

She says nothing. Instead she sinks lower in her chair and finds a cigarette in her desk drawer. Her hand is trembling, but she manages to light up.

"The second thing," I say, going on, piling it on, but still maintaining, "is that it's very possible that there have been other victims."

I'm thinking of Kelsey.

Lauren exhales and fiddles with her necklace. "I'm sure you've never made a single mistake in your life."

"So many," I say, "that I couldn't even count."

"You're judging me now," she says.

"Honestly, Lauren, I'm not. I'm past judging you."

I'm really not. And I'm no longer calm.

"I need you to get your shit together and think a whole lot harder about what you saw on that fucking photograph and who might have taken it."

She doesn't blink at what I've hurled at her because she knows she deserves every bit of it. I would never say that I was perfect. I've lied. I've taken money from friends and family. I've gambled away my future. The one thing I know to be true above all else is that I've never done anything to put another person at risk. I've taken bullets for my sister, covering for my mother with her, pretending that my father's asked about her when he's completely forgotten she existed.

After what feels like a long time, Lauren comes up with something. "There was one other thing in the photo that I wasn't sure about. About the figures I saw reflected in that TV screen. I tried, as I told you, to burn in more detail."

"You saw something?"

"Maybe. Yes. A star and a crescent moon. Part of a star and a crescent appeared in the reflection on the TV. I think someone was wearing a T-shirt that had that on it."

"What did you make of it?"

She sits in silence. I don't want to hear what she's going to say because I've already clicked to it. I know someone who has a crescent moon and star on his right forearm.

"Kappa Sigma," she says. "I was pretty sure that one of the guys in one of the shots was a Kappa Sigma."

Chapter Forty-Two

The basement of the Holland Library is morgue quiet. I wind my way through the stacks to the section where a young research librarian is leading me.

"Everything you ever wanted to know about those people is down here in the Panhellenic section. It chronicles everything that's wrong with this university," he says, before stopping himself and adding, "You're not one of them, are you?"

He acknowledges my sweatshirt.

"No, just another alum," I say. "Just doing some research for a friend. Wants to send her daughter here. I'm trying to convince her otherwise. Nothing against the school. Great school. Just the whole sorority thing. I don't think it's healthy at all."

He offers me a knowing look. We're on the same side.

"Smart move," he says as he leaves.

"Yeah, real smart," I answer back as he vanishes around the corner.

If I were smart, I would have figured this out sooner.

I look up at the rows of booklets, binders, and file folders full of that weird mix of social conscience and naughty nurses that epitomizes the Greek system at universities across the country. I find the section and pull a binder marked 1998 and take it to a table next to a photocopy machine that appears to be a relic from another era.

COPIES. 5C.

On a piece of notebook paper someone wrote "out of order."

I already know who I'll find there. I take my time. My stomach is churning, and I feel as though I might pass out. It's the same feeling I had as a child when I had to go spend time with my mother and her latest boyfriend. I couldn't stop myself from going. It was like being pulled and pushed at the same time. I was both drawn to her and repulsed by what she did. I flip through the pages. Young people. Beautiful young people. Girls with tans and long hair that never knew a tangle. Boys with biceps that popped underneath tight Tees. Page after page. Washing cars for charity, followed by a wet T-shirt contest. A camping trip in Northern Idaho and then a sit-down dinner at a rest home for the elderly. The worlds collided over and over.

And there he is.

He is standing with a bunch of other sorority brothers. His smile is broad and disarming. I've seen those eyes when we've made love. I'd had those arms wrap around me at my lowest point, a time when I'd have begged him to carry me away from the life I was living. To save me.

I was such a fool. An idiot. I was exactly what my mother and sister had told me I was, over and over. "For such a smart girl, you sure have no idea how to pick a winner."

I sit here for the longest time, thinking back to everything that's happened over the past year. I play back each moment of the case that brought me to see Tommy Roberts. The evidence tampering. The false confession. The death of Alan Dawson.

My eyes stay glued to the photograph of the handsome young man with the white-toothed smile.

"Danny," I say softly to myself, "you are such a goddamn son of a bitch. I hate you. You'll never walk free. Not ever."

I tear the page from the book and go.

Chapter Forty-Three

The animal hospital has two doors, one marked "Cats," the other "Dogs." Thinking with an ache of Shelby, I go in the "Dog" door to find Tommy.

A young woman with lemon-yellow hair and pretty blue eyes sits behind the wood grain countertop. She smiles at me through her braces. "Hi," she says. "How may I help you?"

"I'm looking for Tommy. I'm a friend."

"Thomas," she says, correcting me.

I give a quick, polite nod. Unlike Danny, Tommy has elected to use the grown-up version of his name. "Sorry. Right. We go way back," I say.

She calls for him on the intercom, and Tommy emerges smelling like wet dog and looking at me with anxious eyes that I'm all but certain mirror my own.

"Oh hi," he says. "Didn't know you were coming by."

"Thomas," I say, glancing at the girl, "can we talk somewhere?"

"Yeah," he says. "Sure. In here."

I follow him around the counter and into a small examination room. *Cat*, I think. At least, on the farthest wall is a chart showing what seems like hundreds of different cat breeds and the part of the world in which each was developed. On the floor a drift of white fur nudges the bottom of a waste can.

Definitely "Cat."

He shuts the door. "You found something," he says.

I retrieve the page from the Panhellenic book from inside my purse. My eyes stay planted on his. I'll treat the page like a police photo array. While there are names under each image on the page, I won't say anything about who is who. I want Tommy to look at these faces and remember—if he can—what's been locked, dormant, in his memory. Not something I'd plant there by excitedly pointing out the face that's staring up at me.

Mocking me.

"I know it's been a long time," I say, laying the page on the metal-topped exam table, giving him an out and me the chance to be wrong, "but do you know anyone on this page?"

Tommy runs his fingertip across the paper, examining each image. He's deliberate. Thoughtful. A Felix the Cat clock on the wall twitches its pendulum tail over and over. Tick. Tick. Tick. When Tommy gets to Danny's photo he hesitates slightly, but then moves on.

"Do you know any of them?" I ask, unable to resist the need to prod.

He shakes his head. "Not really," he says. "I don't *know* them. I guess I remember seeing some of them around. They were the frat next-door."

"Which ones?" I ask. "Which do you remember?"

I need this. I need something.

"This guy came to the trial," he says hovering a second, before landing and tapping on Danny Ford's picture. "I think he was a photographer for the *Daily Evergreen*. I never talked to him. My lawyer didn't want me to talk to anyone."

Felix stops ticking. At least, I can't hear him anymore.

"Think, Tommy," I say. "This is very, very important."

Tommy sees something in me right then. He knows that this is very personal.

His brow knits as he weighs the look on my face, then taps Danny's picture.

"Do you know him?"

I feel caught. Like Shelby felt when I caught her eating all the jelly beans that I'd bought for a basket I was making for Emma. Trapped. I don't want to lie.

"I think so," I say, finally.

"How is he involved in what happened to Lisa?"

This man's life has been ruined. And God knows I have no loyalty to Danny. Yet I find it hard to say the words. I don't answer right away because I don't know exactly how much I should tell him.

"Nicole," he says. "Who is this guy?"

He needs to know.

"He's a cop," I finally say. "He's a Bellevue cop."

Tommy's eyes widen and he takes a half step backward.

"All those years," he says, reaching behind to grab onto something. He's not breaking down. But he's close. His palms curl over the edge of the counter behind him. He's steadying himself. He doesn't want to fall. His face is suddenly pale.

"All those years," I repeat. "What do you mean, Tommy?"

"One of the guards at the institution thought I'd been given a raw deal by the parole board. Once I became eligible it was supposed to be a slam dunk that I'd get out. I'd pled guilty. I didn't need to allocute. No one thought that I was lying when I said I didn't remember. Even the prosecution agreed. But every time I went before the board for release, they came back and said no. Jerry—the guard—looked into it. He said that he could lose his job if he told me, but that someone from law enforcement had it in for me. Kept the pressure on to keep me inside."

"Did he say who it was?" I ask, a cat hair now lodged in my throat.

"No. He just said it was a cop from Bellevue. Some guy who'd gone to school at WSU when it happened and said the case is what made him decide to be a cop. Said that I was a danger to society and that I'd offend again."

My ears are ringing. Danny. *Danny.*

"I'm sorry," I tell Tommy.

The color and calmness has returned to his face. "Not your fault," he says.

Deep down, I feel as though it is. I should have investigated Danny instead of Angela. Danny was the perpetrator here. He'd set up Tommy and Alan to take the fall for something he'd done.

If he were free, I'd kill him.

My cell finally finds service outside of Fruitland and I pull the BMW over to make some calls. First to Julian, who picks up right away.

"Holy crap," he says, "I've been trying to reach you all day."

"My phone died. Just recharged now." I debate whether to say anything. Julian seems hyper. Almost manic. "What's up?"

His words come from him in a rush. A joyous rush. "Angela's lawyer called," he says. "I'm going to get a visit. An unsupervised visit."

Now is not the time to bring up Danny. Julian has gone through a nightmare, and I cannot ruin his happiness.

"Jesus, Julian, that's huge," I say. "I'm really happy for you."

"I haven't had my boy for months. I'm on my way to get some things at the store."

"That's so great."

"I know. You were always hopeful," he says. "You kept me from giving up. You know that, don't you?"

"I guess so," I say. I want to say more. Much, much more. Instead I tell him that I'll be back in Bellevue that night. I want to say *home*, but that word feels so funny and so presumptuous.

"Did you find out anything out there?" he asks.

"Not really," I say.

We talk a bit longer, but the truth is I really only listen. He's so happy. He deserves to be. I can hear his love for Samuel in every syllable. I cannot imagine the hurt that Angela caused him. And while I'm now sure that Danny's involved in the crime, I know she played a part in it too. *She had to have.* Static clicks on the phone, and we say good-bye.

Next I dial Evan's number. It goes to voice mail after three rings.

"It's Nicole," I say. "I've been over at WSU. I think I know who's behind Kelsey's murder. It was never Alan Dawson. Evan," I say, "I'm pretty sure Danny killed her. I'm on my way to Julian's. I'll be there in a few hours. Going over the pass. If you don't reach me, you know where I'll be. But I'm telling you: *It was Danny.*"

I hang up and realize that tears are streaming down my face. I wipe my eyes and make one more call. I call Stacy. She's the only family I have, and despite our differences, she's my go-to whenever I feel like the world is against me. My counselor, Melissa, says I'm a masochist to reach out to my sister, but I can't help it. She's my lifeline.

"Stacy," I say, then can't figure out what to say, where to start.

"Nicole? What's the matter? Have you been drinking?"

"No," I answer. "Not drinking. Stacy, I need to talk to someone."

"What's the matter?" she asks. I hear her swallow. Wine, probably. If either of us has a drinking problem, it would be her. "Have you been gambling?"

My lifeline is made of spaghetti. I know it, but I keep coming back.

"No, Stacy," I say, louder than I need to. "Let me talk."

I hear Cy complaining in the background.

"Now is not a good time," she says to me. "Cy's packing for an overnight trip to San Francisco."

"Stacy, I was at WSU. I found out who killed Kelsey. It was *Danny*. Danny killed her."

She doesn't say anything.

"Stacy?" I look down at my phone to make sure the signal strength hasn't evaporated.

"I'm here," she says. "I'm just in shock, that's all. Are you sure?"

I wrap my free arm around myself. The phone stays pressed against my ear. "As sure as I can be. I've already called it in to Cooper."

"What did he say?"

"Voice mail, as usual."

"I'm stunned," she says.

"Me too."

"Be careful," she tells me.

I sit here in my borrowed car as a caravan of truckers pass by. In a weird way I feel elated and scared at the same time. It's the same kind of feeling that came whenever I perched on the edge of my chair in front of *Masterpieces and Double Diamonds* and listened for the sound of rain. The sound of a win. I was always sure that it was going to come. I was sure that everything I'd ever wanted would arrive in flashing lights and the excitement that comes with a big win. And even when it did, there was always the feeling, deep down, that it would only be fleeting.

Or that it might never come again.

Just as I cross over the mountain pass, my phone chimes, service restored.

My Gmail account has finally synched up with my phone.

With one hand on the wheel and one eye on the road, I click open the email from my only friend, Truthsayer.

The killer didn't work alone.

CHAPTER FORTY-FOUR

I pull up the steep incline to the top of Somerset. The Seattle skyline sparkles like a socialite's evening gown. I pause after I open the garage door and park under that dangling ball. Though I've barely eaten all day, I feel so sick. I wander out of the garage, where I vomit behind some Tropicana roses. The smell of my vomit and the heady evening scent of the roses make me cough up the remainder of whatever it was that I ate. Chips from a North Bend minimart, I think. My sides hurt. I splash water from the utility sink on my face and rinse my mouth.

Danny did this.

He had done it before.

He had help.

Of course he did.

I catch my reflection on a gleaming garden spade that's never seen a gentle push into the soil. Angela's never grown a thing in her life. I look like hell. My eyes tell the story. They flash fear and disappointment. I thought that finding out the truth would save me.

Save Julian.

Fix my broken life.

That's never going to happen.

The calls to thwart Tommy's release came from the Bellevue Police Department. It could have been Danny, of course. But if Danny were working with someone, his buddy Evan would have been a good fit. I remember how quickly Evan got Danny out of the department, into protective custody, then somehow orchestrated the plea deal on the obstruction charge. It was so, so fast. At the time I thought it was because the department couldn't survive another scandal. They'd had a huge one the year before, when one of the sergeants pilfered a fund set up by the community for two officers killed on duty.

And Julian. I could never find my way to believe that he could have been behind his daughter's disappearance. The man that I knew was broken because of his loss. That I'd even thought he might have been connected to what happened to Kelsey makes me sick.

"Nicole?"

It's Julian. I turn around and face him. He looks at me with eyes that for a beat seem to hold little recognition. It's as though whatever it is that's on my face has made me a stranger.

"Julian," I say, moving toward him. "I think I know what happened to Kelsey."

He looks at me with those sad, beautiful eyes. He's dressed in sweat-pants and a T-shirt, but for some reason, he looks put together. Sweat collects on his temples and ear buds dangle from his neck. He's been exercising.

He puts his arms around me and holds me. Tight. It's as if he's try-ing to keep my heart from beating out of my chest. I push away a little. I don't feel clean, and I don't feel right about his embrace just then. I'm unnerved. Unsure.

"Let's go inside," I say. "I need a shower. Let's talk after I get out."

He presses his hand gently on my shoulders, and we go inside. I brush past the kitchen and a bunch of kid-friendly groceries on the counter. I drop my bag in Samuel's room, but I doubt I should sleep there. Samuel is coming home, and his father doesn't need to explain who I am and why I'm here. I'm not sure where I'll sleep tonight. Maybe on the couch. Maybe over at Stacy's.

Chapter Forty-Five

The water in the shower runs over me. It's nearly scalding. A million hot ice picks coming at me through the oversized showerhead. Instead of moving aside for relief I stand there and take it. I feel as though I've earned the burning sensation somehow. That it will erase all of the shame and confusion I have over Danny. And Julian. And Evan. I am a poor judge of men. My sister is right. I open my mouth and let the hot spray rinse my teeth. I long for my toothbrush and a bottle of Scope.

I now believe that it was Evan and Danny who were involved in Kelsey's death. I just don't know *why*. Evan had lobbied hard for a deal with the prosecutor's office when Danny got caught compromising the evidence on the Dawson case. He kept telling me that while Danny had made a mistake, that didn't mean he was without redemption. That after he served his time, he'd hoped that I'd be among the friends that would help him get his life going. That was before I was shoved out into the cold, of course.

When I step out onto the white bath mat, my skin is red and sore. I pull a towel from the rack by the door and face the fogged-up mirror. I want to see this stranger in front of me. I want to see the woman who could be so easily fooled. I rub my palm on the mirror to wipe away the condensation and the medicine cabinet door pops open.

Inside, Angela's diaphragm greets me.

I feel a jolt, cattle prod. A Taser. It wasn't there when I'd foraged for aspirin one night I couldn't sleep.

I do something next that's so embarrassing I'll never tell another soul. I open the case and touch the latex surface.

It's wet.

Angela's been there. Julian and Angela had sex. I am the biggest fool in the world.

I wonder if she's still in the house, or just snuck out while I was showering. If Julian hadn't been exercising at all. I steady myself on the fucking amazing marble counter. Jesus. Help me. I imagine the two of them tangled in those expensive sheets spun of Egyptian cotton and trimmed in Irish lace. While I know that she could never love him— she's incapable of loving anyone—maybe in his messed-up mind, he still thinks that he has a chance to fix his family. Stupid. Stupid.

Julian has opened a bottle of red wine and poured two glasses. He sits on the sofa that faces the view, but his eyes stay on me. My hair is damp and I've put on a pair of jeans and a T-shirt. I no longer give a shit about how I look.

"Before you tell me what you've found," he says, indicating the wine, "I need to tell you something myself."

He seems uneasy. But I offer no words of comfort. I won't say one word to make him feel better. I might not even say what I know about Danny. *Why should I?* Julian's betrayed me. Even as that thought comes to me, I want to reel it back in. We weren't a couple. *God.* He acted like he cared about me. He rescued me from a shelter. We've made love twice, though in this very moment I amend that to mere fucking. None of what we've gone through is the basis for a relationship. Angela might have been with Michael Bennett, but that didn't mean Julian was really with me.

Or ever could be.

"Angela came over today," he tells me. "I thought it was about Samuel coming to visit tomorrow, but it wasn't. It wasn't that at all."

The wine in our glasses looks like blood. I drink mine in a big gulp and listen. Still seething inside and not doing a very good job of hiding it. I wonder if he sees that or if he's telling me this because he wants to—not because he's been caught. I wonder if he sees my heart beat through the T-shirt.

"She told me about the insurance money," he says, keeping his eyes on mine. He seems nervous, but determined to spit out whatever it is. And though I care about Samuel and Kelsey with all my heart, I want to fast-forward whatever he's saying to the part that indicates how Angela's diaphragm became wet.

He goes on as my mind races.

"She said that she'd forged my name because I was traveling so much and she was worried about finances. She took out policies on all of us. Honestly, I didn't know a thing about it."

This is not the news flash that I was expecting.

"It was a lot of money," I say.

He looks surprised. "You knew about it?"

I nod. "Yes. I saw the insurance salesman."

"You did," he says. A funny flicker comes across his face. I don't want it to be so, but he suddenly looks very, very uncomfortable.

I hold the beat. I am so angry. So burdened. So betrayed.

"Yes, he thinks he sold the policy to you and Angela, but he's half-way blind and I don't know who was there for sure. I mean, I know it couldn't have been you."

"Michael Bennett," he says. "That bastard is up to his thick neck in Angela's shit."

"That's what I was thinking. He said one thing that really got me thinking. He said that Angela was a blond."

That flicker again. Or am I imagining it? "She changes her hair color a lot," he says. "I used to leave for the office and not know if I'd come home to a redhead or a brunette."

He's trying to make me laugh, but it doesn't work.

"She hasn't changed her hair color in a year," I say.

Julian shrugs. "Angela's got other things on her mind. Being behind our daughter's murder will do that to a person."

I don't say it, but inside I'm thinking, *Get on with the part that you just fucked her.*

He sips and thinks. He's building himself up to tell me about it. I think of a daytime TV talk show my dad watched before the synapses in his brain went on strike and refused to fire. The host was holding a manila envelope and about to pull out paperwork proclaiming that some nitwit player was about to be proclaimed the father of a baby.

Julian heaves a sigh. "Despite everything she's done—and I really don't know any more than I've told you—I still have feelings for Angela. It's messed up. I know that. I no longer want to be with her."

The words are bombs, hurled at me by a man I wanted to love. Or maybe did love.

He drinks more of his wine, then sets his glass on the coffee table.

I could cry. In so many ways he's everything I've ever wanted. My sister and I used to sleep outside on the porch and talk about our lives and the men we hoped to find. It was only talk, of course. Stacy wanted a rich, handsome husband. She was all about the things she'd have because of him. She was on a mission even at twelve. I would agree with her when we sat outside and looked at the stars over Hoquiam and plotted our way back to Seattle. I'd say that whatever attributes she ran by me as we watched the stars swipe across the sky were ones I shared. But really, I just wanted to find someone who fit into my life. Julian,

I'd thought, could've been that guy. Something terrible had brought us together, but that didn't matter. There was something deeper at work.

Stacy had been smart. She went after things she wanted. I went looking for something more elusive. And now, I know, it is once more, and very suddenly, gone.

"Look," he says, "you might not believe this, Nicole, but I'm falling in love with you."

My wine splashes as I set down my glass. Like a child, I press my hands against my ears. "Stop it," I tell him. "Just stop it."

He leans over, touches me. "It's true. It's how I feel."

"She was here today," I spit out. "Angela was here."

I wonder if he knows that I know everything.

"Right," he says, pulling back. "Just to clear the air."

The walls close around us. "Don't lie to me, Julian. I don't deserve it, and you are a better man than that."

"That's all it was," he says.

I'm shaking, but I drop my own bomb anyway. "Then why did you fuck her?"

His face is the color of the Cabernet. He follows me to the kitchen where I stare out the window. A gauze of fog now shrouds the Seattle skyline. The Olympics are gone. The lake in the foreground has lost its moonlit shimmer. What had been so breathtaking was a mirage. He puts his hands on my shoulders, but I push him away.

"It was a mistake, Nicole. A final mistake. She said she still loved me and that when we get the money we'll be able to move away from here. She was desperate."

"Do you want to be with her? After everything she's done?"

"No," he says, his voice full of what I'm hoping is genuine regret. "But I wanted my son back. I thought if I played along with her she'd let me have Samuel. She'd stop being a bitch and think about him. You understand that?"

I have no children. I probably never will. Deep down, I know that part of me is a mother. I felt that way toward my sister when our mother first left. I could never understand how she could forsake us for her own needs. I used to dream that she'd come back for us, and Dad would forgive her. Anything to bring us back together as a family. No matter the betrayal.

"You slept with her, Julian," I say.

He's caught, but he doesn't look away. "It was stupid, and I was weak and it will never, ever happen again."

"You're right," I say. "It won't."

I notice that his eyes now seem to shimmer with emotion. "Haven't you ever made a mistake, Nicole?"

It wasn't meant as a cheap shot. I don't hate Julian enough right now to think that everything he flings at me is a poisoned arrow. He knows very well that my life is in ruins. He knows that every part of what I'd been before I sat in front of those glittery machines at the casino has been carpet bombed into oblivion.

I start for the door. He follows me, but I can be fast when I need to be.

"Where are you going, Nicole?"

The question is fair. But I have no answer. I don't have anywhere to go. I pull what's left of the money he gave me from my purse and let it fall to the tile before the front door. I'm shaking. Scattered. Angry. But more than anything, I'm brokenhearted. Being homeless was better than being betrayed. And being betrayed by someone with whom there was only a spider web of connection was the ultimate in foolishness.

"You can take the car," he calls out.

"Keep your wife's fucking car, Julian."

It's dark as I walk down Somerset Hill. I pass by windows illuminated with scenes of lives that I would have thought were happy. A couple dines. Some kids watch TV. A man blows smoke from an open window. A woman waters a flower box. Each person in these beautiful homes is living on a tightrope and none know it. One day the unthinkable will visit them. It's just the way it is. A couple of cars pass, and I consider hitchhiking. With each step away from Julian's house I feel a little bit stronger. I stick my thumb out, and a teenager in a blood-orange-colored Mustang pulls over. The driver's window rolls down.

"Where you headed?" a boy with geek-chic glasses asks. I open the passenger door. The interior reeks of pot, and the bass on his stereo is so amped up that it feels like I've slid into a paint shaker at a home-improvement store. Even so, I'm grateful for the ride.

"Anywhere but here," I say.

He rolls his eyes and nods knowingly. "Tell me about it."

Chapter Forty-Six

When you have nowhere to go, you'll go to the last place on earth you want to be. While I could return to the shelter to punish myself one more time, instead I cajole Josh, the kid in the Mustang, to drop me off at my sister's. It's a big ask, but he says he knows of a party nearby and doesn't mind the extra stop.

"No one cool will be there now anyway," he tells me.

We barely speak on the drive. The music is like a fortress around me, and it gives me time to think. I have no idea what I'll tell Stacy or if I should tell her anything at all. I can see her wagging her finger and running me down, and then me pretending that I've misinterpreted what she's said or meant, when really she'd just poured dirt over me until the light of day was blocked, and I was fully buried.

When I get out of the Mustang, I notice the new ambient lighting that Stacy told me they were having installed. She saw a spread on Jennifer Lopez's house in *Los Angeles Magazine* when she and Cy were there on vacation last year. She'd blathered on about how important landscape lighting could be.

I was about to lose my house at the time, and I wanted to say something about how crucial it was to have *indoor* lighting, but I didn't. The

Bank of Sonntag, as she once famously told me, was closed. I only asked for money one time—a regret that hovers somewhere in my personal top ten.

Top five.

"Nicole," Stacy says, opening the door, "what are you doing here?"

"Can I come in?"

She looks at me, then at the driveway. I smell the chardonnay on her breath. She's on glass number four, I think. "How the hell did you get here?"

"Long story," I say. "Can I come in or not?"

She swings the door open. "Cy's away on business. Yes, sure. Be quiet, though. Emma's asleep."

I shut the door behind me and follow Stacy to the kitchen, where I see an open bottle.

"You look like shit," she says.

"I'll have what you're having," I say, ignoring her remark. "Unless you have something stronger."

"Scotch. Vodka. Whatever. I have no idea what Cy has in the liquor cabinet. I don't drink the hard stuff."

I know my sister is an alcoholic. I have never confronted her about it. She started drinking heavily a year ago. Somehow, I think she has it in her mind that wine isn't really a problem. And yet, I've seen the empty bottles in the recycling bin, and I know that she has to notice the growing number as she drops empty bottle after empty bottle into the trash.

"Scotch," I say, helping myself to a double. "No ice."

Stacy looks at my glass.

"You must have had quite a day."

Understatement.

We sit quietly for a few minutes. The vibration of the running dishwasher soothes me somehow. Although Stacy has to know that something awful has brought me there, she insists on filling me in on all that she's been up to. New wallpaper coming from some exclusive place in New York, Emma's done something amazingly "advanced," and Cy's in line for some major promotion at Microsoft.

"Chief of cybersecurity or something," she says.

"I'm happy for him. For you both," I say. It isn't a lie. I really am. I love her enough to hope that whatever it is that she wants for herself and her family, she finds it. I know that she's still figuring things out, that behind the gloss of her life there is an unhappiness that she's still trying to rid herself of. Like a snake sheds its brittle skin.

I finish the scotch and pour another. I want to talk about Danny and Julian and Tommy and the murders of two little girls. Instead, I just pour the booze down my throat.

"Slow down, Sis," she says, of my drinking.

I nod. "Can I stay over?"

"What's going on with Julian?" she asks.

"Can I stay, Stacy?"

"Of course. Emma's room. She's sleeping in my bed again tonight."

"She does that a lot," I say.

Stacy stares into her empty glass. "Yeah, she does." She surprises me by putting her glass in the sink and recorking the bottle. "We've been having some issues."

"What kind of issues?"

"Family stuff," she says, watching me closely. "Nothing we can't handle. What about Julian? What happened there?"

I could kill myself right now. A tear rolls down my cheek. And my self-absorbed sister comes to me. She puts her arms around me. I feel her warm breath against my neck.

"I'm sorry, Nic," she says.

She doesn't say "I told you so" or that I'm a complete idiot or anything at all. Instead she just holds me for a minute. *Damn her.* Whenever I think our love/hate relationship is locked on hate, she pulls the rug out from under me. She gives me the kind of support that I need most. After Mom left, after Dad's brain went dark, after Danny betrayed me, Stacy was all I had. And that isn't saying much.

"He slept with his wife again," I say.

"Target Mom?"

"Yeah, her."

"He's a fucking idiot," she says. "A total loser."

I nod, though I really don't feel that way.

"You are better off without him, Nicole."

I don't want to wallow, but the alcohol has taken over a little, and I can't help myself. "I know it's stupid," I say, "but I think I love him. He's kind, thoughtful, decent."

"He screwed her," she says. "Not kind, thoughtful, or decent."

She's right.

"You were on a major rebound. Your whole life was fucked up. You broke up with Danny, lost your job, lost everything! You were looking for a way out of it, and he came into your life."

She's right.

I tell her, "As mad at myself as I am—and I *am*, big-time—I'm glad that I got to know Julian. I'm glad that I started to dig into the case. I have you to thank for that, Stacy."

"Me?" she asks in that clueless way that she always does when she's trying to wriggle out of something.

I give her an appreciative smile anyway. "You told him where I was. He found me near the shelter. If that hadn't happened, I might have lost myself forever."

Stacy fiddles with the *Tiff*. "I don't know anyone smarter than you, Nicole. I mean that. I know that you can figure out what happened to Kelsey Chase. You can fix this."

I want to tell her more about what I found out at WSU, but I hold back. I'm drunk. I'm tired. She's probably feeling the same way, but she's used to drinking to excess. We'll talk more in the morning. She leads me into Emma's room. Elsa, Anna, and Sven smile from every corner.

"What's going on with Emma?" I ask. "Why is she afraid at night?"

"She just is," Stacy says, disappearing to get me a nightgown.

She returns and perches on the edge of the bed. I feel drunk and sick to my stomach, but I can tell Stacy wants to talk.

I put on the nightgown and climb into bed.

"I'm sorry, Nic," she says.

My eyelids droop. "About what?"

"I always wanted you to believe that Mom rejected you, not me. That I was her favorite. The pretty one. The fun one. The one that she thought was most like her. But that's not how it was. Not at all."

She stops, and even in the haze of my sleepiness, I see those tears of hers. This time they seem almost real. Maybe they are? I want them to be. I *need* them to be.

"What are you talking about? How was it?" I ask. "How was it with Mom?"

She sits still and looks right at me. "It wasn't just you and Dad she ran away from. It was all of us. She didn't love any of us, Nicole."

I don't believe her.

"She told you that you were just like her," I say, pushing back. "Smart. Pretty."

Stacy slowly pecks out her words. "Right. That's what I wanted you to believe. That's not the truth. I called her one time and begged her to let me come and live with her. I told her that I could be her assistant or something. That if she became a big star on TV or in the movies, maybe I could be just like her."

I hold my breath, and my sister's words crash against the quiet of Emma's bedroom. Each ragged syllable hangs in the air as my younger sister pulls herself together and digs in deep to tell me something that she's held as a secret. *A secret weapon,* I think.

"She told me, Nicole . . ." She stalls, then goes on. "She told me that I just didn't have it. That I was more like Dad, a background player. Like you. Someone whose sole purpose was to make her shine. A chorus girl. She said that in a lineup, I would only be good enough to be on the very end in case they needed to crop the shot tighter."

I couldn't count all the times I had lain in bed thinking of what it must have been like for Stacy to be idolized by the woman who'd rejected me and our father. But she'd been rejected too. Hers might have been the deeper sting. Everyone had thought otherwise, and over and over she'd been told how lucky she was.

How she wasn't plain or average like her poor sister. How no one could deny that she was destined for something great.

All the while, she lived with the knowledge that our mother didn't love her, either. It had pushed her away from me and our father. She'd been spun up in our mother's web, unable to free herself.

Even though she let that lie fester all of our lives, I couldn't help but feel sorry for my sister. When I'm not in the throes of hating her, I know I love her more than anything.

◆　◆　◆

Danny and Kelsey visit me as I sleep. Lightning flashes over and over. I stand at the end of a long, dark corridor. I try to speak, but no words come from my lips. I try to move, but my arms and legs are frozen. Flash after flash. The rush of a wind comes at me. It blows so hard at me that I can barely keep my eyes open. Another flash. Kelsey starts to laugh, like she's being tickled or something. I open my eyes the best that I can. She's not laughing. More lightning. I look right into a camera lens and try to scream.

Then it stops.

CHAPTER FORTY-SEVEN

The Sonntags' magnificent home is quiet. Electrified from my dream and miles from sleep, I listen to Stacy's soft snore as I pass her bedroom. When we were kids, I teased her about the nearly purring sound she made when she slept in the bed across from mine. I lied and told her she sounded like a lumberjack. I don't know why I did that, except at the time it was the only flaw that I could find. I had so many. Each target was hers to hit whenever she wanted. She had none. I wasn't jealous at all. I was grateful she had something just a little annoying.

My head is pounding. I get a glass of water and wander around the house, the glow from the outdoor lighting casting soft light through the sheers. My life was upended by Kelsey's murder. I didn't know it at the time, of course. I couldn't have known that the man that I once thought cared about me had been a part of the crime. I fish through the kitchen cabinets for some aspirin, but find none. I pass by Cy's office on my way to the bathroom. The lights of his router twinkle like slot machines.

Finally, aspirin. I take two with my water and stand there in the near dark, the router lights twinkling from across the hall. I can't sleep. My head hurts. My heart is broken. I hear the purr of my sister's snore, and I find myself sitting at Cy's computer. I wonder if the Microsoft people at his office know that he uses a Mac. The irony brings a faint smile to my face, but it doesn't last for long.

The Eastside Crime Watch opens when I move the mouse.

The only thing I hear as I read is my beating heart.

Then it occurs to me that the snoring has stopped. I turn and Stacy is standing behind me.

"Nicole," she says, "we need to talk."

I have never seen her like this. The frivolousness of her demeanor has been eclipsed by a seriousness that's so foreign I can barely recognize her.

"I don't understand," I say, looking at her, then back at the long thread about Angela Chase, the Target Mom.

She slumps onto the floor. "I didn't, either. Not at first."

I touch the screen. "What are you doing on this site?"

"At first I was looking for a reason not to believe," she says, keeping her voice low. "That changed. It all changed. Everything has changed."

"To not believe what?"

"Cy."

"I'm confused. What about Cy?"

"That Cy was mixed up in something like this."

I swivel toward my sister. She looks at me with those eyes of hers. Those very, very pretty eyes. Our mother's eyes. There's something in them now. I can't quite make it out. Resolve, maybe? I can't be sure. My heart continues to pound. My mind is no longer on my jackhammer headache. How I wish it were.

"Cy," I repeat.

"I'm Truthsayer, Nicole," she says.

I forget to breathe for a second, then gasp. I get up and go to her. We're both sitting on the floor. She's looking right at me, unapologetic. Stronger in a way than I've ever seen her.

"You, Stacy?"

She nods. "Don't hate me."

"I don't understand any of this. If my head didn't hurt like hell right now I'd say that this is a bad dream."

"Not a dream," Stacy says. "A nightmare."

"Tell me."

She stands up and takes my hand. "I'll show you."

The Sonntags' garage is one of those detached carriage house affairs. I've never been inside before. Stacy turns on the light to reveal a space that is as nice as the house—a guest quarters that has never been offered to me, not even in my darkest hour. I say nothing about that. I'm sure there are many more things that I don't know about my sister.

She hands me a gold throw from a maroon camelback sofa and I wrap it around my shoulders as I survey the space.

Over a gas fireplace is a painting of a cougar. Near the flat-screen is a sculpture of one.

Without another word from Stacy, I'm reeling.

"He calls this his lair," she says, barely taking in my reaction. "It's like WSU threw up in here."

I understand the reference. Cy has never been the flag-waving Coug fan Danny is, but when Apple Cup time came around—the annual football game between the University of Washington Huskies and WSU Cougars—both were fully invested in Team Cougars.

Cy and Danny were in the same fraternity, but never made a big deal about it. As I stand here now, I wonder how often it's been mentioned. Maybe once or twice. If they've ever even mentioned its name, I can't recall it.

If I were on a game show and had a chance at a million dollars, I would be rich if called upon to guess it now.

Stacy walks over to the wet bar.

"I don't want to drink," I say. "I want you to tell me what's going on."

"When I had the kitchen cabinets redone, we used the same guy that did this room for Cy," she says. "Cy was off in Thailand doing God knows what, and Ernesto asked me if I wanted anything Harry Potter."

"Harry Potter?"

"Right. *Harry Potter.* I did just what you did. Same response." She points to the wall. It's paneled in cherry. "He tells me that he could make a secret place for me. Something like what he'd done for Mr. Sonntag."

I look at the wall that my sister is indicating. "What was he talking about?"

"I pretended I knew. I told him yeah, maybe something small. A cabinet that I could store some valuables in. You know, our best stemware or something. I rattled off a list of things, but the whole time I was thinking about what it was that Cy would have built. I knew where, but not what."

Stacy turns to me. She's not upset. She's cool.

"It took me a week to figure it out," she says, running her fingertips over the wood surface like a TV supermodel. "Want to try to open it?"

I brush past her shoulder for a better look, but the wood—so rich, so satiny—appears seamless. I don't see a latch, a handle, or anything that could actually open. I look for a smudge that would indicate where others had touched. I think about my old fingerprint kit from the academy. That would probably reveal where to touch.

"I can't see anything," I say, running my hands over the wall.

"That's because you're only looking at eye level. I made that mistake too. And you know, Nic, I'm no mechanical genius. I found the way in when I sat here and drank a glass of wine. I don't know why I tried so hard. I just had to know what it was that Cy was hiding from me. I had no suspicions about him before Ernesto mentioned the secret. But then, I don't know—I thought maybe he had a stash of money or gold or something. I never expected to find what I did find."

Stacy stops and points to the floor. It's hickory. One plank closest to the wall has a big knot. It's almost like an eye. She bends down and presses it.

A door swings open.

Inside there are racks holding probably twenty quietly humming servers. All flickering. On a table is a stack of *Seattle Times*.

My sister lingers, and I enter alone. The space is the size of a child's bedroom. The server racks line one wall. The newspaper on the top of the heap is the last one in which Kelsey Chase made the front page. It's been more than a year and the pages have yellowed a little already.

"I don't understand," I say.

The room is spinning. My sister touches my shoulder.

"This kind of ugly can never be understood," she tells me.

I see some photographs on the desk.

"Do yourself a favor, Nicole," Stacy says, pulling me back. "Don't make the same mistake that I did. Don't look at those pictures."

It's too late.

A girl. A boy. An adult male. As a police officer, I have seen things that have to rival the worst things soldiers encounter in wartime. A woman from Cherry Crest stabbed so many times that her face had to be reassembled at the morgue. A car accident on 405 that left two children charred with faces frozen in agonized screams from being burned alive. But my sister is right. This is the worst.

"What's going on here?" I ask, barely able to breathe. I scan the room. A large chest freezer draws me close. I open it, but it's empty. I think of what Christine told me about Kelsey's body, how she was sure that it couldn't have been frozen on Rattlesnake Ridge.

"There hadn't been snow for two weeks," she had said.

I shut the freezer.

It wasn't Danny and Evan working together, but Danny and Cy.

"The best that I can tell is my husband is trafficking in child porn," Stacy says. "Well, no. It's not a guess. Not really. I'm not a detective like you, but I know what I know."

I flash to Cy's trips to the Far East. To conventions in Europe. I think of his expertise in cybersecurity. Predators learn what they have to do to survive. They go where they can find victims. They become teachers. Priests. Those who offend at a grand scale learn how to avoid getting caught.

I immediately think of my niece.

"Emma?" I ask.

Stacy shakes her head. "I told Cy that she was having bad dreams and needed to sleep with us. The first night she did, I poured warm water all over the mattress and said she'd wet the bed. I did it three nights in a row. He was disgusted and moved into the guest room. I can't risk having her sleep in her own bed anymore. I don't want him near her."

"He doesn't know that you know?"

"No," she says, shaking her head. "What good would that do?"

I feel it in my bones. Stacy's endgame here is something dark. Very.

"He couldn't deny it," I tell her. "You have proof."

"Right. Proof. I have that. But I'd also lose everything I've ever wanted. You've lost everything, Nicole, how does that feel? Imagine having a daughter and needing to start over."

Our father had two.

I want to sit, but I just stand there. "You wouldn't lose everything, Stacy. He'd go to jail."

"The money," she says. "The money that has paid for all of this is mixed in with his side business. I didn't know it. I was an idiot. I thought everyone at Microsoft was pulling down a couple of million a year."

She pauses, and I let her collect herself. I say nothing, mostly because I can't think of the right thing to say. Stacy has always been about *things*.

"And really," she goes on, "I guess I could live without most of this. What I couldn't live with is Emma growing up knowing her father was a freak and that her mother let him get away with it for a long time."

Finally I speak. "How long?"

"Too long," she says, allowing the barest crack in her polished veneer. "Kelsey. She changed everything. I think she was here."

I lose it. "Here? You didn't say anything?"

"I didn't think about it until later. When I read that autopsy report online. The one that said what Kelsey had eaten before she died."

The report said tater tots and a cheeseburger. Angela said the last meal she fed her daughter was pizza.

"Emma wasn't eating cheeseburgers at the time. She was living on chicken. I found the wrapper in the trash. Cy lied to me. I knew it was a lie. At first, I thought he was covering up for himself. Mr. Healthy. Mr. All About Appearances."

Her dream husband.

One of the servers whirs, and then another.

"He's trading files," she says, her eyes shifting from mine to the flashing components.

"This was a little girl, nearly the age of your daughter. And you thought she was here? You let this happen, Stacy."

"Not at the time," she says, pleading. "Later. Nicole, I'm a lot of things, but if you know me at all, you know that I would never in a million years turn my back on a child. Never. Tell me you believe me. Tell me!"

I really don't know what to say. I can see that she's on the thin end of the wedge and despite all of our differences, I want her to know that she and I are still something. Sisters. Family. Whatever. Our bond is tenuous at times, but it is also undeniable.

"You tell me, Stacy. When did you know Kelsey was here?"

My sister takes me by the shoulders. Rocks me. She really needs me to believe. But I'm thinking about the freezer, and my reaction to it. I don't know why, but it just called to me the second I saw it. I felt a connection to Kelsey. I did. I really did.

"God, Nicole," she says, "After. *Long after.* I didn't know any of this when it would have made a difference. The kitchen remodel with Ernesto was after. You and the case were falling apart. I didn't think you could take one more thing, or I might have said something sooner. The girl was dead. She was gone. Alan Dawson was dead. I didn't know what to do, but I knew that I had to do something. Sometime. Just *when*. I didn't know the when."

"You have been living with your murderous, pervert husband for months, Stacy. Just when did you think would be the right time to stop him?"

Silence consumes the room, save for the fans from the servers.

"It was when you were talking about the sheet that she'd been found in."

I don't say a word. She needs to say all of it.

"You and Cy were talking about it and I was fixing dinner or doing something with Emma, and I thought it was weird when he said he'd never heard of that brand of linens. Boll and Branch, right?"

"Right," I say. "That's the sheet."

"I thought I misheard; it was so not right."

"What are you telling me, Stacy?"

"It's the only brand he lets me buy. Nothing else will do."

The lights flicker again, and I wonder what child somewhere in the world is being violated.

"Was it a top sheet or bottom sheet?" she asks. "The one Kelsey was found in."

It had never been in the papers. I'd never said it. Danny might have. Danny might have done whatever he could to save himself.

"Are you missing one?" I ask.

She nods. "We were. One sheet in the set."

"Which sheet was missing, Stacy?"

"The bottom sheet."

No one but Danny, Evan, Christine, and I knew. Kelsey Chase was wrapped in a bottom sheet.

I look hard at her. "We need to call the police," I say. The words feel strange. I used to be the police.

"It would only be an inconvenience. People like Cy have resources. A network. Money. Lawyers. It will drag on and on."

I know where this is going.

"If he doesn't run, he might get jail time for the child porn," she says. "But he'll never do any time for Lisa or Kelsey's murder. A good lawyer will get him off. You know that, Nicole."

I do.

I know what she's suggesting. I just don't know how.

"We can make it look like an accident," she says.

I stand there looking at my sister. She's serious. In a way, I'm okay with what she's thinking. I tried to like Cy because my sister loved him. I really, really tried. But there was never any denying that he was a pompous ass. And that was before I knew he was a killer and a child pornographer.

"What are you thinking?" I ask.

She takes one more look at her husband's operation and leads me out.

"Emma has a playdate with Sidney. We'll go over everything when she's gone. Go back to bed, Nicole. When you wake up you can tell yourself this was just a bad dream, or you can help me."

Words stick in my throat. I say nothing.

Light seeps through the slits along the edge of the window as I lay in my niece's bed. I heard the garage doors rise and close some time ago. Stacy and Emma are gone. I'm alone in the house, and I know that what happened last night was not a dream.

I scroll through my text messages. I read the same text over and over.

> You are wrong about Angela and me. You know me, Nic. You have been with me every step of the way. From the day that I found you at the shelter, I knew that you were the opposite of Angela. You are real. I do love you. Samuel is coming today. I want you to be here.

I don't respond. My heart tells me that two broken people like Julian and I cannot mend each other. Never could. Not in a million years. In that moment, I want more than anything to get in a car and drive to the casino. My fingers long for the touch of the flashing red button. It's like I'm one of those amputees that can feel a missing limb. It feels good and wrong at the same time.

Just then Stacy's car pulls in. *Stacy.* She's been a part of all of this in a way that I could never have imagined. Stacy told Julian where to find me. She posted those prompts on the crime blog, directing me to find out what she wanted me to know. She knew that my investment in finding out what happened to Kelsey would lead me to Cy—and what she needs done. My sister was always manipulative, but she is also smarter than I ever knew.

Stacy could have stepped in and stopped my downward spiral at any time, but she didn't. She wanted me to fall as far as I did. It's like one of those kids held captive by some freak for years, but suddenly doesn't bolt when given an afternoon at the mall. Tear me down, to build me up. Set me free to do what she wants done.

Killing Cy.

She knocks on my door and enters.

"You up?"

"Yeah," I say. "Just trying to pull myself together."

She's dressed to the nines. Playdate moms in her neighborhood have standards.

"It's a lot to take in," she says, setting a cup of coffee on the nightstand. "I'm right about what needs to be done. You know it."

I don't. Instead, I sit up and drink the coffee. It's nearly beige with some god-awful French vanilla creamer in it, but I swallow it anyway.

"Take a shower," she says, studying me like a lab rat. "I put some clothes in the bathroom for you."

I nod.

"I'll tell you my idea then."

"Okay." But I stay right where I am, and so does she. "How did you know about Tommy Roberts?" I ask.

She sits on the edge of the bed. "I've known about that for years," she says. "I walked in one time when Danny was over, and he and Cy were talking about something that had happened when they were in Kappa Sigma. I heard them mention Tommy's name. Some fraternity brother, I figured. Which was odd, because they never, ever mentioned they were in that fraternity together. At least Cy never did."

"Danny didn't, either," I say.

"Right," Stacy says. "And that's always struck me as weird. Most fraternity guys—at least the ones I dated—replayed their frat exploits on one boring, continuous loop."

"So they just mentioned Tommy's name?"

"No," she says. "It was more than that."

My sister does that thing she always does. She holds back, like she's holding a dog treat and wanting me beg for it. As a child, Stacy played with food. As an adult, she toyed with information. Letting it out. Keeping it inside. Just when she was ready.

I wait.

She takes a breath, then locks her eyes on mine. "I heard Danny laugh and say how lucky they were, getting away with murder."

I can hear my pulse pounding in my ears. Finally I say, "That's pretty direct."

"I took it as an exaggeration—you know, like he was talking about how they'd egged the dean's house or something."

"And you're sure it wasn't?" I say, setting down my cup.

Stacy shakes her head. "No. When we had Cy's fortieth-birthday party, I thought I'd surprise him by inviting friends from the past. I remembered them mentioning Tommy's name. When I searched online for him, I found the reports about his little sister's murder. I thought it was strange that Cy hadn't mentioned that at all. A little girl's murder is a big thing."

"So you knew then?" I ask.

Again she shakes her head. "No, I didn't. After the party, I mentioned that I'd wanted to get more of his old friends there—the Microsoft people are completely cliquish. I told him that I'd tried to find Tommy. I didn't say anything more than that. That I'd just tried. I was curious. Having a buddy in prison for murder isn't something you don't mention to your wife. Do you?"

I don't imagine so.

"What did he say to that?"

She keeps her eyes on mine in that Stacy way she has. She never flinches. Never gave up when we played stare-down. "That Tommy died in a car accident on the highway between Pullman and Moscow. Drunk driving. Which I knew was a complete lie. I didn't push him on it. I don't know why. I think part of me knew that there was something terrible behind that kind of lie. I almost didn't really want to know."

"But that changed."

My sister nods, then gets to her feet and disappears. A few seconds later she's back holding a stack of pillowcases and a flat sheet. I know right away what they are.

"Yes," she said. "It changed. It wasn't one thing, but when I found these underneath a Goodwill box that I was collecting—and I knew I hadn't put them there—I knew something was off."

Stacy starts to crack a little. She's tough. But not as tough as she wants to be.

"At first I wanted to believe that he'd had a woman over and screwed her in our bed and maybe stained the sheet. I even asked him about it."

She sits still, and I put my hand on hers. She's holding the sheets like a mother cradles a baby. She's steady, not shaky. But she doesn't pull away like she's done most of the times I've reached out to comfort her.

Her eyes stay on the linens. "He told me that Emma had wet the bed again, and he tossed the sheets."

"She isn't a bed wetter," I say.

Stacy lets my hand stay on hers. "No," she finally says, looking up at me. "That's where I got the idea. That's how I kept him away from her."

I understand. I know so much more about Stacy's world now. I know that her chardonnay is a calculated escape. She didn't drink to forget. She drank so that her husband wouldn't bother her. She drank so she could plot a way to keep everything she had.

Everything but him.

I take my hand from hers, give her a hug, and head to the bathroom.

"Cy comes home tonight," she says.

I know what that means.

My sister's perfect life has been worse than the disaster I've made of my own.

CHAPTER FORTY-EIGHT

It is nearly noon when I emerge from Emma's room. Stacy sits at the dining table in the place where I'd gouged the surface the last night she let me stay here before Angeline's shelter. I wonder if she knows that I did that. I suspect she does. My sister is more than I ever thought she was. She's changed into a white cotton blouse with pearl buttons and dark jeans. Around her neck are our mother's pearls. I wonder why she's wearing them, now that I know she hates her as much as I do. Her hair is perfect and her makeup is fancy lunch with the other millionaire wives of the Eastside.

Stacy has always liked to look her best. Special occasions have always mattered to her.

"You could do what you want to do without me," I say.

She nods. "Sure. Of course. You'd be surprised what I'm capable of, Nic."

Not anymore.

"Your logic is twisted, Stacy," I tell her as I take my place across from her. "You'll get caught."

"I don't think so," she says. "I've thought of everything."

We sit in silence. It's a chess game, I suppose. It's her move.

"It will look like an accident," she says.

Her eyes are begging me to ask for details, so I do.

"What kind of accident?"

"An explosion."

"A bomb never looks like an accident," I say. "You know the Unabomber and Timothy McVeigh and those Boston brothers who detonated those pressure-cooker bombs? All either dead or in prison."

She pushes a newspaper toward me. "I said an *explosion*. Not a bomb, Nicole." She taps a fingertip on a story at the bottom of the front page. It's about a house in Ellensburg that was nearly flattened by a leaking propane canister. Two people died.

I slide away from the table. "Too dangerous," I say. "That could kill your neighbors."

Her eyes are riveted to mine. "The Johnsons are on a month-long cruise," she says. "They won one." She pauses to let it sink in. "They were so excited." She smiles right at me. "People with a lot of money like free things even more than the poor do."

I don't need to ask. I know that Stacy was behind their surprise win.

"The Yangs were more difficult," she tells me of the neighbors on the other side of the Sonntag house. "Turns out the house was infested by termites. Cindy Yang can't stand bugs. They've moved to a condo for the fumigation and renovation."

"Termites," I repeat.

Again the smile. "Did you know you can order them on the Internet?"

That doesn't surprise me. But what my sister is telling me does.

"What's your plan?" I ask.

"I've set three canisters in his lair. His twisted Harry Potter room. He has a barbecue grill he hauls out when he has his friends over—pervs too, I bet. When he opens that secret panel, that half of the carriage house will blow sky-high, taking that motherfucker and his treasure trove of filth to hell where he belongs."

I have a million questions, but I hold most inside. I think of what she's saying and what the true risk is. Arson investigators will look at the blow site as a matter of course.

"It won't work," I finally say. "Trust me, I know what they'll look for."

Her gaze stays steely. "I thought you'd say something like that, Nicole. And yes, I'm taking a chance here. But I think the risk is minimal. You told me that as long as there is no marital discord, as long as there are no financial problems, no other parties involved in the marriage, that a lot of what appear to be accidents could be homicides."

"I was talking about drowning or slip-and-falls at home," I say. "Not about a bomb."

"Not a bomb," she says. Her eyes drill into me. She's steel. "An accidental explosion like this one." She looks at the paper again. "I wonder if that one was a murder? I read online that the son of the victims bought a house in Maui."

"Too dangerous," I say.

"I need him gone. I need every trace of the evil that he's collected obliterated. I need a clean slate."

"Too much of a risk, Stacy. You could get caught."

"*We*," she says. "We won't get caught."

I shake my head. We're not a *we*, not in this. So why can't I say as much to her?

"Think of Emma," she says.

Again I'm mute, and again she pushes. She's playing every button on my personal machine, hoping to hit the jackpot.

Her eyes penetrate mine. "You know what he did to Lisa Roberts? Don't you?"

I shake my head and shrug to say no, I'm not sure.

Stacy won't be denied. She's determined to reel me in.

"You *do*, Nicole. I know it. When you called and said that Danny was the killer, I knew you would have killed him if you were in the same room with him. But it wasn't just Danny. I know it had to be Cy too."

302

"You can't know that for sure," I say.

"Oh, I know it. I know it the way I know that he killed Kelsey. He made a deal with Angela Chase to buy that little girl, and Danny helped him. That's how sick they are. And there have been others. You know that, Nicole. People like my husband don't stop doing what's in their DNA."

"How do you know Angela made a deal with Cy?"

"As smart as my husband is about cybersecurity, he's a careless fool too. When I thought he might have had sex with some woman here and ditched the sheets, I looked on his computer. He'd been emailing her. I saw the emails."

Cy *is* stupid. And a pompous prick. A pervert. A killer. The list is growing.

"Are you in or out?" Stacy asks.

I just stand there mute.

"Think of Emma," Stacy says again, her voice cracking now. Her eyes glistening. This is the little sister that I know. This is the girl who could turn me into mush with a flood of tears and then turn them off when I was just out of view. Like a light switch. Just off and on. I know that she's really thinking of herself just now, but she's right. I have to think of Emma. Someone has to.

"Okay," I find myself saying. "I'll help."

She lets a tear splash on the table and quickly rubs it dry. "I knew I could count on you," she says.

She knew she could use me. Oddly, I don't care. I know that Tommy went to prison for something he didn't do. That Angela set her daughter's death in motion by handing her off—or selling her. I know that Danny and Cy were behind Alan Dawson's death and frame-up. I know that Kelsey Chase's murder will never be avenged.

"What time does he get home?" I ask.

"His flight gets in at four," Stacy says. Her mood is lighter now. Like we're planning a lunch date. "I told him that Emma and I were going to a ballet recital and to dinner. We'd be home late. I wanted him to have time to go look at whatever it was that fuels his disgusting obsession."

My phone buzzes. I look down at a text from Julian.

```
Samuel's here. So far it's mostly good.
Wish you were here. Only weird thing was
that he freaked out when he saw that WSU
shirt you left. Said the cougar was the
monster. He must be a Husky, LOL. Call
me. Love, J.
```

Of course.

All along the cougar was the monster.

Chapter Forty-Nine

I'm outside my brother-in-law's secret space. Stacy stands just inside the hidden, seamless doorway. She shows me how she'll twist the knobs on each of the white steel canisters she's procured, only a little. The leaks need to be slow ones. Silently, the propane will pool on the floor under the server racks. The flammable gas will envelop everything in that space, holding the sickening electronic media that Cy collects and sells like a coiled snake waiting to strike.

Stacy wraps her arms around her torso as she observes me. She is sure she can count on me. When she'd stay out all night with a boyfriend, I slept in her bed with the covers over my head, knowing Mom would only look in on her favorite. I wrote her essays to get into college. I said I was the one behind the wheel the time she hit a tree when she took a corner too fast.

There is a lot about her that I didn't know until last night. I still wonder if I can really trust her. I know that she's selfish, no matter how she couches all of this as an act of love for her daughter and retribution for those whose lives her husband has ruined.

"You didn't take out a huge life insurance policy on him, did you, Stacy?"

"I'm not that stupid," she says.

"Good," I say, hoping that she's not lying.

"I mean, he does have a $2.5 million policy from work. But that's standard. The real money is what he's made from all of this. He has an offshore account. I have what I need to get that money."

I don't ask how much.

"Did Danny get a share of all this?"

She shakes her head. "No. Cy controlled him. Danny did all kinds of shit just to hang out with his buddy, hoping for some crumbs, I guess. When he found out I had a sister, Cy was so pissed off that he made a play for you. He told me he didn't like his friends mixing with family."

I wonder if Danny only went after me to get closer to Cy.

"Where's your detonator?"

Stacy holds up a pair of wooden matches. "Strike anywhere," she deadpans. "I've tested this ten times and never have had a failure."

Who is this girl?

"How?" I ask.

She bends down and places the matches just under the ledge of the opening to the secret server room and secures them with a piece of tape that she's taken from the desk.

"When he pushes open the door the matches will ignite," she says, pulling the tape and lifting the matches away.

"And he'll be gone," I say. "That's your plan."

We stand there, then she eases the door shut. I reach for my sister's hand, and she gives me a gentle squeeze.

"You can't do this, you know," I say.

She stares me down. "But I can," she says.

"I know what you are capable of, Stacy. But it isn't this. You can't do this. And really, I can't live with this."

"What? You'll tell on me like you told Dad when I had the abortion?"

"Not Dad," I say. "The police."

She drops my hand from hers. "You are such a goody-goody," she says. "You care more about doing the right thing than doing what's right."

"You can't kill Cy."

"I *won't* lose everything. And I won't allow Emma to grow up with a monster for a father. I'm not having that."

"The law will do right by Emma."

My sister laughs, but it isn't the kind of laugh that invites the listener to join in. It's the type that sends a chill down one's spine.

"Oh really?" she asks. "You know that for a fact, do you? Like it did for Lisa? What about her? What about Angela? Don't you want her to pay for what she did? She's a mother, for God's sake."

"We can turn over the evidence. Cooper will listen. It will work out."

"You are such a fucking idiot, Nicole. It will never work out."

"I won't help you."

"When I need you, you'll be there."

"I won't."

Her face falls. "Maybe Emma would be better off without me and Cy. Maybe you'd be better off too."

This kind of pity party is so not my sister. I ignore her not-so-subtle threat.

"Promise me you won't do anything," I say. "You'll let me figure out the best way to make Cy, Danny, and Angela pay."

She brightens a little. "How?"

"Give me some time to think."

We go back to the house. Emma is due back from Sidney's before dinner. My sister turns on the oven and puts a pan of frozen lasagna on the rack and goes for a bottle of wine. I fall into the sofa wondering which of us is right. She hands me a glass, and we sip from her Baccarat goblets.

"I need you," she says, a trail of tears shimmers on her flawless skin. "You and Emma. I need you."

2

Gregg Olsen

"We've gone over this," I say.

"You've always been there for me. Even when I was a bitch to you."

I want to say, *which is all the time,* but I don't.

"You and me," she says. "That's where we are now."

"You won't make things worse than they are."

"No," she says. "I promise. I'll do the right thing."

"Are you going to confront him?"

"Yes. You and Emma go to the recital. I'll stay here. I'll tell him to get the fuck out of our lives. I'll tell him that we know everything."

"You shouldn't be alone with him."

She dries her tears. "He's weak. I can handle Cy."

308

CHAPTER FIFTY

As the school orchestra plays, the little girls on the stage pirouette and leap in delicate pink tutus and pointe shoes. I can almost feel the tungsten control that holds together every movement they make. It doesn't matter that they are so young. Determination, I know, knows no age. The floorboards vibrate as they sweep on and off the stage.

The theater is dark, but the two of us sit close enough to the stage that the lights illuminate Emma, wide-eyed and enthralled. I see the look of awe on my niece's little face. She's taking it all in. She's moving slightly in her seat as though she's part of the chorus. *Like me.* Or maybe she's the center of attention like her mother. None of that will be known until she's older, until she processes her childhood and makes her own decisions. I watch her more than I watch the dancers. I think of how precious she is and how her world is being shattered right then. She is safe in that seat. Unaware. But this is all very, very fleeting.

"I wish Momma was here," she says, twirling as we leave the theater.

"She and Daddy need to talk," I say, checking my phone for calls. None. No texts. Good. I promised Emma ice cream.

"What's your favorite flavor?"

"Strawberry," she says. A smile as wide as an inverted rainbow takes over her face.

"Strawberry was my favorite when I was a kid too," I tell her.

In fact I hate strawberry. I only filled my dish with strawberry ice cream because when our mom bought Neapolitan, it was the only flavor Stacy didn't like. I let her have the chocolate and vanilla. Always in that order too.

Later she told me that she hated chocolate but took it because she knew it was my favorite flavor.

After we make our way to Stacy's spare BMW, I overhear some moms talking by the edge of the parking lot.

"Did you catch the explosion?" asks one, a redhead with a daughter whose hair has been dyed to match.

"No, what happened?" asks another.

The mom reads from her Twitter feed. "They think someone was inside the carriage house."

"Wow, that's terrible."

The redhead shakes her head and swings open a car door so her little girl can climb into her car seat. "Just terrible," she echoes.

The other mom fishes in her purse for her keys. "See you at the pizza place."

I put Emma in her car seat. She has no idea what the women are talking about. I do. Instead of ice cream, I find myself driving to where I know I'll find nothing but trouble.

To my sister.

◆ ◆ ◆

The sirens grow louder as I go past cars that have lined the street leading to the Sonntags'. My heart thumps like tennis shoes in the dryer. I keep my eye on Emma, who sits in her car seat behind me, crying. The prospect of ice cream has been supplanted by the fear that she absorbs from the scene outside the car.

And what comes from the driver who cannot hide her own sense of knowing dread.

"It'll be all right," I tell her, though I know it won't be.

"I'm scared," she says. "I want my momma."

I want her mom too.

As I wedge Stacy's BMW SUV behind a police cruiser, I see Lieutenant Cooper. A familiar face. I jump out and scoop Emma from the backseat. She's no longer crying, but whimpering. It's the sound of a hurt animal. It breaks my heart and yet fuels me at the same time. I nuzzle her as I weave my way through the onlookers and first responders. My heart is about to explode.

Cooper approaches. His face is grim. His eyes full of deep concern. "Your sister's place," he says with a slow, sympathetic nod.

I hold Emma tighter, so tight that she lets out a yelp, which snaps me back to the moment. I see the smoke. I hear the rush of the water from a hose. Yelling. People with cell phones point in my direction as they capture every nuance of what is happening so they can post for clicks later. I scan for others I might know. Lane Perry. Not there. Julian comes to mind too. Not because I think he would be there, but because I know that what happened here occurred because of what my monstrous brother-in-law and ex-boyfriend put in motion when they took Kelsey from Angela's all-too-willing arms.

"What happened?" I say this even though I know exactly what transpired. I say it because if I don't Cooper will wonder why. I want to cry, but I'm so scared right now. So very angry. So fucking pissed off at my sister for doing what she did.

"Explosion," he says. "Maybe a gas leak. It blew the damn lid off the carriage house."

Just behind Cooper I spy Cy's car, a black Lexus that he had detailed twice a week. The windshield is spider-cracked from the force of the blast.

"Where's my sister? My brother-in-law?" I say that last part, again because I'm all but certain that Stacy had set her plan in motion.

As he did when he was my lieutenant, my mentor, Cooper reminds me of my father just now. He puts his hand on my shoulder. I feel a tear roll down my cheek, and I let it roll on top of Emma's head. I thought I'd forgotten how to cry. Absentmindedly, I pass Emma to a female officer whose outstretched arms beckon. I lean into Emma for a second. My breath is on her ear.

"Everything will be all right, Emma," I whisper. "I promise you."

"I want my momma," she repeats.

"I know, Honey."

I feel Cooper's hand on my shoulder once more. It's a gentle tug.

"Blast was bad, Nic," he says as my precious niece disappears behind a curtain of police officers and into a cruiser. "Don't think they made it. Techs found remains outside of the blast zone."

They.

I am immobile. I think that my lips are moving, but nothing is coming out.

"Fire found more body parts in the carriage house. Moving debris now. Looking for your sister and her husband. Thank God you and the little one weren't here."

I stopped thanking God for anything after I lost my job. My house. My old life.

Still no words come. *Goddamn you, Stacy. You are such a selfish bitch. You did this. You fucked up. Goddamn you. What about Emma? Couldn't you think about her?*

He asks me for details about Cy and Stacy and I tell him the basics. I give her full name, age. The same for Cy. I tell him she was a stay-at-home mom and he was an executive at Microsoft. I don't say she was a selfish, conniving murderer and that he was a pervert and a murderer. I have Emma to think about.

312

Damn you, Stacy. You really did it. Her words circle in my brain like a whirlpool that can't stop: maybe Emma would be better off with both of us gone.

I feel myself move toward the driveway. No one stops me. They might be yelling at me. I might be responding. I'm not sure. It seems like a dream. It feels like the dread of the last pull on the slot machine at the casino. I'm waiting as the images spin under the glass. The smoke swirls with water vapor like a cyclone over the house. The water from the hoses send a shimmer over the pavement, now lit by the fancy outdoor lights that my sister had incessantly bragged about. I step around a couple of firemen and see the open doors of the carriage house for the first time. The slot machine stops. The air in my lungs rushes out.

Stacy's car is gone.

She's alive.

"Oh my god!" comes a cry from the crowd.

It's her.

I twist around and see my sister forcing her way through the crowd. She's wearing jeans and a light-blue T-shirt. Her hair swings behind her as she runs in my direction.

"Oh my god!" she repeats. Her eyes dart. "Where's my husband? Where's Cy?" She lunges at me and in a second she's in my arms. "Nicole," she calls out, "where is Cy? What's happened?"

My mother was wrong about my sister's acting ability.

I find the only words that make sense to me. "Stacy," I say as I hold her, "I'm so sorry."

Tears are streaming down her face. She's a mess. Her mascara looks like tar splatter on her white BMW SUV. She's never looked worse. I wonder if she's ever felt better.

"Stacy," I repeat, pushing her away so I can speak to her. "I thought you were gone."

Her makeup-smeared eyes blink out more tears. "I was gone. After you left I decided to join you at the recital . . . then I heard about the explosion and came back here. It was on the news. I just had a feeling that something terrible had happened."

Evan Cooper makes his way over to where we are standing.

Stacy bites her lip and braces herself.

"We think we found your husband," he tells her.

She reaches for me, and I prop her up. I wonder if she's going to pass out.

"Oh God no!" she starts to wail. "Not Cy. What happened? What happened? Why won't anyone tell me what's going on?"

He repeats what he told me they'd theorized in the first moments of the investigation. Stacy continues to sob uncontrollably. She spits out something about the propane canisters being the subject of concern.

Pointing out a potential cause for a death is often a psychopath's mistake. If I had helped her, I would have told her that.

Never, ever tell them what the police need to find on their own. We not only resent it, we look at such disclosures as suspicious. Being too helpful is never helpful at all.

"He never shut them off," she says of the propane canisters, tears still coming and her words coming out in a surprisingly convincing sputter. "I told him over and over that turning off the barbecue is not the same thing as shutting off the valve."

Cooper's eyes meet mine. I can't tell what he's thinking.

"We're going to need a statement," he says.

Stacy pulls herself together and plays the mother card.

"Where's Emma?"

"She's with an officer," I say.

"They took her to the station," Cooper adds.

My sister wraps her arm around her perfect yoga body. She looks small. Lost, even. "I need my daughter," she says. "I need to see my little girl."

A few minutes later, we are in the car. She's still crying. Her hands are on her face and she's trembling. She buckles her seat belt. My sister is very safety-minded. She is also very aware that people are brandishing their phones and recording every move she makes.

"It was an accident," she tells me as I put the BMW in gear and start down the street. "It really was. I listened to you. You were right. You were right."

I give her a look, then return my eyes to the road.

"You have to believe me, Nicole," she says putting her hand on my leg to jog me into listening, accepting.

"I wish I could," I say, not for her, but for myself. I am a party to the murder of her husband. Not turning her in makes me as guilty as she is. All of the reasons I gave her for not killing Cy were unshakable in their truth. Killing Cy would only ensure that Angela and Danny never paid for their roles in Kelsey's abduction and murder.

The car stays silent for the longest time. I'm sick and angry. I have no idea what she's really feeling.

"I'm glad he's dead," she finally says, knowing that I don't believe her. "I'm not going to say that I'm sorry about that at all, but I didn't set the trap. I didn't crack open the knobs on those tanks."

I don't really know my sister.

I probably never did.

"You know what you did," I say, looking straight ahead.

"I swear I didn't do it. I wanted to. I planned to do it. You convinced me. You did. You made me see that killing Cy was a mistake. He needed to suffer. He needed the public humiliation that comes with all that he did."

She's playing me.

"Now Angela and Danny can be made to pay for what they did. Right? That's what you wanted, Nicole. We can think of a way to turn them in. Danny for what he did to Alan. Angela for what she did to her little girl. I swear that I didn't mean for it to go off. I listened to you. You were right. It was a freak accident."

My face grows hot. "It was not an accident, Stacy. You set it up."

She doesn't answer right away. The wheels are turning. I've seen that so many times before.

"But I didn't open the tanks or set the match," she says. "I didn't. It must have gone off some other way. I swear it."

I ignore her excuse. "Where were you?" I ask.

"I told you," she says, her tone now pleading. "I went to Forest Ridge to join you at the ballet."

I shake my head. I've heard it all from her before. The time she slept with my boyfriend in high school. The time she stole twenty dollars out of dad's wallet—and blamed me. The time she asked me to babysit for her at our neighbors, but left me there all night.

"You are such a liar," I say, looking her over. "You would never dress like that if you were going to be out with the other moms."

She shakes her head. "You are wrong. So wrong! That's where I was," she says, before dropping her voice. "Honestly, you are so suspicious."

It's easy to be when it's part of your job. And you know your sister even a little bit.

I ease Stacy's car through traffic as it joins the stream of cars on 405, heading toward the police department. I think of Danny sulking in prison and wondering if I can help connect the dots to what he did without ruining Emma's life. My sister set two traps. One for Cy and one for me. I wonder if anything she told me about what Cy was doing was even true, but I don't bring that up. Not now. Too much to process. Too many lies to unravel. My sister is smart. She knows that if I come forward, I'll be implicated. She'll say that I coached her. Told her how to do it. The prosecutor will come after me, reminding everyone of my problem. That I'm an addict. That I'm no better than anyone else who has committed a crime.

"It'll be okay," Stacy says. "Everything will be okay."

"It is not okay, Stacy! It is not. You killed a man. You went ahead and committed the worst crime imaginable."

She sits silently and the traffic crawls off the freeway to the police department.

"What Cy, Angela, and Danny did was the worst crime imaginable," she says. "It's true that we could go to prison for what I did, but we won't go to hell."

"You're justifying."

"I'm right. You know it. In your bones, you know it."

"I don't."

"You'll feel better after we get something to eat," she says.

I know now that she really is a sociopath.

"I'm not hungry."

"I'm sure Emma is," she says.

"Her father just died."

"Yes, but she's a child. Resilient. Just like me. Like us."

I slide the car into the lot of the place that had been like a home to me. I park next to Christine Seiko's car, and we get out.

"After we get Emma and get something to eat I have a big surprise for you."

I hate surprises.

She smiles at me as we walk, then tugs at my arm like she's trying to snap me out of a stupor. "Aren't you going to ask what it is?"

"What is it?" I say, sarcastically.

She smiles and waits a beat. "That stupid dog of yours."

We stop at the door, and I turn to her.

"Shelby? What about her?"

Stacy holds that same smile, her eyes searching mine. "My housekeeper has her. We're bringing her home."

Shelby? I feel my knees buckle, and my eyes start to flood. My sister might be the most conniving, manipulative, murderous bitch in the world, but somewhere inside beats a heart.

"You like the surprise, don't you?"

317

I don't normally. I like routine. I like facts. I like knowing the outcome of something before it happens. Like the feeling I had when I was winning at the casino. And yet, I do love my dog. More than anything.

"We'll make this work, Nicole," she says. "Won't we?"

I don't answer. My sister is a gambler too. She wants to make sure that I cover for her. She's laid it on the line. Double or nothing. A smile nearly comes to my lips. Stacy is taking a very big chance. She thinks I have nothing left to lose.

And I can't claim that she's wrong.

Chapter Fifty-One

It's dark now. Emma has passed out in the backseat. My sister gave a young officer a statement about her whereabouts before the explosion, but everything is just a formality. Stacy is pretty and pretty gets a pass almost every time. Officer Eyes-All-Over-Her tells Stacy that arson investigators will stay at the scene overnight and well into the morning. She managed to eke out some convincing tears. Some lip trembling too.

At the moment, no one knows what I know.

Or what Stacy did.

I carry Emma to the front desk of the Hotel Bellevue and Stacy fishes for her wallet in her purse. I'd reach for mine to help her, but I have no money. No credit cards. I breathe in Emma once more. Her hair is strawberry blond, and my senses tease me that she smells like a summer berry. So sweet. The registration desk clerk acts as if he's put out by our appearance at his desk. He undoubtedly would rather be reading the *Game of Thrones* novel that we interrupted.

"I'm sure it's in here," Stacy says, reaching deep into Kate Spade's golden jaws. She lets out a sigh of exasperation—the kind of thing she does so well to keep all eyes on her. When she tilts the purse, all of its contents pour to the carpeted floor. Emma stirs and wakes up, and I set her down.

"Let me help you," I say, scooting up the spill and putting everything back into the purse, while Stacy reaches for Emma.

"Where are we, Momma?" Emma asks. Her eyes are crusty from tears and sleep.

Stacy lowers her eyes to meet her daughter. "We're staying at a hotel tonight, Honey."

Emma is on the verge of crying. "Where's Daddy?" she asks.

My sister hugs my niece. "Just for one night," she says, ignoring her little girl's question—one she'll need to answer soon.

Daddy's dead.

Among the makeup, loose cash, sunglasses, tissues, and a bundle of hairbrushes, I see a couple of cards. One is for Starbucks. The other stops my heart cold.

Kirk Whitmore, American Life Ins.

I look up, and Stacy's eyes catch mine.

"You did not buy a policy on Cy," I say.

She turns away from me and presents her platinum American Express card to Game of Thrones.

"Should I get you a room?" she asks me.

"No," I say, feeling anger well up inside. "I won't be staying."

"Suit yourself," she says, then pays. I follow her into the elevator to her second-floor room. The doors shut, and I wedge my way in front of her. I don't care what Emma thinks at the moment. I don't care about anything but the truth. The truth, to me, still matters.

"Stacy, tell me you didn't buy insurance from that guy," I say. "I *know* that guy. He's not just a total crook, he's flat-out evil."

She brushes me off. "Hell, no. I'm not stupid."

"But you have his card."

"I admit that I thought of it," she says as we get off the elevator and she inserts her room key into the lock. She swings open the door, and we enter her suite. It's lovely and nondescript. It's Stacy all over.

I was the memorable one.

"Emma, you need to use the bathroom?" she asks.

The little girl complies, and we're alone.

While I stand there waiting for an explanation, my sister checks out the minibar and then finds a place on a settee by the window. She stretches out her long legs and leans back. It's a pose meant to tell me that she's calm. Cool. That she's not going to crumble.

"I told you," I say, now standing right in front of her, staring her down. Looking for something in her eyes. "Insurance trips up people. Every time."

"Like I said, I didn't buy any insurance on Cy. I swear on a stack of Bibles. God, how I hate that you always try to judge me, Nicole. You always are looking for a way to knock me down."

"You killed your husband, Stacy. You said you wouldn't."

The toilet flushes.

"What does it matter? Really? He was a pervert, and now he's gone. Think of Emma. Think of me. You know that someone who has a taste for that kind of filth can't change. Can't stop. You know that. You really let me down, Nicole. I don't know if I can forgive you."

Forgive me?

"You'll get caught."

"I won't. I never do."

Her words hang in the air. I think of all the times growing up when she did get away with things that no one else could imagine. I'm sure there were things that I didn't even know about. Stealth Stacy. That's her.

"I've had enough. I'm going to Julian's," I finally tell her. "I'll see you in the morning so we can get Shelby." I give Emma a quick hug and shut the door. I stand outside her room as the dead bolt slips into place. My sister went to the most disreputable insurance salesman on the Eastside. I had thought she was clever up to that point. Now I wonder. Now I feel a little sick inside.

◆ ◆ ◆

The Somerset house is an icebox. The thermostat indicates sixty-four degrees, but it feels much cooler. The AC needs a repairman in the worst way. I'd call one if this were my house. If I had money. I feel so low right now that I consider whether my circumstances warrant a trip to the casino. When I felt my worst, when I didn't have a prayer of making it through another day, I could somehow summon the strength to make my way to my machine. And I swear to God, I would win. I really would. Yet as my body shivers, I am unsure if it's really the temperature or the reaction to the day I'd just been through. I am having doubts about my sister. She's bent the truth at every turn. I wonder how many lies she's told with those gorgeous unblinking eyes of hers. There isn't a splinter in my being that believes that she was headed to the dance recital. Not a chance. She must think that I'm seriously stupid.

Or that I'd forgive her for anything.

Sometimes I wonder which it is.

My sister.

My mother.

My life.

It's a painful metronome, and I can't escape any of it.

I pour myself a glass of wine. Even the label on the bottle mocks me a little. It makes me think of Stacy. Same wine that she bought by the case. The pretentious. The exclusive. The one "only those in the know" could get. It tasted no better than the second cheapest wine on the Albertsons grocery store shelf—the kind that I bought when I had a job. I look around. The place is spotless. When Julian leaves the house he makes sure that everything is in order so that when he returns it's just so. The schoolhouse clock's chime sends an echo down the hall. I wish he were home. I need Julian. I need him to tell me that what I was thinking was so wrong. And yet I know, deep down, that I can't betray her. Betraying Stacy would suck me down deep into the vortex that is reserved for people who do the right thing. Like I'd done by turning in Danny.

Fuck Danny!

When I can no longer stand the chill of the air, I take my wine and pad down the hall for an extra blanket.

The closet has nothing but jackets on wire hangers and children's toys scattered among its upper shelf. I see a doll and it reminds me of Kelsey. I wonder if she feels any justice now that Cy is gone. She has to. That's the only thing that will make what Stacy did feel right to me.

Or at least a little right.

I take another sip. I'm certain that I'll drink the bottle dry before I fall asleep tonight. That is, if I can sleep. Angela kept extra linens in her office closet so I make my way there. That's my least favorite place in the house. Maybe in the world. It reminds me how unimportant Kelsey had been to her mother. I wonder how it made her feel when she looked up at the wall of images of her brother.

Fuck Angela!

After digging around, I retrieve a nice fuzzy blanket from the top shelf, and in doing so, a box tumbles to the floor. Photographs spill out and immediately I drop to my knees. The air surges from my lungs. My eyes begin to flood. I feel as though I'm going to throw up. I turn the photographs over; on the back of each one are pieces of double-sided tape. Stuck to the tape are tiny fragments of pink—the color of the walls of that room.

I sit there, looking at each one, trying to process the significance of my discovery.

All were of Kelsey. All of them had once hung on that very wall. All of them had been removed by someone and stored in a box.

I try to catch my breath. I reach for my wine glass and guzzle. The room had been staged. That meant one thing. In fact, it meant everything. The wine rises up, and I fight as hard as I can to keep from throwing up. The glass falls to the floor and shatters.

I am shattered.

This can't be happening. This isn't right. None of it. I start to choke and then cough and then it spews out, in all of its red glory. I slide slowly downward to the floor and sit there, putting together the pieces of the puzzle. In my mind's eye, I see Julian, his handsome face. His arms around me. I shake. I want to cry. I have been so stupid.

Fuck Julian!

At first, he'd been the one telling everyone that Angela wouldn't talk. He said she hated Kelsey.

He said that the housekeeper was off work the day detectives came and smelled bleach. He said that it was unusual for Angela to do laundry.

When Kelsey disappeared, she did so silently. How could that be? Unless it was someone she knew who took her. Someone like her father.

My fingers shake as I collect the photos and return them to the box. I clean myself up and leave. I don't even give the place one last look. I know that I'll want to forget everything. The casino is calling me, but I don't get on I-90. I'm on 405. I'm going to talk to the one person who can probably tell me what I need to know. What I'll do with that information, I have no idea.

The Acadia's lobby is quiet. I wait outside the door for someone to come or go, so that I can slip inside. Finally, a young woman chatting on her cell swipes her key and swings open the door; I follow inside with the kind of assured gait that indicates that I know where I'm going. Angela's unit is on the second floor, and I take the stairs. I wait a moment and try to collect myself. I've hated this woman for a year. I've tried everything

I could to find out what she'd done with Kelsey. And now, as I stand outside her door, I try to come up with the words that I'll say.

She opens the door.

"What do you want?" she says.

"I need to talk to you."

"Michael's asleep. You need to go."

"Angela," I say, opening the box of Kelsey's photos.

Her eyes shift downward, and I see a flicker of emotion.

"You don't know what you're getting into," she says. "He'll kill you. They'll kill you."

"Who?"

"I can't do this," she says. "I can't."

"Please," I beg her, pushing my foot in the door slightly. "Talk to me, Angela."

Angela looks behind her shoulder, then opens the door, and I go inside.

Her apartment is nothing like I'd imagined it to be. The furnishings are chic, of course, but everywhere I look there are signs of Samuel. Toys on the floor. A bowl of dry, sugary cereal on the coffee table. DVDs. A PlayStation. I expected the space to be antiseptic. Cold. But it is warm. Homey.

"There's no point in talking," she says. "I'm living with what I did and didn't do."

I hand her the box of photos.

"You didn't buy life insurance on Kelsey, did you?"

Her eyes widen a little, and I can see for the first time that as lovely as she is, there is something behind the facade. Maybe it had been there all the time, but the world had turned against Target Mom. Everything she did was seen through the lens of revulsion. When she's looking into the box, I turn on the "Record" feature on my phone.

A flicker of sadness comes over her face. She steps back into a chair and slides into the seat. I join her. I've conducted hundreds of interviews, but none like this. None that had a personal stake. At one time I prided myself on my ability to be kind and probing at the same time. I could be tough too. When faced with a witness who wouldn't give up what was so patently obvious, I even had it in me to push the boundaries. Not like Danny. A persuasive push all the same.

I have everything on the line here.

So does Angela.

"No, I didn't buy any insurance."

I start from the edges and work inward.

"Did you dye your hair blond?" I ask, though I know from sifting through the photos in the box, there was no indication that she had.

"In junior high," she says. "It looked terrible. My skin tone is best with dark hair. I was one of the few Miss Washington Teen USA contestants to get that far the year I competed without bleached hair."

She probably never misses a chance to remind everyone she was a top-ten finisher. A framed news clipping of her achievement in a pageant dress hangs behind her. I wonder if she wears the sash around the house.

I press on. "Did Michael buy the insurance on your daughter's life?"

She shakes her head. "God no. He's a good man. He's on my side. On Samuel's side."

I keep pushing. I keep unraveling. I think of all the elements of the case against her. How one story piled on top of the other, each making her look more desperate. More evil. More likely to have done the unthinkable. Angela is self-absorbed. She is pretty. Privileged. She's the kind of woman people love to hate.

People who troll blogs. People who gossip while they watch their kid's soccer game. People who feel good only with the rush of hating someone else.

"You were at that luggage store, weren't you?"

Her eyes stay fixed on me. Pay dirt. "This really isn't a good idea," she says.

"You were at that store," I repeat.

"Yes," Angela says, nearly swallowing the word. "But not for the reason in the press. Not for what they've said on that blog."

I lean toward her a little. Not so much to be intrusive, but to let her know that I'm counting on her to answer. This isn't a game. "It wasn't to put your daughter's body in it, was it?"

She shakes her head. "No, I was thinking of leaving. I wanted to leave before everything happened. When that clerk said *body*, I did freak out. Not because I was going to put Kelsey in it dead. I was thinking I could smuggle her out in the case, alive."

"To save her," I say.

She runs her slender fingers through the photos. "Yeah. To save her."

"But you didn't," I say.

She barely looks at me. "No. No, I didn't."

"What happened at Target?"

Angela's hands tremble a little, and she clasps them tightly together. "What do you think happened?" she asks.

"I think Kelsey was there, but never went inside. I think that you left her in the car so that someone could take her."

She stays mute for a long time. A picture of Kelsey in a pretty pink dress has her attention.

"Yes," she finally answers. "Her father. He and whoever was helping him. I don't know who. I really don't. I couldn't believe it really happened."

"But you left her in the car so she could be taken."

Her eyes leave the photo and catch mine. "Yes," she says. "I did. I admit that. Judge me all you want. I guess I really am a bad mother. I tried to like her, and part of me probably did. But she cried so much when she was born. Day and night. It got to the point where I just couldn't even look at her. I tried to get help. Really. I saw a counselor. I joined an online group for women who had problems with their children. I couldn't fucking be me with that little girl crying all the time.

I was losing everything. If it hadn't been for Michael, I'd have killed myself. Julian would have overdosed me."

That's the Angela I know.

"He drugged you?"

"The night everything happened," she goes on. "I told him that we needed to get her back. I'd changed my mind. But he told me it was too late. That everything would work out."

"I wanted to put a stop to it," she says, tears suddenly streaming down her face. "I told him I would tell the police. He fed me some sleeping pills. I didn't get out of bed for thirty-five hours. When I did he told me that I was a suspect and that no one would believe that I hadn't been the one who'd orchestrated all of this."

"Why did you go along with any of this, Angela?" I ask her. "It makes me sick. Doesn't it make you sick?"

"I didn't want to go to prison. I didn't want to lose my son. When Alan Dawson committed suicide, Julian told me that everything was fine. He kept telling me that if I spoke to anyone—the police, a lawyer, the press—that he'd make sure that I never saw the light of day again. Julian terrorized me. He made sure that no one would ever believe me. Do you have any idea what that's like?"

She helped set everything in motion, yet she thinks her hands are clean. She thinks that I will feel sorry for her. I don't.

"You didn't have to go along with any of this," I say. "You did anyway."

Her mascara has turned into a smear of war paint. She thinks that she'll win me over.

She is wrong.

"I didn't know she was going to die. I would never have done what I did. I wouldn't. You have to believe me."

Before I can tell her I don't, Samuel emerges from the hall. He looks at his mother and then me. He's wearing *Cars* pajamas and a haunted look. I suppress the impulse to go over, scoop him up, and take him out of Acadia.

"Mommy," he says.

Angela spins around to face her son. "Go back to bed, Honey. Mommy will be right there."

Samuel's big brown eyes pass over me, but he doesn't actually acknowledge my presence. He nods at his mom and disappears back down the hall.

"You need to go," Angela says to me. "I don't want my son upset. This has been very, very hard on him."

I want to say something about her little girl being more than upset. She is dead. But I don't. There's only one more thing that I need to know.

"I'll leave," I say, "but I need to know Julian's connection with Cy Sonntag."

Angela gives me an odd look. "There is no connection," she says. "Although I have to admit that when I saw the news about the explosion I was glad he was dead. I wish that Julian's girlfriend had gone up in smoke too."

"Girlfriend?"

Her eyes narrow. I see a smile come faintly to her lips.

"You don't know, do you?"

My heart races. I don't know why.

"Know what?" I ask.

Her smile widens a little. Angela Chase suddenly looks a little happy. She's delivering a poisoned apple.

"Stacy," she says. "Your sister. I thought that was why you're here."

The room constricts, and I tug at my collar as though I can no longer breathe. I survey the room as though I'm in an airplane, looking for a place to land. The casino lights flash in my head.

Stacy.

She'd been the one to tell Julian that I was at the shelter.

Stacy.

It wasn't Angela's diaphragm that I'd discovered in Julian's bathroom. Stacy had been using one because she complained that birth control pills made her fat.

Stacy.

And the wine. They both drank the same fucking, pretentious wine.

There were dozens of signs, and I'd missed them all. I run through a list as I drive. I keep my mind on where I'm going, though I want nothing more than to pull into a bar with pull-tabs. A church with late-night bingo. Scratch tickets at a 7-Eleven. Anything. It's how I've coped. It's part of who I am. And I refuse to be that person anymore. I won't let Stacy pull the strings to define my every move.

I'm so done with her.

There were dozens of signs, and I'd missed them all. I run through a list

I park the car outside the hotel where my sister is sleeping. The rain comes down, but I turn off the wipers and keep the heat on low. I have no idea where I'll spend the night. Probably right where I am. My mind flashes to the keying of her boyfriend's car and how the video showed Angela, but she'd denied it. It hadn't been her at all.

I look up at what I guess to be her room and call her cell.

"It's late, Nic," she says when she finally answers. Her voice is scratchy from sleep. "What do you want?"

"When I come tomorrow, I'll be picking up Shelby and Emma."

"Not Emma," she says. "I'm taking her shopping."

"No, you are not. I'm taking her away from you, you goddam freak."

There's a pregnant little pause, and then she says, "I told you, it was an accident."

"Not Cy," I say, fiddling with the phone to push the "Play" button on the recording app. My battery is low and I feel a surge of panic. I need this to work. "I'm talking about Kelsey. I'm talking about Julian."

Silence.

"Stacy?"

"I don't know what you are talking about."

I tighten my grip on my phone so much, that it passes through my mind that I'll shatter the glass. "I was so stupid about the sheets, about the fucking White Castle hamburger and tots that were Kelsey's last meal. Your freezer was full of them! How you always seemed to know what I was up to, even after Danny royally fucked up the case. You were all over this, Stacy. From the beginning. You, Danny, Julian." Saying Julian's name had been like spitting out a peach pit lodged in my throat. It hurt like hell.

"So what if I was fucking your boyfriend?" she says. "You got over it in the past."

"How long have you and Julian been involved?"

"We met in the summer," she says.

"You're going down, Stacy."

Silence for a beat. "You can't prove anything."

"I'll bet Kirk Whitmore will pick you out of a lineup," I say. "You made quite an impression."

The Stacy I know would consider that a compliment. But I don't know this woman.

"So what?" she asks.

"So this."

I play the recording and sit in the BMW as tears stream down my face. I'm not a crier. I'm not a cop. I'm going to have to start over. I have a sister that I will never see again. I have a father who doesn't know my name. The recording with Angela spilling every last dropped stitch of the case finishes, and there's nothing but silence.

"I'll be there at ten. I don't care what you do. I don't care where you go. But you're done here, anywhere near Emma, Stacy. I'd say something about you and Julian having a great life, but that would be a lie. I hope you rot in hell for what you've done."

Stacy gives it a try. She thinks she can win me back, but her effort is hollow.

By the end, she's just being ridiculous. "You always had it so easy," she says. "You don't know what it's like to be the center of attention and to always feel that whatever you have isn't enough. I did what I had to do to survive. We all do."

"Cy wasn't a pornographer, was he?"

I hear her play with the gold bracelet Cy had given her, the one that she once told me cost more than a half-year of my salary.

"We're not going to have this conversation," she says.

I don't yell, but my tone is more than emphatic. "Yes, we are."

"Oh, Nic, just stop it. Just leave it alone. You don't want to know. You only need to know what I've let you know."

I know my sister. She wants to tell me everything because she thinks whatever she's done makes her smarter than me. I don't need to urge her to continue. It's a game. And I do it anyway.

"Tell me, Stacy. Just tell me."

"I wish," she says. "Cy was boring. You've never had the excitement of a real, full relationship, Nicole. You couldn't possibly understand what it's like to be trapped with someone so far beneath you, yet you stay for the sake of your child."

As far as I could see, she didn't care about Emma. She cared about Stacy. And she loved money. Cy was dull, but he was a good provider, and he adored his little girl. At least that's what I'd thought, from the outside looking in.

"What happened to Kelsey?" I ask.

My sister takes a long pause. I know that she knows exactly what happened to Kelsey, but she wants me to think it is difficult for her to retrieve the memory. It's a game.

"She died, Nicole," she says. "You know that."

Though I am crumbling now, I push anyway. I need to know. "How?" I ask. "How did she die?"

Her soft sigh fills the phone. She waits.

"Your stupid cop boyfriend," she says. "That's how. She wouldn't stop crying. Danny thought the gardener or the neighbors would hear her. He put his hand over her mouth. That's what he told me. I don't know for sure. She was dead and in the freezer. He cried like a big baby, and I had to fix it. He screwed up everything."

I think of Kelsey just then. Like I always do. Danny killed her. Just like he'd killed Lisa, in college. I wonder how much of that Cy even knew. Danny knew how to clean the body so there'd be no trace evidence. Danny and my sister were like a pair of wild dogs hunting together, but betraying one another as they got closer to the bone.

"I need you to know that no one was supposed to get hurt. It was only a way to get the money," she says.

"The money," I repeat.

"Five million dollars," she says, suddenly lifting her voice a little, as though she thinks I understand. "We thought we could get Angela's parents to pay. They are loaded. Import/export money. We never got the chance. Kelsey died that very night she was taken from her mother's car."

She's such a liar. "You bought life insurance," I say. "You and Danny."

"So what?"

"Then Kelsey's wasn't an accident, Stacy. It was part of the plan. Goddamn you! Who are you? *What* are you?"

I'm glad she can't see that I'm crying now. I hate the power she has over me. No one on earth could ever hurt me more than my sister. It has been that way since we were little. I'd give. She'd take. She'd burn me. I'd ask for more. I was so caught up in trying to fix things that our mother had done to us, I imagined that Stacy was just as hurt as I had been.

Yet she wasn't. Not all. She didn't even care. She only saw herself in that universe that she owned.

"You have blood on your hands," I say, now spitting out my words. "You are a part of the murder of a little girl. God, what's the matter with you?"

She shushes me like a librarian. "Settle down. It was an accident, Nicole. I swear it. You know me."

Settle down.

I don't answer. I just sit there in the BMW, the place where Kelsey had been the day she vanished from Target. I feel her just then. It's like a wind blowing through me, reminding me about the girl that haunted my dreams. The girl that I thought I could avenge.

"Have Emma ready tomorrow," I finally say. "You can send guardianship papers from wherever the fuck you go. But Stacy, you need to go. You need to get the hell away and never come back."

I imagine my sister is standing now. Looking at herself in the mirror as she speaks to me. Checking to see that her demeanor is puffer-fish big so that I'll back off and kowtow to her wishes.

"Are you threatening me?" she asks.

"We're beyond threats. You just lost the war."

"I'm not afraid of you, Nic. You're a broken, gambling-addled loser. Always will be. Just go play the slots. Be gone with you."

She's fighting, but I won't lose. I ignore her.

"I want some money too," I say. "Fifty thousand dollars."

I know I could have demanded more, but Stacy is greedy, and I only need enough to start over somewhere else. If I got more, maybe I'd be tempted to put it on the line at the casino and try for double or nothing. With Emma, I can't risk that. I can't risk anything anymore.

"You were always such a bitch when we were growing up," she says. "And so very boring. Fine. I'll give you the money."

I won.

I'm the winner.

"I'm sending this recording to my lawyer's office," I say, my voice surging with resolve. "If anything ever happens to me, you'll be in jail for the rest of your life. Good-bye, Stacy."

I end the call, lean back, and close my eyes.

I imagine Hoquiam and the little house we shared before Mom left in search of stardom. The town doesn't have a mall. There are no good restaurants. The schools need funding. It's a far cry from Bellevue. But it is a place where people are happy with just enough, a good place to raise a family. Starting over with Emma is my last chance. My best hope.

ACKNOWLEDGMENTS

I want to take this opportunity to thank the astonishingly good team at Amazon Publishing for the opportunity to try something new. Or at least a little bit new. Special appreciation goes to Thomas & Mercer's JoVon Sovak, whose unbridled enthusiasm and brilliance make her an author's best friend. And she's fun too. I'm also grateful to David Downing for his thoughtful, precise, and insightful editing. I feel so lucky to have had him on the project. But wait! There's more gratitude to be shared. First to Liz Pearsons, who made such a graceful and savvy entrance to the process of creating this book. And to Heidi Ward for her extremely smart and careful copyedit. It feels great to be in such great hands (yours, too Sarah Shaw!). Finally, I want to acknowledge my partner in crime, my agent, Susan Raihofer, of the David Black Agency. This book marks our twenty-year anniversary as author and client. Much love. Always.

ACKNOWLEDGMENTS

ABOUT THE AUTHOR

#1 *New York Times* bestselling author Gregg Olsen has written over twenty books. Known for his ability to create vivid and fascinating narratives, he's appeared on multiple television and radio shows such as *Good Morning America*, *Dateline*, *Entertainment Tonight*, *CNN*, and *MSNBC*. In addition, Olsen has been featured in *Redbook*, *People*, and *Salon* magazine as well as in the *Seattle Times*, *Los Angeles Times*, and *New York Post*.

Both his fiction and nonfiction works have received critical acclaim and numerous awards, including prominence on the *USA Today* and *Wall St. Journal* bestselling lists. Washington State officially selected his young adult novel, *Envy*, for the National Book Festival, and *The Deep Dark* was named Idaho Book of the Year.

A Seattle native who lives with his wife in rural Washington State, Olsen's already at work on his next thriller. Connect with him via Facebook and Twitter or through his website, www.greggolsen.com.